Pr

"Delivers a delicious batch of supernatural ~~...~~ ... up Texas-style—hot, spicy, and with a bite!"

— Kerrelyn Sparks, *New York Times* bestselling author

"An utter delight. Wickedly entertaining with a surprise on every page. Keeps you guessing until the end. Kimberly Frost is a talent to watch."

— Annette Blair, national bestselling author

"One heck of a debut from Kimberly Frost . . . This is definitely an excellent read, and for a debut, it's nothing less than fantastic."
— *ParaNormal Romance*

"Kimberly Frost's Southern Witch series is destined for great things. Full of action, suspense, romance, and humor, [*Barely Bewitched*] had me hooked from the first page until the last."
— *Huntress Book Reviews*

"Frost's latest Southern Witch novel has all the fun, fast, entertaining action readers have come to expect from her . . . Populated with fairies, goblins, vampires, wizards, rampant plants, and a few nasty-tempered humans thrown in for good measure, there's no end to the things that can and do go hilariously wrong."
— *Monsters and Critics*

"What an amazing author! Kimberly Frost's Southern Witch series is fated for great things. *Barely Bewitched* was full of romance [and] magical havoc, and goes from one wild scenario to another. I was definitely hooked . . . and couldn't put it down."
— *Romance Junkies*

continued . . .

All That Bleeds

Kimberly Frost

B

BERKLEY SENSATION, NEW YORK

THE BERKLEY PUBLISHING GROUP
Published by the Penguin Group
Penguin Group (USA) Inc.
375 Hudson Street, New York, New York 10014, USA
Penguin Group (Canada), 90 Eglinton Avenue East, Suite 700, Toronto, Ontario M4P 2Y3, Canada
(a division of Pearson Penguin Canada Inc.)
Penguin Books Ltd., 80 Strand, London WC2R 0RL, England
Penguin Group Ireland, 25 St. Stephen's Green, Dublin 2, Ireland (a division of Penguin Books Ltd.)
Penguin Group (Australia), 250 Camberwell Road, Camberwell, Victoria 3124, Australia
(a division of Pearson Australia Group Pty. Ltd.)
Penguin Books India Pvt. Ltd., 11 Community Centre, Panchsheel Park, New Delhi—110 017, India
Penguin Group (NZ), 67 Apollo Drive, Rosedale, Auckland 0632, New Zealand
(a division of Pearson New Zealand Ltd.)
Penguin Books (South Africa) (Pty.) Ltd., 24 Sturdee Avenue, Rosebank, Johannesburg 2196,
South Africa

Penguin Books Ltd., Registered Offices: 80 Strand, London WC2R 0RL, England

This is a work of fiction. Names, characters, places, and incidents either are the product of the author's
imagination or are used fictitiously, and any resemblance to actual persons, living or dead, business
establishments, events, or locales is entirely coincidental. The publisher does not have any control
over and does not assume any responsibility for author or third-party websites or their content.

ALL THAT BLEEDS

A Berkley Sensation Book / published by arrangement with the author

PRINTING HISTORY
Berkley Sensation mass-market edition / January 2012

Copyright © 2012 by Kimberly Chambers.
Excerpt on pages 303–324 by Kimberly Frost copyright © by Kimberly Chambers.
Cover art by Melanie Delon.
Cover design by Rita Frangie.

ISBN: 978-0-425-24580-4

BERKLEY SENSATION®
Berkley Sensation Books are published by The Berkley Publishing Group,
a division of Penguin Group (USA) Inc.,
375 Hudson Street, New York, New York 10014.
BERKLEY SENSATION® is a regsitered trademark of PenguinGroup (USA) Inc.
The "B" design is a trademark of Penguin Group (USA) Inc.

PRINTED IN THE UNITED STATES OF AMERICA

10   9   8   7   6   5   4   3   2   1

For Sandy Fiaschetti

ACKNOWLEDGMENTS

I'd like to thank my wonderful family and friends for their continued enthusiasm and support. It means so much to me!

For being there years ago when the seeds that inspired this story were planted, thank you to Sandy Fiaschetti. For being a sounding board as I brainstormed this story, I'd like to thank David Mohan, who is a great critique partner. For reading passages and for all the amazing support they've provided, I'd like to thank Laura Montgomery and Rick Haufe. For her positive spirit and wonderful friendship, thanks to Lorin Oberweger. For writing dates at Java Dave's, thanks to Kim Lenox. For taking time out of their busy writing schedules to read this book and offer quotes, thanks to Janet Chapman and Nina Bangs.

For fantastic book signings and great support of the Southern Witch series, thanks to everyone at Murder by the Book. For a wonderful romance book club, thanks to Karla and Jan and Katy Budget Books. For a wonderful week, thanks to Writers Retreat Workshop. For terrific presentations and a great writing community, thanks to WHRWA and Bay Area RWA.

For saying she'd love to see me write something dark and for giving me opportunities that have helped me grow so much as a writer, many thanks to my editor Leis Pederson. For doing so much to promote the books, thank you to my publicist Caitlin Mulrooney-Lyski.

For polishing my books, giving them beautiful covers, and introducing them to booksellers, thanks to the team at Berkley. For being a terrific agent, thank you to Elizabeth Winick Rubinstein.

And as always, many thanks to my readers.

Prologue

I can't believe this is happening, Alissa thought. She whirled around to face her bodyguard, Mr. Clark. His lean form was rigidly straight, his expression grim as she stepped forward.

"We can't just stand by," she said in a low voice with a quick glance around the house's panic room: it had oatmeal-colored walls, a stocked refrigerator, plush couches, and a bathroom with a cavernous slate-tiled shower. A person could live in the panic room for quite a while, and certainly nothing, not even a demon, could get through the magically-reinforced steel walls that were as thick as those of a bank vault. Yes, safe and comfortable—if they were willing to ignore the slaughter happening in the rest of the house. The Arts & Innovation Benefit had turned into a nightmare. Mr. Clark had pulled her down the hall to safety before she'd realized what was happening.

Alissa took a deep breath. The sterile air had an almost metallic tang. She straightened to her full height and beckoned for Mr. Clark's gun. He ignored her outstretched hand. She inched forward, her pink champagne Balenciaga gown swishing over the carpet.

Beyond the bodyguard's shoulder, the giant screen showed the ballroom, where an enormous demon nearly eight feet tall was holding a roomful of humans hostage. Dead security officers littered the dance floor like discarded party favors. The greasy, gray-skinned demon yawned, its toothless mouth as wide as a cavern. Would he swallow his victims whole? Like a snake? He had no weapon, but with razor-sharp claws and inhuman strength, he didn't need one.

How did the demon even cross into our world?

There had never been an incident like it in Alissa's lifetime. Or even in her mother's time. For the fifty-four years since the muses had inspired mankind to defeat the vampires during the Rising, the world had not tolerated supernatural threats. In the twenty-first century, no vampires existed and no demons rose. Humankind wrote the laws that ruled the world. And everyone had been safe. Until now.

"Mr. Clark, either go out and help those people or give me your gun so I can." Her voice was as sharp as she could make it. She might only be twenty-one, but, as a daughter of the House of North, in a time of crisis she was prepared to lead. She kept her arms tight to her sides in hopes that he wouldn't see them tremble.

"Unless Mr. Xenakis gives the order, that door doesn't open until the creature is gone or dead," Mr. Clark said.

Alissa narrowed her eyes. Dimitri Xenakis, the Etherlin Council's president, would never give an order that would put her in danger, but he also wouldn't have locked the panic room when so many other people were still outside.

"Mr. Xenakis isn't here, but I know he would want us to help. Open the door. I'll go out and distract the demon long enough for people to escape. You can get anyone into the panic room who's too afraid or too slow to run."

Mr. Clark folded his arms across his chest, his black tuxedo jacket revealing the slight bulge on his left side where his holstered gun was positioned. "You expect me to use you as bait?" he scoffed.

"Yes, because I expect us to do something," she said, the irritation rising in her voice.

A flicker of movement drew her eyes to the screen. The creature attacked again. The red violet eyes were wild. And merciless. The victim's bloodied body fell to the creature's feet. Alissa's stomach churned, and she had to swallow against its rising contents.

Be strong! Don't let Clark see weakness. She turned from the screen, clinging to her composure.

She pushed back a strand of hair that had come loose when she'd raced down the hall. "We have to do something," she whispered.

"The silver and iron bullets bounced off it. The creature is invulnerable." Mr. Clark shook his head. "I would still face him if you weren't here, but you are. If I open the door and he catches the scent of your blood, he'll be on you in seconds once I'm dead. You know a muse's blood is irresistible to the Damned." He paused. "Nothing but Mr. Xenakis's direct order will make me open that door."

"But the demon could stay until everyone is dead," Alissa argued, holding out a hand to implore him. "We can't wait. Please. You have to let me try."

"No," he said firmly. "Until more Etherlin Security officers arrive, it doesn't make sense to engage it. This demon started its rampage in the Varden, and the ventala didn't manage to kill it. ES needs to come out in force to defeat it."

"It started in the Varden? I wonder if someone there raised the demon and then lost control of it. I guess that shouldn't surprise me."

The ventala so often displayed bad judgment. They were too driven by impulse and their thirst for trouble.

Mr. Clark shook his head in disgust. "We had our chance to rid the world of them. We blew it."

Alissa frowned. "They are part human."

"So what? I'm in favor of capital punishment for human sociopaths, and ventala—even generations down the line— are more like vampires than people. Natural born killers. Given the chance, they'd recreate the Rising. I guarantee it."

She stiffened at the thought of another Rising. It had been one of the darkest times in human history. In the early 1950s after so many people had already died from the Spanish flu epidemic and in the world wars, shapeshifting vampires in bat form had envenomated and drained millions. Initially, people hadn't realized that the bats were vampires. They'd thought that people were dying from a new type of plague for which bats were the vector.

Eventually, the truth was suspected as un-mutated vampires hunted in the wake of their shifting counterparts, but no weapons were effective against the predators. Human losses were massive. When the muses inspired the development of the V3 ammunition, humans finally began to fight back effectively.

Afterward, the tide of human fury had been boundless, and savvy vampires lacking the "Bat Plague" mutation had stopped hunting and tried aligning themselves with mankind by taking human lovers and having children with them. It hadn't saved the vampires; it had only created a new race of bloodthirsty creatures for the world to contend with: ventala.

A tremor rocked the house, and they looked up at the screen. A figure in black strode into the ballroom. He shrugged off a black duster coat, letting it drop in his wake without slowing his stride.

"Merrick," Mr. Clark mumbled.

"Who's Merrick?" Alissa asked, staring at the dark-haired man on the screen who wore sunglasses despite the late hour. He stopped about twenty feet from the creature, then slid a knife from the sheath on his hip. He was tall and broad, but the monster was enormous.

Mr. Clark leaned forward. "He can't be serious. That blade looks like it's made of ivory. It'll crack long before it gets through a demon's hide."

Merrick's lips moved, and Alissa bent over the controls and pressed a button to unmute the surveillance system.

To the people, Merrick said, "Get out." He nodded to the door, but when they inched toward it, the demon roared and they froze. "Go ahead," Merrick said, even as the creature crouched, ready to attack them.

Merrick clucked his tongue, drawing the demon's attention. "Come, Corthus. I'm your dance partner."

"What'd he just say?" Mr. Clark asked.

Alissa blinked, realizing that Merrick had spoken to the

creature in Latin. She'd translated his words in her head without thinking. "He's goading the demon."

"Not for long," Mr. Clark said grimly.

Without warning, the demon sprang forward. Alissa gasped, her hand flying to her mouth. Merrick slid away, and the demon's claws smashed a chair but didn't get a piece of the man who continued to taunt him. As he fought, Merrick's unflinching confidence and strength amazed her.

Nothing about his body had changed, but he moved like smoke, curling close and then away. The demon cocked its head and looked down. She saw it then, blackish fluid spraying from the demon's side. Merrick's blade had connected.

Merrick smiled at the demon's startled expression. "Come on. That can't be all you've got. I got up before noon to get here."

The demon roared and charged again. Merrick slashed and arced away, his motions fluid, almost acrobatic. The demon crumpled, moaning. Its guttural voice protested in Latin. "Impossible," it said.

"Apparently not," Merrick replied. His weapon rested casually near his thigh for a moment before he struck again, sinking the blade into the demon's skull.

Alissa recoiled, her hands in tight fists. The demon stilled. *He made that look easy when all the others couldn't even wound it. Where did he come from?*

Merrick shook his head at the demon as its simmering flesh rapidly rotted into a lumpy puddle on the floor. "Not much of a peach after all," Merrick mumbled. He turned then and looked around at the bodies before he glanced up into the surveillance camera. He seemed to be staring directly at them, though with his sunglasses on it was impossible to tell for sure. The corner of his mouth curved up.

"You can come out now," he mouthed.

She blushed, embarrassed that he'd guessed that someone was hiding.

"Bastard," Mr. Clark grumbled.

"How could he know we're in here?" she asked.

"He doesn't. He's just guessing," Clark said, walking to the refrigerator at the back of the room. "It's all over. Sit and have some water."

"No," she murmured.

Onscreen, Merrick turned and strolled to retrieve his coat.

Alissa strode to the door and unlocked it, then she darted out and down the corridor before Mr. Clark could stop her. The air from the ballroom smelled like asphalt and sulfur. She grimaced at the stench, but it faded as she reached the foyer.

Merrick seemed taller up close. At least six and a half feet. *Beautiful bone structure.* Even obscured by whisker stubble, she could tell.

"Mr. Merrick," she said breathlessly. He smelled spicy and masculine. Unaccountably delicious. She was almost overcome by the urge to touch him. Was it the adrenaline rush that made him seem so attractive? She extended her hand. "Please accept my thanks—"

Merrick's warm hand closed around hers just as Mr. Clark's voice boomed down the corridor. "No! Let her go, Merrick."

With his free hand, Merrick slid his sunglasses down, revealing eyes so dark they seemed to have no color at all, as black and gorgeous as midnight.

"This is an unusual party. First, a demon. Now, an angel."

"I'm not an angel."

"Me either, as it turns out," he said with a slow smile, then he opened his mouth slightly to touch the point of his tongue to the tip of a fang.

He's ventala, she thought as fear sliced through her veins. Alissa stiffened.

Apparently amused by her surprised reaction to his fangs, Merrick cocked a mocking eyebrow. Alissa tried to withdraw her hand, but he held it. She blinked as the muzzle of Mr. Clark's gun appeared, pressing against Merrick's temple.

"I accept your thanks, Miss—?" Merrick's deep voice hummed over her skin. His breath smelled like mint leaves, making her breathe deeper.

It's a trap. Everything about him lures in his prey.

"Miss North," she said, trying to keep her voice steady as her heart beat a riot in her chest.

His gaze flicked to her neck. She wondered if he could see

her pulse throbbing there. Would he sink those teeth into her throat? Bleed her dry? He might, but he seemed so in control of himself. How was that possible if the ventala were just animals in the face of a muse's blood? She knew she should draw back from him, but she didn't want to.

Innocence and mystery don't last long in each other's company. It was a quote she'd read long ago. She could taste its warning. *Don't forget what he is.*

"V3 bullets, Merrick. Unless you'd like parts of your brain leaking out of the holes I put in your skull, you'll let her go," Mr. Clark said.

Alissa grimaced. She was grateful to have the bodyguard with her, but she didn't want more violence. "This isn't how the night should end, Mr. Clark. We're in Mr. Merrick's debt," she said.

Merrick's smile widened. "Beautiful manners to match the beautiful face." His low voice sent a wave of heat through her. She was attracted to him. Still. Which was foolish and made her angry with herself.

"I bet your boarding school education was expensive," Merrick said.

Yes, very expensive. And where did someone like you get educated? Charm school for killers? Her lips were dry, but she didn't dare lick them. She wouldn't tempt him. Her blood alone should have been a temptation that he couldn't resist. And yet he did, standing there so calmly. How? With a gun pressed to his head, no less.

She swallowed slowly. "If you returned my hand, I think it would ease Mr. Clark's mind."

Merrick stared into her eyes. "Mr. Clark's. Not yours, huh?" The corners of his mouth turned up in a mocking smile.

Be still. He's toying with you.

"Too bad I was so late to the party, Miss North. If I'd gotten here earlier, I could've asked you to dance." His dark gaze seemed to light her blood on fire.

"It wouldn't have made a difference. No matter when you'd arrived, I would have had to say no." She cleared her throat. "Let go of my hand please," she said more firmly.

"Not a peach to be had," he murmured, letting her hand

fall from his. He moved past her in an instant, leaving Mr. Clark's gun pointing at empty air. When Clark noticed, he lowered it.

Relieved, and yet disappointed, Alissa turned to watch Merrick walk through the gaping hole that he'd blown in the front of the mansion to gain entry.

"Why did he come to save us if he's one of them?" she asked.

"He didn't come to save anyone here," Mr. Clark said. "The demon was in the Varden last night, slaughtering them. Merrick came for vengeance. He's an enforcer. A common killer."

Alissa stared at the velvety darkness into which Merrick had disappeared. *Certainly a killer, but not common.*

Chapter 1

Spring 2012

A door slammed, assaulted by the wind that hissed through the house's east wing. Strands of moonlight stretched toward Alissa's ankles as she swept down the corridor. She wanted to check on her father one last time before leaving for the Xenakis party.

Her dad had worsened again, which she continued to conceal along with the fact that she was using her magic illegally to help him. If anyone found out, everything she'd worked for would be lost. And so would he.

No one knows, and no one will.

A lone leaf blew across the floor. She walked on, faster, hoping that this setback was temporary, caused by the upcoming anniversary of her mother's death.

The memory of that day flashed in her mind and Alissa winced. She saw the steaming mug in her small hands. Her mother had been upset, so Alissa had made herbal tea for her. At twelve years old, Alissa already had a keen sense that being a muse involved nurturing the gentle parts of people, not only to foster their creativity but also to soothe their self-doubt. She liked to practice because she wanted to be as great a muse as her mother and grandmother.

Alissa had knocked softly on her mom's door and announced herself before opening it. At first when she'd seen the dangling body, she hadn't understood. The luminous limbs that had been sculpted and painted by countless artists hung limp and lifeless. The face that had graced hundreds of magazine covers was blue and swollen. Not a sound or a breath had escaped Alissa. She'd backed from the doorway and walked, trancelike, downstairs. Instinctively, she'd avoided her father, protective of her mother's image even while in shock. She'd gone to the garage and found her mother's driver and Etherlin Security bodyguard, Mr. Sorges. While they were home, he was always there, smoking, tinkering with the car, and occasionally cleaning firearms.

Alissa had told him in a shaky voice that her mother needed help, and he'd rushed inside, taking charge. As the house erupted, Alissa had sat silently in the garage, holding the cooling tea that would never be drunk.

The memory faded, and Alissa tapped on the door to her father's suite of rooms. In the time before her mother died, he'd jokingly called them kingly accommodations. When Alissa had knocked as a child, he used to call out, "Enter the king's chambers." The laughter in his hearty voice had easily traveled through the solid oak doors. She remembered how much fun it had been to slip into his work sanctuary, which had been decorated with rich tapestries and ornately beaded pillows from Morocco and India. Colored scarves in jewel tones had been draped over the chairs and chaises, while netting and silks had dripped from the bed frame, creating an exotic hideaway for a child to play within.

Tonight her father didn't answer when she knocked, which wasn't unusual. He was often in his own world now. She pushed the door open and shivered at the gust of cold air. He had the balcony doors thrown wide. Pages blew over the barren floor where there had once been a Persian rug. So many of the room's comforts and ornamentations had been torn to pieces and burned in her father's fireplace, as though no matter how high the central heating was turned up, he could never quite get warm.

More than once his impromptu fires had nearly spread to the bedroom or the roof. Careless or intentional? Alissa wasn't completely sure.

As she moved into the room, she frowned at not finding him. There were shards of broken glass in the corner and a sticky film of red wine. Her heart pounded like a horse thundering from the gate. Nothing congealed or thick. No blood, but how had he gotten the bottle? And had he done anything more with the broken glass?

She hurried across the bedroom and spotted him lying prostrate on the floor. Her heart nearly stopped. Alissa rushed to him and knelt, feeling his face. Still warm. Still breathing. She exhaled in relief, then noticed he'd used the wall as a canvas for poetry and ramblings. In his drunkenness, he'd knocked over his inkwell and dragged his fingers through it, creating a swirling black mess, like a sinister finger painting. She flushed, embarrassed by the work Mrs. Carlisle would have to do to clean it. The housekeeper wouldn't enlist the help of the maids for fear that people would learn how unwell he still was. When she returned from the party, Alissa would try to clean most of it before Mrs. Carlisle arrived in the morning.

"Oh, Dad," she said, gently nudging him.

He jerked awake. "Ah, Persephone's twin," he murmured, his eyes peering through strands of unwashed hair.

"There's no Persephone. She was just a myth, remember?" Some legends were true. Some weren't. Her father had difficulty keeping them straight in his mind.

"This dagger," he said, brandishing his fountain pen near her throat and causing her to draw back. "Not sharper than a sword, but with a purpose as true as any." He exhaled stale wine and she grimaced.

"Dad," she said. "It's cold on the floor. Get in bed." She squeezed his forearm. "Please. I'm going to Calla and Dimitri's. I can't be late."

"That blasted Hades. Red-eyed demon. I'll cut him," he said, slashing the air.

With more prodding, she got him to his feet and helped him stumble past his scarred writing desk. Once a beautiful piece from Shanghai, it had been a gift from a devoted reader. Now his admirers had scattered to the four winds—along with his sense.

She led him to the bed, ignoring his mumbled ravings.

"I'll skewer his black heart. I'll reclaim Persephone from the underworld." He looked at his pen as Alissa tucked the blankets around him. "By your eyes, I can read your thoughts, and you're right. Perfectly right. This dagger is not nearly sharp enough. It will take Excalibur, to be sure. Gather words for a crown of poetry to rest upon her head. The Lady of the Lake is not easily impressed. Not easily. Nor should any such as she be." He closed his watery blue eyes, and Alissa slipped the pen from his grip.

"Rest," she whispered, infusing her voice with persuasive power.

For a moment, his eyes flickered open and his gaze was clear. "Alissa?"

A smile spread across her face. She was grateful to have him back for even a moment. "Yes, Dad, it's me."

"Hello, Moonbeam," he said, the smile in his voice.

"Hello."

Then his lids drooped, like shades descending slowly to close out the night.

She set the pen on the bedside table and pressed a kiss to his ink-smudged forehead. "When I become the Wreath Muse, I'll bring you all the way home," she said, wanting it to be true.

The spray from the fountain left faint water marks on the sage green velvet of Alissa's gown as she moved across the rose-scented courtyard. The dots of golden light gave everyone's skin a creamy porcelain glow.

The soft hum of voices mixed with background music. Mozart's lilting notes relaxed her. She stopped next to a table covered in Chantilly lace, pretending to admire it, while her attention was really on the large group of laughing friends across the courtyard.

Cerise Xenakis, her former best friend, held court at the center. Cerise's dark hair gleamed in the candlelight. She wore a daring dress of white leather and pewter lace. From a distance it looked like lingerie, and Alissa had heard that Cerise had taken the dress from a music video she'd starred in for the Molly Times, one of the bands she inspired. The Molly Times's debut album had gone platinum and had been nominated for three Grammy Awards.

Alissa swallowed hard, wondering to whose presentation the EC—the Etherlin Council—had given more votes: hers or Cerise's. Among the people Cerise inspired, there were an Olympic gold medalist, a Heisman Trophy winner, a principal dancer with the San Francisco Ballet, and four multiplatinum musical artists. Among Alissa's aspirants, her writers had won a Pulitzer, three National Book Awards, and two Academy Awards. Her scientific and engineering aspirants had published eighty-four scientific papers and generated nineteen patents, two of which Alissa had been included on. She had transferred her share in the patents to the Etherlin community trust. She was proud that her work on clean energy had generated eight million dollars over four years. That was four million more than she'd made modeling. She wanted to be respected and regarded as a muse of substance, but she was glad to have the modeling income for the community as well. She knew that with her combined earnings, she'd contributed more money to the trust than all the other current muses combined.

Alissa spotted Grant and nodded at him with a smile.

Grant Easton could sail around the world in rough winds, and the blond good looks he'd inherited from his grandfather made most women want to join him. Alissa actually had.

When he reached her side, he brushed his lips over her cheek in what was nearly a kiss. The public greeting was just like the man who'd given it to her: smooth, reserved, and appropriate. She wished that could be enough for her.

"I heard that you and your aspirants gave a great presentation on the desalination project. The council was really impressed."

She beamed. "Were they? I'm so glad. I keep going over the voting members in my head, trying to convince myself that I have enough support. I'm glad that the vote's only a few days away; the past few weeks have been so nerve-wracking."

"Well, despite having two daughters in the running for the Wreath, Dimitri continues to be your staunchest supporter."

"He considers me his third daughter. I'm very lucky in that respect. What else have you heard regarding where people are leaning?"

"I think if they voted today, you'd have it, but there are still lingering concerns about the past."

"They can't really be worried about my stability," she said, frowning. "I've been completely solid my whole life."

"You refuse security detail while in the Etherlin. People wonder why."

"I'm not the only one. All the muses refuse it in the Etherlin. There's no threat here. ES is the best."

He smiled and inclined his head at the compliment to Etherlin Security. ES acted as both police force for the Etherlin and personal security for the muses. Since Grant had been in charge of ES for two years, the praise was directed at him, too.

"I'm sure things will work out the way they're meant to for you, Alissa," he said. "Speaking of the voting EC members, one of them wants you."

She followed his gaze to Dimitri Xenakis, who raised a blunt-fingered hand to draw her over. He was a dark-haired bull of a man. Not very tall, but direct and powerful. In the early days after her mother's death and her father's breakdown, he was the best advisor and surrogate parent she could've wanted. But recently she'd become wary of his interest in her father's recovery. He'd suggested more than once that her father might unknowingly be leeching some of her muse energy. A guilty tremor made Alissa's muscles twitch. Her dad wasn't leeching energy. She was giving it to him, a fact she couldn't let anyone discover, since it would definitely cost her the Wreath if they did. Unfortunately, without her magic, Alissa was sure her father would spiral downward into a suicide attempt. She couldn't bear the thought. He was the only family she had left.

"Are you coming?" she asked Grant as she nodded at Dimitri.

"No, I've got some reports to write tonight. I'm heading out soon."

"All right," she said, giving his arm a squeeze as she passed him.

Dimitri's youngest daughter, Dorie, was at his side. When Alissa got close enough to see the sixteen-year-old, she was startled by the change in Dorie's face. The girl had been born with her mother Calla's proud Roman nose. Alissa had loved the distinctive look it gave her face, but apparently a plastic surgeon had whittled and sculpted it into something very different. Dorie's new nose looked familiar, and Alissa realized with a start that she was seeing her own nose on the other girl's face. Alissa maintained a blank expression, but cringed inwardly. There was always so much pressure to be the council's idea of perfection. It could be overwhelming for someone so young. Alissa, who'd had to battle back from the shame and censure that surrounded her mother's death, was well used to that pressure. She'd developed her own special way of coping. An illicit way.

She wrote letters to Merrick—and enjoyed it. There was the feeling, true or not, that she wouldn't be able to shock him with anything she shared. That he could never condemn her for breaking a rule because he would inevitably have done worse in his life. It gave her an intoxicating sense of freedom, even though it was dangerous. She surreptitiously touched the Art Deco gold and enamel bracelet on her wrist, a gift from Merrick.

Initially, she'd thought writing to him would be a temporary thing, but she couldn't seem to stop. Weeks would pass, and he would send her something, some gift. She would try to ignore it, but then in a weak moment, usually during the night, she went to her desk, unearthed her most elegant stationery, and drafted a letter. She often wrote for an entire hour. She never sent the first letters. They contained too much. She always wrote a second, milder, less revealing version that she actually sent. Except once. Once, she'd sent a first draft. She shivered, thinking of it. That letter had almost pushed them into territory where they could never venture. After the Merlot letter, as she referred to it in her mind, she'd stopped writing for almost six months, but then he'd sent flowers and she couldn't resist acknowledging them. So the writing resumed. The truth was, she loved having a connection, however minor, with someone outside the confines of her own world.

"Hi, Alissa," Dorie said. She pushed back a heavy curtain of black hair that had been highlighted with brassy copper streaks.

"Hello," Alissa said, offering her a warm smile.

Dimitri kissed Alissa's cheeks. "You look beautiful. You should wear that color to the meeting with the Ralph Lauren people."

Alissa's fingers tightened on the champagne flute in her hand. She hoped to be too busy for paid advertising campaigns soon. She hoped to be completely consumed with the Wreath Muse publicity tour and the obligations of the role.

Although there were three other muses officially in contention for the honor, realistically Cerise was the only one who could possibly edge out Alissa. As if on cue, the Act I waltz from *Swan Lake* began, and Cerise's friends encouraged her to dance. She declined at first, then relented. Cerise didn't have the willowy body of a ballerina, but no one could deny that when Cerise danced, she was a wonder to behold. Alissa kept her face blank, though her throat burned as it always did when she watched Cerise perform. A dance recital had ruined their childhood friendship, and Alissa had tried unsuccessfully to mend things between them for years afterward.

"She's amazing, isn't she, Papa?" Dorie asked.

"She dances well."

"Will the Etherlin Council take a muse's personal talents into consideration when voting?" Dorie asked. "Cerise sent the songs I wrote to a music producer. She thinks I'm talented enough to sell or record them."

"The EC is aware of everything a muse accomplishes, but it's more concerned with how well she inspires *other* people. Using the muse magic for personal gain and attention is a good way to not only get yourself taken out of the running for the Wreath, but also to be asked to leave the community."

"I didn't use muse magic! I write music in my spare time."

"You could be using that spare time to study and come up with ways to help foster innovations in the world. You should look to Alissa's example. She just finished her second degree."

Alissa hated being drawn into Dimitri's lecture. She knew he was just trying to motivate Dorie, which, if rumor served, Dorie needed. But the younger girl would certainly resent being negatively compared to Alissa.

"I probably study too much. I often have to fight the urge to collaborate," Alissa said.

"There's nothing wrong with collaborating if it enhances the inspiration you provide your aspirants," Dimitri said.

"Alissa, how's your father?" Dorie asked. "I was walking along the lake, and I saw him messing around in the flower beds. It looked like he was in his pajamas and digging with his hands," she said, wrinkling her nose.

Alissa narrowed her eyes. "He's doing well. He gardens sometimes to relax now that he's writing again."

"Writing? That's good. Not with your help though, I trust," Dimitri said.

"No. It's just exploratory writing and historical research, but it's keeping him occupied, and he's enjoying the process again."

"Took him long enough," Dorie muttered.

"Is that what you think?" Alissa demanded.

How dare Dorie, a girl with limited drive, criticize a man who'd once worked fifteen-hour days to write novels that had won major literary awards, a man whose work had sparked a political debate that led to a congressional hearing and changes in foreign policy. What did Dorie, a pampered teen barely past puberty, know about real pain? When Alissa's mother had died, her father had lost his love and his muse in a single night, a loss so devastating it had tipped him into despair and madness. Her father's current state wasn't his fault. No one had warned him about the dangerous side of muse magic until it was too late.

"Dorie, go and see if Mrs. Rella needs anything," Dimitri said curtly.

"Sure," Dorie said, unperturbed. Her dark eyes bore into Alissa as she passed.

"I'm sorry if that remark hurt you," he said with his characteristic bluntness.

Alissa didn't answer.

"Maybe Richard should stay with us. You know what fans Calla and I are of his novels. She'll be home in a few days, and she'd love to assist in his research and encourage his return to writing, which would allow you to concentrate on your own work."

"I have it all under control. It's the anniversary of Mom's death soon, and we always spend that together." She was sure the impending anniversary had caused her dad's setback, and Alissa wasn't going to let anyone see him until it passed.

If she got the Wreath, she might even be able to restore him to his former self. She longed for that and didn't feel guilty about using a little magic for his sake. The loss of muse magic was what had destroyed him in the first place, so he was owed some consideration. Also, it was the only thing Alissa took for herself. With the exception of the few hours per year that she spent writing letters to Merrick, her entire life was consumed with her role as a muse. Often from the time she woke until the time she went to bed, she followed an agenda that was created to serve her aspirants, the Etherlin community, and mankind at large. *I'm allowed to take care of my own father, too,* she thought defiantly.

"All right," Dimitri said. "Let us know if you need help with anything."

She smiled and squeezed his forearm. "Thank you, Dimitri."

He nodded and excused himself. She relaxed her shoulders and slipped into the house through the French doors. Passing the lilac damask drapes framing the arched window, she maneuvered around the three-foot-tall flower arrangement sitting on a white-stone pedestal. She set her empty champagne flute on a sterling silver tray for soiled dishes, and then turned to the servant standing at the front door.

"If you have a moment, I'd like my wrap," she said.

"Of course," he said with a smile, then walked to the closet. A moment later, he held aloft the ivory shawl that was intricately embroidered with gold. She stepped forward and let him slip it around her shoulders.

"It's quite a lovely piece," he said.

"Yes," she said, cursing the faint blush that rose in her cheeks. Another gift from Merrick that she shouldn't have kept. She wondered what he was doing tonight. Probably something disreputable. Since he seemed to know her taste and always sent beautiful and thoughtful gifts, it was hard not to romanticize him. She had to remind herself that violence lurked under his charming generosity. "Thank you," she said.

"Would you like the car called?"

"Oh no," she said. "It's a beautiful night. I'll walk."

"Very good, Miss North," he said, opening the front door.

The clanging of the gate drew her gaze. A group that included Cerise and Dorie had come out of the yard, apparently going for a stroll. Alissa waited for them to pass before she left the house.

When she was beyond the edge of Xenakis property, she cut down one of the cobbled paths to the lakeside promenade. It was a shorter walk home, and a prettier one. The lake was like glass, moonlight reflecting off its placid surface. She paused to stare at the water. The Etherlin was the most beautiful place on Earth. They were lucky to have built their community in such a stunning place.

A shadow crept over the water. She looked up at the huge full moon. No clouds had drifted across it.

Strange, she thought, her gaze returning to the path, which seemed to darken in front of her. She began walking again, noticing that the night had grown colder, a chill seeping under her skin.

What is it? What do I sense?

She trod lightly but quickly. The silence became oppressive. Her breath quickened, and she dampened her lips. Something slithered around her ankle, and she stumbled, crying out. She landed on the grass, her heart hammering. Black magic as bleak and frozen as a snowcap surrounded her, but that couldn't be. Not within the purity of the Etherlin.

She yanked at the hem of her dress to be certain there was no snake crawling up her leg. Finding nothing tangled in her skirt or limbs, she clambered to her feet and jerked her head to look over her shoulder.

A cloaked figure rushed toward her.

There wasn't time to react.

Chapter 2

Sitting in his office, Merrick's eyes flicked to the flat-screen television that was on but muted. He watched Alissa North climb out of a white stretch limo and walk toward a fountain. Her white dress and white blonde hair glowed in the moonlight, and then she looked over her shoulder as the camera zoomed in on her flawless face. His muscles tightened at the impact of her wide blue eyes staring at him. He must've seen the perfume commercial a hundred times, but he still couldn't look away.

Merrick took a key from his pocket and unlocked the bottom drawer of his desk. Sliding the drawer open, he took the top letter from the pile and opened the envelope. Who in the twenty-first century besides a very rich heiress would use heavy bond, monogrammed stationery and a fountain pen?

He extracted the letter, one of the first she'd sent, and unfolded it.

Dear Mr. Merrick,

As usual, the roses you sent for my birthday were beautiful. As usual, I cannot accept them. Also per routine, your messenger refused to return them or the other gift to you. In fact, he went quite pale at my suggestion that he do so. I can't help but wonder why he was so terrified at the thought. I think it very likely that your management style

*uses a great deal of intimidation—another thing of which
I don't approve.*

Merrick smiled. She'd challenged him in the early letters,
and he'd liked her for it. Just as he'd admired her at that first
meeting, when she'd seen his fangs and stood her ground,
controlling her fear.

He glanced back at the letter.

*I distributed the flowers among the county hospital wards
to patients without family. Did you know that many of the
people in the county hospital are from the Varden? That
makes them members of your community. Perhaps, instead
of sending me flowers and gifts, which I can't accept, you
could write a check to fund one or two hospital programs.
I've heard your businesses are very successful, and chari-
table giving is good for the soul—though I confess that I'm
not certain whether you still have yours. From your reputation, you might have lost it playing cards or while working
for your former employers. If not, I've enclosed the card of
Mr. Robert Wendell, who can discuss philanthropy with you.*

    *When the flowers arrived, I was pleased to find that
you took my suggestion and sent a separate and longer
note with them. Three whole sentences. Shockingly ver-
bose for you. Maybe one day you'll graduate to a full
paragraph.*

He laughed, then rubbed his thumb over his lower lip. He
wondered, not for the first time, how long it would take him to
seduce her if they were ever in the same room together again.

He had never forgotten the way she'd smelled, her vanilla-
scented skin and beneath it her blood, so fresh and pure that
it made his fangs ache. For how long would a drink from her
throat quench his thirst? Months? And how soft would her
naked body feel under his?

He closed his eyes and exhaled slowly. Leaving her alone
went against all his predatory instincts, but they had an unspo-
ken understanding. She flirted with him in the letters because
she felt safe. In person, she wouldn't be bold. In person, she

wouldn't be happy to see him. So he stayed away because he wanted the letters to keep coming.

As ever, I wish you a long and happy life. Please do your utmost to let those around you enjoy the same.

Sincerely,
A.N.

Merrick set the letter on his desk and rested his hand on top of it. If she'd been human, he'd have had her by now. But Alissa North was part of a dynasty. The last heiress of the House of North. The purest of the Etherlin. Descended from the ancient muses . . . inspiration made flesh.

For a member of the ventala, even trying to see her would be a dangerous game. Not that danger would have stopped him if he'd thought she'd welcome his visit. Not that anything would have stopped him.

Someone knocked, returning Merrick from his thoughts.

"Come," Merrick said, and watched the office door open. Ox maneuvered his massive bulk inside, and Merrick raised an eyebrow at Ox's shirt. It was a shiny, seizure-inducing print of dark gold, teal, and black.

"Ox, you looking for a second job?"

"Boss?"

"Well, I figured in that shirt you must be looking for some part-time work as a pimp or a gigolo."

"It's Versace, boss," Ox said, running a hand over his chest.

Merrick smirked. "You think Versace makes clothes in your size?"

"It's Versace," Ox said stubbornly, though a scowl clouded his features. "There's a Versace label. You want to see it?" His thick fingers went for the buttons.

Still smiling, Merrick slipped Alissa North's letter in the drawer and locked it. "How hard do you think it would be to switch a label? To take it out of one shirt and sew it in another . . ."

After a momentary pause, Ox growled, "That son-of-a-bitch."

Merrick's gaze flicked back up as Ox turned toward the door.

"Before you go, you want to tell me why you came up?" Merrick asked.

Ox snapped his fingers. "Sorry, boss. Yeah. Theo Tobin called."

Tobin. The parasitic photographer who trailed Alissa everywhere. Merrick waited.

"He wanted to let us know he's crossed into the Varden through our patch," Ox said.

"What's he doing here?"

"Guess he followed the girl."

Merrick's stillness became preternatural. Even the atoms seemed to slow responsively.

Alissa had never entered the Varden. She was too cautious, too smart. "Call him back. Find out if he's following her and, if so, where they are."

Ox nodded and walked to the phone.

Merrick waited, wondering what could have enticed her to come into his world.

Two calls later, Ox hung up. "He followed her, but he lost the car when it went through a private underground tunnel into Jacobi's territory."

Merrick shook his head and stood, his muscles tight. She would never have agreed to go there. Someone had taken her. *Kidnapped her.* Unbelievable. And unwise. Rage simmered inside him.

"Call Tony and tell him I need an unmarked car. We'll take a ride and have a look." He paused. There would be terrible consequences if they were caught trespassing in another syndicate member's territory. But she was there. Alissa North. On his side of the wall, and in trouble. The temptation to go after her burned in his blood. If she were in hell and the devil was home, Merrick might have stopped short of crashing the gates. Then again, maybe not.

"Ox, let's do this quietly."

"Like a whisper, boss."

Chapter 3

Alissa's head hurt. She squinted. She didn't recognize the dark room, but could feel that she was lying on a bed. She needed something to drink.

Where? She put a hand to her temple. Her hair felt strange, stiff and prickly. Her elbow throbbed, too. *I'm not well. So thirsty. Where am I?*

She tried to sit up, but the room spun. She lay still for several moments, then rolled carefully onto her side and pushed herself onto her hands and knees, breathing deeply. It was better if she moved slowly.

She ran her hand along the wall until she found a switch. She turned it on and looked around at the small, spartan room that contained only a twin bed and chest of drawers.

I'm so thirsty.

"Where in the world am I?" she mumbled, struggling to recall. The last thing she remembered was leaving the Xenakis party.

What time was that?

She looked down at her chest, reassured by the sage velvet. She was still wearing her gown. Glancing around slowly, she realized that her purse wasn't in the room. No cell phone. She glanced at her bare wrist. Her favorite bracelet, the Art Deco one from Merrick, was gone.

Both of her pale wrists had faint blue marks. She touched one and winced. Bruises. Someone had gripped her wrists tightly. Had he, or they, held her down? Nausea roiled in her belly.

She moved to the edge of the bed, dangling her bare feet over the side. Her shoes were gone, too. She put a hand to the throbbing ache in the crook of her left arm and felt small crusted scabs. Puncture wounds? She winced, feeling sick, too afraid to contemplate where she suspected she was.

How? How did I get here?

She stood, overwhelmed by dizziness for a moment. She braced herself against the wall and licked her dry lips. She had to have water.

She turned the small brass handle and opened the door as noiselessly as possible. Down the cool, dim hall, she walked cautiously toward a lit room. She heard a man speaking. She paused, breathless. Every nerve seemed to cry out for her to turn back, but she had to have something to drink.

She moved to the edge of the room and peered in. Hanging above the couch was a horribly graphic picture of a dead naked woman. *Oh, God.* Nausea and dizziness. She gagged silently.

Have to get out.

The brown-haired man who was speaking on the phone had his back to her. If he turned, he would see her. Fear roared in her ears.

Every heartbeat painful, she stood frozen for a moment, then walked silently to the front door. She tried to open it, but it wouldn't give. The deadbolt had been locked with a key. Her breath came and went in short gasps. Her chest squeezed tight.

"Hey there, princess. I'm amazed you can stand when you're a few quarts low."

She spun to face the man. Was he the one who'd bitten her? *He'll pay for it,* she thought, fury mingling with fear. Her eyes darted around the apartment. *Assuming he's caught.*

His wiry build and narrow eyes gave him a ratlike appearance, and the receding hairline and fleshy lips were mismatched, as though his genes had been too generous with some features and not generous enough with others.

"Who are you?"

His smile was pure menace. "I'm your keeper, sweetheart."

No way!

Her legs moved, almost without her thinking. She couldn't get past him to the door, but she could put some distance between them. She staggered down the hall, stubbing her toes. Once inside a large bedroom, she slammed the door and locked it. Her gaze darted around the room. No phone, no way to call for help, but she had to escape.

He pounded on the door, and she jumped.

"Don't make me come in there after you. You won't like what happens when I do."

Her legs burned and her chest wailed, everything cramping like she'd been running for miles. She stumbled to the far wall to lean against it. She didn't want to lose consciousness, but felt so weak. This was shock, she realized, from dehydration. From blood loss.

She grasped the curtains, trying to steady herself, but they crashed down, unable to hold her entire body weight.

"All right, what the hell?" he bellowed.

Without the curtains, she could see the door that led to a balcony. How many stories up? Could she climb down?

She slumped against the wall, trying to catch her breath. Her heart slammed against her ribs. Just breathing was such an effort.

The sound of a key turning in the lock made her muscles cramp in terror. She had to get away from him, but how?

She forced herself to stand. If she could get around him, maybe she could get out of the apartment. If he was ventala, that made him at least half human. Was there enough humanity in him for her to influence with her power?

The door swung open and he stalked in, frowning. "We're not going to play games all night." He gripped her arms and bent his face close, fangs hovering above her skin. Another bite would kill her.

She glared at him.

He ran his tongue along the side of her throat, making her stomach lurch in revulsion. She raked her nails down his arms. The predatory look in his slitlike eyes froze the breath in her chest, but she didn't let fear show on her face.

He pinned her to the wall. "Do you need me to teach you a lesson about who's in control here?"

Alissa let her expression turn to ice. She'd survived things worse than death. Survived with the silent, unshakable dignity that was her birthright. The last muse of the House of North was not going to grovel for some half-breed monster's pleasure.

"Control me?" She shook her head with a grim smile. "That's something you'll never manage."

His frown turned fierce. "We'll see," he sneered, his lips baring jagged fangs.

In the passenger seat of the dark-windowed sedan, Merrick hung up his cell phone. "No one admits to knowing anything," he told Ox.

"Maybe Tobin doesn't know what he's talking about. Maybe the girl's at home, asleep in her bed," Ox said.

"For now, let's assume she's in Jacobi's territory. She'll be delivered to him. Anything else is a suicide play. Drive to Coliseum and Athens and park there."

"Couple blocks from Jacobi's building?"

Merrick nodded.

"If we take a walk through the street, someone's sure to spot us. Especially if something's going down. He'll have more security."

"No doubt," Merrick said.

Ox found a parking spot on Coliseum Street and slid the car into it.

"You're too recognizable. Stay in the car," Merrick said, pulling a black mask down over his face.

"Boss, you can't be thinking of going alone."

"Pop the trunk, and stay sharp. I'm just going to have a look around, but I might be in a hurry to leave when I get back."

"Boss, I could put on a mask, too. You gotta let me do what you pay me for—"

"Tonight, I'm paying you to drive. Stay in the car."

Merrick got out. He opened the trunk and retrieved his enforcer duffel.

"Your life must be so tiring," Alissa whispered breathlessly. If he'd been completely human and she hadn't been ill, it would've been easy to overcome his will. Of course, if he'd been human, he wouldn't have bitten her in the first place. There were those who wanted to kill all the ventala, ridding the earth of them as people had once exterminated all the vampires after the Rising. At the moment, she could almost agree with Grant and his cohorts who said the ventala were a menace beyond redemption. *Except for Merrick,* she couldn't help adding in her mind.

She thrust as much muse power as she could focus into her voice. "You need rest."

The man's lids drifted down, his arms dropping. He slumped to the floor.

She took his keys, swaying dizzily.

Now, get out, she thought, but her body couldn't move as fast as she wanted. And he recovered too quickly, his dazed expression clearing, his eyes narrowing angrily. She tried to get around him, but he grabbed her leg. She jerked free. She slammed the heel of her hand into his nose, all her self-defense training coming back.

Then she grabbed the short security pole from the track of the sliding door. She hit him with it, snapping, "Fall!"

He stumbled, blood dripping from his nose and brow where she'd hit him. She lurched out onto the balcony and wedged the pole between the frame and the door handle.

He got to his feet and tried to jerk the door open. When it didn't move, he slapped his palms against the glass. "You don't have wings, baby," he yelled. "Open this door." He slammed his fist against it.

She locked eyes with him defiantly, even though her breath came and went in short gasps that sliced through her lungs like a knife. Her dry lips cracked, and she tasted a hint of blood. There was barely any blood left to flow through her.

She reached out and held the rail to steady herself as the world spun. She blinked against blurring vision, forcing herself to stay upright by sheer force of will. If death was the only option, she would do it on her own terms. She leaned against the rail, swaying as the view of the drop swam in and out of focus. When the time came, the silent fall to the concrete several stories below would only take seconds.

"You can barely stand up! You need to be in bed till the doctor gets here. Open the damn door! I'll bust the glass if I have to."

Open the door? So she could be a prisoner and a blood whore for him? *Never.*

She glanced at the building's exterior. Glossy black and pearly white. Stark and shocking, so unlike anything in the Etherlin.

Her muscles cramped and her knees gave way. Her skin scraped against the rough outdoor carpet. She raised a palm, staring at the eerie bloodless scratches. *No blood left.*

Burning pain became piercing and lanced through her.

She realized she wouldn't need to jump.

Pain blossomed in her chest. Death was coming.

There was extra security. A guy on the back door. Probably a guy on the roof, too, Merrick thought, looking up. He went still.

There was a body on the penthouse balcony. A blonde-haired, porcelain-skinned body. *That had better not be her,* he thought wildly.

He yanked his binoculars out of the duffel. *She's too valuable,* he told himself as he raised the binoculars. Jacobi wouldn't have gone through the trouble of getting her out of the Etherlin only to kill her on the first night.

Unless the asshole couldn't resist biting her, and he'd drained her dry. Merrick's muscles bunched. *If he did, I'll kill him for it. He'll pay for her blood with his own.*

Merrick swallowed his rage. It was the vampire in him talking. His human side reasoned that he had no claim on the girl. Avenging her wasn't his responsibility.

The lattice of the bars made it impossible to tell for sure if the woman was Alissa North, but whoever was on that balcony wasn't moving.

He should walk away. If she was already dead, there was no point starting a blood feud.

What if she's not dead?

He set the duffel down lightly. He popped a nonkilling clip into his gun and fitted it with a silencer, then he slung the harpoon rifle and its corded nylon rope over his shoulder.

He stayed in the shadow of the opposite building until he was ten feet from Jacobi's. Two shots took the backdoor guard down. That bullet between the eyes was going to give the guy a major headache.

Merrick shot the spike into the underside of the balcony and started up the rope. Alive or dead, he had to know.

Chapter 4

Roses. She smelled roses, which reminded her of Merrick. She dreamed he was standing over her. Beautiful and dark, like a fallen angel. *Fallen.*

Why didn't he smile? In her dreams, he always wore the smirk that she'd never forgotten.

"Smile." Her voice was soft and rough. She tried to raise her hand to touch him, but it was too heavy. He would disappear now. That's what he did in her dreams.

"Rest," he said. He caressed her cheek with his fingertip, which surprised her because he'd never touched her before.

"I'm thirsty."

He smiled. *Finally.*

"I bet you are," he said.

His voice was different than she remembered. Deeper. Her pulse throbbed in her ears. Something was wrong. "Am I—?" She tried to sit up, her eyes darting around the dim room. Rich, heavy fabrics. Eggplant trimmed in gold. The colors were wrong for one of her dreams.

"Where am I?" she croaked. It wasn't a dream, she realized with a stab of fear.

"My penthouse."

His penthouse? How had that happened?

She looked down at the bandage taped to the inside of her

right elbow; an IV sprouted from underneath it. A memory surfaced of another penthouse. Of preparing to die.

"How did I get here?"

"I brought you."

She clutched the thick, velvety coverlet. "I was on a balcony . . ."

He nodded.

"In the Varden. This is the Varden, isn't it?"

"Yes." He moved a plush, deep purple chair next to the bed and sat.

She massaged her temples with her fingertips, trying to piece together the details.

"I don't understand," she said and fell silent. He waited as her mind connected the dots.

She'd survived somehow. Impossible as that had seemed.

She'd been so anemic that her body had gone into shock. But she wasn't suffocating now. Why wasn't she, she wondered.

"Did you give me blood?" she asked sharply.

"Had to."

"Not your blood."

He smiled. "No. Not tainted blood. Clean human blood. I would've given you muse blood, but that's generally hard to come by."

She frowned. It hadn't been hard to come by for the ventala who'd fed on her. "I can't remember what happened," she said.

"Here," he said, holding out a glass. "Orange juice fortified with iron."

She took it and sipped. "I must have been kidnapped—and drugged, I suppose." She glanced at him to gauge his expression.

"Tell me the last thing you remember," he said. His voice was so smooth, so calm and reassuring. She was grateful for that.

"I'd been at a party."

"What happened there?"

"Nothing special. I remember leaving . . . then my mind's

blank, like the memories were erased." She shook her head. "I woke up in a strange apartment. I collapsed on the balcony." She ran her fingers absently over the blanket. "How did you . . . ?"

"Don't worry about how I found you. Concentrate on how you got into the Varden to begin with."

"I don't know. You're the only person in this area that I'm acquainted with—remotely acquainted with," she felt compelled to add. The letters had been reasonably safe, but this definitely wasn't. Being in the same room with him? So much could go wrong. He could lose control.

She didn't completely trust herself either. There was something about him that she found so compelling. She made her tone falsely optimistic. "It's incredible that I ended up here."

She shivered as the circumstances sank in. She was lying in a bed in the home of a ventala who'd been interested in her ever since they'd met. One she'd written letters to. Letters that smacked of a familiarity they were never supposed to have. Of course, he understood the situation. The limitations. She knew he did, because he'd never tried to see her. Not once.

She realized she might be able to overcome the disaster of the night, to save herself from ruin. If she was clever and quick, the Wreath Muse position might not be lost and, with it, her only hope of saving her dad.

"I have to go home immediately," she said.

He studied her in a cool, assessing way. Would he help her or not?

A knock at the door startled her, and she jerked.

He watched her for a moment, ignoring the door. "I know you've been through something and that you're scared—"

"I'm not scared."

He smiled at her bravado, which they both knew wasn't completely genuine. "You're on edge," he offered diplomatically.

She shrugged.

"Well, you can relax while you're in my house. No one will hurt you here."

She ran a finger over the bandage on her wounded arm.

The place where she'd been bitten. "Not even you?" she asked boldly.

He leaned forward so his mouth was very close to her ear. "The only way I'll bite you is if you invite me to."

Her heart raced, and her lips went dry. "I'll never do that," she whispered in a voice that was more breathless than she intended.

"Probably not." He leaned back. "You look good with color in your cheeks again."

He walked to the door. She fisted the covers to brace herself as he opened it. She recognized the waiting man. She'd seen him in pictures. His name was Mr. Orvin, and he was the enormous bodyguard with spiked blond hair who went everywhere with Merrick, as if Merrick needed a bodyguard.

"What's up, Ox?" Merrick asked.

"Cato Jacobi's downstairs, boss. He wants to talk to you. Seems to think we've got something that belongs to him." Orvin's quick glance at her conveyed his meaning.

Alissa's eyebrows shot up in surprise. "I don't know anyone named Cato Jacobi."

"You don't know his name, but you've met him," Merrick said, tapping the inside of his left elbow as he looked at her. Her hand drifted to the sore spot. "I picked you up from his balcony."

"He's the one who kidnapped me?"

"My guess is that he'll have a different version of events," Merrick said, cool as ice. Merrick nodded toward the next room and said to Orvin, "Tell them to give Cato a drink, and let him know I'll be down in a few minutes."

Orvin disappeared from the doorway, and Merrick closed the door.

She studied him. Was he on good terms with the man who'd kidnapped her? Perhaps Merrick had even arranged it, she thought, horrified. She had been playing with fire by sending him those letters.

She exhaled forcefully and leaned back against the cushioned headboard, trying to recover her strength. "Were you involved in the plot to get me into the Varden?" she asked.

"A plot that involved someone else biting you?" he countered, and shook his head.

"Maybe that wasn't part of the original plan, but someone couldn't resist. Ventala aren't exactly known for their restraint."

"If I'd wanted you kidnapped, I wouldn't have trusted anyone else to do the job. I'd have come for you myself."

"How very reassuring," she said dryly.

"Cato Jacobi's here to retrieve you. What does that tell you?"

"That he's a presumptuous, psychotic bastard?"

The corner of Merrick's mouth curved into a smirk. "What else?"

"That he thinks you'll negotiate with him. You won't, will you?"

He shook his head. "Think things over while I'm gone. Try to remember what happened," he said. He strode out and closed the door behind him.

Chapter 5

Ox stood when Merrick walked into the living room.

"Lotta things in life are a disappointment. Not her though. She's better in the flesh than in pictures, huh?" Ox said.

Merrick nodded.

They strolled into the hallway, and Merrick locked the door, punching in a nine-digit pin to set the security code. If he'd wanted to get in and hadn't known the pin, it wouldn't have stopped him, but it would stop most people.

"Jacobi's here to reclaim her. What does that say to you, Ox?"

Ox shrugged massive shoulders. "Says he thinks he's entitled to her."

"Exactly. Why would he think that?"

"Must've paid someone to deliver her to his place."

Merrick nodded. "And who but someone from her inner circle could've delivered her to him?" he asked as they walked down the hall.

"Doesn't she know who it was?"

Merrick punched in another code, and the elevator doors slid open. He barely glanced at the sleek steel walls or framed white orchid painting. "She can't remember, but she doesn't seem to suspect anyone she knows," Merrick said.

Ox's pale brows rose. "Why not?"

"Because where she's from they don't betray each other that way. They're like her. Pure of blood and heart, focused on helping mankind and on giving money away to any cause they consider worthy, which is practically anything."

"Sounds too good to be true. And obviously it is, since somebody sold her out."

"Right. So what do you think would happen if I sent her back there alone?"

Ox shrugged. "The guy might be too scared of getting caught to betray her again, or he might not. I'd say even money."

"Fifty-fifty? I don't agree," Merrick said. "Whoever betrayed her has gotten paid, and Jacobi wants what he bought. That's what he's doing here. You think the kidnapper will be allowed to walk away from the deal?"

"You got a point. The guy who took her has either gotta disappear himself or he's gotta turn over the girl."

Merrick nodded.

"So what are you going to do with her?" Ox asked.

That's the question, Merrick thought. He knew what he wanted to do with her. It certainly didn't involve sending her to the Etherlin unprotected. Or sending her to the Etherlin at all. "She thought I might give her to Jacobi tonight."

Ox's laughter echoed around the elevator.

"You find that funny?" Merrick asked.

"Yeah, boss, I do," he said, barking out another laugh. "If Jacobi showed up here demanding a half dozen rats from our sewers, I don't think you'd give them to him. I know you're not turning over the only girl you send flowers to."

"Roses are cheap," Merrick said lightly.

"Not the kind you send."

The elevator stopped at the ground floor.

"Look sharp," Merrick said as the doors slid open to reveal the nightclub he lived above. His club.

The Crimson's décor was inspired by its name. Large framed black-and-white prints of glamorous women hung in corners, the only color being their merlot-colored lipstick. Small vases of crimson roses sat on each black marble-topped table. One wall was papered in smoky pewter with deep red crushed-velvet vines crawling across it. On the balconied second floor, plush burgundy couches and chaises encouraged people to recline and do things better left unnamed.

Merrick wondered what Alissa would think of the place when she saw it. Would it be too dramatic and sensual for her? The only thing he could recall about the inside of the Etherlin mansion he'd been in was that the place had been brightly lit and unremittingly beige.

He nodded to the bartender and walked to the back of the club. He opened the door to a private room and found Cato Jacobi and two of his guys sitting at the copper table. They each had a drink in hand, and Candy, one of the Crimson waitresses, was topping off Cato's tumbler.

He and his guys stood when Merrick and Ox entered.

"You mind if we get right to it?" Cato asked when they were all seated.

"Go ahead," Merrick said.

"You violated the rules tonight. Came into my territory uninvited. Took something that belongs to me."

"You're misinformed," Merrick said.

"You deny it?" Cato scoffed.

Merrick simply stared at him, causing Cato to explode into curses.

"Look, I know it was you," Cato snapped as he pulled out a small manila envelope. He opened the clasp and dramatically pulled out several photographs, slapping them on the table in front of Merrick.

Merrick spread them out, glanced them over, and restacked them. The pictures had been taken from a security camera outside Cato Jacobi's building, and they showed Merrick carrying an unconscious Alissa North away from the building, but there was nothing about his clothes to identify him, and his face was covered by the mask.

"Who's the girl?" Merrick asked.

"You know who she is!" Cato snapped. "I want her back. And I want a big friggin' payout since you came into my territory without talking to me."

"She looks familiar. She looks a little like that heiress from the perfume commercials, but I know it can't be, because only a moron would think he could get away with kidnapping a muse from the heart of the Etherlin. That would open the Varden up to the biggest crackdown we've ever seen. Extremely bad for business."

"Oh, no," Cato said, showing off a crooked smile. "I've got it covered. An insurance policy. They're not going to come after her."

Merrick narrowed his eyes. "Why not?"

"None of your goddamned business. Just get her ass down here. And I'll take fifty grand to start for your little joyride across the border."

Merrick slid the envelope to him and stood. "Nice of you to visit tonight, Cato, but don't make a habit of it."

"We'll bring my car around back," Jacobi said. "Your guy here can bring the girl and the money down to it."

Merrick shook his head. "The guy in the pictures could be anyone."

"The hell it could!"

"And if she's so important, maybe you should've tried a little harder to hold on to her."

"You son-of-a-bitch," Cato shouted, pulling out his gun.

Merrick slammed Cato's wrist to the table, causing the gun to drop with a clatter. "You don't want to do that, Cato."

Cato panted, saliva dripping from the corner of his mouth. "What are you going to do, Merrick? Kill me? My father knows I'm here." When Merrick didn't answer, Cato narrowed his eyes. "Go ahead and do me then. See what it buys you. You may have been a great enforcer, but you're still only one guy. And you're not popular these days with the syndicate. They'd like an excuse to take your head."

Merrick picked up Cato's gun and tossed it to Ox, who caught it. "Thanks for the gun. Have a safe drive home."

"You're making a mistake!" Cato shouted as Ox ushered him and his men out of the room.

It took about ten minutes for Ox to reappear. When he did, he was grinning. "You're slick, boss," Ox said. "There's no way they can prove it was you."

"What's the most interesting thing Jacobi said tonight?"

"What caught my attention is different than what caught yours, boss."

Merrick cocked his head. "Yeah?"

"Well, he said the syndicate's pissed at you. That's because you won't take any more enforcer jobs, and you're the best. They thought when they gave you this part of the Varden you were going to stay their boy. They see it as payment."

"How do I see it?" Merrick asked.

"You paid a boatload of money for this patch of concrete. I think you figure you bought it outright and don't owe the syndicate anything."

Merrick nodded.

"It still gets my attention," Ox continued, "that they're pissed at you though, because it's my job to make sure no one cuts off your head. But since having people gunning for you never bothers you, I know that's not what interested you about what Jacobi said."

"You're right."

Ox grinned. "See. I told you that you wouldn't be sorry for taking me on. I can almost read your mind these days, boss."

"So then you know what I'm going to say."

"Well," Ox said sheepishly. "I know you wanna know why Jacobi's so damn convinced the family of the baby-doll upstairs is going to write her off."

"Exactly, but I think we can guess what's involved."

"We can?"

"Call Tobin. Get him here and put him on ice until I'm ready to talk to him."

"What are you going to do, boss? Nothin' that will give the syndicate an excuse to take you out, I hope."

Merrick shrugged. "I've never had much of an appetite for playing it safe, Ox. Besides, what's the point of me paying you, unless I expect the syndicate to send a crew for my head one of these days?"

Alissa peeled the tape from the crook of her arm and exhaled slowly as she slid the intravenous line from her vein. A small drop of dark blood welled in the hollow until she bent her arm up tight.

Still a bit woozy, she emerged carefully from the cloud of bedding. She wished she could stay resting, but knew she shouldn't. She needed to get home before she was missed.

At least she'd made the muse-powered suggestion to her father that he rest. Between that and his depression, he'd be asleep for at least twelve hours. Considering her situation, she was glad she didn't have to worry about him until morning.

She padded to the door and pushed it open. Her gaze darted around the dimly lit parlor, drinking it in. The black-and-white furniture. The highly polished metal and silver blue accents. A small bronze statue of a dancing Egyptian girl charming a snake. Another of a half-naked female huntress. Art Deco, she realized. One of her favorite periods. She regretted that she needed to leave so quickly.

She looked around for a phone. Etherlin Security had a helicopter, and when Grant learned she'd been kidnapped, he'd keep her visit to the Varden a secret. Would there be a place for him to land? On the roof, perhaps? Should she check it before she called?

She wondered if he would be able to get out of the Etherlin without people noticing. Her future depended on Grant's discretion, but things wouldn't be completely under his control. The community—Her thought broke off midstream as she thought about Etherlin Security. How could Cato Jacobi or any ventala have managed to get her out? If she'd been awake, she'd have fought. Someone should've noticed. And why couldn't she remember? It seemed like the drugging must have preceded the abduction. But how?

The words hung there. She didn't want to finish the thought, but couldn't help herself. Had someone helped this Jacobi? Someone she knew? The vote was only a few days away, and she was favored to win. She thought of Cerise, Dorie, and Ileana, the other three Etherlin muses, any of whom might benefit from her being out of the way, but she couldn't imagine any of them knowing someone from the Varden, let alone helping him kidnap a muse.

A soft beeping startled her. A moment later, the main door

opened and Merrick stepped inside. There was no one with him, and the expression on his handsome face was inscrutable.

"What did the kidnapper say? How did he get me out of the Etherlin?"

"We didn't get into those details."

"Have you heard anything? Has there been a news story about an assault on the Etherlin? Maybe someone detonating a part of the wall?"

"No."

Her hand rested lightly on a console table, and she shook her head in confusion. "How could he have gotten in, found me, drugged me, and gotten us out?"

"There are only a few people in the world who could've broken into the Etherlin undetected. Cato Jacobi isn't one of them."

"Are you?"

He nodded. "But if I'd taken you, you would have woken up here. Not at his place."

She sank into a chair. "I don't understand what happened."

He leaned against the wall, watching her. "There were traces of black magic clinging to your skin."

She looked down at herself.

"It's gone. I washed it off you. How'd it get there?"

"I have no idea." She shook her head. "There are no practitioners of black magic in the Etherlin. I must have been exposed to it in Cato Jacobi's apartment."

"His place wasn't the source. When I was on the balcony, I would've been able to tell if it had come from inside."

She shrugged. "Then I'm not sure."

"You've never used it for anything? A ritual or a rite?"

"Never. I wouldn't."

"So it happened during the time period that you can't remember. It was probably used to alter your consciousness."

Someone had forced black magic on her? Used it in a way that made her lose her memory, like a date-rape drug? She shuddered, wishing she could stand under a hot shower and scrub her skin for an hour. What else had been done to her? There was no soreness between her legs. She didn't feel as if she'd been raped. Apparently, Cato Jacobi had felt the time was better spent drinking her blood, but the way he'd acted in his apartment suggested that he would've gotten around to rape quickly enough. Maybe he'd wanted her to be awake for that part. *Sleazy bastard.*

She glanced at Merrick, experiencing another rush of gratitude. She was incredibly lucky that he'd found her.

"Mr. Merrick, I don't have any real experience getting out of trouble because I don't normally get into it. May I hire you? I need your advice and expertise."

The corner of his mouth curved up. "There's only one kind of work-for-hire that I do."

She frowned. "I understand."

"No, I don't think you do. I said you can't hire me. I didn't say I wouldn't help you."

She raised her eyebrows. "What would you hope for in return?"

"Longer letters?"

She laughed softly, surprised and charmed. "I don't believe for a minute that that's the only thing you hope to gain."

"I'm going to have a drink. I'll make you one, too. Then you can tell me what illegal or immoral activities you've been involved in."

"What?" she exclaimed. "Why would you say that?"

"Cato Jacobi came here to get you back, effectively announcing that he'd had you kidnapped. He wouldn't have done that if he expected repercussions from your side of the wall. What could he know that would make your family and friends refuse to come after you?"

"Nothing . . ." She trailed off, thinking of her father. Even if someone had found out about that, she couldn't imagine anyone helping a ventala to kidnap her. That was effectively being an accomplice to murder, since most ventala would have bled her to death—as Jacobi almost had. She clenched her teeth. Had she really been betrayed by someone she knew? If so, that person couldn't be allowed to get away with it. Alissa would have to find out who had done it, and why.

Merrick stood at the bar, his back to her. The sound of ice

sliding along the walls of a cocktail shaker filled the air. "We don't have a lot of time."

"Mr. Merrick, if you give your word, do you honor it?" she asked.

"Yes."

"I've heard that you do . . . keep your word, despite the way you make your living." She paused, sitting up straighter. "Will you give me your word that you'll keep what I tell you a secret? And that if you're not inclined to help me, you won't prevent me from leaving?"

"I *will* be inclined to help you, and I will let you leave," he said, his voice as smooth as the polished steel of the shaker. He strained a mixture that looked like hazy sunlight into a chilled cocktail glass.

She took a deep breath and exhaled, rubbing her forehead. *This subject makes her weary,* Merrick thought.

"I've been secretly using my influence to help someone. I've lied about it. If anyone from the Etherlin found out what I've been doing, I would get into a great deal of trouble."

He walked over to her and held out the glass. "Who have you been helping?"

She tilted her head, her pale blue eyes widening slightly in an innocent expression that made Merrick both hungry and wary. "I'd rather not say."

"All right. Leave that for now. But ultimately, you're still doing good. As a muse, that's your thing. What's the problem?"

"To be entitled to a muse's energy and efforts, a person has to work extremely hard and has to have talent or intelligence, ingenuity and drive. Do you understand? There aren't a lot of muses. Our focused attention facilitates the greatest inventions, the greatest works of literature, feats of athleticism, scientific discoveries . . . If a muse expends energy on someone who isn't capable of doing something extraordinary with it, then what happens to the person who could have created a masterpiece or the next technological revolution? It's actually a weakness in my character that I haven't stopped."

Merrick suppressed a smile. This was her big secret? That

she was helping someone? Even if it was the wrong person, he couldn't believe that if she were caught, her community would throw her out.

"You're quite the rule breaker," he said diplomatically.

She ran a hand through her hair. "Apparently so. I sent letters to you."

"I don't think Cato Jacobi's insurance policy against retribution is that you're misusing your magic. There isn't anything else?"

"Only the letters, but if someone from the Etherlin knew about them, they could just expose me. They wouldn't need to get involved with a ventala."

"Maybe Jacobi has leverage over someone there."

"Could this Jacobi have found out about my letters from someone who works for you?"

"Nothing's impossible, but it's unlikely."

"Because you're very discreet and keep the letters locked up?" she asked hopefully.

"Yes, but more important, because I have a reputation. When I was an enforcer, I found whoever I hunted. *Always*. Besides, if Jacobi knew about the letters, he'd have said so tonight. A connection between you and me would be more evidence to support a charge he wants to make against me."

"What charge?"

"That I stole you from his balcony."

Her brows shot up. "You rescued a kidnap victim. What charge could he possibly make and who could he make it to?"

He returned to the bar. "Trespassing, for one."

"That's ridiculous," she snapped.

He smiled. On the surface, Alissa North looked like an ice queen, but underneath she was pure fire. It was an irresistible combination. He poured scotch, then squeezed the juice from a lime wedge into the glass.

"Scotch Lime. Mr. Hemingway invented that," she said.

"How do you know?"

"I've seen memories of him in Key West."

He glanced over his shoulder at her. "Seen memories? That's some magic you people have."

"Yes," she said, smiling. "I'd rather not lose my place in

the Etherlin. Me being here, being bitten, getting an un-screened blood transfusion . . ." She shuddered. "Even though it wasn't my fault, there would be unpleasant consequences for me."

He'd heard rumors, had seen how cautious the muse-heiresses always were. The risk of being tossed out of their community was always there.

She took a sip of her drink. "This is very good, by the way." She swallowed slowly. "You were able to get into the Etherlin once. Can you get me home without anyone knowing?"

He wanted to say no. The darkest part of his soul did not want to return her to where she belonged. It wanted to keep her. The vampire's blood wanted to lock her in a tower with stone gargoyle sentries. Those rose-petal lips and crystalline eyes were a temptation that gnawed at his insides. He moved his hands behind his back so that he could clasp them into fists without her seeing.

"I can't take you back the way I'd go in," he said, and waited for her reaction. He wanted her to accept that she'd have to stay with him. Of course, that wouldn't be her reaction, but he still held his tongue.

"I'm sorry to hear that," she murmured, tilting her head, soft blonde hair skimming her shoulder. "I do have a friend who I'm sure will help me conceal that I've been here when I tell him about the kidnapping. But he'll be wary and watch-ful. For a while, he'll probably insist on overseeing my work and my life. I won't be able to risk sending you letters." She studied his face. "For a while," she added. "I could write again later. If you still want me to."

He liked the way the statement implored him to respond in the affirmative. He would have anyway, but there was no denying that the lilt to her voice was pure muse. It had a pull, a sway, that spoke to the human half of him.

"There won't be an interruption of the letters. If I don't hear from you, I'll wonder if you're all right, and I'll be inclined to come and check," he said.

"It's dangerous for me to have any connection to you. You know that. If anyone learns that I've been here—"

"No one from your side will know. I can't take you the

way I would use, but there's a way for you to get back without calling your friends or family to help smuggle you in." He thought of Lysander, who he'd already summoned. Merrick hoped it took all night for him to arrive.

The tip of Alissa's tongue caressed her top lip, making his mouth go dry, his fangs descend, and his groin take notice. He clenched his fists tighter, fighting for control.

"Well? Are you going to tell me how? Or should I guess?" she asked with a smile. "I warn you, my lack of experience will probably get tedious after the first fifty unsuccessful guesses."

"Hard to imagine anyone finding you tedious."

"Mr. Merrick, I—" She paused, putting a hand to her throat.

Merrick wondered if she was unconsciously protecting herself with that move.

"It's nice to find that I wasn't wrong about you," she said.

He arched an eyebrow in question.

"You've been charming to me, and sometimes I questioned whether it was a game to get me to trust you, so that I would be tempted to come here if you asked me to. And whether, once I was away from the protection of the Etherlin, you'd drain me dry and laugh at how gullible I'd been."

It was such a reasonable suspicion, what could he possibly say?

"But I'm here, unprotected, and you're still charming, still inviting me to trust you." She lowered her fingers from her throat. "I do. Whatever else you are—despite what you are—I consider you my friend."

She extended her hand. The hell of it was, he knew if he took it, there would be no power on Earth that would keep him from pulling her to him, and she'd learn how misplaced her trust in him could be. Then he'd be forced to see the disappointment in her eyes. God help him, despite what he was, he didn't want that.

He swallowed against his dry throat and shook his head at her offered hand.

"Too much of a temptation?" she asked, drawing her hand back.

The corner of his mouth quirked up into a rueful smile. "Yes. Every inch of you."

"I'm sorry . . . but flattered," she said, as she took a step back. "Should I go into the bedroom? We could talk through the closed door." Her voice had a slightly playful note to it.

He liked it when she flirted. Liked it too much. Unfortunately, she was everything he'd built her up to be in his mind. How the hell could he go back to just the letters?

He unclenched his cramped fingers and went to the bar, where he poured himself another drink.

"Honestly, should I go into the room and close the door?" she asked, all teasing gone.

He squeezed lime juice into the glass, watching it slither into the liquor. "It wouldn't do any good. I'd come in after you." *And we'd be closer to a bed.*

"Mr. Merrick, what's your first name?"

"Just call me Merrick. Everyone does."

"But isn't that your last name? You can call me Alissa, and I thought I could call you by your first name. Just for this evening, since we're the only ones here."

He poured the scotch down his throat in two slow swallows, then looked over his shoulder to find her watching him. "Do you think it's wise to invite that kind of intimacy?"

"Not normally, but I think this may be the only time we'll ever be in a room together."

Don't count on it. He set the empty glass down and moved toward her casually, so he wouldn't put her on her guard. He liked that she was relaxed around him.

"I'd like to talk to you as a friend would," she said.

A friend? His intentions could hardly be considered friendly. He watched her mouth move. There was a very good chance that if he kissed her, he'd be able to let her go if she resisted. He took another step in her direction. She was only a few feet away. One swift lunge and the struggle with himself would be over.

She smiled, tantalizing him. Another step. She was within reach now. He glanced at the rug. Expensive, but not soft. The couch was nearer than the bedroom.

He'd seduce her. He could probably keep himself from

biting her. At the moment, her blood was diluted from the transfusion. Plus, control was one of his strengths—normally. The danger was that he'd waited such a long time to taste her. Who'd have thought letters could be foreplay?

"I'm curious about your life and your past," she said. "I'd love to ask—"

She didn't see him reach for her because the thump on the balcony drew her attention. He clenched his jaw, his fangs scraping his lip. He swallowed the blood and let his hand fall before it touched her.

Lysander's here. She's safe from me.

And soon she'll be gone, he thought with a frown. Temptation swamped him. The temptation to talk to Lysander on the balcony, to send him away, to barricade the doors, to keep the entire world out . . .

The balcony door opened, and the archangel ducked his dark blond head to come inside.

Too late, Merrick thought, exhaling. *No turning back now.*

He'd arranged this because it was what she wanted most. Unfortunately, at the moment, it was also what he wanted least.

Chapter 6

"My God," Alissa whispered.

That Alissa herself was descended from a legendary being didn't prepare her for the sight of the entering creature. She stared as the light fractured around him, bending toward him, then blurring away. Her eyes strained to absorb every spectacular detail. Seven feet tall, broad, shirtless, and scarred. His shoulder-length hair hung in haphazard dark gold waves around a heartbreaking face that was both young and hard. His face was marked with three scars; there were two thin ones along the left side of his forehead, like sinister echoes of his brow just below them, and then a longer scar that ran from in front of his left ear to his jaw. The third slash seemed to continue through the air, picking up at his right collarbone and crossing his chest before stopping at his right nipple. What kind of blade had made that mark? How deep had the wound originally been? And how had he survived such brutal attacks?

Other scars crisscrossed his chest, punctuating the spectacle of his muscled torso. And then there were the wings that folded behind him. Ivory-, amber-, and sienna-colored feathers overlapped each other in a stunning array of harmony from chaos.

With a sucking sound, his wings disappeared. Fascinated, she tilted her head, wishing she'd been standing behind him to watch them fold into his back. His hand moved to the right calf of his worn leather pants. A moment later, he skinned a knife from its sheath and sported a dagger with a foot-long blade.

In the blink of an eye, he'd halved the distance between them, then came to a dead stop.

He murmured something in a language almost as old as time. Muses had the gift of tongues, but it took a moment to translate in her head.

"A girl," he'd said.

She needn't have worked so hard to remember Etruscan. A moment later, he repeated it in Latin.

He backed away, turning his upper body so that he could look at Merrick.

"If you need my help killing her, you're sorely out of practice," the angel said.

Alissa leaned forward, studying the creature.

"You're not here to kill her," Merrick said.

"You woke me." The angel pointed the tip of the dagger at Merrick. "You summoned me. If not to kill a demon, then why?"

"I want you to do something."

The angel sheathed the knife and went to the kitchen. He didn't bother to look at her or Merrick. Instead, his entire attention seemed focused on a polished silver serving bowl full of small oranges. He took one from the top and tore the skin from the fruit, then downed it in two large sections, his powerful jaws only chewing a few times before swallowing. He ate a second orange in the same way.

Then he walked through the living room toward the balcony doors. She watched with fascination as the two ridges on his scarred back opened and slick wings poked out.

"You want my help when the time comes. This is my price," Merrick said.

The angel stopped and turned. He studied Merrick with smoky green eyes. "Your price?"

The angel moved with such force that a gust of air disturbed the papers on the desk. He slammed Merrick into the wall, closing a huge hand on Merrick's throat. "Are you bewitched?"

Merrick didn't struggle, nor did he attempt to answer.

Alissa took a step toward them, grabbing a marble obelisk to hit the angel with.

"She comes," the angel said softly.

"No, Alissa," Merrick said in a rasp of a voice. "Stay back."

She hesitated. "I don't— Are you—?"

"Look at me," the angel commanded, studying Merrick's face. "Are you bewitched?"

"Do you want me to answer? Or would you prefer just to choke me?" Merrick rasped dryly.

The angel let go. "Not bewitched," he said thoughtfully.

"As I've told you before, magic doesn't penetrate me."

"You're half human," the angel said dismissively. "You can't know that all magic won't. Hers smells especially good." He turned toward Alissa and focused his arresting gaze on the marble object still clasped in her hand. "You should put it down. Wielding a weapon against me is dangerous."

Merrick walked to her and took the obelisk. "Her intent was to help me, not to attack you," he said, setting the obelisk back on the small table behind them.

"She wanted to rescue you," the angel said and smiled. His face was radiant with it. She had been told endlessly how beautiful she was, but she knew she was nothing compared to him. Killer or not, the angel was simply the most compelling creature on earth.

"Are you fearsome then?" he asked her. "Skilled enough to interrupt a fight between an arcanon and the ventala he trained to kill demons?"

"No, not at all," she said. "Trying to help Mr. Merrick was instinctive because he's my friend."

The angel's grin faded as he dipped his head in a nod. "Loyalty is good if it's sincere." Then he glanced sideways at Merrick. "You're reckless. If she kills you in your sleep, don't expect me to avenge you."

Merrick laughed softly. "If she kills me in my sleep, I'll die happy. No avenging will be necessary."

"Tell me the favor."

"I want you to fly her home."

The angel's brows drew together, making the thin forehead scars stretch. "Like a winged horse?"

Merrick rolled his eyes.

The angel shook his head at Merrick in exasperation. "You summoned *me* to help *you* with a *girl*. Apocalypse?"

Merrick chuckled.

"Seriously, you were wrong to summon me for this."

Merrick shrugged.

"Some day we may have a disagreement that one of us doesn't walk away from."

Merrick shook his head. "You can't kill me. There's that prophecy you want me to help you with."

"Yes, try and live long enough for that. I invested a lot of time training you," the angel said.

"Sure," Merrick said with a smirk, "but you've got nothing but time."

Alissa studied them with frank curiosity. Were they friends? Not precisely, but they were something to each other. She wanted to ask questions. She wanted to sit down with them and untangle their mysteries. Exactly what did the angel know of the afterlife? Of the secrets of ancient times? There were some original legends buried among the memories contained in the Wreath, but they were reportedly fragmented and hazy. When she'd tried on the Wreath, she hadn't seen them, though she would have liked to.

The angel turned to her and touched his chest. "Lysander," he said.

"Alissa," she returned.

"Are you afraid of heights?"

"Not usually."

"Then you're welcome," Lysander said. He walked out onto the balcony, and she heard the rush of air as his wings burst out of his back.

She stared after the angel for a moment, then she turned to Merrick. "So an archangel. Why did he call himself an arcanon?"

"Because he's fallen."

"Didn't all the fallen angels become demons?"

"Apparently not."

She glanced at the balcony doors. "I suppose I shouldn't keep him waiting." She started to go, but then turned back. It might be the last time she saw Merrick. The thought saddened her. She crossed to him and kissed him on the cheek, then backed away quickly, feeling the way he tensed.

"Obviously I don't know the full extent of what it cost you to summon him, but I appreciate it. I appreciate everything you've done for me tonight." She held up a hand as if to wave good-bye, but couldn't quite bring herself to do it. "Even if I don't see you again, I won't ever forget." She touched her fingertips to her lips and extended them in a brief makeshift kiss.

His gaze caressed her with an unveiled hunger that made things deep within her tighten. Laconically he said, "Stay."

"I wish I could," she whispered, the words slipping out before she had time to stop them.

"Alissa—" Her name had come from both directions.

Ignoring the impatient archangel, Merrick extended a hand. She struggled against the urge to take it, backing away slowly.

"I really have to go home. My—people are counting on me," she said.

He didn't drop his arm. He waited, as though he'd pull her back by sheer force of will. He almost did.

She fisted her hands. "I'm sorry," she whispered. "I just can't."

Ruthlessly steady, his hand continued to reach for hers, stubbornly wanting to bridge a chasm not meant to be bridged.

Her body rigid as she battled her desire to stay, she finally forced herself to turn and step out into the night. She closed the balcony door and leaned against it, exhaling. Lysander hovered above her, his wings slowly beating the air.

"Now I understand," he said.

"Understand what?"

"Why he wants you so badly."

Alissa stared up at him blankly.

"You're as reckless as he is."

Merrick clenched his fists and closed his eyes, trying for calm. Within him, dark emotions warred.

Frustration. Discord. Jealousy.

She'd wanted to stay, but she'd gone. He hated the Etherlin for its hold on her. Hated her commitment to duty, to history, to destiny. Really hated the way she'd looked at Lysander.

Merrick ground his teeth together. Fallen or not, Lysander had been crafted from heaven's ether, had been touched by the hand of God. Only Lysander's own sin had tainted him, and as irresistible as the blood of muses was to vampires and ventala, that's how irresistible Lysander was to humans. Alissa might be part muse, but she was many generations down the family tree; she was many parts human. If Lysander had been standing in the living room with his hand out, Alissa North would never have stepped onto that balcony.

Merrick leaned his head against the back of the couch and stared at the ceiling. But did he want her to stay under those circumstances? Compelled by magic rather than desire?

Yeah, under those circumstances or *any*, he thought savagely.

Merrick grimaced and rubbed his eyes. She was a muse, and he was ventala. There was no future for them. He knew that to the marrow of his bones.

The problem was that he didn't care. He wanted her.

Tightening his muscles until they ached, he wondered just how far inside him this obsession with Alissa North had burrowed.

"You'll get yourself killed. Her, too, probably," he murmured, as if saying the words out loud would help convince him—would somehow hold him back from what he wanted to do next.

The vampire in him weighed the risk of death and destruction and gave its cool and expected response. *Give me what I want. I don't care what it costs.*

Most of the time, the human side of him won out over the vampire because Merrick took pleasure in crushing vampire urges, the same way he took pleasure in crushing vampires. Unfortunately, in this case, Merrick's human side wanted Alissa North, too.

He rose. Time to suffocate in magic.

Lysander stood on the railing, towering like a flesh-and-blood Florentine bronze, his massive wings spread behind him.

"You'll face the ground, so you can feel what it really is

to fly." He leaned forward, caught her upper arms in his hands and lifted her. For a moment, her bare feet rested on the glossy black rail, and her breath caught in her throat. Then, with the snap of his wings, they rose. Above the windows and the rooftop, above the black-and-white buildings, into the murky sky, and higher into soft, clean air.

Neither of them spoke. She pointed the way home, and they glided and swooped, rose and dove, amidst treetops and rooftops until she knew she would dream about flying for the rest of her life.

He landed where she indicated, within a collection of trees near the lake. It was a place that she didn't think the security cameras would easily penetrate. When her feet were on the ground, she faced him.

"Thank you, Lysander."

He nodded.

"How did you and Merrick become friends?" she asked, wanting to sate her curiosity and to delay his departure.

The archangel's gaze shifted to the right. "I smell something. Not a demon, but something that's touched what lies beneath. If you walk around the lake, avoid that direction," he said.

Alissa looked the way he'd pointed. It was the path she'd taken between the Xenakis house and her own. If there were lingering traces of black magic, maybe she could follow it back to the person who'd betrayed her. "What do you mean? What exactly—?"

His wings flapped, lifting him a few feet off the ground. "There's a subterfuge to you. I don't know whether you conceal things to protect yourself or for some more sinister reason."

"I—"

"Don't defend yourself. Time will reveal your character better than words. Just understand something. I need Merrick to do something, and he's promised he will. Also, he's my friend—the only friend I've chosen to have in hundreds of years. So when I said that if you killed him, I wouldn't avenge him, it wasn't true."

"I'm a muse. I help people. I don't kill them."

"You are well aware that power can be used to inspire violence as easily as peace. Have a care for his safety, because where you are concerned, he clearly does not." He didn't look down as he rose into the night.

With his departure, the cold engulfed her. She shivered as she thought about Lysander's implication. What retribution would Merrick face for rescuing her from Cato Jacobi's balcony? That worried her. Jacobi was clearly very dangerous. She didn't want Merrick to be hurt because he'd helped her.

Merrick can take care of himself. You know that. Everyone knows that.

The thoughts reassured her as she left the woods for the lakeside path. The entire night had been so surreal. It was hard to drag her mind back to the Etherlin, to normal life, but with the dawn, the sun bathed the world in a tawny glow.

The splendor of her neighborhood hit her all at once, reminding her of who she was and of the danger in standing around in daylight where someone might see her. She needed to cover her arms. She couldn't let anyone see evidence of the bite or the subsequent transfusion.

She looked upward again, her eyes traveling along the puffed clouds that dotted the sky toward the Varden and Merrick. She wished that, like Lysander, she had wings that would carry her through the night undiscovered. Then she could go wherever she wanted, could see Merrick whenever she liked—which she suspected would be often.

She dragged her gaze back to Earth, to reality.

You didn't work so hard for so many years to throw it all away in one night. Forget about black-and-white penthouses and iron balconies. Forget about the Varden, Cato Jacobi, and Lysander. And especially, for your dad's sake and for the sake of your future, forget about Merrick.

You're back where you belong. Be grateful for that.

She turned from the path and strode to the front of the house, stopping halfway up the walk when she realized that on the doorstep was her former best friend and current Wreath rival, Cerise Xenakis.

Chapter 7

The wind tousled Cerise's hair as she bent to set down a large document box.

Egyptian princess meets girl gladiator, Alissa thought, noticing Cerise's kohl eye makeup and her strappy boots. With Alissa's feet bare and Cerise already five foot ten before the tall boots, she'd noticeably tower over Alissa, possibly raising questions about where Alissa's shoes were. Alissa hung back, grateful that the gown's skirt skimmed the ground, hiding her feet.

"Hello," Alissa said calmly, posing herself as elegantly as possible. The first rule of being a public figure was *never appear rattled.* Alissa laced her fingers together behind her back so that her arms were hidden, the hollows of her elbows shadowed and protected by the sides of her body.

"You're still in your dress. Where's your coat?" Cerise asked, her gaze skimming Alissa from head to hem.

"I fell asleep still dressed," Alissa said with what she hoped sounded like an easy laugh. "I wanted to watch the sunrise, so I came out."

"No wrap? It's chilly out here."

"It is. Colder than I first realized," she said, inching slightly closer. "What did you bring?"

"It's an unfinished manuscript and some research materials of your dad's that were at our house. Dorie said your dad's writing again. I thought he might want them. I know the musicians I work with keep song notes for years. Sometimes something sparks an idea years after the original lyric was written."

"What was a manuscript of my dad's doing at your house? How old is it?"

"Old. My dad brought it home from the Dome. Your dad left it there a long time ago."

"At the Dome?" Alissa echoed. The Etherlin Council's headquarters housed some important historical documents on-site, but there wasn't a library for a writer to use. "When?"

"A long time ago." Cerise's hooded expression made Alissa's eyes narrow.

"There's no place to write there."

"My parents said he was using a conference room while he waited for your mother, who was there for a meeting."

Alissa looked at the box. It made sense that her father would have wanted to work near where her mother was, but why wouldn't he simply have waited for her to get home from the meeting she was attending rather than lugging a manuscript and materials to the Dome?

"When *exactly* was this?" she asked.

Cerise hesitated. "A few days before your mom died, I guess."

Alissa shuddered.

"The date and time are in the manuscript header from when he last saved. Or maybe from when he printed it out."

A few days before she died . . .

Why would her dad have forgotten his manuscript at the Dome? If it had been after her mom had died, his misplacing his work was plausible. He hadn't looked for anything but her then. But before? It didn't make sense, and Alissa didn't remember him ever going to that building to write.

"I can put this inside for you."

Alissa was careful to keep her arms turned inward as she passed Cerise. She opened the door and held it. Inside, Cerise set the box on a console table. Alissa crossed her arms in front of her to keep her elbows safely bent, but Cerise's gaze settled on her arms and stayed there.

She couldn't have seen the bite, Alissa thought nervously. Alissa forced herself not to move, not to change expression.

"Is that a bruise on your wrist?" Cerise asked.

She'd forgotten about the bruises.

"Yes, a little bruise. I actually tripped and fell when I was walking home last night. Not exactly the picture of elegance," Alissa said with a roll of her eyes. "I'm glad no one from the EC was there to see me."

Cerise smiled, but still looked thoughtful. "It's really from falling? The outside of the wrist is a weird place to bruise in a fall."

Alissa shrugged.

Cerise took a half step closer. "Your other wrist—"

Alissa opened the front door. "Thanks for bringing that by." When Cerise didn't walk to the door, Alissa added, "I'm going upstairs to shower and change."

"Is your dad up?" Cerise asked, glancing over her shoulder toward the staircase.

"No," Alissa said with a forced smile. "He keeps late hours."

"A lot of artists drink and have violent tempers. I don't remember your dad being like that, but he hasn't been the same since your mom died, has he?"

"He's fine. He's much better."

"Not violent?"

Distracted by all the things she was trying to conceal, it took a moment for Alissa to realize what Cerise was asking. Cerise thought the bruises were from her father.

"Oh, no," Alissa said. "Of course not! Everything's fine."

Cerise didn't speak for several excruciating seconds. The urge to explain what had really taken place nearly overwhelmed Alissa. She couldn't stand for Cerise to think her dad had hurt her. But Alissa knew she couldn't possibly explain. That would cost her the Wreath.

"If you say so," Cerise said, still skeptical, finally moving toward the door.

"Cerise, I don't expect to hear rumors about my dad or any mention of these bruises."

Cerise's concerned expression hardened, and Alissa immediately regretted her warning.

"That's not why I was asking," Cerise said coldly. "But trust you to worry that smearing your image is my ulterior motive. Appearing picture-perfect for the council has always been your top priority."

Alissa opened her mouth to deny it, but stopped herself. It wasn't in her best interest to prolong the conversation, though the accusation opened an old wound. Alissa closed her mouth, pursing her lips against the things she wanted to say and to stop herself from trying to restore the fragile connection that had existed a few moments before. Alissa had craved the restoration of her friendship with Cerise for so long, but she couldn't pursue it after a night in the Varden.

With a curt nod, Cerise stalked out, leaving an icy emptiness in her wake.

Alissa closed the door and locked it, then bent her head, trying to prevent the tears from coming.

It wasn't until Alissa was scrubbing her skin under the warm shower jets that she realized she'd been lied to. Not by Cerise, but long before. When Alissa had asked questions about her mother's final weeks, she'd been told that her mom had been depressed and had managed to keep it from her family. Helene had supposedly stopped working, causing a sudden withdrawal of magic from her collection of aspiring authors, actors, and artists, many of whom then slipped into despair. The EC, alarmed by her erratic behavior and deep depression, tried repeatedly to help Helene, but she refused to meet with them. Those were their exact words. *We tried to help her, but she refused to meet with us.*

Leading up to the end, Alissa remembered there being tension in the house, hushed conversations between her parents, but her mother hadn't seemed depressed until two days before she killed herself. Alissa had come home from school on Friday afternoon to find that there'd been a sudden shift in her mom's personality; so startling in fact, that at first Alissa had thought her mom was physically ill.

Alissa knew her mom's crying jags had lasted throughout Friday night because she'd heard the servants discussing it. They were as shocked as Alissa. No one had ever seen either of her parents break down before.

The crying stopped sometime Saturday, giving rise to silence and a blank expression that lasted the rest of Saturday and the first part of Sunday. And then suddenly, about forty-eight hours after the melancholy first consumed her, Helene North was dead.

So the question was, what had her mother's meeting in the Dome been about? And why had it been kept secret from Alissa? Had it somehow caused what followed?

Alissa went through the box Cerise had brought, looking for some clue as to why her mom and dad had been at the Dome, but there were only manuscript pages and research notes. All the papers were labeled and neatly clipped together. Very neatly. As though someone had been through them.

She paced for almost thirty minutes before going to her dad's room and nudging him awake.

"Here you are," he said, rubbing his eyes. "You got me out of there just in time."

"Out of where, Dad?"

"Oh, no." He grimaced. "You're sweet for acting interested, but I wouldn't . . . People who insist on telling their dreams are among the terrors of the breakfast table."

She laughed. "Who said that? Beerbohm?"

"Perhaps. Can you tell me something?" he asked.

"Of course, then maybe you can tell me something. I have questions for you."

He raised his head from the pillow and looked around as if someone might be hiding in the corner, eavesdropping. "Will there be real bacon today? Or only more bird meat in disguise?"

"Probably turkey bacon," she said, smiling. "I don't know how you can even taste the difference. I can't."

His head thumped down on the pillow. "I've failed you as a parent in so many ways."

She squeezed his hand. "Not true. You stayed. Even though it was hard."

He frowned. "She's on the banks of the river. I hate to keep her waiting."

"She has nothing but time now. I'm the one who needs you. If you go, I'll be all alone in the world."

He studied Alissa's face for a moment. "Whoever is delighted in solitude is either a wild beast or a god."

"I'll try to keep that in mind. I have to ask you something. Do you remember Mom having a meeting at the Dome just before she got sick?"

"Meetings," he said, his tone bitter. "They never left her alone."

"What was the one before she died about?"

"Be not too hasty to trust the teachers of morality. They discourse like angels, but they live like men."

"I'm sure you're right, but could you be more specific? Who are the teachers of morality? The Etherlin Council?"

He sat up and climbed off the bed. "She was Wreath Muse. If she wanted to learn something—anything—about the history of the muses, that was her right, and it was none of their business. Their investigation pushed her." He spun to stare at a dark corner. "It did. It did push you!" He scowled and then took a deep breath in and blew it out.

He's getting worse again, she thought. "Pushed her to what? To suicide?"

He turned and, to Alissa, he said, "Someone stole the back brush from my shower. The one with the smooth wooden handle."

"That was a while ago," she said. "Dad—"

"How long?"

She sighed impatiently. "About a year and a half. You swung it like a bat and shattered the bathroom mirror."

He paused for a moment as if trying to remember, then said, "Well, who wants to live in a wilderness of mirrors where no fact goes unchallenged? And what's my back supposed to do without a brush? Wash itself?" He disappeared into the bathroom, and she stood next to the bed, shaking her head. His outbursts were erratic and violent, but the violence was never directed at people, only at defenseless objects. Still, she was afraid that ES would find out and become concerned for her safety. Would the EC force her to put her dad in an institution? She shuddered. He'd never survive there. He needed to be near her and near her mother's things.

Alissa wondered who she could ask about Helene's meeting at the Dome. No one was very comfortable talking about her mother, and Alissa couldn't really afford to remind people about her mother's suicide when she was vying for the Wreath.

"Facts are daggers."

Alissa jerked her head to find that her dad had come back into the room. "Are they, Dad? In what way?"

He waved a hand vaguely. "Experience has to teach that lesson. But if you're going to pursue the truth like it's got a price on its head, you should look for what she was looking for. Just don't tell anyone. You mustn't let them find out."

"What was she looking for?

"She made notes in her private journals. I hid some in the library. Behind Chekhov, Carroll, Palahniuk, and Poe."

He disappeared again into the bathroom, and this time she heard running water. She hurried to the library. She knew her mom's cabinets had been emptied of all her important papers, but Alissa realized that the things that had been relinquished to the Muse Antiquities Society for preservation had been work related. The community didn't have a right to a Wreath Muse's personal diaries as long as she kept a separate set of muse journals. Since Alissa had never seen any private diaries, she'd assumed that her mother hadn't kept any.

Several times, Alissa had requested access to her mother's Wreath Muse journals but she had never been given clearance to read them. She'd been told that the EC thought it would be too upsetting for her. As if Alissa needed to read journals to encounter painful reminders of her mother's death. Her mom's memory was everywhere in their house, and her father mentioned Helene every day.

Alissa removed books by the four authors her dad had indicated, and she found a collection of journals hidden behind them. She thumbed open the first leather-bound book. The handwriting was beautiful, a really elegant script that she remembered as her mother's. Glancing at the dates, Alissa flipped the journal closed and pulled others from the shelves.

They spanned fifteen years. Unfortunately, the final one that should've included 1998 to 1999 was missing. Alissa went through each book again to check the dates, then she checked the shelves again. Soon, she was systematically removing all the books to check behind them.

Hours passed, but she didn't find it. Her mother's final journal, which might have contained some shred of information about what had led to her unexpected depression and death, wasn't there. Had her dad hidden it somewhere else? Or destroyed it? The house was huge, and he couldn't be relied upon to answer questions coherently or with any sort of timeliness. She might never find out what had happened to the final diary.

Alissa rested her head in her palms. Her father had implied that her mother had done something controversial at the end of her life, causing the EC to question and investigate her. What could it have been? Dimitri and the other council members obviously never intended for Alissa to find out the truth, despite the fact that, as a muse and a daughter, Alissa had a right to know.

Chapter 8

Of all the letters Alissa had sent him, the one written on her twenty-fifth birthday was Merrick's favorite. It rested against his thigh as he sat in the chair next to the bed where she'd lain. Her scent lingered on the air, and he wasn't ready to leave it. Though he would have to go to his own room soon with dawn's heavy fist about to come down.

He ran his thumb over the letter's top page. Three drops of wine marked the upper right corner. When he'd first opened it, he'd catalogued the information. Alissa liked dry red wine, and she must have been a little buzzed when she wrote the letter because a few drops had sloshed out of her glass and rained down on the paper. Also, the handwriting stretched the words out and was much less careful than usual. She'd included the time. 3:31 a.m. When he'd gotten the letter, he'd wondered what he'd been doing while she was writing it and what she'd thought of the birthday present he'd sent: a one-of-a-kind 1920s bracelet. He hadn't wondered long. He'd seen it on her wrist in plenty of photographs afterward. The days where she claimed to give away the gifts he sent were over.

Merrick glanced at the letter. The wine had melted the ice-princess façade and underneath was the real girl. She talked about her disdain for the emphasis placed on her looks, though she also called them "her protection." She confided that she missed her former best friend and envied the other girl's eclectic style and natural athleticism. Magazines and designers almost always chose Alissa to model for them over Cerise, which Alissa thought showed a lack of imagination. She claimed that pictures of her friend were often more compelling than the ones of her.

Merrick had smiled at that. Apparently she hadn't been in the mood to recognize that imagination and everything else often took a backseat to profit. Everyone knew that the Alissa North image was one of the most valuable brands on the planet.

She confessed that she'd tried to look bored in her pictures, but rather than getting less work, she was told that her "aloof" images worked as well as her friendly ones. Subtle self-sabotage was as far as she allowed herself to go though, so she was trapped in an endless parade of photo shoots, lest she lose the favor of her council supporters.

She conjectured that it must be nice to be Merrick, who probably never worried about what anyone thought of him. Merrick had agreed, but had amended the statement in his mind. He didn't care about what anyone thought, with one exception.

She mentioned that she'd heard interesting rumors about him lately. Good things that might not be true, but that she liked to believe were. He could've guessed the things she'd heard. He'd given a lot of money to a foster-care program. One that she supported. Normally, he would have donated anonymously, but for once he hadn't hidden it because he'd wanted her to find out.

In the letter, she went on to talk about her obsession with the environment and the courses she'd taken to assist her in inspiring and fostering the careers of her young scientist aspirants. She'd studied so much that she'd begun dreaming about nanotechnology and more efficient ways to desalinate water. Then, suddenly while writing, she'd apparently gotten irritated by his silence, saying: *These conversations are ridiculous. They're not even conversations since you never write more than a couple sentences back, and you never tell me anything about yourself. I've told you what occupies my thoughts. What about you, Mr. Merrick? Do you dream? And, if so, about what? Please don't say bullets!*

I take that back. Tell me what's on your mind—no matter what that is. What do you think about, Merrick?

You, he'd thought, but his response had been to send her orchids with a card that read:

> *97% of the time—Sure, bullets*
> *2% of the time—Salt water and nanotechnology*
> *1% of the time—The wall I'd like to knock down to*
> *reach a certain girl who writes me letters.*

The following night he'd gotten a bouquet of black dahlias with a card that read:

> *I thought so. What kind of bullets?*

He'd laughed out loud when he'd read the card, making everyone in the staff lounge stop what they were doing.

"Secret admirer?" Tony had asked.

"Just business. The electrician's grateful I hired him to rewire the underground club."

Which, of course, had been everyone's cue to pretend that the boss wasn't flirting with some girl bold enough to send him black flowers.

He'd sent a dozen lavender roses with the note: *All kinds.*

For the rest of the night, in every spare moment, Merrick had been consumed by one thought: *I want to see her.*

Just before dawn, he'd sent a dozen white roses with a note. *It's time to discuss salt water in person. Name the date, and I'll make it happen.*

She hadn't answered. She'd gone to San Diego for an eco summit with a troop of ES bodyguards, and there had been no letters for fourteen weeks. The message was plain enough. No meeting.

A part of him had spent hours thinking of ways to corner her alone, just to prove he could do it anytime he wanted. But another part of him knew she'd had seven stalkers since she was twelve years old and that was a crowd he didn't intend to join, no matter how satisfying it would be to see her in the flesh. So he'd waited, and then he'd sent flowers and a note with a single word. *Understood.*

A week later, she sent a letter as if nothing had happened.

They were back to the long-distance flirtation, though occasionally for a line or two, the ice melted again, the banter disappeared, and he was given another glimpse into her private life. A glimpse, her hints implied, that no one in the world was ever given except him.

Somehow, for a very long time, that had been enough.

Exhausted by her ordeal and by the night's fragmented sleep, Alissa should have been able to fall asleep immediately, but she couldn't. Her thoughts darted between the abduction and wanting to talk to someone about her mother's meeting at the Dome and the missing diary. Unfortunately there was no one in whom she could confide.

She started a letter to Merrick, but knew it was too dangerous to include any real details. She wished she could somehow arrange to see him again.

With an image of Merrick in her mind, she finally started to drift toward unconsciousness. So when the phone rang, she thought it would magically be him, though of course he'd never be foolish enough to call her house.

Still, she expected to hear his voice, and her fevered craving for it worried her. She wanted too much for it to be him.

Instead, it was Theo Tobin.

"How did you get this number, Mr. Tobin?"

"Look, I know you're still angry with me over those sailboat pictures, Alissa, but don't you think you've punished me long enough?" he asked.

"I was fifteen. I used bad judgment in wearing a thong. Since the captain and crew were women, I didn't think it would be a problem, but you proved with your long lens that when you're around I'm not allowed to make a mistake without having the world find out about it. Did you expect that to make us friends?"

"I'm sorry I sold those pictures to the tabloids. I needed the money."

"So be it. I'm hanging up."

"Wait! I can make up for it now. I have some pictures that they made me take last night."

The blood drained from her face. "Who made you take them?"

"Listen, there's more going on with this ventala syndicate than the Etherlin realizes. I can't talk about it on the phone. The bastards are trying to figure out where I am right now. I need to keep moving," he said, fear lacing his voice.

"Come into the Etherlin. You'll be safe inside."

"I can't. They'll grab me before I get to the gate. But I could get home if you helped me."

"Helped you how?"

"First, you have to talk to Merrick. He's looking for me, too. You have to tell him not to kill me. I wasn't involved in taking you. I swear it."

Her heart slammed against her chest, but she kept her voice cool. "Why does he think you were?"

"Because I was there. How was I supposed to know what they had planned? Jeez! I've been covering your family since I was eighteen and got my first telephoto lens. Like I'm gonna do something to destroy you? Never! But Merrick's not going to listen. He warned me once. You have to talk to him."

"I don't have any influence over him. We barely know each other."

"Alissa, don't play games with me. He really will kill me unless you call him off."

"Listen, I can't call him from here. The phone bills go to the Dome. With the vote a few days away, people are scrutinizing everything I do."

"I'll send Merrick a message. He can get a phone to you that can't be traced."

She bit down on her lip. She did really want to speak with Merrick again.

"After you talk to Merrick, we'll meet in the Sliver. I'll show you the pictures and tell you what I know, and you'll give me a ride back to the Etherlin."

"The Sliver's outside the wall. I would have to bring a security detail, and we couldn't talk in front of them. Not to mention that my coming to pick you up would look really suspicious."

"We don't have a choice! This needs to happen. You'll have

to come up with an excuse. I'm telling you, you won't get the Wreath anyway if news about last night comes out, and if the Jacobis get their hands on me, it will."

Her mouth went dry and her mind raced. "I can come up with a reason to visit the Sliver, but we'd need to pretend that you and I crossing paths happened by chance. We'll have to wait until we're back in the Etherlin to discuss things."

"Yeah, fine. That makes sense. Be at Handyrock's at eight tonight."

"I'll try to be there."

"If you're not, I'm dead and you're ruined, so you'd better try hard."

Chapter 9

Dusk's failing light glinted off the ends of the sniper rifles pointed at the square in front of the Infi-Moderno building, headquarters of the ventala syndicate. Merrick appreciated the irony. Years earlier after a breach of the building, he'd been asked to consult on security upgrades. He'd made several suggestions, including that men with Special Forces training be added to the staff and positioned on the rooftops as snipers. Now those men's weapons were pointed at him.

He slid his sunglasses down so that the camera above the entrance could capture his eyes. A moment later, he punched in his code and opened the door.

The brunette sitting at the reception desk was flanked by two paramilitary guards. She swept her hip-length hair over her shoulder and smiled.

"Hello, Merrick."

"Hello, beautiful."

"Nice suit. Do you really pay ten thousand dollars for each one?"

He shook his head, and she looked disappointed. "Fifteen."

"Fifteen?" She gasped. "Are they really worth it?"

"You tell me."

She made a show of looking him up and down, then grinned. "You do look good in a suit, but I bet you look better out of one. And it'd be a lot cheaper."

"Sure, but where would I keep my pens? I'm a business-man now, you know."

Her grin widened. "I do know. Everyone's noticed how well you're doing. South of Firenze was the worst part of the Varden. Used to be, people tried to claw their way out of there before they ended up dead. Now look at it. There's a waiting list to rent, and if you want a high-rise apartment, forget about it. I bet if I wanted to live on Delphi Saint near the Crimson, I'd never find a place in a million years."

"There's always room for another pretty girl." He put his palm over the scanner. "Call the club and talk to Ox or Tony. They'll take care of you."

"Thanks, Merrick." She leaned forward and lowered her voice. "Listen, be careful up there. Cato's been stirring it up all afternoon about you. Then he got in a shouting match with Tamberi and smashed his fist through the display case in her office. Broke half a dozen pieces of her millefiori collection. She shot him twice in the shoulder with that old Colt .45 she keeps in her desk. You know how the old guns make that popping sound like firecrackers? Everyone heard it and came out to see what was going on. The bullets were only lead with copper jackets, but he bled all over the new gray carpeting."

"So Victor's in a good mood then," Merrick said, making her laugh before he went to the elevator. On the way up, he glanced at the photo of boss Victor Jacobi with his son and daughter. Tamberi's black hair was buzzed short in the picture, but when combined with the sexy suit she wore, it worked somehow.

In the hall on his way to Victor's office, Merrick passed the workmen who were already replacing the carpet. Victor's efficient sixty-one-year-old secretary gave Merrick a pained looked and waved him through.

"They're in a meeting downstairs, but I'll let him know you're here."

"Thanks, Sil."

"The snack in the office is for you. Don't hesitate if you're thirsty."

He raised his eyebrows. That was surprising. There'd been

tension for months, and hospitality had been pretty thin whenever he'd been summoned to headquarters recently.

He was only a couple steps into the office when he went still. Standing at the giant silver-framed window was Alissa North.

Cato cursed as Tamberi wrapped the bandage tightly around his wounded shoulder. He glared at her, but she only shook her head and didn't say a word as she taped.

"You fucking had to shoot me twice? You got my attention the first time."

"Lost my head," she said.

The break in conversation lasted several moments before he said, "Me, too. I'll buy you some new glass."

"Sure. I needed to do some shopping in Venice anyway."

The phone rang, and Tamberi clicked on the speakerphone. "Yeah, Sil?"

"He just walked in."

Cato clicked a button and the wall of screens blinked on.

They both studied Merrick's expression, which gave away nothing.

"Cool as a fucking cucumber," Cato said, but Tamberi pressed a button to amplify the pulse wave sensors. They listened to the rhythm of the beating hearts. Both were thumping about eighty times per minute.

"You were right," Tamberi said. "He's got a thing for her."

"You think?" Cato asked.

"Absolutely. Merrick's resting heart rate is thirty-five. Remember that time John Grange jumped across the table to kill Dad with the ice pick, and Merrick grabbed Grange and slammed him to the ground? Thirty seconds after it was over, Merrick's heart rate was only fifty-seven."

Onscreen, Merrick said to the girl, "Hey. You lost?"

"Smooth. I told you he wouldn't slip. He knows the office is wired. Even if he's shocked, he's not gonna show it," Cato said.

The girl turned so that she could look directly at Merrick. "No, Mr. Merrick. I've been waiting here for you."

"Look at her face. That surgeon did a *good* job," Cato said.

"Yeah, pretty good. But he realizes now," Tamberi said, and they both listened as the span between the beats of Merrick's heart grew longer and longer. "Sixty-two. Fifty. Forty. And thirty-five," Tamberi said. "So Alissa North revs his engine more than fighting or killing."

"I told you! He doesn't do anything without a reason. He's gotta be bangin' her."

"Well, if he was, it's over now. He'll have to make do with a replacement."

Cato held up a hand as the girl tipped her head to the side and exposed the smooth skin over her carotid artery. "No matter how good she tastes, it won't be the same. Muse blood is like ventala springwater. I haven't had a single pang of thirst since I drank from that bitch."

"Yeah," Tamberi said. "Me either."

Merrick took in everything about her in a few seconds. The neck wasn't as long. The eyes were darker blue. The nose was perfect, but the entire face was a little wider. The tiny dimple in the left cheek when she smiled was missing, and the teeth were different—smaller. The haircut and color was spot-on, but how hard was that to fake?

"What's your name, sweetheart?" Merrick asked.

She widened her eyes and smiled. "It's Alissa."

"Sure it is. So, Alissa, whose discovery do you think had the bigger impact on public health, Snow's or Fleming's?"

"I—Well, they both made important contributions."

"Sure. How about this century? Do you expect the most important developments to be electronic or ecological?"

The girl didn't answer even though Merrick had fed her the exact questions that Alissa North had answered and discussed on multiple occasions. There were hundreds of available sound bites from interviews she'd given over the years. Anyone who'd done any kind of prep work for the role of Alissa North should've been able to parrot back Alissa's answers.

The voice was wrong as well. Too high. The skin was

wrong. It didn't smell as fresh and the tint wasn't as pale and creamy as the real thing.

A copy, but not a very good one.

She moved close to him and pressed her palms against his chest. "You don't actually care about those things, do you? I bet we could find some more interesting topics to talk about. Or not. Talking is overrated."

He dipped his head so that his mouth was near her ear. "I appreciate the offer, but I'm here on business. Why don't you run along and let Victor know that I'm leaving in five minutes whether I've heard what he has to say or not."

The girl threw him a wounded look as she strode out of the room.

There were a lot of girls having their faces cut to look like Alissa North's, but the syndicate wouldn't invest in creating a ringer as a novelty item. They had a reason. Merrick suspected the Alissa look-alike had been part of their insurance policy. The girl didn't have muse magic and wasn't a good enough impersonator to send anywhere as a live copy, which meant they'd intended for her to turn up as a body. If Alissa North were dead, no one would look for her, and Cato Jacobi could have kept her as a pet for as long as he wanted. At that thought, Merrick clenched his jaws and glanced in the direction of the hall. If Cato wandered by, Merrick would cheerfully bust every bone in the asshole's body.

Don't get distracted. There's more to this than just keeping her as a blood whore. If Jacobi and the syndicate had kept Alissa North prisoner long-term, someone in the Varden would have found out. Rumors would have eventually filtered back to Etherlin Security, who would have certainly investigated. Maybe the syndicate had planned to move Alissa outside the Varden?

Merrick's thoughts were interrupted by the arrival of the head of the ventala syndicate. At five foot six, a hundred and fifty pounds, Victor Jacobi didn't look like much. Plenty of fools had underestimated him and ended up with their windpipes crushed.

"Merrick, it's good to see you," Victor said, briefly clasping Merrick's hand between both of his before moving around his desk and sitting.

"And you."

"Sit," Victor said with a gesture.

Merrick sat in the large leather chair across from Victor's desk and waited.

"So here we are," Victor said. "I remember when you came to see me when you were seventeen. We were having that problem in Puma Park. Five murders and nobody could catch the bastard. You said if I paid you, you'd take care of it for me, and I could be the hero who hired you." Victor laughed. "Cocky little bastard. So skinny you could've fallen through a crack in the sidewalk."

"That was my secret. I turned sideways, and the quarry couldn't see me coming."

Victor barked out another laugh. "You didn't look like much back then, but the eyes don't lie, and you had it—that stare the old vampires have."

Victor knew Merrick wouldn't consider that a compliment, but Merrick stayed with his back resting casually against the chair.

"I think maybe that's why you always wear sunglasses around humans. So they don't see it."

"What can I do for you, Victor?"

"We go all the way back, Merrick. You're an asset that I brought into the syndicate. I'm sentimental about that kind of thing."

Merrick smirked. Snakes were more sentimental than Victor.

"Which is why I'd really hate to kill you."

Merrick's expression didn't change. No need to get agitated when they were just getting started with this dance. If Victor had made up his mind to have Merrick killed, he would never have let Merrick into his office where he'd be too likely to take Victor to hell with him.

"Conversations are like drinking packaged blood: the longer it takes to go down, the worse it tastes," Merrick said. "If there's a problem you want me to fix, lay it out."

"We know you took the girl from Cato's balcony. You can

deny it, but c'mon, Merrick. Nobody else is that smooth. Get into his territory, put the guards down, get the girl, and get out. Practically blending with the shadows? Plus, there's the way you move. With such economy, like an animal or a machine. No motion wasted. You probably don't even know you do it, but it's your signature as sure as your palm print or that vampire stare most ventala don't have."

Merrick waited. Something was coming, but Merrick wasn't sure what.

"Two things I don't know. The first is why." Victor rested his arms on his desk and leaned forward. "Why do it? You're a stubborn, cocky son-of-a-bitch, but you're not a trouble-maker, Merrick. Not without reason.

"And the second thing is, after you had her, how did you put her back in her house without anybody on her side of the wall finding out?"

"I'm still waiting to hear what you want done."

Victor sighed. "See, this is why the rest of the syndicate wants to kill you. You never come on board. You're always out there on your own, keeping secrets, breaking rules like they don't apply to you. You've got this idea that you're above everyone else and don't have to answer to anyone. That's just not true, Merrick. For that to be true, you'd have to kill me and take over everything. But then to run things, you'd have to have meetings and make conversation for more than ten minutes at a time, which is about nine minutes more than you can stand."

Merrick glanced at the pearl-handled letter opener and wondered if putting it through Victor's hand would make him get to the point or at least end the meeting. Out of habit from his enforcer days, Merrick followed that line of thinking, speculating on how he'd get out of the secure building after a hit.

Victor would alert security. Guards would take about three minutes to come through the door. Plenty of time for Merrick to create an exit. If he swung the desk chair hard enough at the plate-glass window, he'd shatter it. He'd get to the roof using the cable concealed in his belt. Take out the sniper on the Infi building to get control of his gun. Then shoot—

"Why did you want your own territory, Merrick?"

Idly, Merrick again glanced at the letter opener.

"The more I think about it, the less sense it makes," Victor continued. "You've never wanted roots. You make more money as a boss, but you don't spend like you need it. Enforcing paid for your suits and then some. There's power in being a regional boss, but what do you need it for? As an enforcer, you were like a rock star; girls threw themselves at you from sundown to sunrise. So why the hell did you fight for and pay so much for what used to be the most filth-infested piece of the Varden?"

Merrick rested his hands lightly on the arms of the chair and thought about his reason. There were six-hundred-thread-count Egyptian cotton sheets on all the beds in his apartment because skin as soft as Alissa North's shouldn't be wrapped in anything less. The odds of her ever being in his place had been long, but sometimes fortune favors the prepared mind. It was how Fleming had discovered penicillin.

Merrick had wanted a permanent address so she had a place to send her letters. And so that if she'd ever wanted to slip in through an open window, there would be one for her to come through.

"I think you wanted that territory because you found a way in and out of the Etherlin. I think you wanted to seduce and drink the blood of the world's next crowned muse. You're just arrogant enough to think you could pull that off. And maybe you did pull it off, because it took you less than two minutes to figure out the girl in this office wasn't her. How would you know that unless you've been up close and personal with the real thing?"

Merrick gave the letter opener serious consideration. If the syndicate started prying into his relationship with Alissa North, she would end things immediately. Of that, Merrick had no doubt. He contemplated ways to divert their attention from her.

"You know her, don't you? So help me, Merrick. If you hold out on us where a muse is concerned, there will be hell to pay."

Merrick leveled a stare at Victor, then raised a brow.

"You're right. I seduced Alissa North. Went right past the Etherlin Security command post, the security cameras, into her house and convinced her to ruin her life and give up her bid for the Wreath that all the muses would kill for.

"Since that night, I smuggle her in and out of the Varden all the time. Nobody from her side ever notices she's gone. We use the piled-pillows-under-the-covers trick to fool the staff. Works every time. Etherlin Security and the hundreds of people in the club and on the street outside my building never notice her coming or going because no one pays very close attention to what Alissa North does or where she goes.

"As a precaution, sometimes I turn her invisible. Having unlimited power comes in handy. People say it makes me cocky. I don't see it," Merrick said. "Since you and I go way back, I'll confess my identity. I'm the sits-on-high, betrayed-by-my-favorite-angels creator of heaven and earth." Merrick stared coolly at Victor. "You can call me God for short."

Victor blinked and then roared with laughter.

Merrick stood and stretched his legs.

"Not so fast."

"I like you, Victor. Don't make me smite you."

"Hey, we're not done," Victor said, grabbing Merrick's arm.

Merrick slammed Victor into his chair, then adjusted his shirt cuffs. He stared Victor down, all humor gone from his voice when he spoke. "We are done. We were done before you asked any questions. You say you know me, but you don't act like it. If you knew me, you'd have realized something by now." Merrick paused. "I don't apologize, and I don't explain."

Victor's face turned to stone. "I know it was you on that balcony."

Merrick shrugged. "So?"

"Cato and the syndicate have to be compensated or you have to die. That's what we're left with, and for the—"

"How much?" Merrick demanded.

"It's not just the money. You have to return the girl."

Merrick laughed.

Victor held up a hand. "Don't answer. I want you to think about it. You can get in there. You've done it before."

"I can get in. Myself, alone. I can't get her out."

"Take some time. You'll think of a way."

"What is this about? This isn't about Cato scoring the ultimate blood slave."

"No, it's not. The syndicate needs her for something."

"What?"

Victor shook his head. "Can't tell you that."

"She hasn't won the Wreath yet, so you don't have to have the lead muse. You could use another muse in her place."

"She's the only one without family. All the rest, even if there's a scandal and the community rejects them, they have family—people who will want them back. She's the only one who doesn't have anyone."

Yes, she fucking does. She has the most dangerous protector of all. Me. "Her father's alive."

"The guy's lost it. He's ready for an institution. He won't be a problem for us afterward. That's why she's the right choice. She's alone. And if you've got some connection to her, that just makes it easier. You can lure her here."

"Tell me what you want her for."

"Not a chance, but I will offer this. She can stay with you. You'll keep her until we need her. And afterward, you can have her back."

Merrick paused, tempted by the thought of having her to himself for good. But of course, he wasn't going to share her with the syndicate. Not for a day. Not for an hour. Not for a second.

"Think it over. Because if you don't do it, we'll kill you, and when we get her without your help, she goes back to Cato."

Chapter 10

Alissa slept for several hours and felt better when she woke, until she remembered that she'd agreed to leave the Etherlin. What if Theo Tobin was luring her outside the wall so that Cato Jacobi could abduct her?

The Sliver was a small stretch of four city blocks that lay between the Varden and the Etherlin. When the wall around the Etherlin had been built, the owner of the Sliver had declined to be enclosed within it, fearing that he would lose control of his property. Later however, as the ventala bought and took control of everything west of him, he regretted being outside the wall. His children and grandchildren had become attorneys and police officers and fought to keep the area ventala free. No Sliver real estate had ever been sold, rented, or leased to the ventala, so it was considered neutral territory where visiting humans from around the world who couldn't attain access to the Etherlin directly could stay in hopes of gaining the security clearance needed to get inside and meet a muse.

Although ventala weren't welcomed as residents of the Sliver, they could stay in the hotels and visit the bars there, so it would be possible for Cato Jacobi to lay a trap for her.

She paced the carpet in her room. If she took Etherlin Security with her as bodyguards, they would report back to the council about her visit with Tobin and whatever happened. On the other hand, she didn't dare go alone.

Alissa paused from her pacing when her phone rang. She was surprised to see the display with Mrs. Carlisle's name, since she was working downstairs.

"Hello?"

"Yes, miss, sorry to interrupt your evening. A delivery-man from Pead's Florists wanted you to sign for some flowers. I told him you don't sign for deliveries and had to threaten to summon ES to convince him to leave. I've unwrapped the flowers. They're lovely pale purple roses and seem to be okay—nothing dicey in the box with them or anything."

Lavender roses. Merrick.

"Is there a note or a package?" she asked, hurrying to the door and rushing from the room. Normally, if he wanted to send her something very discreetly, the messengers delivered the flowers to her while she was out, but she hadn't been out all day. She should have realized that she needed to leave the house for them to deliver a package to her.

"There's a note. Garden variety admiration, quite liter-ally—"

"Hold on to the note. I'll be right down. I suspect I know who the flowers are from. An eccentric admirer."

"Well, he needs to learn the protocol! As if we'd interrupt you every time someone sends you a gift! You'd never get any work done. I wouldn't have disturbed you about this, except the boy acted so odd. I wanted to know if you wanted me to call Mr. Easton about it. You know what he always says. Anything suspicious, however minor, should be reported. And I agree with that! There are men who would pay anything to get their hands on you. Deliverymen, even from Pead's, would be tempted by the kind of money they'd offer. The thing is . . . your father's been roaming all over today, and he's more talkative than usual. I wasn't sure—well, I thought you might want to go and talk to Mr. Easton at his home rather than have him come here."

"Mrs. Carlisle, you protect us so well." Alissa stepped into the kitchen, spotted the gray-haired dumpling of a house-keeper, and flipped her cell phone shut. "You know the coun-cil maintains all the household accounts, so I can't simply give you the raise you deserve. Please accept the sapphire earrings I tried to give you in December. You can take them to Dusselburg's, and they'll give you the cash value. It'll be a bonus. You deserve it. We couldn't manage without you."

Mrs. Carlisle frowned. "Miss Alissa, I've told you so many times! Your mother did more things for me and my family than I can ever repay. What would she think of me if I—No, I won't. She had the best heart. She really did, and you're the same way." Mrs. Carlisle dabbed her moist eyes and her voice turned steely. "I'd look after you for nothing and feel lucky to do it. Those Xenakis girls aren't half as pretty or talented, and they've got twenty-five people or more looking after them. The same for Ileana Rella. You're going to be the Wreath Muse, and you did it all yourself. I like to think that my helping with your dad and the house let you concentrate a little better."

She'd known that Mrs. Carlisle prized her position, but she hadn't realized how much pride she took in Alissa's accomplishments. "It did help me. I couldn't have managed alone."

Mrs. Carlisle smiled. "There's my bonus. And when I see you wearing the Wreath like a crown princess, that'll be my bonus, too."

"I still have to get through the voting," Alissa said.

"You will. You'll come out on top as you always do. Now, what about tea and some shortbreads?"

"I'll have tea, but no cookies. I have to go out for cocktails tonight. I should have dinner early so that I've got something substantial in my system. May I have the note that came with the flowers? Where are they, by the way?"

"Front hall on the console. The note's with them."

"Thank you," Alissa said. She walked to the front and smiled at the lavender roses that had stunning indigo tips to their perfect petals. She picked up the note.

You're as lovely as cherry blossoms. M

There were two cherry blossom trees on the grounds. That Merrick knew the landscape made her shiver. What else did he know about her home? And how did he know it? The council hadn't approved pictorial spreads or Internet images of the muses' homes since one of Alissa's stalkers had managed to get almost to her front door before Etherlin Security realized the invitation and identification he'd used to get past the security checkpoint at the wall were fraudulent.

They'd used a taser to subdue him before anyone had opened the door for him, but the contents of his duffel bag, which included duct tape, KY lubricant, a straight razor, and a journal outlining his plans in horrific detail, had upset everyone. Phrases like "forced seduction" and "achieving the afterlife as one" were among the man's chilling goals. He'd intended to tape her mouth shut immediately so she couldn't use her magic to confuse him or talk him out of "bringing them together forever."

Strangely, the security force took the experience harder than she did. As a muse, she understood the way passion could rage out of control, that a spark could smolder into a dangerous and irrational obsession. She'd seen firsthand the devastation the magic could wreak. Unfortunately, becoming a target for emotions run amok was a necessary risk if she were to perform her duties. She'd accepted that early on in life. All she could do was take precautions and hope for the best.

She went to the hall closet and slipped on a jacket and walking clogs and went out, but paused about fifty feet from the trees. Thinking about the stalker who'd gotten to the front door made her trip to the Sliver without an ES detail seem ridiculously risky. What would Cato Jacobi have done with her if Merrick hadn't gotten her off that balcony? She'd been dying, but what if Jacobi had been the one to give her a transfusion to keep her alive? She shuddered.

The muses had all been trained in self-defense, but the training wasn't likely to be effective against a supernaturally strong and swift ventala. Her palm-to-the-nose strike had temporarily stunned Cato Jacobi, long enough for her to escape to the balcony, but she doubted she'd be able to take him by surprise again.

The muses had had weapons training, too. When Cerise traveled outside the Etherlin, she was often armed, but Alissa had resisted that path, knowing that viewing people as potential threats who meant to do her harm would negatively influence her ability to help them. She was a muse. A vessel of inspiration. Closing herself down from connecting with people wasn't an option if she wanted to be the best muse she could be—and if she wanted to win the Wreath.

That thought brought her full circle. Someone had conspired against her. Someone would do whatever it took to keep her from getting the Wreath. If she had no idea who that was, how could she protect herself? She needed Theo Tobin's information.

She walked to the trees and circled them, easily finding a small package wrapped in brown paper that blended with the color of the tree's bark. She sat on a bench that looked out over the lake and opened it.

There was a single number programmed into the small black phone. She pressed the button and, a moment later, she heard Merrick's voice.

"It's me," she said.

"So it is. What can I do for you?"

"I need another favor."

"Then ask."

She lowered her voice and gave him a full account of her conversation with Tobin. "What do you think?"

"I think you should stay on your side of the wall tonight."

"He has something they want. Something that could be damaging to me. If I don't help him get home, eventually he'll be found."

"I'll take care of it."

"He said you threatened him."

"You mentioned that."

"You understand that if I send you to Handyrock's in my place and you hurt him, I'll feel responsible."

"Hmm."

"So I'm asking you not to."

"I'll keep that in mind."

"Mr. Merrick—"

"Yes, Miss North?" he said in a smooth, mock-formal tone.

She couldn't understand why she almost smiled. They were talking about a man's life. They were talking about her life's work. There was so much at stake.

"If you could see your way through to avoiding violence, I'd be grateful. I'd write you a letter that was at least ten pages long and, in it, I'd tell you what I liked best about your apartment and what I liked best about you."

He laughed. "After a letter like that, I'll have to change my name to Narcissus."

"What do you say? Do we have an agreement?"

"I'd love to say yes. Narcissus is a great name."

She smiled.

"Listen, I hate to cut this short, but I've got a few things to take care of," he said.

"I'd like to hear that we have an agreement about how you're going to handle Tobin."

"Alissa," he said, his tone soft and affectionate.

It gave her an odd thrill to hear him use her first name. "Yes?"

"It would be better to let this conversation end."

"It can't until you clarify things."

"Are you sure it's clarity you want?"

"Yes," she said, though she wasn't certain at all.

"Tobin knows you're under my protection. We had an agreement that if he ever found out anything that would put you in a compromising position, he would come to me and I would pay him to not sell the information or the pictures elsewhere. I also told him that if I ever found out that he'd done something to put you in harm's way, I would kill him. At the time, I was thinking about high-speed car chases through French tunnels, but the threat was definitely broad enough to include abduction by another ventala syndicate member."

She leaned against the bench and tipped her head back to stare up at the sky.

"When I meet with him, I won't hurt him unless I think he deserves it. But if he conspired to put your throat under Cato Jacobi's fangs, no one can save him. Not even you."

The conversation pressed down on her like a massive weight. "People can never make a mistake? You never give anyone a second chance?"

"That would depend on the person and the mistake."

"Please try," she said, her voice creaky with emotion. "Your friendship means something to me. I don't want to lose it."

For several moments, he said nothing. She waited.

"All right. I'll let you tie my hands," he said.

"May I call you later?"

"No. When we're done with this conversation, erase my number and get rid of the phone."

"Oh," she said, unable to hide her disappointment. She enjoyed hearing his voice. She wanted more of it, of him. "I don't think there would be much increased risk in me keeping it for the night."

"I'll be in a dead zone for cell service for the next few hours. You won't be able to reach me again on my cell before the charge on that one runs out."

"I see."

"If you want to talk again by phone, I'll arrange for that to happen. Is that what you want?"

Yes. She ran a hand through her hair. "I suppose it would be safer to wait until after the vote. But then, yes. I'd like that."

"So would I." There was a brief pause and he added, "Stay in tonight with the doors locked."

"I will, and thank you for going to Handyrock's."

"You're welcome, Alissa."

Merrick hung up and walked out of his office. He took the elevator to the basement and used a key code and his fingerprint to enter the safe room. The room was mostly metal. Reinforced steel tables, chrome and halogen lights, and a few chairs, including the uncushioned one with wrist and ankle clamps. It was bolted to the floor with the seat positioned directly over a drain.

It was a hard room in every sense of word. It had been designed to feel uncompromising, merciless, and final. Merrick, retired from work as an enforcer, had hoped never to use it, but this had to do with her, and while he might be reckless with his own life and future, he found he could not be that way with Alissa's.

Ox sat on one of the two stainless-steel tables. The white boxer's tape that covered his knuckles was tinted pink, and he was cleaning his nails with the tip of an eight-inch, razor-sharp blade.

Sweating under the lights, the guest of honor's hair was plastered to the sides of his face and hanging down over his swollen left eye.

"I can see that you encrypted the last photos you took and mailed them to yourself before you erased them from your hard drive. So how about those passwords?" Merrick said.

Theodore Tobin shook his head. "You're going to kill me either way. If you see the pictures they made me take, you'll just do it slower."

"You're still going with the story that you were in the wrong place at the wrong time?"

"I'm telling you. The guy they had was a rank amateur. When they saw my camera with some shots I'd taken of her on the memory card, they shot him in the head and pointed the gun at me. It was take the pictures or die. When we were done, Jacobi stood over me while I emailed the files to him, but he didn't understand that in the transfer, I put them through my custom software. It's insurance to make sure I get paid. The first photos are infected and degrade to random black and gray pixels in hours. He's got nothing. I swear. And no one ever will. I would never sell that trash to anyone."

"Yet you kept the original files."

Tobin sighed. "I wasn't thinking it through."

"I think you were. You decided those pictures were your life-insurance policy if he caught up with you."

"I'll erase them. You can watch me do it," Tobin said breathlessly.

"I don't need you to erase them. I'm going to do that myself just as soon as you tell me your passwords."

Ox chugged a bottle of water, then cracked his knuckles. "We might want to try out the hook. I could work the body for a while, so I don't knock him out again."

Merrick gave a short nod.

Ox went to Tobin and unlocked the clamps. Then he hauled the guy up and hung him from a hook that was over a second drain in the floor.

Merrick gave Tobin his most cold-blooded stare.

"You don't have to do this," Tobin croaked.

"You're right," Merrick said. "Ox has ten thousand dollars'

worth of gym equipment. He doesn't need to beat you to a pulp to get a workout. And I had a full schedule that's fucked ten ways from Sunday by this interruption." Merrick rubbed a thumb over his lip and shook his head. "It's pretty inconvenient."

Ox stepped forward and slammed his fist into Tobin's ribs. Tobin wailed, and Ox stepped back.

"I only care about one thing, Theo, and it's not you."

Tobin hung his head, wincing and wheezing. "If she ever finds out you did this . . ."

"I know."

"Eventually she'll see how bad you really are."

"Probably."

"And she'll never have anything to do with you again."

"That's very likely."

"So why are you doing any of this?"

"She's under my protection. Period."

Tobin sighed, taking a few wheezing breaths. "Come here," Tobin rasped. "Come over here."

Merrick stood in front of him.

"Look me in the eye, and give me your word that you'll erase them," Tobin said.

Merrick raised his brows and stared into Tobin's bloodshot eyes. "Is that what you're worried about? That I'll keep them? As leverage?"

"She's a good kid, and she doesn't deserve any of this. The world's fucked with her enough."

"Has it?" Merrick glanced over at the computer and then back at Tobin. "After the pictures, you can make me a list of names. Settling old scores is a hobby of mine. As for the pictures, yes, I swear I'll erase them."

Merrick looked at Ox and tilted his head toward Tobin. Ox lifted Tobin off the hook and set him on the chair.

"One more thing," Tobin said. "I want your promise before you see them that you'll make it quick. One well-placed bullet. I don't want to feel it."

Merrick nodded. "You have my word."

Chapter 11

The corners of Grant's lawn were perfect right angles, edged with military precision, Alissa noted as she walked to his front door and knocked.

Intelligent, handsome, and well-spoken, Grant was one of the most eligible bachelors in the Etherlin, though his bachelor status was up for debate, considering that many expected him to marry Alissa.

They'd been together, of sorts, for years. It had started well, with a flush of excitement and infatuation on both their parts. After they'd dated a few months, he'd invited her for a monthlong sail along the East Coast. She'd learned to cook, learned to sail, and turned nineteen on his boat, and they'd cemented their close friendship forever.

Over lobster bisque and jalapeno bagels, she talked openly about her ambition to become Wreath Muse, and they'd discussed the things in her favor and what would be counted against her. He'd shared his ambitions, too, and they'd worked together to devise strategies to achieve their goals.

While she honed her skills as a muse, he'd gone to a military academy, returned and rose through the ranks of Etherlin Security, and went to law school. For a long time, they'd continued to date with an eye toward eventual marriage, but from the moment she'd met Merrick, she'd realized that something was missing between her and Grant.

Alissa loved Grant as a friend, but nothing more. She

sensed that he felt the same way about her. Sometimes she thought he might suggest they date other people, but he never did. As longtime friends and allies, they were fiercely loyal to each other. She was always on his arm for the important functions, and she never argued with him in public over his conservative political views or criticized his rigid adherence to the rules. She admired Grant for his steadiness. It was probably what she needed most in a life partner. Unfortunately, it wasn't what she wanted. She knew that for certain now.

She knocked on Grant's door again and when he opened it, she smiled at him as cheerfully as she could.

"Hello. Are you busy?"

"Not too busy for you. Come in," he said, waving her to follow him. He wore a crisp white shirt with navy trousers, part of ES standard issue. He would be going into ES headquarters then rather than to court. On court days, it was power suits.

She glanced around at the colors, the cream and taupe with gold accents. The tasteful elegance of Grant's home echoed many of the council members' houses, but it failed to move her. After the boldly painted treasure chest that was Merrick's penthouse, everything was bound to look a little dull in comparison.

She sat on the couch, smoothing her skirt before clasping her hands on her lap. "Grant, something happened. The fact is . . . someone drugged me and tried to kidnap me."

He jerked forward. "What? Who?"

"I don't know."

"When?"

"After the Xenakis party."

He stared at her. "Last night?"

"Yes."

"I haven't heard anything. You didn't make a report?"

"No."

"Well, what were you waiting for? I've been home all day. Why didn't you call me earlier?"

"I don't want to report it."

"What do you mean? Of course, you have to report it."

"I have my reasons for wanting to wait."

"I don't understand. You're here now. Where were you taken? How did you escape?"

She shook her head. "How I managed to get home isn't the important part. How I was taken and who did it is."

"Alissa, I'm going to need the details. All of them."

"I was drugged. I don't remember the details. It happened after the party. Either someone followed me from Dimitri's or someone anticipated that I'd walk home along the lake and waited for me."

"And you have no idea who it was?"

"None. I suppose it was someone trying to sabotage my bid for Wreath Muse. I'd like to look through the security footage from last night. Would you take me to headquarters and show me the video files?"

"You don't have security clearance for that."

"I only want to see the files of me walking home."

He shook his head. "No, but I'll certainly look into it and let you know what I find."

She pushed down her frustration. Why shouldn't she have access to footage from cameras pointed at her own property and the public walkway leading to it? She and the other muses allowed their privacy to be constantly and continuously invaded. Shouldn't there be some relaxation of the rules when she'd been abducted?

"You think it was someone from the Etherlin? That's hard to believe. You've had stalkers. Someone must have gotten in."

"It wasn't a stalker."

"How do you know?"

"It was the wrong kind of an attack for a stalker."

"Have there been any recent threats?" he asked.

"Nothing out of the ordinary. I've forwarded everything to your office, as I always do."

"Do you think the Xenakises had something to do with it?"

"Not Cerise. I'm sure she wouldn't have. And Dimitri, of course, would never do anything to hurt me. I think Dorie's too young to pull off something like that on her own, but . . ."

"But what?"

"They are friends with Troy Rella."

"So are we."

"I'm not."

"Troy's council."

"I know he's on the EC, but he's also Cerise and Dorie's friend and Ileana's brother. He doesn't like me. If I were gone, whoever got the Wreath would suit him better."

"Why don't you and Troy get along?"

She shrugged. "We just never clicked."

"Alissa, if you don't confide in me, I can't help you."

"Just check the surveillance footage. That will be a huge help. Find out who took me from the path."

"That I will definitely do."

She nodded with a tentative smile. "Thanks."

He leaned back and shook his head. "I can't believe something like this happened on my watch."

"No one would've suspected this kind of treachery from anyone in the Etherlin. It's not us." She smoothed her skirt again, then forced herself to look at him. "Grant, there's something else I wanted to talk to you about."

"Of course."

"It's been a long time since you invited me to spend the night. Why is that?"

"You're always welcome to stay over, Alissa."

She studied him. That hadn't answered her question. "If there's someone else in your life—"

"Of course not," he said too quickly. "Is there someone else in your life?"

"What I wondered is . . ." Ever since he'd come back from college, Grant had spent most of his time with the other ES officers, who were generally fit young men. Like Grant. Was his choice to spend time with them job dedication? Or something more?

Alissa had never broached the subject because having Grant as her boyfriend suited her image, and she'd thought that if there was something to tell her, he would in his own time. But things had changed since she'd been abducted. She couldn't pretend they hadn't. Grant was too good a friend to keep locked in a relationship with her when she was more attracted to someone else, especially if Grant would be happier out of the relationship as well.

"It's just that as one of your oldest friends, I hope you know that you could confide in me. I will never turn my back on you, Grant."

"Thanks," he said with an easy laugh. "But I'm not the one who's been distant. I've been here the whole time."

"I'm sorry. You never seemed to—"

"To what?"

"To miss me."

He smiled. "We've known each other a very long time. It's not hot and heavy like when we were teenagers. How could it be? What we have is easy and comfortable. It's good for both of us. We would have great kids together. There's no rush, but it's what's meant to happen between us. Unless you've met someone that you think is a better match for you?"

A better match? She almost laughed. No, definitely not that. Half the ventala were sterile and the other half had kids who grew up to be violent criminals. Not exactly great marriage material. Merrick couldn't even set foot in the Etherlin where, as Wreath Muse, she would live for the rest of her life.

Thinking about the hard reality of the situation left her feeling cold all over. "No, I haven't found a better match than you, Grant. You're wonderful, and our lives are well suited."

"Good."

She frowned. So he wasn't going to admit what she was sure he knew as well. If he wouldn't meet her halfway, she'd have to do it alone.

"I have to be honest though." Her heart thudded in her chest. Grant waited. "You and I—we're more friends than lovers. I worry—I suspect that neither of us has met our soul mate yet. I think staying together could prevent that from happening, which would be a shame."

Grant folded his arms across his chest. "Who is he?"

She kept her expression neutral, but extra color stained her cheeks. She couldn't tell Grant about Merrick. He would never understand, but she also couldn't deceive a loyal friend. "There's someone I'm attracted to, but this is not about him. I haven't slept with him, and I'm not going to. It's just made me wonder how you and I could be right for each other when I feel something intense for someone else."

"Is it Dimitri?"

"What?" She choked out a laugh. "Of course not. He's been like a father to me."

Grant shrugged.

"Why would you ask that?"

"Because he's always saying how much you look like your mother. That you're just as beautiful as she was. I thought he might have seduced you, the way he seduced her."

The blood drained from her face, and she gripped the arm of the couch. Her voice sounded far away as she said, "That's not true."

"Hell," Grant said, moving quickly to her side. "I'm sorry. I thought you knew."

Alissa's rigid body resisted Grant's attempt at comfort when he put an arm around her. The icy rush that washed over her whenever she had to face prying cameras or unkind scrutiny returned reflexively.

"If you're going to slander her, you'd better have evidence, Grant. And if you do, I want to see it."

Chapter 12

Merrick had sent Ox upstairs and had taken Tobin out of the room with the drains. With its lead-lined walls, there was no way to get a cell or Internet connection. It had been done on purpose, so that no tracking devices would operate inside its walls.

But with Tobin spilling information, Merrick had moved him to a room down the hall. Tobin sat next to Merrick, downing painkillers and pressing an ice pack to his swollen eye.

The pictures were what Merrick had expected, and he controlled his reaction, even if he couldn't suppress it.

Alissa's body had been artfully posed. Head tipped back, mouth slightly open, eyes closed. A pillow hidden under her back created an arch. Cato Jacobi's tongue licked blood from the puncture wound on her arm while his fingers splayed over an exposed breast or thigh. Image after lascivious image. Even though her expression never changed and Merrick was sure she'd been unconscious, it was impossible not to be stirred by the way she looked. Tobin was a great photographer, and Merrick wanted to kill him for it.

Merrick focused on Jacobi. When Merrick had first seen the bite mark on Alissa's arm, he'd wondered why Jacobi hadn't bitten her throat, which would've been more intimate and a greater show of dominance. Merrick had thought it might be because Jacobi wanted a wound that could be concealed, but that wasn't it. Jacobi had chosen to bite her arm so that his body wouldn't obscure the camera's view of her.

Merrick clicked through the pictures as they became more graphic. A slow burn licked through him. He couldn't kill Cato Jacobi so soon after they'd squared off, but things would die down eventually. Merrick could be patient when he had to be.

He glanced at Tobin and noted the intent way Tobin studied the pictures, his pupils dilated. Tobin admired his own work.

"Go sit over there," Merrick said, nodding to the couch.

Stiffly, Tobin moved away.

Merrick erased the files, erased the emails, permanently emptied the computer's trash, and changed the account passwords. He erased the browser history and systematically deleted all Tobin's files from the hard drive. Then Merrick ripped the laptop open and yanked the drive out, pushing the empty computer casing aside.

"So who from the Etherlin helped Jacobi?"

"I don't know," Tobin said woodenly.

"Guess."

Tobin shrugged. "Most likely one of the other muses. Or one of their family members or friends, supporters. Someone who wanted to eliminate the frontrunner from the competition."

"Which of them has connections outside the Etherlin? Who makes trips to this side of the wall?"

"None of the girls themselves come this way often. People watch their every move. They'd never be able to party in the Sliver without someone finding out." Tobin leaned back, warming up. He sold plenty of pictures to the tabloids; peddling gossip was as natural as breathing for him, and this was a final chance to show off what he knew. "But if you're asking if one of them could be in secret contact with someone from this side, you know the answer to that, Merrick."

Tobin's tone was snide, but Merrick didn't react. If Tobin wanted the satisfaction of poking the tiger before it ripped out his throat, so be it. Finding out what the weasel knew was more important than knocking him out.

"Which one? If you had to pick?" Merrick asked without missing a beat.

"Ileana Rella is a cold fish. She'd gut her parents for the chance to be Wreath Muse, and her brother Troy and Alissa aren't friendly. The Rellas could've orchestrated something like this." Tobin's hands folded together, and he tapped his thumbs against each other.

"Alissa has always outshined Cerise Xenakis. Could be Cerise finally got sick of it. She's got a huge following, and some of them are on this side of the wall. Any hungry musician or athlete from the mean streets hoping to make the big time would kill for a shot to work with Cerise. She'd just have to say the word, and it would get done. The little sister, Dorie, just joined the scene. She's too busy enjoying the attention and learning the ropes to cause real trouble yet."

"What about Dimitri Xenakis? I've watched him testify at hearings about crime in the Varden. He's got a killer instinct," Merrick said.

"He does, but Xenakis is Council President and totally elitist. He wouldn't spit on Cato Jacobi, let alone conspire with him. Besides, Alissa's his girl."

"What do you mean?"

Tobin gave a little shrug. "Xenakis was crazy for Helene North, but the husband was always in the way. Now, Helene's dead. The father's a recluse. Uncle Dimitri's been there every second since. Grown up, Alissa's a ringer for her mother. You do the math."

"So what about his wife then? Would she make a deal with the devil to get rid of the North women for good?"

"Maybe. Never heard that Calla Xenakis has connections Varden-side, but she's a quiet one, so it's hard to know. She's been out of town for almost a month though, so unlikely."

"What about Grant Easton? Alissa's had him on ice for years and won't commit. Is he bitter about it?"

Tobin smiled. "You wouldn't mind that, would you? Me helping you pin a target on the boyfriend's back?"

Merrick gave Tobin a steady stare. "Do I look worried about Easton?"

Tobin's smile faded. "You're first-gen ventala, making you

half vampire. Any humanity you might have been born with got choked out of you by that vamp blood a long time ago. So no, I don't think you look worried about Easton. I doubt you ever look worried about anything, Merrick."

"In favor of Paragraph Seventeen, were you?" Merrick asked coolly, referring to the one part of the Human Preservation Act that had been struck from the bill. In the Varden, they called it the Genocide Clause because it had proposed killing the ventala along with their vampire parents.

"Vampires are the ones who went on a killing spree," Tobin said. "You can't blame people for wanting to protect themselves from another Rising."

"Survival's a universal preoccupation," Merrick agreed to keep the conversation flowing.

"You know who's really in favor of Seventeen? Easton. So no, he wouldn't conspire with Jacobi. If Easton ever met Jacobi, his first order of business would be to cut off Cato's head."

"Jacobi would carve up Easton and use him as fish food."

"Think so? You might be right. You and Jacobi probably don't need to worry about him outside a courtroom, but Alissa does. If he finds out she's cozy with you, she's done. Grant likes her as much as he likes any woman, but he's a straight arrow. The Wreath Muse is the most important symbol of the Etherlin. If he finds out Alissa's been pen pals with a ventala, the council will hear about it before she has time to lick the seal on another envelope."

" 'As much as he likes any woman.' If he's gay, who's his lover?"

"The guy's not sloppy. He's head of Etherlin Security and an assistant DA. Next, he'll be DA. Then he'll be on the council and eventually Council President. This guy has a plan. He'll marry the right wife. He'll have the right kids. If he swings both ways, he's gonna keep that secret well buried."

"Nothing stays buried if there's someone around who knows how to use a shovel. Who's the lover? Your best guess."

Tobin shrugged. "Couldn't say. All I know is that Easton doesn't stay over at her place, and she doesn't stay over at his. I've staked the places out tons of times, trying to get a shot of them kissing each other good-bye. Now I ask you, what straight guy with Alissa North as his girlfriend is going to let that relationship turn platonic? Unless she's an ice queen in the bedroom, but if that's the problem, you'd think he'd have a girl on the side."

Alissa had certainly felt warm enough to him. It would be convenient if Easton were gay. Alissa could be Easton's beard, and Easton could be hers while she was with Merrick. Also, there would never be reason for Merrick to kill Easton out of jealousy, which was good because killing the director of Etherlin Security would've been a complicated thing to achieve without getting caught.

Tobin pulled his arms into his body and rubbed them with his hands. The room was a few degrees warmer than a fridge, but not many. The chill was getting to Tobin now. He hunched his shoulders as the grim reality of his situation set in again.

"Any other inside information I should know?"

"You want to know the best way to protect her? Leave her alone."

Merrick walked over to the door and unlocked it. He swung the door open. "I suggest heading straight to the airport. Jacobi's third-generation ventala, but the extra humanity doesn't seem to have made much of an impression. He gets his hands on you, and his fish are going to eat well for a month."

Tobin stayed in the chair, staring at the door. "Are you kidding?"

"Well, I'm no expert on fish, but you're what? Two hundred and fifty pounds? Even piranhas would take a while with you," Merrick said. He knew what Tobin was really asking, but didn't want to dwell on the fact that he was going to let the prick go.

"You're letting me live?"

"Unless ventala-assisted suicide appeals to you. In which case, just say the word."

Tobin raised his eyebrows and a slow smile turned up the corner of his busted lip. "You promised her, didn't you?" The guy's tone was almost smug. "Promised that you'd let me go?"

Merrick's gaze slid over him, recalling the pictures Tobin

had taken of Alissa. There hadn't been a mark on Tobin when Ox had found him, so Tobin hadn't even put up a token resistance to taking them. Had he set up the lighting and helped Jacobi pose her for the best effect? It had looked that way. The extreme close-ups made Merrick think Tobin had enjoyed having her helpless and exposed for his lens.

Rage seeped slowly into his veins again, and Merrick's eyes narrowed.

"There are a lot of ways to make a body disappear, Theo. I know them all."

Tobin's triumph melted away.

"And what I promised was that I wouldn't kill you when I met with you in the Sliver. The Sliver's what? At least eight miles from here? Also, there's Ox. When you were checking into my past, did you hear how he came to work for me?"

Tobin licked his lips and looked nervously at the doorway.

"This used to be the most dangerous part of the Varden. The cops wouldn't drive into it after dark. People had bars on the windows and locked their houses up around seven every night.

"There were a dozen underground nests that kids and young women were dragged into. They were kept chained for easy use. Rogue vampires that escaped extermination controlled the underground. Anyone who tried to stop them was slaughtered, and his family was murdered in retaliation.

"When I took power here, I started raiding the underground. Naturally, the predators and their clientele came out in force to stop me from disrupting their way of life. The price on my head was so high, the oddsmakers gave me a life expectancy of about two weeks.

"Ox showed up with a little local muscle. He said he'd work for nothing if I let him keep me alive long enough to raid every nest. I don't know which one his little sister was in. Those kids were in such bad shape when we first got them out, you couldn't tell one from the other, and Ox never said." Merrick popped his knuckles.

"I'll tell you this though: the Varden oddsmakers still like taking bets on life expectancies. For a rapist or pedophile who tries to move into this slice of the Varden, it's about forty-eight hours. It takes about a day and a half for word to get to Ox and then about six to ten hours for him to take care of them.

"Which is why I know that if I mention to Ox that while Alissa North was drugged unconscious, you stripped and photographed her, he'll tear you to pieces with his bare hands."

"They forced me—"

"You were there. You didn't try to stop it. You kept the pictures." Merrick gave him a hard look. Pausing for effect between the last four words, he repeated, "He will *tear you to pieces.*"

The color drained from Tobin's face, and he shifted in his seat.

"What I suggest is that you start running and don't stop. I may have promised I wouldn't kill you today, but I never said I'd keep you safe." Merrick swept a hand toward the doorway. "The airport's that way."

Chapter 13

Grant didn't have any proof that Alissa's mother had had an affair with Dimitri. ES's supposition that there had been an affair was based on the fact that Dimitri and Helene had apparently spent a lot of time together, often at night. But their meetings had been at their respective houses, sometimes when their spouses were in town. Who would conduct an affair that way? If they'd wanted to see each other in secret, they could've met out of town or even in the Sliver. In her mother's time, passing the wall wasn't considered nearly as dangerous as it was now.

Chastened by her anger, Grant had been conciliatory and agreed to review the security footage after she left and to show her anything he found that might be useful.

On her way home she got a text message from Theo Tobin, thanking her for handling Merrick and saying it was essential that she be at Handyrock's. There were certain things he would only tell her and no one else, and she needed to hear them immediately.

She didn't understand how he knew that she'd spoken with Merrick. Had Merrick already talked to Tobin? She frowned, trying to remember if she'd made it clear that Merrick should help Tobin get back home.

Tobin's text suggested that she invite some of her current aspirants, many of whom had come to town for the upcoming retreat and banquet. Meeting with the aspirants would be a good cover, since it looked like she would still have to go to the Sliver herself to find out what was happening.

The question was whether or not to take Etherlin Security officers with her. Normally she would have, but the talk with Grant had made them seem as gossipy as teenage girls. Also, with them hovering, there would be no way for her to discreetly talk to Merrick, assuming that he hadn't yet seen Tobin and would be at Handyrock's, too. If he was going to be there, his bodyguard Mr. Orvin probably would be as well. Then she wouldn't need an ES detail because Merrick and Mr. Orvin certainly seemed capable of handling any sort of trouble.

The key, she decided, was to be sure that everyone else arrived before she did, so she wouldn't be sitting there alone.

She called Pead's Florists. They answered immediately.

"Hello, this is Alissa North."

"Yes, ma'am," a male voice said.

"There was a young man who delivered flowers to my house today. Is he still working? I'd like to speak to him."

"That was me. Robin."

"I didn't see you today, Robin. We've met before, right?"

"Um, yeah. I delivered the . . . um, package to you on February the thirteenth and the one on January tenth."

"Do you know who sent them?"

"They were sent anonymously. Dropped off by courier to the shop with instructions. Anonymously," he repeated.

"It's funny that you're always the one who gets those deliveries. And it's interesting how you usually catch me on my way in or out of the house or at Bick's Café with them."

He didn't answer.

"It would be easier to just drop them at the house."

Again there was silence.

"A couple years ago there was another young man who did the deliveries, and he sometimes helped me send a return message to people who sent me things anonymously. Do you think you could help me with something like that?"

"Yeah, um, maybe."

"I'd like to send a note tonight."

"Tonight?"

"I realize it's not convenient, but I'd like to take care of it right away. I'd certainly compensate you for your time and trouble."

"I think today's stuff came from pretty far out," he said nervously. "And maybe they wouldn't want me showing up uninvited, since it was sent anonymously. There are kind of a lot of instructions about keeping things private."

"Yes, I'm sure they value their privacy, but I don't think they'd mind if you were bringing a message from me, do you?"

"Um." He paused. "Maybe not."

"You're not comfortable. It's okay. We won't worry about it."

"Um, listen. What I can do is check if it's okay to bring a message. I've got a number to call in case of emergencies, if there's any kind of question or problem with the delivery. Like I was supposed to deliver the package to you directly today, but you didn't go out and that housekeeper lady wouldn't let me hand it to you. So I called, and they said to leave the one package by the trees and to change the note. You got the package, right? Not just the flowers?"

"I got it. Thank you. And actually, if you're calling, you don't need to deliver a note at all. You can just deliver my message by phone. How would that be?"

He exhaled audibly. "Better. Yeah, a lot better."

She smiled. She didn't blame him for not wanting to go into the Varden alone at night, uninvited.

"What's the message?"

"Tell them that I'm going to have to take that eight o'clock meeting after all."

"Yeah, okay. No problem." He repeated the message once, then repeated the time again.

"Yes, great. When you're out making deliveries tomorrow, please stop by the house. I'll leave an envelope for you. Something for your trouble."

"Um, you don't have to do that. Tips and everything are all covered with those deliveries. I'm not supposed to take money from you."

She almost laughed. And what if he did? Early morning firing squad? She wondered if Merrick had personally terrified the delivery boy or if it was just his reputation that had done it. She guessed she should be grateful that the boy was cautious. If he hadn't been so afraid of Merrick, maybe he'd have told people about the deliveries.

"I understand, Robin, but this wasn't one of their deliveries. You're sending a message for me. This time, you should take a tip from me."

"Um . . ."

"We can keep the envelope just between us. I'll leave it with the housekeeper, and you can decide if you want to pick it up or not."

"Thanks, Miss North."

"You're very welcome, and thank you for delivering my message."

Alissa closed the phone and looked at the clock. Plenty of time had passed for Grant to have checked the security files. She wondered why he hadn't called her yet.

She fingered the phone. It would be helpful to have some answers before she left for Handyrock's.

She called, and he answered in his official voice. She raised her brows.

"Is this a bad time?"

"No, it's as good a time as any," he said, and she heard him close a door. "I reviewed the footage. I found some of you leaving Dimitri's. You reached camera twelve, which is the first one that would pick up someone walking from his place to yours, but after that there's nothing."

"What do you mean, nothing?"

"I mean that you don't appear again until hours later on camera eleven, which is closer to your house. There's a collection of trees between cameras seven and twelve. It seems as though you might have wandered off the path into the wooded area, stayed there during the night, and returned.

"So someone could've just carried me through the trees to a waiting car and taken me anywhere from there without ever appearing on another video camera? It would be that easy?"

"No, there are several cameras pointing at those trees from all directions. The lights are motion activated, and there are no real blind spots around that patch of woods."

"So who entered the woods? Have you checked?"

"I'm going through the footage now, but I've gone back for two hours from each of the cameras and I've found nothing."

"Did the lights go on around the woods?"

"No."

"Could someone have tampered with the cameras?"

"Any manipulation of the cameras or lights sends an alert, and none went off last night."

"Who has access to the footage? Who could tamper with the feed after the camera records it or with its storage?"

"That would be a complicated process."

"Who has access?"

"ES and the EC."

"What about tech support? Computer programmers who designed and maintained the system?"

"Sure."

She sighed. "Well, someone covered his or her tracks, but I doubt they did it alone. Can people get remote access? Can the security files be looked at from the Dome?"

"If you have clearance on the network, yes."

"Can you trace who accessed the files last night and today?"

"Alissa," he said tightly.

"Yes?"

"I know how to run an investigation."

After a moment, she said, "Yes, of course. I'm sorry. You're doing everything you can. Please call when you find something."

"If you weren't in the woods all night, Alissa, where were you?"

"You'll tell me when you find out who was involved?"

He was silent.

"I'll speak to you soon, I hope. Good night," she said, closing the phone after he said good-bye.

She shook her head. There was no doubt that whoever had orchestrated her abduction was well-placed. It might have been an ES officer or technician who'd acted alone out of deranged loyalty, but somehow she doubted it. More likely, the perfectly executed plan had been conceived by someone

close to her. An Etherlin Council member or a muse. Someone who'd been at the party . . . near enough to touch her.

Standing in his office, Merrick glanced at the door when
someone knocked.

"Come," Merrick said, shuffling the papers he held into a
stack.

Ox entered, and Merrick handed them to him.

"What's this?" Ox asked, glancing down.

"Instructions. I'm going to be away for a few days. Maybe
longer. I know you know the drill for when I'm gone, but this
time the syndicate might try to come down on you, looking
for information about where I am and what I'm doing."

"Where are you going?"

Merrick stared at Ox, unspeaking.

"I'd never betray you, boss. They could cut me into
pieces—"

Merrick held up a hand. "I don't doubt your loyalty, Ox."

After a pause, Ox nodded.

"Let's run the list."

"Sure," Ox said, and Merrick went through the instructions
that were new, like what Ox should do if the syndicate tried
to force their way into Merrick's building or grabbed some
of Merrick's people for leverage.

"Don't worry, boss, we've got it covered here. If you'll be
gone though, you might want to send a warning to your girl.
Been hearing her name whispered a lot in connection with
the syndicate. I wouldn't be surprised if someone tries to
make another run at her."

"Any details?"

"Nah, sketchy stuff. Nothing useful. But speaking of her,
that's what I came up to tell you. She sent a message."

"Where is it?" he asked, putting a hand out for the envelope.

"That's the weird thing. She didn't send flowers or a letter.
She had the kid who delivered the flowers call the contact
number I gave him. I just heard the message."

"What was it?"

"She said she's got to take her eight o'clock meeting after all."

Merrick jerked his head toward the clock. It was already ten minutes to eight.

"Not sure why she'd want you to know about her Etherlin schedule. Not like you can score an invite—" Ox continued as Merrick grabbed his duffel from the floor.

"Get the V3 clips and meet me in the parking garage."

Ox's mouth dropped open. "Are we—?"

Merrick didn't hear the rest of Ox's question as he crossed the room in heartbeats.

Chapter 14

Alissa wore a jade dress with silver and peridot jewelry to Handyrock's so the surrounding colors would complement her choice. The two-story club was filled with furniture the color of limes and fresh snap peas. The chocolate brown wood accents and framed mirrors were all hip and friendly. The music vacillated between pop hits and edgier rock, and pockets of dancers in small nooks were framed by pale green sheers hanging from polished brass ceiling rods.

Her aspirants were gathered around a corner table, laughing and drinking their way through a rainbow of cocktails. Apparently book people and ecoscientists went together like gin and olives. As she watched them, she wished she'd brought them together sooner.

"What are you doing here?"

She glanced over her shoulder to find Troy Rella. Troy had sleek dark hair, a square jaw, and perfect olive skin. In his twenties, he'd modeled for Versace and Armani Exchange before becoming an EC member and the Etherlin's head publicist. He could write an article about bumping into her at Handyrock's that would be picked up by the Associated Press and go out to a billion media outlets around the world. He'd never make a muse look bad in print, of course, but he could make her look bad for the council, depending on what he saw and heard when she met with Tobin. The power Troy could wield, among other things, made her wary.

Despite a thumping heart, she smiled at him. "I'm visiting with some of my aspirants. A couple are new and don't have their security clearance yet to come into the Etherlin."

"They don't have clearance so you came out here to meet them?" he asked disapprovingly.

"What are you doing here?"

"The Handyrock's owners are friends of mine. I'm going to do some publicity work for them. Not that they'll need me to. They just hit the exposure jackpot."

She knew what he would say next, but widened her eyes as if she didn't.

"A picture of you here," he said.

Alissa didn't respond to Troy because she spotted Theo Tobin and was shocked on two counts. First, he didn't have a camera, which was normally attached to him like an appendage. Second, his battered face and rumpled clothes made him look like he'd slept in a cardboard box and had been hit by a truck while emerging from a Varden alley.

"Wow," Troy murmured. "What happened to him?"

Tobin hurried straight to them. "Miss North—"

"Mr. Tobin, this is Troy Rella. Ileana Rella's brother," she said, cuing him to watch what he said.

"Sure, I know who he is," Tobin said with a cursory nod at Troy. "Nice to see you." Tobin's gaze darted back to her. "I need to talk to you."

"You don't look well, Mr. Tobin. Maybe you should go to the emergency room."

"I'm fine."

"Are you sure?"

"Can we talk privately?"

"I suppose so. I'm having drinks with some of my aspirants tonight. Let me say hello to them, and I'll drop by the bar for a minute."

He nodded and strode to the bar, looking around nervously.

"It was nice seeing you, Troy. Have a pleasant night."

"Where's your security detail?" Troy asked.

Alissa walked away without answering. With Troy's scrutiny, the night had taken a dangerous turn. She strode up to the table, and all the aspirants sprung up to greet her. After smiles and hugs, she made her excuses and sent one of them to the bar to tell Tobin to meet her at the valet stand. She couldn't afford to wait for Merrick to arrive. And she couldn't afford to be seen acknowledging him when he did arrive.

She spotted a staff member with a camera that Troy was sending her way. She glanced around. If she ducked into the bathroom, they'd just wait for her to come out. She and Troy locked eyes, and he gave her a Cheshire cat smile. *Damn him!*

She assessed which wall would make the best backdrop and crossed to it, crooking a finger at her aspirants. They loped over, still in high spirits. She arranged them quickly.

"Miss North, it looks like you know what I want," the staffer said with charming sheepishness.

"Of course. I'm pressed for time, so only two shots please."

"We really appreciate this. You have no idea what this will mean for the club. Let us know if you'd like to move your group to the VIP room upstairs. And of course, we'd like to comp your table's tab. I'm Neal, one of the owners."

The aspirants erupted with cheerful thanks and goodwill.

"That's lovely of you," Alissa said. Her eyes followed Tobin as he made his way to the front door. When he paled and stopped suddenly, her eyes swung to the entrance. The fierce young woman who came through the door set Alissa's heart racing. Black buzzed hair, high cheekbones, and scarlet lips. A flash of memory tried to surface. Gravel-voiced and dangerous. When and where had she met the woman? She struggled to remember, but that effort burned away when she saw the man with her. Cato Jacobi wore a black suit and a determined expression.

Alissa's heart hammered against her ribs. She was tempted to duck behind one of the columns and to try to circumnavigate the club to get out behind Jacobi as he moved inward, but her feet stayed firmly planted. North women weren't seen running from bars or hiding under tables. She had a room full of witnesses and the handgun she'd stashed in her bag before leaving. If she was going to be ruined, she'd be ruined with her chin up.

She kept her eyes on Cato Jacobi and tipped her head toward the Handyrock's owner.

"Neal, I need a favor. That man's ventala, and I can't be in a club with one of them. Can you ask him to leave?" At the persuasive power in her voice, determination lit Neal's face and he snapped around, waving at some bouncers.

Jacobi spotted her and smiled. She maintained a cool expression, watching as the Handyrock's employees blocked Jacobi's path. The woman with him never slowed. She moved smoothly around the men focused on her companion and walked directly toward Alissa.

The memory, muted but chilling, emerged. Words in a gravelly voice. *Pretty earrings, Barbie.* And the cold slither of a tongue licking Alissa's earlobe and jaw. Alissa shuddered.

She's with him. She's one of them.

Alissa popped the clasp of her Prada bag and shoved her hand inside. She closed her fingers on the gun, then moved the bag in front her body. It would be a shame to put a hole in the beautiful purse, but a bigger shame to have the pretty psychopath put a hole in her neck.

"Well, hello. Nice to see *you* again, Miss North," she said, and licked her red lips in a way that was lascivious and menacing.

Alissa's thumb clicked off the gun's safety. Her eyes held the woman in focus, but Alissa inclined her head toward Jack and Hank Erdman, the sandy-haired twins who played folk rock on acoustic guitars and who were going to solve the world's energy crisis with her help. "Guys, it's getting very loud here. Let's see if we can find that VIP room."

The woman caught Jack's arm in a vise grip. "Move and you'll lose one of your pets." She retracted her lips to show off her fangs. The aspirants, suddenly sober, went silent around her.

"Hurt him, and I'll make you regret it."

Black eyes clashed with blue. Alissa didn't blink.

"Attacking humans and a muse in a club? In front of a hundred witnesses? That'll be an automatic death sentence for you, and a quick way to get Paragraph Seventeen resurrected."

Fury flashed in the woman's eyes. "He'd still be dead and so would you." The woman grabbed Phyllis, one of Alissa's writers, by the hair and jerked hard enough to make Phyllis yelp and fall to her knees.

Alissa's muscles clenched, but she swallowed her gasp. The female ventala lived up to their reputation for explosive rage. A violent twist of Phyllis's hair made the writer shriek in pain. Alissa had to stop the ventala before she did permanent damage.

"You don't want this," Alissa said, thousands of years of muse magic distilled into her every word and breath. "You're smart, calculating, cool. Your reserve is to be admired."

The red mouth slackened ever so slightly and the expression softened. Fingers slipped from Phyllis's hair, and Jack jerked his arm free. All the aspirants backed out of reach. Alissa remained still as the woman's dark eyes blinked and cleared.

"You bitch," she sneered. "I'm going to—"

"You want to sit down. You want that now. You're exhausted."

The woman's shoulders slumped, and her body sagged. Alissa jerked the gun free of her bag and pressed it against the woman's chest a few inches below her left clavicle.

When the woman's eyes cleared, she roared with fury.

"The gun is loaded with V3 bullets. If I pull the trigger, they'll tear holes through your heart. I don't want to hurt you, so back up slowly. You're relaxed, calm, and you want to step aside and let me pass."

The woman started to move, but then shook her head and clamped hands over her ears, growling. "Bitch, I am so going to kill you."

Three things happened almost at once. With her scarlet mouth open, the woman lunged for Alissa's throat; Alissa's finger pulled the trigger; and the woman was jerked through the air by Merrick.

The bullet went through the woman's arm to embed itself in a column, leaving a bloody spray. With his left arm around the woman's waist, Merrick's free hand shoved Alissa's forearm down, so the gun was pointed at the floor. The woman shouted curses as Merrick flung her through the air. She landed on a couch, but erupted off it, pulling a blade loose as she launched herself toward him like a Fury.

Merrick crouched and rose in a blindingly quick move. His left arm deflected her right, making the blade miss his throat, but it still slashed across his shoulder as her body connected with his.

The woman's eyes widened in shock, and she crumpled. Merrick lowered her to the floor, and Alissa watched his right hand emerge from under her. The long blade in his hand was stained the red of a cocktail cherry.

Cato Jacobi, whose mouth dripped with the blood of his victims, wailed, "Tamberi!"

Merrick slid his blade back under his pant leg and yanked open the woman's suit jacket. Crimson bloomed from her torso like an opening rose. He thumped his palm down in the center, compressing the wound.

"Put it back in your purse," Merrick said.

Alissa's eyes darted to the gun, and she shoved it away. Cato Jacobi slammed his way past bodies, ready to attack.

"She'll be all right!" Merrick said, making Jacobi come up short. "Here," Merrick said. "Press here."

Cato dropped to his knees and shoved his hand over the wound.

"I stopped short of her heart."

"I'm going to kill you," Cato rasped.

"You're welcome."

Merrick stood, and Mr. Orvin appeared right behind him, shaking his head. "It's a bloody mess. He killed a couple of them."

"I saw," Merrick said. "These are yours?" he asked Alissa, nodding at her aspirants.

"Yes," she said.

Merrick glanced at the shredded shirt and bleeding wound on Ox's thick neck. "How bad is that?"

"A scratch. He tried to get a bigger piece, but didn't."

"Take these people to the front and wait for the cops. Cato may lose control again. You've got your gun. Use it if you need to. Leg wound if you can since he's Victor's kid, but if you've got to kill him, I'll have your back until it's over."

Ox nodded gravely. "Thanks, boss, but no worries. I won't let it go there."

"Man plans. God laughs," Merrick murmured and turned to Alissa. "Miss North, I'm your escort if you need one."

"Yes. Thank you."

She followed him in silence. Neal's body and two others lay in pools of blood. Her stride faltered.

"Oh no," she whispered.

Merrick's hand closed on her arm and stopped her from going to them. "Keep walking."

"I—"

"You can't help. Come with me. Let me get you out."

She allowed Merrick to pull her along. "He's dead because he tried to help me," she said, guilt and grief threatening to consume her.

"Then don't let him have died for nothing."

They exited through the glass door, and Merrick strode directly to the valet stand. "Miss North's keys," he demanded. The startled valet fumbled for them as several black sedans pulled up. Sirens wailed in the distance as she took the keys from the boy.

Several men in black suits leapt from the cars.

"Merrick," the leader said. "What's the situation?"

"See for yourself," Merrick said, walking her away.

"I'll take her," the man said, gesturing for the others to go in.

Merrick moved so that she was on the far side of his body. "Witnesses saw me walk her out. She goes back where she belongs."

"I have my orders," the ventala said.

Without breaking his stride, Merrick whipped a gun out and pointed it at the man. "And I've got an alley and a stubborn streak."

The other ventala stepped back. "Easy, Merrick."

"It can be," Merrick replied. "Get the door, Miss North." Alissa pulled open the heavy door, not sure where it led to. "I'm right behind you," Merrick said.

She raced down the poorly lit stairwell into an underground parking structure. She spotted her car and rushed to it. Her hands shook slightly as she opened the door. She looked over her shoulder and found Merrick approaching.

"You'll drive," he said, striding around the car while scanning the area. He waited until she was in the leather bucket seat with the door closed before he climbed in himself.

Belted in, she started the car.

"Head there," he said, pointing. She pressed the pedal, and the car roared forward.

"This car's all engine," he said.

"Yes," she said, distracted by her racing thoughts. "It's a prototype. A V-10 engine that runs principally on solar and electric power." She was so upset; she wasn't sure why she was talking about cars or why she was talking about anything. The image of the fallen men kept flashing before her eyes. She pursed her lips, knowing that she'd missed whatever Merrick had just said. She needed to concentrate on driving.

"What?" she asked.

"It's okay," he said, squeezing her arm gently. The touch helped focus her.

She stopped at the security arm blocking the drive. It didn't open. "We may have to go the other way." She shifted into reverse as he opened his door.

"Be right back." He got out and snapped the wood gate, tossing it aside. When he climbed back in, he said, "At the end of the drive, turn left."

She didn't hesitate. Down the drive and onto the road, she followed his instructions without question. He took them on a twisted path through the Sliver, down dark streets, through alleys and neighborhoods, but, with a pounding heart, she drove like a race car driver on the final lap. The need to get behind the Etherlin's protective walls consumed her.

With one last turn, the shining silver and iron gate appeared fifty feet in front of them. Halogen and ultraviolet lights blazed bright.

Home. Relief flooded through her.

"Stop," he said.

The car jerked to stillness at her tap on the brake. With adrenaline licking her veins, she felt like she'd biked to the gate rather than driven. She forced her breathing to slow.

"Nice driving, North."

"Nice navigating," she said. She glanced at him. He was

handsome and thoroughly disreputable looking with his five o'clock shadow and the dark sunglasses he slid on to shield his eyes. "Thank you for the rescue."

"I was in the neighborhood." He opened the door, but paused when she laid a hand on his arm. He pulled the door closed again.

"I owe you so much. I want to give you a 'thank-you' gift. What can I send? I don't know what you'd like. A car like this? A year's supply of bullets in a rainbow of metals?"

He flashed a smile.

"Seriously. What does someone like you need? Please tell me."

"Another time." His voice was smooth, but she felt a vibration that stirred her muse senses. A secret lay under the surface of his easy reply.

She nodded absently, studying his face. "A part of my talent relies on me being able to read people."

"And?"

"And you're very difficult to read, Mr. Merrick, but you're still part human."

"Again, and?"

"I think you already know what you want. Unless it's something you know I can't give, ask for it."

"This isn't the place."

That had the ring of truth. "All right." She stretched a finger out and slid the sunglasses a few millimeters down the bridge of his nose. "If I kiss you good-bye, will you lose control?"

Dark eyes stared into hers. "Only if you want me to."

Her fingertips rested on his jaw, and she leaned forward. She inhaled his breath: liquor and cloves. His vampire magnetism pulsed, making her body tighten in anticipation. She brushed her lips over his, her lids fluttering closed. He tasted of expensive scotch with a spicy hint of lime, and underneath something delicious she couldn't name. Him, she guessed.

Her other hand rose to his throat, feeling his steady pulse thump under her hand as her tongue explored his cool mouth. She felt the razor scrape of his fangs, and the dilemma of whether to end the kiss arced through her. Sense warred with its age-old enemy: temptation.

She tipped her head back, sucking the drop of blood inward and swallowing it. He exhaled roughly, and she felt the rigid clench of his muscles.

"Your control is amazing," she whispered.

"Seems that way, does it?"

"Yes, it does."

He leaned back in his seat, pushed his sunglasses up, and took one more long breath.

A crack of noise on the roof made her jump.

"Took them longer than I expected," he said.

"What?" she asked, blinking. The car was parked in the shadows and, with the tinted windows, no one could've seen inside, but she had been too distracted to notice anyone approach.

The door was pulled open and, when the ES officers identified her passenger, the muzzles of automatic weapons pressed against Merrick's head from both sides.

Chapter 15

Victor Jacobi sat in a chair in the surgical intensive care visitors' area. Cato paced back and forth, cursing and shaking his fists.

"You have to let me go with the hit squad. I have to be there when he buys it."

Victor clenched his jaws, trying to control his rage. His kids attacking humans in a public place? Merrick gutting his daughter like a fucking fish? Victor wanted blood to spill till the rivers turned red.

When the call he'd been waiting for came, it saved him from having to talk to Cato, whose head Victor wanted to slam against the wall.

"Yes?" Victor said.

"Well?" the voice asked.

"No, she's back on your side of the wall. She was armed. What the fuck was that?"

"That's not my problem. You've had her delivered into your hands twice without a security team."

"Well, we're going to have to try again," Victor said angrily.

"I don't think so. The Handyrock's incident will be known. There will be a security crackdown even in the Etherlin."

"Well, you'll find a way around it."

"No, I won't. You obviously can't get the job done. I heard she had help from one of your own syndicate members."

"Yeah, we'll take care of that."

"Do it, and I'll talk to you again at some point." The connection went dead.

Victor shut the phone.

"Who was that?" Cato asked.

"Never mind. That's my goddamned business, not yours."

"What about Merrick?" Cato demanded. "You can't let him get away with this."

"Forget Merrick. I ordered the hit on him yesterday."

Etherlin Security wore navy trousers and maroon blazers with a silver crest over the heart. To Merrick they looked like overgrown prep school boys. In spite of the attire, they were well trained and well armed. There were three of them, which were odds he could survive if he took a stand, but he'd have to kill, and she'd seen enough violence for the night.

He rested his hands on top of his head and let them take his weapons. They barked questions at him, which he didn't answer, and he covered his smile when she defended him.

They were respectful toward her, but also tried to hustle her away. She stood her ground. If he'd been in their place, the temptation to pick her up and transport her bodily into the Etherlin would've been pretty strong. As soon as the Sliver police arrived, she'd be taken to the station for a statement and stuck on the dangerous side of the wall. If he'd been ES, they wouldn't have been standing around in the street.

One of them pressed an earpiece and took a step back. A moment later, he explained the situation to whoever was on the other end.

"Yes, sir." He turned. "Miss North, let's get you back into the Etherlin. Why don't you drive your car through?"

"What about Mr. Merrick?"

"Director Easton would like to talk to the ventala. We'll escort him to the post."

"He's not a prisoner. He saved my life and, likely, the lives of my aspirants. Give him back his weapons and let him go on his way."

"Director Easton—"

"Doesn't have jurisdiction out here and can't detain Mr. Merrick. Let him go."

"I'm sure he won't mind accompanying us."

Alissa marched over to the one holding his weapons, retrieved them with a firm jerk, and walked them to Merrick.

"Mr. Merrick, I apologize. Thank you for seeing me safely home." She handed him his guns and knife. "Good night."

"Night," Merrick said.

Taking note of the fact that ES had their guns on him again, she said, "I'll wait here until you're safely on your way. Take my car."

The stone-faced looks of the ES guards made him smile.

"I've got my own way home," Merrick said, tucking his weapons away as he disappeared down the alley.

He waited until she was safely on the other side to make his way south toward the creek. He paused periodically to be sure he wasn't followed. Near the water, he stripped down to the superfine neoprene he'd worn under his suit. There was a slice through the fabric where Tamberi's knife had cut him. She was becoming as much of a problem as Cato.

He wiped down the weapons and then dropped them and his suit into a Dumpster. An expensive loss, but there was no help for it. If he went home to drop them there, he'd risk being picked up by the police for questioning, or by the syndicate for a brutal interrogation and probably worse. He had other plans for his night.

He ran a hand over the chest of his wet suit, feeling the packet that was sealed against his skin. It was critical to his plan. He hoped the amulet's magic wouldn't be affected by extreme temperatures.

He climbed through the trees growing up from the bank, and his bare feet sank in the damp ground. He stretched his muscles and lowered himself into the cold water. As a half-vampire, he could tolerate the cold better than humans. He knew from experience he could still concentrate and function when his body temperature dropped as low as twenty-six degrees centigrade. Extreme heat was a different story. The hot springs had nearly boiled the flesh from his bones the last time he'd tried to cross this way.

He took several deep breaths and submerged. He swam down to the barrier between the Etherlin and the Varden. He'd cut through two iron rods on his trial run. Now he slid through the opening without a problem. He swam more than a mile without surfacing. If he'd come up for air sooner, the sensors monitoring the water's surface would've triggered a security alert that meant visible and ultraviolet lights turning on, security camera activation, and a team of Etherlin Security being dispatched to hunt for him.

If this had been a short trip, as when he'd come in for the demon, he could've blown a hole in the wall, gone over it, or used any number of other methods for gaining entry. Getting in wasn't that hard. Getting in without anyone knowing he was in: that was very difficult.

His muscles burned, and his heart rate increased. Merrick dove deeper. The water got warmer, then hot. He felt for the rock opening but couldn't find it.

He dragged his hands over the surface, cutting one of his palms. He was in the right place and should've felt it.

The ache in his muscles worsened as his temperature rose. His skin burned and stung. He realized that rocks had fallen and covered the mouth of the underwater cave.

He worked quickly to shift them, his body hungry for air. His pulse throbbed in his throat. He made an opening and rammed his body against it, pulling himself forward. His shoulders wedged between the rocks, and he couldn't move.

He kicked hard with his legs. Even ventala couldn't go without air forever.

Desperate for oxygen, his body took an involuntary breath and water gushed into his lungs.

Once she'd closed and locked her front door, Alissa walked into the family room with its bamboo floors and butter-colored silk drapes and pillows. She sank down onto the eco-friendly oatmeal-colored couch, trembling with adrenaline and a maelstrom of conflicting emotions. Plagued by regret over the Handyrock's incident, excited by the drive and the kiss with Merrick, and concerned about the encounter with

Etherlin Security, she folded her hands on her lap but couldn't remain still. She rose and paced the floor.

When she reached the edge of the room and turned for the third time, she was startled to find her father standing in the doorway. He'd showered, shaved, and slicked back his wet hair, which she took as a good sign. He wore hunter green flannel pajama bottoms and a Peter Max Earth Day T-shirt under his worn navy blue bathrobe. His pockets bulged with pens and Post-it notes and scraps of paper.

"Hi, Dad. Have you been writing?"

"Still am. And you? Are you working?"

She smiled. Her dad was one of the few people she knew who understood that staring out windows and thinking could be serious work.

"Would you like to write here for a little while? I'd enjoy the company."

He took out a pen, slid it behind an ear, and sat in front of the recycled-wood table. From his pockets, he extracted sticky notes and bits of paper, uncrumpling and arranging them. She sank down on the couch and curled into the cushions.

She looked at the various colors of her dad's notes, watching him move the Jadar River note to the beginning as he mumbled bits of the story of a young soldier who would try to secretly shield his lover's brother from being killed during the Srebrenica massacre in Bosnia. And of the aftermath . . . the emotional devastation of not succeeding, of having his lover find out that he'd participated in the genocide of the lover's people.

Her father rearranged the scenes of moments of normal life interspersed with events like digging up the mass graves to redistribute the bodies. She closed her eyes as her dad narrated, his prose as fluid and devastating as ever. He would take his readers on an amazing and raw emotional journey if he could shake his madness and stay an author long enough to complete it.

She rose and retrieved a netbook from the corner table. She powered it on, created a file, and typed as he dictated. At moments, he paused, and she whispered magic-laced encouragement and suggestions.

Forbidden love was fragile enough, but when the truth of the soldier's hand in the brother's death broke over them, the lovers screamed recriminations at each other, their hearts shattering into too many pieces to ever be fully mended.

All the precious loves that Alissa had been unable to hold on to came rushing to memory. Her mom hanging, Cerise's back as she rushed out of the dance studio, her father fleeing unseen ghosts down empty hallways while Alissa called after him. And then there was Merrick, whom she wanted but could never really have except in dreams and letters.

The tragedy at Handyrock's rose in her mind, too. Just as in her father's story, in the coming days, families would bury their young sons. Tears spilled, and her throat contracted. She wished she'd never gone to the Sliver. She closed the netbook and set it on the table.

"Stop. Please stop," she said.

Awakened from the fever of creation, her father, slightly misty-eyed himself, blinked and looked at her.

"What's wrong? Not good?"

"No, it's amazing. Too good. I'm feeling sad, and the story . . . it's too much tonight."

He sighed and nodded. "Nature's first green is gold. It's especially hard to lose the young. I mourn them—the ones I sacrifice for the story's sake."

"Tell me an old story, Dad. Tell me 'The Poison Cup-cake.'"

"Ah," he said softly. "A different type of story, that." He rubbed her ankles, cleared his throat, and began. The voices of her favorite childhood characters from the stories she and her dad had written together filled the air.

The stories featured an exiled princess named Briselle who lived in a mobile home with her affectionate aunt, uncle, and cousin. In each story, Briselle was drawn into some drama. In Ohio, Briselle rescued children who'd been kidnapped using a magical merry-go-round. In Texas, she thwarted a terrorist plot to blow up a football stadium. In New York, she foiled an assassination plot while staying at the Waldorf Astoria.

Alissa's favorite adventure had been when Briselle discovered a magic park swing. When she jumped off the swing, she landed on the wisteria-draped Japanese footbridge in Monet's garden in Giverny. As soon as Briselle landed in France, her father lapsed into French, explaining how Briselle captured the thieves who stole Monet's canvases from the Musee de l'Orangerie by an elaborate scheme that included a small dog, cupcakes with sleeping pills baked inside, and a mannequin's dummy in a French police uniform.

Alissa and her dad laughed together through all the outrageous and ridiculous parts and were almost to the story's satisfying conclusion when the doorbell rang and they both fell silent.

Her father's brows drew together, his body still like a deer in headlights. Then he jerked into action, his fingers moving in a frenzy to recollect his Post-it notes. He stuffed them in his pockets, saying, "With Pandora's jar spilled on my pages, they might have sent someone to take them. Words aren't safe here. Not for many years."

Her mother's missing diary sprang to mind. "Who takes them?"

"Lost gardeners and intelligence operatives disguised as water sprites." He smashed the notes against the bottoms of his robe's pockets. "Spare keys are a mistake. They're never returned." He looked around to be sure he'd collected everything. "Let's go. I'll barricade us in the library. Hades' thieves have stolen their last book from this house," he announced.

She squeezed his hand and walked with him to the stairs as someone got impatient with the bell not being answered and began knocking loudly.

"It's late. You go up to your room and rest. I'll send whoever it is away."

"I'm not sure it's safe for you here."

"I'll be fine," she said, giving him a gentle push toward the stairs. "You don't want to come back down here tonight," she said, infusing suggestive power into her voice. His lids drifted down, and he turned and climbed the stairs slowly. "You'll dream about your new book and tomorrow the story will pour out of you onto the page."

She waited until he was out of sight before going to the

door. Outside, three formidable men waited. Dimitri, president of the Etherlin Council, Grant Easton, head of Etherlin Security, and Troy Rella, tasked with preserving and promoting the Etherlin's pristine image. They were not disguised as whimsical water sprites, and their expressions were grim. A part of her, recognizing the danger, wished she'd agreed to let herself be barricaded in the library with a lifetime of books.

Chapter 16.

Merrick jerked his body until the rocks loosened. He dragged himself through the narrow passage, tearing a deeper wound in his shoulder, and stretched his head above the surface, choking and retching up water. He wrapped his arms around a jutting rock and locked his hands together so the loop of his grip held his sagging body in place. Eyes bulging, throat burning, muscles screaming, he breathed through the pain.

A few moments later, he'd recovered and pulled himself onto a rock. He looked around. The climb was three stories, with the last part being nearly vertical, which meant when he reached the top, he'd have no leverage to dig or push his way through. If there were rocks covering the opening, he didn't have a prayer of getting out of the cave's peak.

He stretched his body and found the handholds he needed to get him started. He climbed quickly. It had taken him three hours to find the right set of handholds the last time he'd tried the climb. Twice he'd fallen off the wall, breaking two ribs and dislocating a bone in his wrist. That wouldn't happen tonight.

Lysander called it muscle memory. People taught themselves how to move so they could balance on a snowboard, hit a tennis ball into a square, or run and leap while catching a football. For them, it required hours of practice and repetition. Lysander's body only needed to do something once to achieve mastery. Merrick needed more practice than Lysander, but not as much as ordinary people. So having made the climb before, Merrick trusted his body to make it again, despite the wound.

The constant movement refused to let the ache in his shoulder die, but long experience with bearing pain allowed his mind to accept it. He fixed his focus on the goal. *Alissa.*

As Merrick pulled himself through the top of the cavern, the inky darkness of the cave was replaced by a faint smattering of stars. He immediately moved deeper into the wooded mountainside.

He paused for a few seconds to let his body rest, then he started the hike. Since there was no trail, it would take him at least eighty minutes. The difference in the temperatures of his hands made him stop again. The water running off his left hand was warmer. Mixed with blood, he realized. The shoulder wound had gaped open as he climbed, but he hadn't realized the bleeding was so brisk.

He unzipped the wet suit to retrieve a Swiss Army knife that he'd secured inside. Using the knife, he cut a slip of cloth from the suit and created a makeshift tie around his shoulder. The wound location was awkward to bandage. He used his teeth to help him secure it. Afterward, he moved the arm and shoulder slowly. No bleeding, but the tight wrap would probably have to be adjusted and secured again periodically. And moving the arm carefully would definitely slow him down and affect his timeline, which was dangerous. He had to reach the house before dawn.

He picked his way through the trees. The shoulder was going to be a problem during the final swim. After hiking through the woods, he'd end up on the side of a cliff. He'd dive off into the lake and swim across, coming out of the water at the back of Alissa's property. That was a long time to have his shoulder in an arm-numbing tourniquet or alternatively to have it bleeding steadily from not being bandaged. He wished Tamberi Jacobi a slow and painful recovery.

Calculating time and distance, he couldn't be sure that he'd reach her place before sunrise. He'd never actually crossed the lake. The risk of being caught was too high to attempt it twice. He contemplated turning back, but the taste of Alissa's blood on his tongue during that kiss and the sounds of her whispers echoed in his head. Someone in the Etherlin wanted to destroy her. Would he leave them to it? *No.*

Of course, he'd be no good to anyone if he ended up dead or in ES custody. He needed to make it in time. *In time,* he thought. That phrase brought to mind the fact that he'd almost arrived at Handyrock's too late. Alissa had been minutes away from being dragged out of the club or killed by the Jacobis. It was like a punch to the gut to think of Alissa falling into syndicate hands again, of Jacobi's mouth on her, of them using her or hurting her until she broke. Merrick's blood ran cold, and his legs pumped hard as he ran through the trees. He was driven to reach her, driven in a way that surprised him.

She'd sat in the car with him, sweet-skinned and warm and pulsing with life, and asked him, *"What do you need?"* His normal answer to that question would have been, "Not much." Blood. Air. Water. Only things essential for survival. But a different answer had sprung to mind, as unexpected as Athena springing from the head of Zeus.

What do you need?

With inexplicable passion, he'd thought, *This. Just this. To be where you are.*

Alissa let them in, of course. Then she made them wait. She needed time to compose herself, so she'd claimed she was shaky from low blood sugar and had escaped to the kitchen. She wished Merrick were there to make her that sublime cocktail he'd fixed her at his apartment and to talk to her in that deep, calming voice. She also wished he were there to spar with the trinity of frowns darkening the living room. She suspected he wouldn't have answered any questions; he'd just stare them down until they took their bleak expressions and went away.

Returning with a platter of food, she found them shifting impatiently in their seats. They ignored the small plates and napkins, trying to begin the conversation.

Still picturing Merrick's face, she went to the bar and poured herself a Tanqueray and tonic. She drank about half before she returned to them. She knew she'd stalled as long as possible when Dimitri asked her to sit down for the second time.

She did so and watched them silently as she nibbled smoked salmon wraps and sipped her gin and tonic while they talked. Eventually, she fielded the expected questions.

"Of course, in retrospect, I should have taken a security detail, but there hasn't been a single violent incident at a club in the Sliver in the past decade. Ventala aren't exactly welcome in that section, and most of the ventala have their own clubs, so why should they have been there? Troy was there without ES as escort."

"I'm not a muse," Troy sputtered. "I'm not ventala catnip. I'm not vying to be the face and future of the entire Etherlin. If I get myself killed or involved in an incident in the Sliver, it might make papers around the state. You're international news, and you know it."

"Alissa, why would you go out of the Etherlin without a security detail? You never have before," Grant said.

"In the first place, because ES can feel like a military presence, which tends to dampen a celebration and interferes with the creative spirit I try to inspire in my aspirants. Secondly, this was a spur-of-the-moment thing. I didn't want to fill out forms and wait while an advance team went to scout and secure the location. As I've told you before, I think the predeparture protocols are too time-consuming."

"Do you think that? Do you really?" Troy demanded. "Considering what happened tonight?" He shook his head furiously. "A friend of mine is dead."

Alissa paled. "I'm very sorry about that, Troy. Of course, I am. I know that no amount of money can compensate the families of the men who were injured or killed, but I'll create a memorial fund for each of them."

"Using discretionary funds?" Dimitri asked.

"Of course not. My discretionary funds aren't enough for something like this. I'll need to access my earnings."

"Your earnings are in the Etherlin accounts. They belong to the community."

"Right, but this is community business. Those men fought

to protect me, and it was my poor judgment that led to what happened. I asked them to confront the ventala and to force him to leave. If I had not been there, they'd still be alive."

"Maybe," Grant said. "Maybe not. Ventala are violent and unpredictable. The male ventala who did the killing has nineteen arrests. He could've ended up attacking those men whether you were there or not."

"How do you know about his arrests?" she asked.

"The Sliver authorities are sharing information with us since we've agreed to help them with their investigation and with bringing that ventala into custody."

"Which is the way that we'll support the Sliver community. You're not financially responsible for the actions of a vampire half-breed," Dimitri said.

"Well, I feel partially responsible. If the EC won't authorize a financial offering to the families, I'll do it myself. I have jewelry and vintage clothing that can be auctioned. The emeralds my grandmother wore to the White House in 1962 and the diamond-encrusted mask she wore to Truman Capote's Black and White Ball are worth at least half a million dollars, which is a good start. Christie's can take care of the sale for me."

Dimitri grimaced. "Do you really want the council to hear that you're planning to auction off pieces of muse history? You know how the EC will react to something like that. The vote is three days away."

"Then please help me compensate the families. Even if we're not obligated to do this, it's right. What if I take on some modeling work and specifically earmark the income for a memorial? Wouldn't that be good publicity for the Etherlin? The Estée Lauder people have been really lovely to work with. They've offered very generous contracts in the past."

"It *would* be good publicity to offset any backlash we get for ES not being there to handle the situation," Troy said.

"I'll propose it to the rest of the council and see what they think," Dimitri said. "Now, there's the other matter."

"What other matter?" she asked.

"You drove to the gate with a ventala. Did he force his way into your car?" Dimitri asked.

"No."

"Then what was he doing there?" Grant asked.

"He saved my life. I wasn't certain whether other ventala would try to prevent me from returning to the Etherlin. I trusted him to get me back to the checkpoint."

"Why?" Troy demanded. "He could've been trying to get you alone, to separate you from witnesses. Going with a strange ventala makes no sense."

"It does if I know him."

They all gaped at her.

"He killed the demon at the 2007 Arts & Innovation Benefit. He didn't attack anyone else while he was in the Etherlin. Not humans and not me. I was a foot away from him when I thanked him. He never tried to hurt me."

"That night an ES officer had a gun to the ventala's head," Grant exclaimed. "I've read the report. There is no reason to believe that given the same opportunity while *alone* with you, he'd behave the same way."

"Except he did. He saved my life and helped me get back to the gate."

"And it cost you nothing? Not a drop of blood?" Troy asked.

She shook her head.

"Let us see your neck and arms," Troy said.

She glared at him, her heart thumping in her chest. The bruises and scabs from the kidnapping were still visible. Did Troy know about the abduction? Did he know about Cato Jacobi biting her? Had he been involved in the plot? It would make sense. She and Troy had a history—an unpleasant one.

Despite the flush rising in her cheeks, she kept her expression defiantly neutral.

"ES said your car was parked for twelve minutes before they approached it. What were you doing all that time?" Grant asked.

"I was talking to him. He'd just saved my life for the second time. In such cases, it's appropriate to offer a few words of thanks, don't you think?"

"He didn't save your life at the ball. You were in a safe room," Grant said.

"Well he saved the lives of my friends and aspirants, including Troy's sister, who wasn't in a safe room. That demon would eventually have smelled Ileana's blood and found her hiding place."

"Be that as it may, you were alone with him in the car for quite a long time," Troy said.

"Did anything happen?" Dimitri asked.

"I thanked him and said good-bye."

"That took twelve minutes?" Grant asked.

"I was rattled. It took a few minutes for me to pull my thoughts together. Then pleasantries and small talk were exchanged. Simple courtesy."

"He's part of a crime syndicate, you know," Grant said.

"No, I didn't," she lied.

"Well, he is."

"And they never do anything for anyone without compensation. He either wanted blood or he'll want a favor from you in the future," Grant said.

"If he wants a favor, as long as it doesn't put me in danger and isn't criminal, I'd be inclined to grant it. On two occasions he has saved lives and performed a service to me and the community."

"He's a blood-swilling thug," Troy said. "Any connection to him—any at all—would be pure poison from a publicity standpoint and would be a terrible and dangerous example to set for the rest of the Etherlin community. There is no way you can wear the Wreath now."

"Troy," Dimitri said in a calming voice.

"No, Dimitri, you heard her. She'd do him a favor. She'd consort with a ventala. That's grounds to remove her from the competition."

"You'd like that, wouldn't you?" she demanded. "Cerise is your friend. Ileana is your sister. My removal is what you've been hoping for. I wonder what you'd be willing to do to make that happen."

"Meaning what?" Troy snapped.

"Meaning, how did they know I was there? Did someone tip them off? I notice you're unharmed. You've got muse blood in you, yet you weren't attacked. Where were you while your friend was fighting them?"

"Alissa," Grant exclaimed. "Troy wasn't armed."

"If it had been Cerise, I would have helped her."

"Cerise isn't your friend," Troy snapped. "She can't stand you."

Alissa winced. "It's true that we're not friends anymore, but I would still have tried to help her. What does that say about me? And you?"

"You're an ice-cold bitch!" Troy shouted, jumping up.

"That's enough," Grant said, grabbing Troy and pulling him back. "Troy, enough!"

Dimitri rose, too. "It's late. Everyone's upset. We're going." He embraced her briefly, whispering in her ear, "If the ventala tainted you, you must withdraw from Wreath contention. We'll find a way for you to save face and remain in the community, but no more talk of doing favors or consorting with ventala. Never to anyone. Or I won't be able to protect you. Understand?"

She nodded, feeling sick and shaky. She waited until the door closed behind them and sank down onto the couch. She sat, awash in numb regret, for more than an hour. Finally, she wandered upstairs to her room.

In the bathroom, she washed her face and rubbed her eyes. She'd been struggling with the decision. If getting caught was inevitable, she should probably withdraw from the competition before it was too late. But if she did forfeit the Wreath, Cerise would get it and might never let Alissa have access to it. Her dad would never get the chance to recover. He'd probably get worse. The pain of that thought left her breathless.

The Etherlin had been founded in order to concentrate muse magic, which was never as strong when the muses were separated. If Alissa was thrown out of the community, what would happen to her dad?

She couldn't withdraw; she absolutely had to remain in the competition for her dad's sake. But then what about Merrick? Was she supposed to stay silent when people said all ventala were vicious creatures who should've been exterminated with the vampires? Was she supposed to never address the fact that one of them had risked his own life to help her?

In bed, she lay awake with churning thoughts, exhausted but unable to sleep. Her cell phone rang at five forty in the morning. She contemplated the unidentified number. It might be Tobin. She didn't feel like talking to him, but still needed to.

She answered wearily. "Hello?"

"Still want to know what I need?"

She froze at the sound of Merrick's voice. It took a moment for her to answer. "It's very late," she managed. *And things are extremely complicated and dangerous for me.*

"So the offer's expired?"

She hesitated, but finally said, "No. Like you, I keep my promises. What appreciation gift would you like me to send?"

"Shut off the security system and come to the garden door."

She sat bolt upright, heart slamming. "Are you—? You're not here."

"See for yourself."

Oh my God.

Chapter 17

When Merrick ended the call, Alissa's mouth went dry, half in dread, half in anticipation. If he was downstairs, she shouldn't open the door for him, but could she afford to leave him wandering around outside her house?

She glanced down at her silk nightgown. She grabbed a pair of black slacks and a blue knit shirt. She changed quickly and hurried down. She disabled the security system and opened the back door.

The quiet darkness was velvet smooth with no signs of movement, not even the wind. Had he been joking? She stepped back and began to close the door when he stepped into view.

She gaped at him. His dark hair dripped onto the shoulders of a black wet suit that looked painted on. There was mud on his hands and feet and blood trickling down his left arm.

"I need a shower, help bandaging my shoulder, and a place to sleep at dawn."

"I—you can't stay here. You can't be here."

He raised an eyebrow.

"Of course you can take a shower, and I'm happy to bandage your shoulder, but you know you can't be found here."

"I won't be found. Shower?"

"This way." She closed the door, but he stilled her hand from bolting it.

"One more thing. There's a box that was shipped to the gardener."

"He doesn't come until Tuesdays."

"I know; that's why I sent it to him. Your staff opens packages sent to you, and I couldn't ship something to myself at this address, now could I?"

"What's in the package?"

"A duffel bag of my stuff. Where would the staff put something for the gardener? In the tool shed?" Merrick grabbed a handful of paper towels and pressed them against his shoulder.

She stared at him. "You planned this? Why didn't you tell me?"

"Because you would've asked too many questions and tried to say no. The conversation would've been really long." He grimaced as he put more pressure on the shoulder wound. The paper towels were falling apart in his fingers. "Pointlessly long, since I would've come either way."

"It's my house. You need my permission to stay here."

"Are you going to call Etherlin Security to drag me out?" he challenged.

She frowned. "I might surprise you."

By his expression, he certainly wasn't concerned.

She grabbed a dishtowel, shoved his hand away, and pressed down hard on the wound. He let out a hiss of pain.

"Toughen up," she said lightly.

He grinned. "You're some peach. And after I saved your life. Twice."

"Saved it so you could ruin it."

"Would I do that?"

"How should I know?" she said, pulling him with her. He followed her into a guest room. She turned on the shower and brought out a stack of towels.

"I've lost quite a bit of blood. Maybe you should join me in the shower in case I need help." His voice was pure seductive lilt. It almost made her smile, but she knew it wasn't a good idea to encourage him.

"I bet you'll manage. Scrub that shoulder with soap and water while you're in there."

He quirked a brow. "I wouldn't have expected it of you," he said, unzipping the top of the suit, revealing a chest of hard, perfect muscles.

"Expected what?" she asked, glancing too long at his body.

"Sadism."

She blushed, then glared at him. He flashed her a smile.

"What are you doing here? You know I can't possibly let you stay." She said it softly, imploringly.

"You will." He pulled free a small packet that had been taped inside the suit. He unwrapped a scorpion amulet covered in black stones and put it over his head. The minute it touched his skin, the light shimmered and her eyes blurred. When she focused on him, she was staring at a younger, plain-looking man. Medium brown hair and eyes. Ordinary features and build. Nothing noteworthy.

"What is that? And why do you look familiar?"

"It's an Ovid Medallion, created about a thousand years ago by a practitioner of magic who was a fan of the Metamorphosis stories. I acquired it about ten years ago. I look familiar because this image first belonged to Len Mills."

"Of course, Mr. Mills. The security consultant ES always uses in California. But if you had that, why didn't you just come through the gate?"

"They've got devices that can detect magical implements. I'd never have made it through the checkpoint."

"I still don't understand what you think you're doing here."

He lifted the amulet off and exhaled, his looks shifting back to normal. "Someone here betrayed you." He set the amulet on the edge of the sink. "You need a bodyguard you trust."

She ran a hand through her hair. "You think I trust you?" she demanded.

"Yes."

They locked eyes.

Could she really let him stay in her house? Would that magic trick of an amulet really fool Etherlin Security? "I just don't know," she murmured. Seconds ticked by with him just watching her.

"It's James," he said, unzipping the suit, causing her eyes

to trail down. She forced her gaze back to his very dark eyes. He peeled the suit from his arms, leaving his entire torso bare. "You wanted to know my first name. It's James."

"No one ever calls you that."

"No one but you."

Alissa found the box that had been shipped to the gardener and retrieved Merrick's duffel bag. She set it on the bed in the guest room while he showered. She gathered first-aid supplies, and, when she returned, the bathroom door was open. Merrick stood with a towel wrapped around his hips, looking like an ad for an action movie.

When she joined him in the bathroom with the supplies, he sat and turned his shoulder to her.

"You're ventala, so this will heal without scarring?"

"Right, I don't scar."

"That's lucky. I do have that potential, so if I get even a tiny cut, the council sends a plastic surgeon rushing over as if one of my limbs were dangling off."

"You could say no."

"Not if I want to be Wreath Muse. Believe me, I've rebelled to the limit of what they'll allow." She rubbed peroxide onto his wound and peered inside. "This is pretty deep. And there's a little pumper," she said, compressing the small artery. "I can have the plastic surgeon give you a few stitches just to close it, so it doesn't keep bleeding."

He shook his head.

"Let me hold pressure. I'll see if I can get it to stop."

He watched her with a steady, unnerving gaze. A dark lock of hair fell across his forehead and her fingers longed to brush it back and, in doing so, to sample its wet texture. She looked away, licking her lips.

He's the living embodiment of temptation. When she looked at him again, she found his gaze more intense than ever. She nearly leaned down to touch her lips to his.

"Let's see," she said, examining the wound. The spurting blood had stopped, so she wrapped a bandage around his shoulder and upper arm, keeping the wound compressed. "How does that feel?"

"Fine," he said.

"Have you ever been wounded badly enough to need stitches? Or surgery?" she asked.

"I don't remember."

She smiled. "Is that a polite way of asking me to mind my own business?"

He returned the smile. "No, it's a way of saying that when you're standing this close with your hands on me, I don't care about anything else."

She stepped back. "I don't want to waste my opportunity to talk with you, so let me know how far away I need to be for you to concentrate."

"Wyoming's probably far enough."

She laughed softly and left the bathroom. In the bedroom, she sat on an elegant periwinkle velvet slipper chair, tipping her head so she could still see him.

"Tell me one story about your life."

He rose and leaned against the doorway.

"Tell me how you met Lysander."

"If I do, what will you give me?"

"I'll share one of my secrets in return."

"I met Lysander in jail." He walked to the bed, unzipped the duffel, and pulled out a pair of black boxer shorts.

"That's not a story. That's a hook. I want the whole story." She closed her eyes as he dropped the towel.

"The beginning will make you sad."

"I don't care. Tell me anyway, *James*." She liked the intimacy of using his first name. She liked being able to tease him with it, the way he teased her by calling her by her last name alone, which no one ever did. She was always Alissa or Miss Alissa or, most frequently, Miss North, the valuable Etherlin asset and longed-for muse and mentor. She never got to be just a girl. Except, perhaps, with him. The irreverent way he used her last name made her feel like she'd been released from the role she always played.

"Please keep going," she said from behind her closed lids.

"My father married my mother and had me to save himself. Before she got involved with him, she was a biochemistry professor. Afterward, she was in a coma."

Her smile melted away. She leaned back, resting her head against the chair so her face tipped toward the ceiling. Did she want him to keep going, she wondered. *Yes.* She wanted all of it. No matter how awful. This was her chance to really know him.

"He made sure there was no one for the court to put me with except him. The body count was high. When he realized that the Human Preservation Act was going to pass without Paragraph Seventeen, he was jealous. He was going to die, while I got to live. He hated me for it, though that didn't make me special. He hated everyone.

"I was a kid, so I did what kids do. They try and try and try, no matter how futile something is. I wanted to win him over, but since he couldn't have what he wanted, no one should.

"He tried to beat me to death, but I was the son of a vampire. Hard to kill. When he came for my head with an ax, I ran away from home. Living on the streets was easier. By then I was numb. I met a lot of nasty characters, but no one more vicious than him.

"I got in trouble. I was in and out of the juvenile detention centers and headed for an early grave. I didn't care.

"One night, I fought off some guys. Lysander was on a nearby rooftop. Afterward, he told me he recognized me from a prophecy I was going to help him fulfill.

"Since he had watched me fight four guys alone and hadn't bothered to help, I told him to go fuck himself. That was the beginning of our close friendship," Merrick said with a rough laugh. "Anyway, I got scooped up on a B&E, and Lysander got himself thrown in jail with me. Assaulting a police officer, I think the charge was. They couldn't hold him. He slipped out whenever he felt like it. They had no idea the scars on his back covered wings.

"I was the only one who knew that, and the only person he talked to. In fact, I could not get him to shut up. Most of the time he spoke Latin and other dead languages. After a while, I couldn't take any more. I told him I'd join any fight he wanted if he'd just stop talking about things that happened five thousand years before I was born."

She opened her eyes, expecting him to be fully dressed, but he wore only the black boxers. Apparently he thought that nearly naked suited him. The trouble was that she agreed.

"How old were you when you met him?"

"Fourteen."

"Whatever happened to your mother?"

"She passed away without waking up."

"That's why women and children are safe in your territory. You protect them the way no one protected you and your mom."

"Who says women and children are safe in my territory?"

"Everyone."

"Oh, that guy again. He talks too much."

She smiled. "Thank you for confiding in me. Since your usual participation in our dialogue consists of sending gifts . . . or shooting things, I appreciate the extra effort." She offered a sly, teasing glance as she stood.

"Where do you think you're going?" he asked.

"We're moving upstairs. I can't have the staff finding you like Goldilocks, asleep where you don't belong."

She pulled the bathroom trash bag from the bin and knotted it. She bunched up the towels and his wet suit and walked out. He stayed with her as she disposed of the wet suit and trash and put the towels down the laundry chute.

Upstairs, she took him to the room that adjoined her suite.

"Beige," he said, glancing in the guest room.

She quirked an eyebrow, her gaze dancing over the stunning hand-painted Napa Valley mural that covered two walls.

"Well, it's not solid eggplant, like being cinched up in a Chivas Regal pouch, but we manage to soldier on," she said, bolting the door that had hallway access. "If you keep this locked, the only way they'll be able to get in here is through my room, which they won't come through without my permission."

"What about when they clean?"

"I do these rooms myself most of the time. I like having a

place to myself, where no one pokes around in my stuff."
When she returned to her room, he followed. She put a hand
out to stop him, but he kept coming until their bodies nearly
touched.

"It's almost dawn, Merrick. Let's get a few hours' sleep."

He moved her out of his way and proceeded to lock the
door to her bedroom that opened to the hall.

"You didn't need to do that. They don't barge in on me."

"Which bed?"

She laughed. "You're kidding, right?"

He glanced between the rooms. "Guest room's darker."

"Merrick, I'm not sleeping with you."

"You owe me a secret. If you want to leave after you tell
me one, you can."

In the guest room, he pulled the covers back and got in bed.

"What happened to 'People talk too much'?"

"Change into whatever you wear to bed and get in here."

She stared at him. His audacity just kept knocking her off
balance.

"If you force me to come and get you, Alissa, you won't
get off with just telling me a secret."

She flushed, her belly tightening. How did he make threats
sound delicious?

She went to her room, dug through the drawers to find the
pale blue flannel pajamas she'd worn for a "sleepover" photo
shoot when she was a teenager. She put them on in her bathroom.

When she returned, he shook his head. "You just ruined
every fantasy I've ever had of going to bed with you."

"That was the idea." She lay on the bed next to him, and
within moments, he maneuvered her against his side. His right
arm felt solid against her back and the bare skin of his chest
and stomach invited touching. She closed her fists to restrain
her hands from wandering over his gorgeous body.

This was the closest she'd been to anyone in a very long
time. It made her hungry for foreplay . . . and the things that
followed.

She licked her lips and resisted. His fingers on the back of
her head beckoned her close. She rested her cheek against his

chest. He smelled so good, of warm, freshly washed male skin. Her teeth wanted to nibble, to tease a reaction from him.

She clenched her jaw. *Don't be insane. If you start anything, you will not be able to stop it. He's a ventala. He can't be played with.*

"So, a secret?" She closed her eyes, enjoying the feel of his muscles against her cheek. "You fascinate me," she murmured.

"That's not a secret."

She laughed. "You're so arrogant. I didn't realize it before, but you are."

"That's not a secret either. The whole Varden knows that." His fingers pressed against her side, creating a riot of sensations throughout her body. "It's almost dawn, North. Get on with it."

The challenge rattled the gates inside her, and almost without a thought, she unlocked one. "I let the wrong man seduce me once." She let the statement hang on the air, but he didn't reassure her that the same thing was not happening again. Nor did he pull back in any way.

"Go on," he said.

"I was struggling to prove myself as a muse. My dad was very sick, and I was having trouble sleeping. This smart, powerful, respected older guy gave me sleeping pills and comfort. He gave me advice at a time when I needed it. The people I was closest to had abandoned me for an extended business trip and family vacation. I was on my own, which I'm sure appealed to him as much as it terrified me.

"He coerced me into doing things I didn't want to do." She paused, thinking back, then continued softly, "I sacrificed pieces of myself and sobbed through every shower afterward. And later, after I'd done everything he wanted, he treated me worse than I would ever treat a stranger, let alone someone I'd claimed to love.

"He went on to undermine people's confidence in my skills. He claimed I'd exaggerated my muse successes—which I never did—and that I was promiscuous, which I wasn't. I'd worked so hard. I'd trusted him so much. I felt betrayed. Very badly betrayed.

"The emotions built into a fury that consumed me. I thought, 'I'll show him. Let's see who really has what skills.' So I went to see him, and I used my power to make him despair. I watched him push aside the draperies, open the fourth-story window, and lean out. I very nearly let him jump." Her lashes were wet with tears as she blinked. "The only reason I held back in that moment was because I wanted him to realize how powerless I'd made him. So he would know how it felt."

A tear spilled over her cheek. "It's so evil, so wrong to use the gift to hurt someone. I was sick about it for weeks afterward. I was also afraid he would tell the EC what I'd done and get me thrown out of the Etherlin forever. He didn't. Looking back, I'm sure he knew the EC would've asked me why I'd done it and, with nothing to lose, I would've told the truth and destroyed us both."

She took a deep breath and exhaled, trying to let the tension of the memories drain out of her. "I've never misused my gift that way again. I've also never let one of them seduce me again, though they try. It was a hard lesson to learn, but I learned it."

"What's his name?"

"Why?" she asked, wiping her eyes. "I didn't confide in you so that you would do something to him. I've already had my revenge; it was more than I could stand."

"How old were you?"

"Old enough that I should've known better." She pressed her lids together.

"That young, huh?"

"Fifteen."

"And he was?"

"Don't expect me to give you a number."

"But significantly older?"

"Naturally."

"You're not what I expected."

"I'm sure," she said with a rueful laugh. "You thought you were going to get to corrupt a snow-pure Etherlin princess. I bet it's disappointing to learn I've already been completely corrupted." Her voice sounded hollow, just the way her insides felt at times.

"Completely corrupted? Have you forgotten who you're talking to?" His fingers stroked her hair. "I've read all your letters, remember? You take dreams of a better world and make them true. You reach out to redeem people who don't deserve it and deal almost exclusively in hope and optimism. Are you really going to describe yourself as corrupted? I thought your vocabulary was better than that."

"You don't understand."

"Sure, I do. Someone took your innocence, then tried to convince you it was your fault, that you should be ashamed for falling for his lies. That game's as old as Lysander.

"It's easy to see the world as a great place when it's never shown you anything but deference, Alissa. That's how I assumed you came by your optimism. But the truth is you've been tested in ways I never realized. You've been betrayed. The ultimate trial by the fire. The pain couldn't break you; it couldn't bend you into something you weren't meant to be. The past may still hurt, but it doesn't own you. I respect that. So should you."

New tears formed. She blinked them away, realizing this was what she'd wanted from him all along. That he should know her true lapses in judgment and yet treat her as though she had never had them. The knots in her muscles, in her conscience, loosened. Here in the dark, with the most unlikely of confidantes, she was her true self. She exhaled her relief as a sigh and felt tenderness and also responsibility. Real friendship had to be reciprocated. It had to be guarded and protected.

"Please be careful, James." She laid a hand on his ribs and pressed for emphasis. "I think as a ventala you're immune to the addictiveness of muse magic. I believe I could have you and let you go without destroying you, but I can't be completely sure."

He smiled. "If destruction is the chaser to being had by you, pour me a glass and watch me drink it down."

She raised her head to look in his eyes. "I'm serious. It's a warning that shouldn't be taken lightly."

"Maybe not, but fear overplayed its hand when I was a kid. At some point, I stopped caring whether I was living my last day. Since then I haven't met many warnings that interested me. What does interest me though is what 'being had by you' entails. I'd like to hear about *that* in detail."

She smiled, wanting to put all her faith in the fact that he could handle whatever came, that she could flirt with him without reservation. She bent her head and bit his unwounded shoulder hard enough to leave a small red mark. "You are temptation's fruit, James Merrick."

He stole a deep kiss, then let his head fall back onto the pillow as he glanced at the window. "Morning has the worst timing."

She smoothed a lock of hair back from his brow as dawn broke over the Etherlin. His eyes closed, and his breathing settled into an even rhythm. She kissed his lips softly and whispered, "Please be strong enough."

Chapter 18

Alissa slept deeply, following a path of dreams that progressed darkly until she woke in a nightmare.

"Oh," she said with a gasp as her eyes adjusted. Her father stood over the bed. He'd taken an antique dagger from the library wall display and was holding it to Merrick's throat. She'd missed what her father had said, but knew from Merrick's reply that it was something to do with suspecting him of being Hades.

"Where's a helm of darkness when you need one?" Merrick said, his voice a low rumble.

"I smell pomegranate. If you fed her a single seed of that blood fruit, I'll spill the juice from your throat."

"Dad, everything is all right. This—"

Merrick's hand snaked up and caught her father's around the wrist, holding it steady at the left side of his neck. "I'm not Hades, though that would've been a more interesting disguise than a security consultant from San Diego."

"I'm sorry. Don't hurt him," she said softly to Merrick, which seemed ironic since her father was the one standing over them with a knife.

Her father's free hand thrust forward and compressed Merrick's windpipe. "The door is never locked. Never. Until today. Think I'd let you hold her prisoner in her own house?"

Alissa put her hand on her father's arm. "He isn't holding

me prisoner. He came to help me." She squeezed tighter. "Please let go."

Merrick's face was impassive as he studied her father. She was grateful that he didn't fight to free himself.

Her father let go of Merrick's throat but didn't withdraw the dagger. "Hades can disguise himself. All the gods can," he said, then looked back at Merrick. "If you're not Hades, prove it."

Merrick smiled slowly. "How would I do that?" Merrick's gaze flicked momentarily to the dagger. "By showing you that I'm not immortal? Like a witch trial where they tie you up and throw you in the water, and if you drown, you're innocent?"

"The doors are never locked. I come in every night through these doors to watch over her."

"You didn't need to come in. Last night, I was watching over her."

"Who are you?" her dad demanded. The tip of the blade nicked Merrick's skin, and Merrick pushed her father's arm back and sat up in one continuous motion.

"You tell me," Merrick said. "After a long journey of many obstacles, destiny gave me the opportunity to rescue her from a titan. I've waited a long time for this chance." Merrick's eyes locked with her father's. "He conquers who endures."

Her father's expression shifted from serious to amused. He stepped back, pulling his wrist free and lowering the dagger. "You've mixed Perseus with Persius." The unkempt eyebrows bobbed as if nodding. "Hades is a trickster, but he's not possessed of wit, clever or otherwise. So you need not die to prove you're innocent of the first charge. Congratulations."

How had Merrick known about her father's love of quotes? Or exactly how to handle her dad?

"Now, show me your teeth, because I suspect I know what manner of creature you are. Modern, I think," her dad said.

Alissa, who was now also sitting up, put a hand on Merrick's shoulder, leaned near his ear, and whispered, "You don't have to. Give me a moment with him."

"It's all right," Merrick said, drawing his lips back, letting his fangs show.

"It's against the law for you to be here," her dad said.

"Ius summum saepe summa est malitia," Merrick said.

"Extreme law is often extreme injustice," Alissa translated.

Her father tipped his head to the side. "I know that quote . . . Terence the Roman playwright. I used it once in an essay." He pointed the tip of the dagger. "Fifteen years ago."

"You warned of the danger of creating a new second-class citizen," Merrick said.

"The ventala were the new second-class citizen?" Alissa asked.

"Yes, by virtue of having a special set of laws that pertain only to them," her dad said.

"I didn't know you felt that way," she said.

"The counterargument was that blacks and women, who were granted equal rights, are not driven by genetics to hunt and prey on their fellow human beings. My suggestion was that any special laws for ventala should be confined to protecting humans in a very direct way. Laws restricting other things, like travel, I postulated were going to be considered oppressive, and oppression always leads to insurrection." He flexed his wrist, making the dagger's tip move up and down for emphasis. "That article was never published. I withdrew the rights to print it at the request of the EC. Where did you read it?"

"A file."

"Why are you investigating me? Who's helping you? Is it that damned Hermes? Or J. Edgar Hoover? He's a problem. Keeps files on everyone."

Merrick stood and walked around her father, who turned to keep his eyes on Merrick.

"Andromeda, Dimitri's here for you," her dad said.

She snapped her head up. "What? Dimitri's downstairs?" Her father nodded.

She winced. "Did you talk to him, Dad?"

"No, I was busy breaking in here," he said, watching Merrick warily as Merrick dressed. "Why are you spying on me?"

Merrick shook his head.

"You deny it? I stand by my word choice," her dad said. "Mining through manuscripts, quoting quoted quotes, superseding home security. You've invaded my privacy and catalogued my thoughts! That is spying."

Merrick pulled the dressing off his shoulder. The wound was dry and scabbed over. He strode to the bathroom and pitched the bandages into the trash. "The file wasn't about you."

"What was it about?"

"Her," Merrick said with a nod at Alissa.

She stared at him. Of course, she knew he'd taken an interest in her, but to have collected background information on her father . . . That was unsettling. How much did Merrick know and who were his sources?

Merrick slid on a white shirt. It hung open, framing the incredible muscles of his torso. His cavalier attitude toward the dagger seemed almost natural since he looked thoroughly capable of defending himself with his bare hands against all but a nuclear attack. "The medallion goes under the shirt. Think he'll take the change in stride?"

She didn't know how her dad would react to the sight of Merrick shifting appearances. "Hey, Dad, can you wait for me in the reading room?" Alissa asked gently.

Her father gave Merrick an appraising look, then put the dagger in Alissa's hand. "Don't eat any seeds."

After her father left, Alissa turned to face Merrick. Lacking makeup and wearing rumpled flannel pajamas, he still found her beautiful enough to induce aching. She stood as straight and still as if she'd been carved of stone.

"Now you've met the inspiration for my warning. After the muse magic was ripped from his life, he stopped being able to separate facts from fiction."

Despite the father being unhinged, Alissa clearly wanted to keep her dad with her. Merrick bet if Etherlin Security found out that the old man was prone to full-blown hallucinations and skulking around Alissa's bedroom with daggers, he'd be relocated to an institution before she could say Hades.

"He's been getting better," she said. "This is just a temporary setback." She paused. When he didn't respond, she set the knife on the dresser and touched her fingers to a spot on her neck that mirrored where he'd been pricked. "I'm sorry about the dagger."

"I've nicked myself worse shaving," Merrick said.

Her shoulders relaxed. Her smile was tentative, but grateful. He'd never expected that his chaotic and violent childhood would become advantageous, but Merrick was sure he was unique in Alissa's life with his unfazed reaction to her dad's behavior.

"I didn't know he was checking on me at night. I would've warned you—or better arranged things—if I'd realized."

Better arranged things by not sleeping in the same bed with him? He'd have suffered a lot worse violence than a nick before he'd have given up the feel of her hair against his chest and her body pressed to his.

"So, you've been investigating me and keeping a file? I don't know how to feel about that."

"Feel flattered."

She raised a brow.

He smiled. "I thought you were looking for a suggestion."

"About last night," she said, leaving the sentence unfinished.

"Yes?" Merrick said, picking up the medallion.

"I got a little carried away last night."

They were bound to disagree on that point. He set the medallion down again, blinking against the light seeping in from behind the curtains. Midday, he thought.

It was probably natural for her to have second thoughts, but he wouldn't make it easy for her to back away from him.

She glanced at the door. "Dimitri is president of the Etherlin Council. I shouldn't keep him waiting."

The Etherlin calling, pulling her away from him. The impulse to block the door or pull her into bed was strong. Everything in him wanted to reestablish the intimacy of the previous night. "Think this is a good strategy?"

"I don't know what you mean. I have to change and go down to see Dimitri. It's two days before the Wreath Muse vote, so I need to be particularly careful in my behavior."

He stared at her. She held her hands out in a conciliatory gesture. "But you're right. It's impolite to say I'm having second thoughts about something and then not elaborate. I apologize. I'll explain later."

He didn't need an explanation and wouldn't waste their time together listening to one. "Good luck with that." He raised the medallion.

She narrowed her eyes. "What did you mean by strategy?"

His blood quickened at the challenge in her aquamarine gaze. "The prey runs; the predator chases. It's instinct. If you actually want to get away, are uncertainty and retreat your best strategy?"

"I am not your prey."

She might object to the terms, but they were clearly engaged in a ritual as old as time. He quirked a brow.

"Don't patronize me," she snapped.

He studied her. She was angrier than he'd expected.

"I can change my mind. That doesn't absolve you of civilized behavior. Human beings are capable of ignoring their instincts. And before you say that ventala are not human, save your breath. You have more control than anyone I know. People shove blades and gun barrels against your skin, and you don't even react. That completely defies instinct."

"I never said I wasn't capable of ignoring my instincts when I want to."

"Meaning what? That if I tried to run away, you'd *enjoy* hunting me?"

"Well, it's not my favorite of the proposed scenarios. I liked it better when you were going to have and destroy me. But if you lose your nerve and play hard to get, I'll pursue you. Genetically, that's my job."

"As a man or as a vampire?"

"Pick one."

"I don't like being called prey."

"Noted."

"Do you understand why I hate it? Real predators kill their prey. I've been hunted by men I would characterize as predators. Stalkers who were so driven by their impulses, they would rather have killed me than be denied what they wanted. The intensity of their obsession made them feel entitled to me, whether I wanted them or not."

He frowned, finally understanding why his word choice had been a miscalculation. Most women he flirted with wanted him to chase them. Uncovering his predatory nature was part of the thrill. But none of them were muses who'd been the victims of stalkers.

"Do you want me to go?" he asked. He kept his tone even, but his body tensed. This opportunity for them to spend time together might never come again. When it was over, he at least wanted his memories of it. He wasn't ready to be cast out yet.

"If I wanted you to go, would you?" she asked.

Knowing the right answer, he nodded. She wanted to play with fire, but she wanted reassurance that she wouldn't be burned.

She stared into his eyes, weighing his sincerity. He doubted it was a thing she could assess, since he didn't know himself whether he told the truth. Of course, he wouldn't hurt her, but would he leave if she asked him to? If she really wanted that, he probably would. He thought about how he'd let Tobin go so he could keep his promise to her. She had the kind of influence over him that no one else ever had. He needed to be careful of that. Their interests might not always run parallel.

"I'm sorry," she said, exhaling, "for implying that I can't trust you. If you'd wanted to hurt me, you could have already. It's only that I hear the council's warnings in my head. I also wonder if I can really trust myself to be a good enough judge of character, given that I've made mistakes in the past. That reference to being stalked like prey dredged up memories. None of that is your fault, though, so I'm sorry."

"You have cause to be suspicious of any man who goes to extraordinary lengths to get near you, especially one who's half vampire."

She stepped forward and laid her palm against his cheek. "I don't want you to go. Although if you stay, I'm still not sure what I'm going to do with you. Maybe you'll get fed up and leave before I figure it out."

He shook his head.

"Then again, maybe not," she said with a small smile. "He conquers who endures."

Chapter 19

Dimitri sat in a wingback chair with a file open on his lap. His black pinstripe power suit and platinum cuff links signaled the seriousness of their meeting. He was clearly on his way to the Dome.

He stood and embraced her briefly before reclaiming his seat. He set the file on the round side table as she sat down, and she noticed that there were savory breakfast turnovers and coffee there as well. The staff catered to him as if he were at home.

"I'm sorry for my part in last night's unpleasantness," she said. "Troy and I have had some trouble in the past, but I know that exchange was really uncomfortable for you and Grant to see."

"I'm not worried about angry words spoken behind closed doors. Sometimes that helps clear the air. I'm concerned about the implications of the accusations that were made. Do you have any evidence, concrete or not, that Troy put you in danger?"

"No, I spoke rashly. I'm sure that those ventala were there for some unrelated reason."

"They were. According to Theo Tobin, they were looking for him."

"Oh." Her hands went to the chair's arms, but she forced herself to rest them lightly. "Did he say why?"

"They wanted to buy some pictures and information from

him. When he refused, they beat him. He stopped in Handy-rock's on his way back to the Etherlin."

She nodded.

"Though clearly there are some missing pieces of the story. No one with a battered face and body, who's being hunted by the perpetrators that assaulted him, stops in for a drink at a club his assailants might search. Why wouldn't he have simply come home? If he needed a drink, he could've gotten one at a club in the Etherlin or from his liquor cabinet, presumably."

When she didn't answer, Dimitri added, "Any thoughts?"

She shook her head.

"Grant says Theo called you."

"How does Grant know that?"

"He reviewed the phone records."

She pursed her lips. "I was told that allowing my bills to be paid by the community fund did not mean that my calls would be a matter of public record."

"Grant's hardly the public. There's just been a major violent incident. He's the head of Etherlin Security, and he's investigating. I'm surprised that the thing you're worried about is an invasion of your privacy."

She sighed. "I'm sorry. Grant and I haven't been as close lately as we once were, and we strongly disagree about me refusing an ES detail when I'm in the Etherlin. Ever since the attack on the Arts & Innovation Ball, when I became aware that an ES bodyguard would hold me against my will if he thought it was the best way to protect me, I've been uncomfortable."

"But ES has neutralized so many threats. You wouldn't be alive or be able to function the way you do without security. Surely you see that."

"I do. I'm grateful to them. I just don't want to feel like I'm under house arrest or under constant surveillance by people who report to the EC rather than me."

"Do you have something to hide?"

"Does Cerise? Does Ileana? Dorie? They've all been offered permanent twenty-four-hour protection, and they've all refused live-in bodyguards." She folded her hands on her lap. "I do understand the need for security. Especially after last night. As luck would have it, I've become friends with a member of a consultant security firm. For now, I'd like to have him provide additional personal security."

"Who is he? Have you talked to Grant about it?"

"Where is Grant today?"

"He's in the Sliver, assisting with the investigation there."

She nodded. "Exactly." She steepled her fingers. "I've known for a while that Grant's first loyalty is to his ambition. I think he's going to be a wonderful council member one day. He's kind and fair, and he cares so much about the community. Unfortunately, I sometimes feel that as he focuses on the big picture, he forgets that I'm not just a muse. I'm also a young woman who wants a voice in all the decisions that affect her immediate surroundings. Mr. Clark was a very qualified ES officer, but he was also uncompromising and often condescending. When it comes to a personal bodyguard, I need to be the one to choose him."

"Who's the security consultant?"

"His name is Len Mills. His firm was selected and vetted by ES, so I think he's a good compromise."

"It's natural to want to exert your independence, but by doing this, you'll appear critical of ES and, by extension, the Etherlin Council. Is that the impression you want to give as we head into the vote?"

"I'm not planning to flaunt my decision. I respect ES, and I'm very grateful to the Etherlin Council. The work you do allows me to do my work without having to concern myself with so many other things. I really value that. I know my mom did, too. As a muse, I want to spend my time studying and working with aspirants. I don't want to manage a household or choose financial investments. I really am happy to leave that in the council's hands.

"I just don't want to feel like I'm being watched and judged every moment. I know we're in the middle of the competition now, but afterward, I expect to be able to work in peace. I'll certainly always do my best to represent the Etherlin well, and I won't take needless chances. You can be sure I'll never leave the Etherlin without security again. But as an adult muse, I need a say in decisions that pertain to me."

"By raising this issue now, you're putting your life's work in jeopardy."

"My work speaks for itself. I'm the most accomplished muse. I'd also make the best leader, since I'm the most open to working with the other women. I won't try to exclude anyone, thereby squandering valuable talent." Her implied meaning didn't need to be stated. Dimitri already knew that any of the others would try to close ranks, leaving her out of any combined muse efforts.

"I know you're intelligent and savvy about these things, which makes me wonder why you're courting controversy now."

He's going to keep pressing the issue of the timing. If you really want to keep Merrick here in the guise of Len Mills, Dimitri will have to be convinced an outside consultant is necessary.

"I don't have a choice." She studied Dimitri's face, wanting to gauge his reaction to what she would say next. "Someone attempted to abduct me recently, and someone I know may have been involved."

He looked genuinely shocked. "What?" he sputtered. "Were you hurt? Who—?"

"Grant's looking into it. I haven't said anything to anyone else because I don't want to disrupt the Wreath Muse activities and the EC's vote. I know ES is supposed to be unbiased, but the individual officers have their favorites, I'm sure. That's the reason I'd like additional security from outside the Etherlin."

Dimitri stared at her. "I can't believe you didn't tell me about this immediately."

"I didn't want you to worry."

A clock in the hallway chimed, and he looked up. "You're leaving in the morning for the retreat center?"

She nodded.

"I'll make sure we send extra security. I can't be there myself until tomorrow evening. If you need to reach me, don't hesitate to call. One other thing. Is there any possibility Theo Tobin was involved?"

"I don't know. Why?"

"Because Tobin's going to be among the photographers."

Despite being keyed up, Alissa had lunch with Merrick. She noticed that he ate very little and licked his lips numerous times as though they were dry. She remembered reading that repeatedly licking their lips was an early sign of bloodthirst in a ventala. At the moment, it was difficult to get a sense of how he was feeling since he was buried beneath the heavy glamour of the Ovid Medallion. It took some getting used to. She missed his real face.

"You bled quite a bit. Will you need blood? The retreat center's isolated, and I'm sure you realize there's no blood-derivative available in the Etherlin."

He didn't look worried, but his silence felt evasive. He probably hadn't anticipated losing blood. How long until he'd need to feed?

"Will the lack of blood supply be an issue?"

The shake of his head was barely perceptible, and her instincts told her he wasn't being honest.

"The retreat center—tell me about it," he said.

She eyed him. If he didn't want to talk about the blood situation, she couldn't force him, but it made her uneasy.

"The center's incredible," she said. The retreat center had been her idea, and it was one of the few projects about which all the muses had been excited. "Ileana Rella, whose area is architecture, helped inspire the most amazing design. You'll have to see it to appreciate it.

"The drive takes a few hours, but it's worth it. Normally I'll have several rooms at my disposal, but on this trip there will be some members of the media photographing the new center and writing articles about it and us. Etherlin Security might want to house you with their security officers."

When Merrick didn't answer, she glanced at him. He licked his lips and drank a couple swallows of tomato juice that had been fortified with iron powder.

"That's okay, I take it?"

"I'll be in the room that best allows me to protect you."

"The rooms might already be assigned."

He shrugged as if that wouldn't be an obstacle to his rearranging things.

She leaned forward. "There's more to a disguise than changing your looks, you know."

He glanced at her as he drank more juice.

"There's an air about you that's too much your own. You need to act like we're friends *and* as if you work for me. People will expect you to behave a certain way."

He squinted at the light streaming in through the dining room windows, then stood and turned his back to them and slid on dark sunglasses.

She frowned, realizing that despite the human visage, the daylight still hurt his eyes. "I didn't think this through. There will be times at the center when I'll have to be outside. There's so much reflected light off the snow. It's blindingly bright in some places."

He drank the rest of the juice while standing, saying nothing in response.

Since he was a consultant, ES would be watching his every move. They were bound to notice his sensitivity to light.

He set the glass down. At her sigh of exasperation, the corners of his mouth quirked up.

"This is not a game, Merrick. If we're caught—"

"I know what happens if I'm caught."

"Listen, it's all right to admit this was a mistake. You made your decision to come too quickly, without knowing what would be involved," she said, striding toward the door. "I can arrange for someone to drive you into the Sliver. You'll be able to get home from there."

"Alissa," he said softly.

She paused. "What?"

"Relax. Wearing sunglasses isn't unique to ventala. Light burns my eyes and makes me feel sluggish, but even in bright sunlight, I'm faster than a human being will ever be. When the sun rises, I do have to sleep at least a couple hours. Are they going to expect you to work at sunrise?"

She shook her head.

"Then it's not a problem. And don't worry about the way I'll come across. Mills is a former Navy SEAL who works for an elite private security firm. I promise you that high-profile clients want their bodyguards to be seen, not heard. ES will expect him to be watchful, not chatty, while on duty."

He was right, of course. "I'm nervous," she said. "Your frequent sphinxlike silences are unnerving."

"You'll get used to it."

"I don't actually want to get used to it. I want you to talk to me, like you did last night."

"Last night I had an incentive."

She narrowed her eyes. "I shouldn't need to bribe you to talk to me. What do you have against conversation?"

He shrugged.

"Like now. I'd really like you to tell me what you're thinking."

He pinned her with a look. Even with someone else's face, there was something dangerous in his eyes. "I'm thinking," he said, lowering his voice to a whisper—a very intimate whisper, "that we have unfinished business from last night."

Her heart thudded behind her ribs. He licked his lips and glanced at her throat, where she was sure he could see her pulse thrumming beneath her skin. She blushed.

"I'm thinking," he said, and paused deliberately, leaning close, "that if there were a lock on the dining room door, we could take up where we left off."

Her jaw dipped open, and she drew in an unsteady breath. The idea had its allure, but they really couldn't. A lot of staff milled about on the ground floor during the day. Anyone could come in or notice the drawn drapes. Her eyes darted between the floor and the door, then back to him.

The way he watched her made her body temperature rise another degree. She swallowed.

"I could move the dining room table to block the door." He lifted a corner of the long, heavy table experimentally. "I could barricade us in—"

"Point taken." She shook her head with a small smile. "You can stop talking."

Chapter 20

Merrick said he wanted to see the area she'd walked through on her way home from the Xenakis party, so she led him out the back door to the lakeside path.

"Tell me what it's like to wield the muse magic."

"You expect me to answer questions when you don't?" she asked.

He shrugged, the hint of a smile playing at his lips.

"That hardly seems fair."

"If life were fair, we would've been lovers the first weekend we met," he said.

She slid a glance at him and raised her brows. If he thought he could continue to throw her off balance by flirting, he was mistaken. She was, after all, an experienced public figure, and she was certainly used to being propositioned by men. The only reason he'd flustered her at all was because she was attracted to him, too. But she realized there was an advantage to his being different. With a lot of men, she had to walk a tightrope by flirting in a way that made them feel good without promising too much. Yet Merrick flaunted his unflappable control, making her trust it. Also, being outside, bathed in the afternoon light, their walk was very public.

She smiled at him and widened her eyes with mock innocence. "From the very first weekend?" The back of her hand brushed his arm in a light caress. "And, if it had started then, would we still be lovers after all these years? If life were fair?"

"What do you think?"

She paused thoughtfully, then shook her head. "I doubt it. By nature, muses flit. Lots of passionate love affairs. Men, though not always prone to monogamy themselves, don't like to share. Long relationships are hard to sustain. Before my parents' generation, muses either didn't marry or they married *a lot*."

He smirked.

"Ventala aren't known for their long attachments either," she said. "Our correspondence probably lasted much longer than a full-blown affair would have. Maybe we're lucky there was a wall," she said. "What do you think?"

"Anticipation can eclipse actual events, and I do like my letters. The way the ink soaks into the heavy bond paper. The sexy sweep of the letters." He licked his lips. "You'll have to work pretty hard to be better in the flesh."

She laughed. "A challenge. I do like challenges." She glanced at the lake, a glacial blue stretching to the far shore and a thick forest of evergreens. "You asked what it's like to wield muse magic. The magic can be used in a couple different ways. The side effect of having it is being able to infuse my voice with persuasive power to influence people, but I don't use that much because it borrows power that should be used for greater things. Using power for persuasion is also against Etherlin rules, but you may have noticed that I occasionally break Etherlin rules," she said, shrugging her brows.

"Using it for inspiration with aspirants, that begins like a dance, an exchange of energy and ideas. I can almost share their thoughts and follow them forward. I start talking, filling the empty spaces. Encouragement washes over them like rain, enlivening them to the possibilities. Hunger follows, a need to reach a conclusion, to see what hasn't been seen before. Anticipation builds, and the power ignites in a frenzy of thoughts and impulses. The few spoken words mean infinitely more than what's actually said. It ebbs and flows, until there's a rush, like being intoxicated, and then there's a crescendo. It's orgasmic, I suppose, but more intense. Afterward, the buzz continues for hours and there's a sense of satisfaction and bliss, a knowing that something has been created that will ripple through the world and touch people's hearts and minds, possibly shape their lives. The aspirants are giddy and manic and grateful, while I feel connected to all mankind. In those hours, I'm powerful and humble at the same time. And there is complete clarity. No matter what else I waver about in life, there is one thing I know with absolute certainty. I was born to be a muse. Setting that blaze of inspiration makes me truly happy."

"There wasn't always an Etherlin," he said. "Why did the muses create it?"

"People think it was created to separate us from the world, but quite the opposite is true. Or was true initially. The muses noticed that their powers had faded over the generations, but the magic was strengthened when they were in close proximity to each other. They met several times a year to cultivate that enhanced strength. During World War Two, many of them came to the United States before it entered the conflict. We always try to avoid choosing sides during wartime; no one wants to inspire a weapon that results in human casualties. When the U.S. entered the war, Fleming's discovery of penicillin was ready to be exploited and the muses used their influence to inspire mass production, which, of course, continued long after the war and saved millions of lives.

"The muses of that generation, my grandmother's, were all very close friends. They decided to live in the same city. One of them was involved with a real estate developer, and they bought the property for the Etherlin and developed it.

"When the first casualties of the Vampire Rising were discovered, everyone thought it was a plague with bats as the vector. The combined power of the muses helped scientists to realize they were mistaken. Seven million deaths could've been twenty or forty." She brushed a strand of hair behind her ear.

"Why the wall? Ventala weren't always here."

She frowned. "Don't you know?"

He shook his head.

"It's not a nice story," she said, wanting to give him a chance to avoid hearing it, the way he'd given her one before talking about his childhood.

"They never are," he said, shrugging, then nodded for her to go on.

"Some of the un-mutated vampires moved to Colorado. They were searching for ways to save themselves and hoped to graft inspiration from the muses. Unfortunately they found themselves desperately drawn to muse blood. More and more of them arrived, and their behavior became erratic, swarming around a muse whenever they encountered one, trying to cajole or intimidate her and her security detail. Finally, they killed a pair of ES officers who were guarding a muse. They dragged her into the shadows and raped her while they drained her dry. It was kept relatively quiet because there had been talk of having the Secret Service take over the duties of ES, and the council and the muses thought the incident would force changes the muses didn't want. We never want to be beholden to a specific government—for protection or anything else. And so, a wall."

"Did the muses lend their influence to the Human Preservation Act?"

"I'm not sure. It was before my time, of course. Americans had just suffered through World War Two and were plunged into the Cold War. Paranoia and McCarthyism were prevalent, and then the Bat Plague killed off several million more people. Even when the mutated vampires were defeated, people couldn't relax. They carried around that primal fear that's etched into the souls of all human beings—the fear that the human race will be wiped out. The muses might have supported the HPA, but I don't think they inspired that legislation. It was the inevitable result of all that post-traumatic stress and lingering fear."

"No one tested the DNA."

"What DNA? The mutated vampire DNA?"

He nodded. "Scientists didn't have the technology at the time. The idea that the Rising came from a deadly evolution of the vampire species was a theory."

"What are you suggesting? That something other than a mutation caused those vampires to turn—for the lack of a better term—rabid?"

He shrugged.

She slowed and looked at him. "What are you saying? You can't just make a statement like that and stop talking. The Rising was a devastating moment in human history. No one thought vampires existed anymore, and then they mutated and came out and swept across the land like locusts. And the un-mutated ones seized the opportunity and came out to hunt, too. Men, already weary from war, had to organize themselves for a different kind of battle, one against nature, on a scale which they'd never before fought. It changed the face of the world. If you know something—if you have some secret knowledge of those events—you're obligated to disclose it."

He raised an eyebrow and she fumed.

"There's no law saying that you must, but it's a moral obligation!"

"An obligation to the people who stripped away my basic rights?"

"Your basic right to hunt and kill, you mean?"

He shook his head. "To feed from a person who's consented."

Her heart thumped a horrified rhythm. "Why would you want to do that? Blood is processed perfectly now. I know early on it caused salt and mineral imbalances that made the ventala sick, but it's been perfected."

"So they say."

"Meaning?"

"Meaning they don't have to drink it."

"So tell me. Does it make you sick? Does it make your muscles cramp?"

"No, but it doesn't fully satisfy the thirst."

"It's whole blood. They're able to preserve ninety-four percent of what's in human blood. The proteins and cells and fluid. It's an almost perfect match."

"Our bodies know the difference and crave the real thing."

"You know where that leads. Vampires and ventala lose control during direct consumption, and human lives are lost. Packaged blood outside the donors is the only safe alternative."

"So they say."

"Do you know differently? Do you have some personal experience to share?"

He shook his head, but she couldn't be sure whether he was denying the experiences or just denying the inclination to talk about them.

"Let's defer the discussion on the blood-drinking issue and return to what you said about genetic mutation not being the cause of the Rising. Explain that."

"I'm not a geneticist."

"But you do know something. What?"

"Lysander said it wasn't a mutation."

"What . . . what did he say it was?"

"He didn't."

"Maybe that was just conjecture on his part."

"Maybe, but when Lysander mentioned it, I remembered that once my father had said the same thing."

She rounded a curve in the path and stopped walking. "This is huge. Do you realize what you're saying? It's like saying that the world isn't round. We—everyone—believes the mutation theory to be true."

"What does it matter? All the shapeshifting vampires who caused the plague were wiped out. Their bodies were burned to ash. Next, you had the Human Preservation Act, where all the other vampires were killed and their bodies burned to ash."

She tipped her head back, staring at the sky. "You're saying people made a mistake? That killing them all means the truth will never be known?"

He shrugged.

"I understand why you're angry at people for killing the vampires. That's your heritage."

"I'm not angry about that. They were right to do it."

"But you resent the current restrictions on you?"

He flashed a smile. "Of course. What's good for the world isn't necessarily what's good for me personally. Take the wall. It couldn't prevent me from hunting muses and feeding off them. It just keeps me away from the woman I'm interested in. On the other hand, it does prevent others of my kind from coming across a muse and being overcome by an impulse to bite her. Not all ventala have enough control. So the wall makes sense for your community, even if it's inconvenient for me personally."

"What makes you different from the others?"

"My will."

She studied his profile. "And why do you think that's so different than theirs?"

"Because my father said I would be like him. The hunger and the rage would eventually consume me. In the end, I would let them because it would be too exhausting to fight my own nature."

"And yet?"

"The kid I was, the one with the broken bones and almost broken spirit, swore he'd defy that bastard till the bloody end. I told myself I could control that much. Turns out I was right."

"But you became an assassin."

"That's different."

"How?"

"I kill ventala and demons and occasionally evil human beings. I don't attack people in fits of rage or thirst. I don't strike without provocation. I never prey on the innocent."

She reached for his arm and squeezed it. "So you won. You're not like him. Does that give you some peace?"

"No, but it gives me satisfaction."

She nodded. "You know, I think you haven't become all you can be yet." She studied his face. "Maybe fate brought us together. Maybe I was meant to become your friend, so I could inspire you to create a different future for yourself."

"I'm not in a hurry to get to the future."

"No?"

"Why would I be? You're finally close enough to touch."

She smiled. "Yes, but this can't last."

He shrugged.

She glanced around to be sure no one was coming. There was a copse of trees that could block them from view, and she drew him off the path into it.

She kissed him softly, an inexplicable need curling through her. She wanted more and more and more of him. "I'm afraid it's going to hurt . . . when I have to let you go."

He licked his lips.

"Sometimes it hurts just wishing things could be different," she said, but she didn't wait for him to respond. She forced herself to return to the path and to walk on to where there were no trees.

"Hold on," he said, stopping in an area of smooth lawn.

She slowed, wondering if he wanted her to risk another kiss. The truth was she might have, but he'd paused where the path had snaked away from the lake so there was grass on either side of it, no cover at all.

He rubbed his chest. "The medallion's spell acts as insulation, but I can smell black magic from here. Are we close to where you were abducted?"

"Very close, I think," she said, pointing to a spot on the embankment where there was another large cluster of trees. "About there."

He walked off the path and went down on one knee on the grass, bending his head and inhaling. He trailed his fingers over the lawn and plucked a few blades. He slid his sunglasses down and examined the grass.

"Animal blood. Goat, maybe. Not freshly slaughtered. It was in a mixture. There's dandelion root and pine to cover the stench. There's also something greasy—" He drew his forefinger and thumb back and forth. "Animal lard—lamb, I think. And sulfur-scented ash that reeks. The ash came from the site where a demon was slaughtered."

He dropped the grass and rose. "That'll help me narrow it down. Only a powerful witch could track down the site where a demon had been slaughtered. Most supernatural creatures can't smell the ash. The only reason I can is because Lysander trained me to hunt demons."

"A witch who could find demon ash," she murmured, shaking her head. She couldn't imagine who that could be.

"There are no demon-hunters in the Etherlin. So whoever betrayed you didn't do a rite himself. He or she had to buy the potion from a witch who deals in black magic. And before he or she used it, they had to store it somewhere. Something so strong will have left traces. Let's go to the Xenakis house and see whether that's where it was kept."

"Even if there are traces there, it won't help us. Their house was full of people that night. Anyone could've been carrying it."

"Right, but the party was downstairs. If that's the only place there are traces, it won't tell us anything, but if the original source was in the house, the traces won't only be downstairs. The container that held the potion would've been hidden where no one would come across it by accident. In a safe. Or someplace private the staff wouldn't be rummaging through while cleaning or getting ready for the party."

She hesitated.

"What's wrong?"

"The Xenakises are like family."

"Two of the three muses that are your competition for the Wreath live there, along with their parents, who probably want their daughters to win."

"Calla's away, and Dimitri's my biggest advocate. Cerise and I aren't close, but she wouldn't—" She paused. "I know Cerise and don't think she would arrange for something so terrible to happen to me. Dorie's so young. She's barely been out of the Etherlin."

Merrick waited.

"If it has to be a muse, I'd like it to be Ileana," she said wistfully. "Better still, her brother." Alissa shook her head at herself. This was a time when it was nice that Merrick was circumspect, because the fact that he didn't argue or give her a skeptical look allowed her a moment to come to terms with the truth: investigating the Xenakis house first was sensible and practical.

I don't want them to be involved, but that doesn't mean they aren't.

"If wishes were horses, beggars could ride." She moistened her lips and nodded. "Tell me your plan for getting upstairs, and I'll do what I can to help you with it."

Chapter 21

Merrick scanned the path and the Xenakis property as they approached it, but he had to force himself to concentrate on the details—entry and exit strategies, security cameras. His thoughts tried to remain on something else entirely.

He still felt the kiss she'd given him, still heard her alluring words, still breathed the scent of her skin and hair and blood. He didn't look at her now, but despite her location in his vision's periphery, she loomed larger than the mansion in front of him. She was like the sun: he didn't need to look directly at it to witness its power, to feel its skin-scorching warmth. Without looking up, he always knew when the sun was overhead, and that's what it was like with Alissa. He felt her presence next to him, felt it so hard that awareness of her jackhammered through his body and brain.

If the Xenakises had betrayed her, he'd deliver the consequences. But did Alissa have to know the truth about them, a truth that would hurt her? He wanted to protect her from more than physical threats now.

The front door opened and a housekeeper stood in the doorway. She was dark and stout with a slightly crooked smile and a faint mustache on her upper lip.

"I know that Mr. Xenakis is at the Dome working, but I wondered if the girls are here?" Alissa asked.

"The girls are at Ileana Rella's house. They went for lunch

and to help Miz Ileana choose a dress for the reception tonight. They won't be home for about an hour."

"They're spending time with Ileana. That's nice."

He heard the slight catch in her voice. The other muses were together, and she hadn't been invited to join them. Merrick's jaw tightened, but he swallowed the vampire instincts. He calculated the hours until he would have her alone in her room. When they were alone, he'd make her forget the rest of the world entirely.

"I seem to have lost my bracelet when I was here the other night," Alissa said. "I was hoping they could help me look for it. Could you help me?" Alissa's smile was so sweet, her voice so persuasive, that the small woman nodded immediately. "Are there other servants who could help, too? I think it might have fallen off in the courtyard."

The little housekeeper obligingly gave them an accounting of where the servants were and, as he'd suspected, the timing was good. The house had already been cleaned, the laundry done and put away. Since it wasn't mealtime and the family was out, the security detail was gone, and nonessential personnel—everyone except the housekeeper—had left for the day. The girls' stylists, who were coming to get the muses party-ready, wouldn't arrive for another hour. It was like the Xenakises wanted him to search their house.

He noted the camera position on the main floor and calculated the blind spots. He followed Alissa and the housekeeper as far as the doors to the courtyard, then melted into the background. He waited until he was satisfied that the housekeeper hadn't noticed that he wasn't joining the search, then grabbed the spindles of the staircase railing and pulled himself up. He was sure that Dimitri Xenakis wouldn't have security cameras on the upper floor when he had pretty young daughters wandering between bedrooms and dressing rooms while young male security guards manned the monitors, but Merrick's gaze panned left and right, checking to be sure.

He inhaled deeply. No black magic. He smelled citrus and jasmine, and under those, he detected the unmistakable vanillalike scent that he associated with Alissa.

He found one of the girls' rooms—the one that smelled like jasmine. He opened and closed the drawers and checked the closet. There was nothing demonic inside.

After a quick walk-through of a pair of guest rooms, he went into the room that smelled of oranges and cream and vanilla. He made a systematic search and found the Alissa source. It was a locked box of mementos containing ticket stubs, hair ribbons, and old cards and letters in the loopy child's handwriting that apparently had once belonged to Alissa. There was also a gold charm of ballet shoes with the words *Best Friend* engraved on the soles.

He closed and relocked the box, finding it interesting that Alissa hadn't been the only one to treasure the friendship she'd shared with Cerise. He couldn't help but wonder why there had never been a reconciliation. How bad could a fight between a couple of little girls really have been? When Merrick was a teenager, Lysander had forced him into a fight-to-the-death battle with a demon, and Merrick and Lysander were still friends. By their nature of being beautiful, charismatic muses, shouldn't Alissa and Cerise have been drawn back to each other? Alissa wanted to rekindle the friendship. Why not Cerise?

He shook his head. Since when did he care about the fights of little girls? Or even of adult women, for that matter? His policy was that when any kind of drama started where no one needed killing, it was time for him to ride the elevator back to his penthouse for a scotch and lime while the club bouncers dealt with the problem.

Merrick passed the stairwell on his way to the opposite hall. In the master bedroom there was very little scent at all that he could detect. It wasn't unexpected. Calla Xenakis, Dimitri's wife who normally shared the suite with him, had been away for a couple of months.

Merrick opened and closed the drawers and closets, detecting no demon odors. He found a wall safe behind a painting. He glanced at the door. It would be nice to have a look inside, but without tools it might take a while.

Merrick laid his palm against the safe's face, hoping to detect the vibration or click of the tumbler as he used his fingertips to turn the dial.

Minutes ticked by as he worked. He heard Alissa's voice downstairs. At the housekeeper's insistence, they were searching the front hall and foyer for the bracelet. Then the front door opened, and he heard other female voices. The muses were home.

It was time to get out, but Merrick was pretty sure he had two of the numbers. He walked to the door of the master suite and closed it, then returned to the safe.

He turned the dial slowly. *Snick. Snick. Snick.* He heard the sound of light footsteps on the stairs. He waited. He could drop and roll under the bed if the feet moved toward the master bedroom's door. The feet didn't approach.

Snick. Snick. Snick. Tick.

A minute or less now.

He tried the numbers in different orders. On the fourth combination, the safe opened, and when it did, it rewarded him with a scent he knew well. *Demon.*

Alissa hadn't been able to delay Dorie from going up to her room, but Cerise had been more polite.

"I'm surprised that someone didn't come across your bracelet during the cleanup after the party," Cerise said. "Maybe it fell into one of the large pots. It was a tight squeeze at the northwest corner after the caterers rearranged things. We should check the greenhouse, too. Some of the flowers were brought out for the party."

"Would you mind if I looked now? Do you have time to come with me?" Alissa asked.

Cerise glanced at the grandfather clock. "Yes, it's no problem."

Before they could go, the front door opened. Dimitri was home.

"Oh, hello," Alissa said, crossing the foyer to kiss his cheek. "You're home early, aren't you?"

"No one scheduled late-afternoon meetings. People wanted extra time to get ready for the reception. Speaking of which, shouldn't you be home doing the same?" he asked, his arm still around her shoulders.

"I lost a bracelet the other night."

"It *is* getting late," Cerise said, and, without another word, she turned and started up the stairs.

"Cerise, could I see your gown?" Alissa asked, groping for a reason to distract or detain her.

"You'll see it in an hour," Cerise said without looking over her shoulder.

Dimitri frowned. "Showing Alissa your dress wouldn't take more than a minute."

Cerise ignored him and turned to the right just as Dorie reappeared at the top of the staircase. Alissa's heart raced. This was a disaster. How was Merrick going to get out now with the girls milling about upstairs? She held her breath, cringing inwardly, waiting for Cerise to discover him.

"Daddy, I sent Mom a picture of the dress, and she said I should wear her rubies in the white gold instead of Cerise's diamond pendant. She says the pendant's too modern for the dress. What do you think?"

"Put on the dress. I'll get your mother's necklace from the safe. You can try it with both and we'll see."

Dorie nodded and rushed back toward her room.

"Now what have you lost? A bracelet? Was it one of your mother's?" he asked Alissa.

"No, one of mine. A favorite, actually."

"I'm sorry. And you think you left it here?"

"I might have."

"Well, the sun's already going down and we've got the reception tonight, so we'll have a good look first thing in the morning, all right?"

"Well," Alissa said hesitantly. Blood raced through her veins. She could ask him to talk in the living room. If neither of the girls had found Merrick, didn't that mean he was in Dimitri's room? Or maybe he was hiding in a guest room and would just wait until they all got dressed and left.

"You've got lots of beautiful pieces to choose from for tonight. What's this about? Because I don't think you're only here about a bracelet. Are you nervous?"

Yes! "Yes, I'm nervous about the next couple of days. I just wanted to see you."

He gave her upper arms a reassuring squeeze. "And my daughters didn't exactly make you welcome. Listen, when the competition's over and you're all working together, everything will change." He kissed her forehead. "You can come upstairs if you want. You can sit in the bedroom while I change in the bathroom, and then Cerise, Dorie, and I will walk you to your house and wait while you dress, and we'll all drive to the reception together."

Dimitri was always so good to her. Tears stung her eyes. She felt wretched for allowing Merrick to search Dimitri's house. She hugged Dimitri, who squeezed her and patted her back reassuringly, which made her feel even guiltier.

"No, I'm fine. I'll see you there in a while." When she got to the door, she paused and turned back. "Thank you, Dimitri, for always being here for me."

He smiled. "I do it for myself. What man wouldn't want to have three beautiful daughters instead of two?" As Dimitri turned, Alissa glanced up and saw Dorie standing at the railing, glaring down at her.

Alissa smiled sheepishly and left the house. Her muscles were tight as she walked, a part of her still waiting for sounds of a commotion at Merrick's discovery. She stopped at the property's edge with a pounding heart, wondering whether to go home and get ready for the party or to wait for Merrick and risk being seen. If he were caught, she knew he wouldn't implicate her, but it would appear suspicious if she were found pacing outside the house, waiting for him.

She heard the courtyard gate open and spun, expecting to see the housekeeper, but instead Merrick walked toward her as Len Mills. She gaped at him.

"How did you end up in the courtyard?" she demanded when he was close enough to hear her despite her lowered voice.

"I went out a window and across the roof. I wanted to drop on the grass in a surveillance camera blind spot. The best one's in the back."

"I think I had three heart attacks while I waited for you." He smiled.

"And I bet it was all for nothing," she said, starting around the lake path.

"For nothing?" he asked.

"I told you that you wouldn't find anything. You didn't, did you?" Her voice held more accusation than she meant it to. She had agreed to go along with his plan. It wasn't fair to treat him like she'd been an unwilling participant just because she'd felt guilty and afraid once it was under way.

"I was in the middle of breaking into his safe when people started coming upstairs. I didn't find traces of black magic in the drawers or closets."

She nodded. "You wouldn't have found anything in the safe either. Dimitri's the last person who would ever hurt me, but if he wanted to, he'd do it the simple way, by shunning me and turning the vote against me. He doesn't need to resort to black magic and deals with ventala syndicate members."

When Merrick didn't answer, she turned her head to look at him. "Sorry. You know I didn't mean you."

The corner of his mouth quirked up. A wry smile? she wondered. He was so hard to read.

She stopped walking. "You do know I didn't mean you, right? I was referring to the syndicate members who think it's okay to kidnap women and to prosecute someone for trespassing when they're trying to rescue a victim."

Merrick continued walking, which made her start again to keep pace.

"They'd done all that work abducting you. Me coming in and scooping you up after the fact had to be frustrating," he said, mock serious.

"Right, their anger was clearly justified. Anyone psychotic—I mean reasonable—could see that."

"There you go, trying to hurt my feelings again."

"Do you have feelings? It's so hard to tell sometimes."

He smiled and so did she. They finished the walk home in silence. At the door, she realized that she was no longer upset about searching Dimitri's because Merrick had distracted her. It seemed to be part of an emerging pattern. No matter how bad things were, as soon as Merrick was with her, they got better. It was a fact she found both amazing and concerning.

Chapter 22

Merrick swept through the house to be sure it was secure and dropped Alissa at her bedroom door.

"I'll be back in a few minutes."

"Where are you going?"

"I thought I detected something off the path on the way back. I'll have a closer look."

"I could've gone with you."

"You need time to get ready for the party."

She nodded.

"What's wrong?" he asked.

Her fingertips skimmed the back of his hand, and she whispered, "Nothing, just be careful, James."

His heart thumped like she'd reached in and trailed her fingers over it. He stared at her intently, the impulse to kiss her roaring through him. He cleared his throat. "Easy, North. I like giving you what you want, but if I'm too careful, there goes my reputation."

She parted her lips slightly, tantalizing him. His mouth went dry, and he clenched his hands to keep from reaching for her.

"What gave you the idea that I cared about your reputation?" she teased.

He couldn't concentrate well enough to come up with a retort. So this was what it felt like to be tongue-tied. "I'll be damned," he murmured.

"Oh, I hope not," she said, touching a finger to his lips before she stepped back and closed the door.

He rested his palms on the frame, fighting the urge to enter the room, to chase her and pull her into bed, to trap her body beneath his. He breathed deep until lust loosened its grip. She needed to attend her reception. He'd have her alone after that. He could wait. He didn't want to wait, but he could—barely.

He forced himself away from the door and took the stairs two at a time. He crossed through the kitchen to get to the back of the house and went outside. He didn't need more time on the path, but he wanted her to jump to the wrong conclusion about where he'd gotten the smooth chunk of stone in his pocket. He walked the path until he was sure he was out of sight.

He doubted she would stand at her window and watch him, but the best lies and deceptions contained some truth. He pulled the three-inch flat piece of limestone from his pocket, bringing it close to his face. He inhaled deeply. It had definitely touched demon blood or ash, but he didn't smell spices or lard or animal blood. He inhaled again. There was an incredibly faint trace of something beautiful, but he couldn't make it out.

He lowered the stone and studied the front. Etched onto its face was a round Celtic symbol made of intertwining thistles. If there was special significance to the symbol, he didn't know it. He flipped the stone over. The undersurface had been ground flat, except for a boltlike square nub protruding from the center, which looked like it would fit into another piece, tongue and groove.

He raised the stone once more, but despite drawing in a deep breath, he couldn't make out the underlying scent. He needed to get the Ovid Medallion off because it obscured his senses. He pocketed the stone and returned to the house.

When he got upstairs, a grinding sound drew him down the hall. He opened the library door and found Alissa's father dragging furniture into a circle.

The older man climbed on the seat of a chair and looked down at the arrangement. He shook his head and stepped down, grabbing a heavy table covered with books.

"Hang on," Merrick said, stepping up and gently shoving Richard aside. "Where?" he asked.

Richard stared at him for a moment. "Ah, Perseus." He nodded. "Having more than one face . . . that's usually figurative, implying treachery, rather than being meant literally. In your case, however, two faces, not figurative. Curious. Perseus was never depicted as a shapeshifter in the myths." Richard studied him thoughtfully. "The difference between fact and fiction, I suppose. Here," Richard said, pointing.

Merrick moved the table and then righted the books that had fallen over.

"Perseus," Richard said, motioning Merrick over to an enormous bookshelf. "Would you mind?"

Merrick raised his brows. "Up against the wall is a good place for that one."

"Too heavy to move like this?" Richard asked and began removing the leather-bound volumes and setting them in stacks.

"Wait," Merrick said. He walked over and tested the bookshelf. There was some give. It wasn't bolted to the wall or floor. "Get on the other end to help keep it steady."

Richard ran a hand through his silver hair, walked to the end, and nodded. "Ready."

Merrick grabbed the frame and pulled. The floor groaned as he dragged the heavy case over it. "Wait," Merrick said, squatting to examine the floor. He ran his fingers over the scratches. They were deep enough that it would take more than polish to remove the marks.

"No," Merrick said, standing. "She's not going to be happy if I tear up the floor." Merrick pushed the shelf back into place, feeling a sharp pull in his shoulder. He grimaced. The muscle wasn't completely healed from the stab wound. He paused, letting the ache fade.

"I need that wall," Richard said, peering at the bookshelf, clearly disappointed. "Books don't write themselves," he murmured. "But the hard is what makes it great. Maybe if I wedge—"

"Where do you need a wall?" he asked.

Richard stretched his hand out to indicate an area near the room's center.

"Does it have to be solid? Are you going to ram anything into it?"

"No."

"Give me fifteen minutes. I'll make you a wall."

"You're a prince among men," Richard said solemnly.

Yeah, that's what all the madmen say. "Just so you know, Richard. If Alissa doesn't like the room's new look, you did it all yourself."

"Yes, all the credit. None of the blame. Got it," Richard said with remarkable lucidity in his pale blue eyes.

"Exactly," Merrick said, flashing a smile. "I suspect we're going to get along fine."

Richard turned his head and stared at an empty corner. "Hmm, blood. Like Lady Macbeth?" He paused, apparently hearing a voice to match the invisible presence. "Ah, no. Well, beggars, choosers, you know." Richard looked back at Merrick. "You may be right about us getting along. Unless you're a villain." Richard looked him over. "If you are a villain . . . well, I know where you sleep."

Merrick laughed softly. "There you go, Richard. Keep your options open."

Alissa dusted another layer of shimmery gold powder over her cheekbones as the bedroom door opened. She didn't want Merrick to see her until she was ready. She stood and walked to the door of the dressing room that connected to her bathroom.

She opened the door a crack and spoke through the opening, "Hey."

"Yeah?" He walked over, but didn't attempt to open the door. She loved how intuitive he was. He understood that if she'd wanted to be seen, she would've opened the door all the way.

"I need a little more time to finish getting ready. After you're dressed for the party, can you wait for me downstairs? There's a tuxedo for you in your room."

"Just happened to have a spare lying around, huh?"

"I'm a muse. I have stylists on standby around the clock."

"All part of the muse magic. Able to generate formal wear with a single phone call?"

"Exactly," she said with a laugh. "I'm the envy of super-heroes everywhere. See you downstairs in a few minutes." She closed the door with a gentle click. A group of agitated butterflies flitted around her belly. *Insane,* she thought and shook her head. It was only two nights before she might be crowned Wreath Muse, and the thing she felt most nervous about was how well her evening with Merrick would go.

She sat in front of the mirror, finishing her makeup. She ran rose pink lipstick over her lips and turned her face to each side, examining her work. Her upswept hair lay smooth against her head, held in place with unseen pins. Around her throat, she fastened an antique gold and diamond necklace that twinkled in the light.

She uncovered her vintage strapless gold gown. Shimmering scalloped lace rested on a lining of flesh-colored satin. She stepped inside the fabric, raised it, and drew the zipper up, sheathing herself in luxury.

She glanced at the crook of her arm where she'd placed two tiny round bandages over the bite marks. They were almost invisible against her skin, but she slid on pale gold satin gloves that reached her biceps. She slipped on shoes that matched the gloves.

She opened the door a sliver. "Are you there?" she called softly. As she'd expected, Merrick was efficient in all things. He'd already dressed and gone down.

She emerged and found a Post-it note he'd left on the inside of her bedroom door.

For when you say good night: Richard—library.

She smiled. Merrick's memory of the small details of her life flattered her. She'd mentioned in a letter that she had her little evening rituals, like always saying good night to her dad. What she hadn't said was that she often tucked him in now, their adult and child roles reversed.

Knowing where her dad was saved her time. She wouldn't have looked for him there at first, and she was already late. Alissa swept down the hall, around the corner, and into the library, finding it transformed.

She paused at the bronze silk sheets hanging from subtle ceiling hooks and took in the large potted plants arranged like clusters of trees. Flour coated the floor, creating the illusion of a light dusting of snow.

"Hi, Dad."

He turned and smiled. "Well, well, well. You're beautiful tonight, Moonbeam. A gilded goddess."

"Thank you."

"Careful of your dress. It's snowy," he said, indicating the flour.

"I thought the landscapers were gone for the day."

He looked at her blankly.

"How did you hang these sheets?"

"Well—do you mind? Why should you? It's my library. We share it, of course, with all these authors. I wanted props. I'm working, you know."

"I don't mind, but you didn't climb—" She looked around. There was no bookshelf close enough for him to have climbed.

"Oh, no. I don't have keys to the shed with the tools. The infernal Mrs. Carlisle's rules. I don't have access to my own ladders or drills or the most useful pieces of equipment, but fortuitously she left me with the most dangerous thing of all. My pen," he said with an impish smile. "I may write her a note bitter enough to pickle her ears."

"No tools, then how did you . . . ?" She glanced at the door. *Merrick.*

"Well, I'll tell you. That Perseus may have blood on his hands, but he's Svengali with a hammer."

She sighed. "Mr.—Mills isn't here to do carpentry work, Dad."

"I know, but the titans will have him soon enough. Might as well get something useful out of him before they crack his bones to splinters."

She winced. "He's very adept at taking care of himself."

"No doubt, but you should always kiss him good-bye when he goes. Even the warrior sons of Ares need that before they die."

A shiver of uneasiness ran through her. "Speaking of a kiss good-bye," she murmured and stepped forward. She hugged him and kissed his cheek. "I love you, Dad. Get lots done and have an inspired night."

Outside the library, she took a moment to shake off her dad's warning. On a deep breath, she rounded the corner.

Merrick can take care of himself. It's not his life, but this visit, this time with me, that's fleeting. Yes, kiss him when he goes, but also kiss him before that.

She slowed as she approached the top of the staircase. She let her heels click the floor so he turned. She paused for a few beats, not exactly a pose, but long enough for him to take in the lines of the dress and how she looked in it.

He watched her descend, never blinking, never moving.

The skirt whispered *swish* as she came to rest a few feet from him. He studied her in silence, but this silence differed from his usual wordlessness. In its depths, nothing existed save their two bodies, their beating hearts and slow breaths, and the alluring gravity that drew them together.

With the lightest possible touch, his fingertips grazed her skin just above her jaw, making her shiver.

"Real and earthbound," he confirmed. "You don't look it."

"No?"

"No." His stare consumed her. "In that dress, you're heaven's mist. I can't decide whether to fall to my knees and worship from the ground up, or to start at your tendrils and work my way down."

She slid her arms around his neck and kissed him in a lingering exploration of his mouth. He held her long after, her soft, satin-sheathed body pressed to the hard planes of his.

"Tell me a secret," she whispered in his ear.

"Exploiting your advantage? That's not very angelic of you." His mouth sucked the side of her neck, making her warm, then flushed.

"You said you wanted bribes. Doesn't the way this dress fits suffice?"

His low laugh vibrated against her throat, and her belly tightened. She wanted to peel off his clothes and the medallion and to become the Alissa of his dreams, a memory he would never forget.

"Never mind," she said softly. "You don't have to talk if you'd rather not."

"It's all right," he murmured. "It turns out, you're the one person in the world I enjoy talking to."

"Thank you," she said, kissing him again. "That was a lovely secret."

Alissa needn't have worried about Merrick. He'd introduced himself to the on-duty ES officers and joined one of their tables. She regretted that he couldn't sit with her. The night should have been about her last chance to charm the council members but, for her, it was about him.

She smiled and laughed and posed through two courses of food, wondering the entire time what Merrick thought of dinner. She felt his eyes on her often, which was simultaneously reassuring and unsettling.

When the muses were escorted from the room, he joined the ES officers standing guard. Inside a private room lit with candles, rich fabrics were draped over most surfaces to act as a neutral backdrop for their dresses.

Surprised to find Theo Tobin among the handful of photographers, Alissa's gaze settled on him and refused to budge for several moments. The other women were shocked by his bruises, but he lied smoothly, telling them he'd been in a car accident.

The muses were arranged in a series of poses, where it was clear that she and Cerise, who wore a body-hugging gown in metallic indigo, were most often the focal point. Ileana, demure but boxy-looking in ivory, and Dorie, in terrible, severe makeup obviously intended to make her look older and a voluminous red dress that nearly swallowed her, were seated at the sides and eventually photographed separately.

As a change of lighting and backdrop were arranged, Theo Tobin beckoned her. When they stepped behind a decorative Chinese screen, she discovered the room had a second door.

"Let's go into the hall," he whispered.

"I don't think that's a good idea," she said.

"You want to take a chance that the other girls will overhear our conversation? Because I don't."

What she wanted was for Merrick to be within calling distance. She opened the back door and glanced out. At the far end of the long hall, a security officer stationed at an exit door nodded at her. Tobin or an accomplice wouldn't be able to drag her out of the building. Tobin followed her into the hall, and they closed the door.

"How are you?" she asked.

"I'm sore as hell, but I'll live, and that's a bonus after yesterday. Listen, those ventala, they had me take really damaging smutty photos of you. They planned to use them to make it look like you'd willingly taken a walk on the wild side."

She winced. "Which means they could still use the photographs to create a scandal anytime they want."

"No, the photographs were destroyed, but the ventala aren't done with you."

"Mr. Tobin, Grant Easton and Dimitri Xenakis know me well. They would have realized the photographs were staged. Etherlin Security would've retrieved me."

"If they'd gotten to you in time."

She thought about lying on the balcony, dying. They wouldn't have been in time. They hadn't even realized she'd been taken.

"It seems like a lot of trouble to go through for a couple gallons of blood."

"That's just it. I don't think they wanted only your blood."

She frowned, thinking of Cato Jacobi's tongue on her throat. "Well, it's a lot of trouble for anything." She paused and shook her head. "It doesn't make sense. There are so many beautiful women they could've taken more easily. The EC has powerful friends. Dimitri has the ear of world leaders. It's shortsighted to abduct a muse. If people didn't buy the ventalas' ruse that I'd been willing, and of course, at some point when someone asked I would've told them I'd been kidnapped—"

"Exactly," Tobin said in a frantic whisper. "Cato said, 'We'll make sure this one gets it right. Just like her mother.'"

Alissa pursed her lips. "They planned to drive me to

suicide? Again though, what would've been the point of taking me if they only planned to kill me? Unless they want someone else to be Wreath Muse. Someone they believe will be more sympathetic to their political interests or something?"

"I don't know."

"Mr. Tobin—"

"Theo. Call me Theo, for God's sake. You saved my life. We can be on a first-name basis, don't you think?"

"Saved your life? You give me way too much credit. That diversion at Handyrock's that allowed you to get home certainly wasn't something I orchestrated."

"I'm not talking about that. Although, that cluster-fuck did distract the syndicate so I could make it to the checkpoint."

"If not that, then what?"

"You saved me from Merrick. You made him promise to let me live."

"How do you know? You never saw him, did you?"

"Never saw him?" Tobin laughed bitterly. "Who do you think did this to my face?"

She stepped back, her stomach lurching like the floor had fallen out from under her. "The Jacobis."

He shook his head. "Merrick."

Chapter 23

The rest of the photo shoot had been a blur. Alissa returned with the others to the ballroom and didn't make eye contact with Merrick when she passed him.

You knew what he was when you started this, she thought, angry at herself for being shocked and upset. There had been so much talk of killing, the word had temporarily lost its meaning. But when confronted with the aftereffects of his violent nature, she felt anything but desensitized.

Back in the ballroom, she danced with various council members, prominent community leaders, and aspirants. With effort, she concentrated on talking to them, but within the conversational gaps, her mind returned over and over to the image of Theo Tobin's face.

After the shoot, Tobin had left through the second door. For a split second, she'd thought he was avoiding Merrick, but, of course, Tobin hadn't known that Merrick was among ES. She wished Merrick wasn't. She needed time alone to think, but with the party winding down, he'd be coming home with her.

She strode into the women's lavatory and sat on a cushioned bench in an alcove.

"Tired, Alissa?"

She turned her head. Dorie strode in and stopped in front of the mirror. Dorie touched her severely coifed hair, then retouched her wine-colored lipstick.

"This lipstick is pretty dark. I probably should've gone brighter to match the dress."

Alissa didn't comment, but agreed that the girl's makeup was too dark. It was also laid on very thick, like stage makeup. What had the stylist been thinking?

"You look pretty tonight," Dorie said, sitting on the bench next to Alissa. "I like those gloves. Can I try them?" Dorie clutched Alissa's fingers and pulled on her left glove, which slid down to the elbow.

Belatedly, Alissa remembered the puncture marks. She jerked her arm back, a flood of adrenaline pouring into her veins. "Do you mind? I came in here for a moment of quiet."

"It'll just take a second. I'm trying to decide whether—"

"Dorie, enough," Alissa said, pulling the glove back to its original position as she stood. "I appreciate the fact that you're trying to develop your sense of style, but imitating me isn't the answer. We're totally different types."

Dorie tilted her head and smiled, looking far older than her years. Suddenly the dark makeup didn't look as inappropriate. "So that's a *no* to me trying the gloves?" She paused. "You wore your hair up. Shows off your bare throat and collarbones, but your arms are covered. And, of course, your legs. I've heard we'll be wearing bathing suits for the photo shoot by the retreat's tropical indoor pool. No gloves or long skirts for that session."

Alissa turned and left, knowing that Troy had shared his suspicions with Ileana, Cerise, and Dorie. Had Cerise confirmed that Alissa had had bruises and marks on her arms? If the EC heard, would they demand that her arms be examined?

Outside the bathroom, she ignored the ballroom, striding straight to the exit. She'd had enough of the banquet for the night, and enough of the world.

Merrick wondered again what had happened. Alissa hadn't looked his way once since the closed-door photography session, and when she returned to the hall from the bathroom, she hadn't even checked that he was with her before she left the building.

"You forgot something, Miss North," Merrick said, walking up to her and the valet. "Your wrap's still inside."

Next to him, Alissa didn't reply. While the valet went to get the car, Merrick studied her. "Are you going to make me guess?" he asked.

With barely a glance at him, she said, "Pardon?"

"Are you going to make me guess what's wrong?"

"It's been a long night. These events tire me out."

"Yes, all that smiling must be exhausting."

"Well, it's not as physical as your work, to be sure, but keeping up appearances can be a strain."

The car arrived, and she took the driver's side. "I'll drive so you're free to shoot. Isn't that the way it's done?"

He glanced around and got into the passenger seat. She said nothing on the drive home, but her stiff posture communicated plenty. He went over the night. He'd made nice with the ES officers, introducing himself and complimenting them on their reputation and organization. Under the guise of wanting to keep his new job as Alissa's personal bodyguard, he'd asked a lot of questions about operations, finding out the names of the officers working the night of the abduction. He'd never felt that his questions had been viewed as anything more than professional interest, but maybe taking names had made someone suspicious?

He'd acknowledged the women who'd looked directly at him by nodding, but he certainly hadn't flirted with anyone, so there'd been no cause for her to get jealous. Maybe whatever she was upset about had nothing to do with him, but the vibe he got from her was that it did. She'd become distant. He didn't like it. She'd been so free in their recent conversations, he'd gotten used to that intimacy; craved it, in fact.

With the car parked, they went inside the North house. She locked the door and set the alarm. He followed her to the staircase, to the exact spot where a few hours before she'd kissed him. Twice.

"Now that it's known that you're here as a bodyguard, it

wouldn't look appropriate for you to stay in the room adjoining mine. The guest room down here where you showered last night would be better. You can lock the door when you take off the medallion. No one will disturb you."

He waited, saying nothing.

"Well, good night." She turned and ascended the stairs.

He followed silently. When she got to her door, his hand prevented her from closing it on him.

She raised a quizzical brow, then said, "Oh, your things are up here."

He ignored the impulse to pull her to him. Sudden and direct didn't seem the right approach at the moment. When they were both inside, he closed the door and locked it.

She folded her arms across her chest. He did the same, but because she still looked every bit as beautiful as she had all night, he felt at a disadvantage. He hid that fact behind an impassive expression. When it came to staring people down, experience was on his side. After several long moments of silence, she shifted uncomfortably.

"I don't want to talk about it," she said. "I just want to be alone."

He continued to stare at her, waiting. She finally walked to her dressing table and took off her jewelry. She set the pieces in their cases and pushed them aside.

"I saw Theo Tobin at Handyrock's. I assumed he'd been beaten by the Jacobis."

Ah. Tobin had cried on her shoulder. A parting gift to Merrick on his way out of town?

Alissa looked over her shoulder at him. "Do you have anything to say about that?"

He shook his head.

"He says you were the one who hurt him. Confirm or deny?" she asked.

She rested a hand on the back of her neck, rubbing her fingers over her spine. He would have liked to have done that for her, and the fact that Tobin had ruined their night was something Merrick would remember if he ever saw the little weasel again.

"I don't know what I was thinking getting involved with

you," she said when he didn't answer. "Tobin was forced to take some incriminating pictures, but he destroyed them. He seems to have done the best he could to help me."

"He didn't erase the pictures. He kept them."

"He said they were gone."

"They are."

"You?"

"That's how his face ended up looking like it does. He would've kept them, but I didn't give him the choice."

Several silent moments passed. Finally, she said, "I believe you. Even when I was young, he tried to get inappropriately provocative pictures of me. If he took some graphic ones the other night, he'd never have given them up without a fight. Though the fight seems to have been pretty one-sided, from the look of things." She unfolded her arms and let them drop, lacing her fingers together. "The pictures, what were they like?"

Merrick shook his head.

"Bad?"

Yes, he thought, but he only shrugged.

"You won't tell me?"

He shook his head again.

"Why not? The more outraged I get, the more I'll think he got what he deserved."

"He did deserve it," Merrick said evenly.

"So why not tell me? I have a right to know." Her voice had a cool, distant quality, as though she hadn't been a victim, but was instead asking about something that had happened to someone else. Despite that, he saw the pulse pounding in her neck and a flush rise in her cheeks.

"I don't want you to hear the details. I think it would upset you, just like seeing Tobin's face did. I worked to erase that night because I don't want anything to hurt you."

Her eyes shone bright, and she looked away. "It was hard to see Tobin's face and feel somewhat responsible. I don't know if I can be okay with what you do, even when it's for a good reason."

He strode to her and put his arms around her from behind, drawing her against him. "You know why they chose you?"

He paused. "It was because they thought they could get away with it. I'm the reason they weren't right."

"Everything is so hard," she said with a catch in her voice that made his heart clench.

"I know."

"Sometimes I think maybe my mother killed herself so she could rest," she whispered.

He picked her up and walked to the couch. He sat with her on his lap. Her head turned toward his shoulder, and he felt her body shake as she silently cried. He held her tighter, relieved that the wall of ice between them had melted again.

Chapter 24

During the few minutes when she'd gone quietly to pieces and put herself back together, she was grateful for Merrick's silence. His even breathing and the slow, steady thump of his heart had been the comfort she needed. She didn't usually allow herself the luxury of breaking down. She'd always been afraid that if she ever started crying she wouldn't be able to plug the dam.

"I think I'll wash my face," she said, getting up. "Would you like a drink?"

"Where's the liquor cabinet? I'll bring up a tray," he said, tossing his tuxedo jacket on the arm of the couch.

"You don't need to do that. I'll go down for it."

He shrugged. "Bartending was the first job I ever had. Now I own a nightclub. If nothing else, you can always trust me to make you a decent drink."

"Just don't make me too many. I shudder to think how inappropriate I'd become, considering how free I've been with my emotions tonight. I'm sorry about that, by the way. I'm normally stronger."

"Even the strong have weak moments, and you've had to be stronger than most."

"Is that so? Everyone has weak moments? When was the last time you wept?"

He smiled. "It's been a while, but if I thought you'd be the one comforting me, I might try to remember how it's done."

"Sure you would," she said with a soft laugh, going into the bathroom. Honestly, she wouldn't have wanted that. With the exception of seeing the evidence of it on Tobin, Alissa liked Merrick's strength. "The wet bar's in the living room. I'll have one of whatever you made me in your apartment," she called.

"A Maiden's Prayer," he said, and she heard the door open and close.

She washed her face and took the pins from her hair. Running a brush through the curls didn't quite tame them, but the loose waves suited the night. The sleek, razor-sharp angles of her normal hairstyle belonged to Official Alissa, Professional Muse Alissa. Not to the soft Alissa who let herself cry on someone's shoulder or had drinks with a ventala in the sitting area of her bedroom.

She curled her lashes and ran a tinted lip balm over her lips, but otherwise left her face bare of makeup. *Symbolic,* she thought. She'd let him in and wanted to keep letting him in, despite Tobin's battered appearance and all its dark implications.

She glanced down at the beautiful dress and considered changing, but she wouldn't go that far. They were having an old-fashioned nightcap; a quiet, calm end to the roller-coaster day. Wearing lingerie would take away her options.

She reentered the bedroom and found Merrick setting down a silver tray that held a whiskey decanter, a dish of sliced limes, a pitcher of Maiden's Prayers, a pair of crystal highball glasses, and a small ice bucket.

"That was fast," she said.

He dropped an ice cube into her glass and poured her drink. Then he unbuttoned the top two buttons of his shirt and removed the medallion, tossing it aside. She took a sip, watching his own image return. Len Mills had nice enough looks, but Merrick's were better. It was a shallow thought, but she didn't condemn herself for it. She'd fallen for Merrick over months and years, for his steady pursuit of her and for the way he paid attention to every detail of her life as though what she really wanted and needed mattered to him. It couldn't be wrong to enjoy the looks of a man who cared that much.

He made himself a drink and sat back on the couch where

they'd been. She started to sit next to him, but he shook his head.

"No?" she asked.

His left arm, drink in hand, rested on the armrest. His right extended to her. "Come back," he said. It was so like that moment in his apartment when he'd held out his hand to her and asked her to stay. She couldn't then, but now . . .

"Sit here, and I'll tell you about the road trip I took with Lysander to Nebraska."

"You and Lysander went to Nebraska?" she asked.

He nodded.

"You drove there?"

Again a nod, the continued outstretched hand a tantalizing flame to her moth.

"Why?" she asked, taking a sip of her drink.

"If you sit here," he said, "I'll tell you."

She looked at him through her lashes and smiled. "Will I ever get a story out of you without a bribe?"

"Probably one day. But not tonight."

She lowered herself onto his lap. He leaned back, and her body followed, so she was curled against his chest. His arm snaked around her legs and moved them so they rested on the couch. It was dangerously cozy.

"So the road trip," she said, taking another slow swallow.

"I was sixteen. Lysander was the age of mankind, give or take a century, though he never acted it. His emotional growth's stunted. I think the concussion he got when he fell from grace must have been a direct blow to the frontal lobe," Merrick said with a roll of his eyes.

"He got a car, gave me the keys, and said, 'Drive us to Omaha.' To which I said, 'Why the hell would I want to go to Omaha with you?' And he said, 'Because I left some money in Omaha, and I need to retrieve it before I forget where I hid it. I'll pay you to drive.'"

"How much?" she asked.

"How much money did he leave in Omaha? Or how much was he offering me to drive him?"

"Both, of course. That's why I left the question open-ended."

"He didn't know how much. The 'money' was in the form of gold coins—Spanish doubloons, to be exact—and a handful of Peruvian emeralds."

"No."

"Yeah. He'd been the only survivor of a shipwreck. He didn't think the fish would have much use for gold coins, but he knew he might."

She laughed.

"That's how he lives. He'd never steal someone's wallet or their car, but if he works in a diamond mine, some diamonds go into his pocket. He says, 'Minerals come from the Earth, and no piece of the Earth really belongs to any one man. Men only rent space here.' "

"I bet his bosses, the landowners, feel differently."

Merrick shrugged. "You can't argue with an archangel."

"Why? Would he get violent?"

"No, he'd just get bored and fly away."

She laughed again. "So how much did he offer you and how did the trip go?"

"He offered me a sack. Of course, after living on the street and barely being able to pay my rent while bartending, I said, 'How big a sack? What will it be worth?' He sighed and said, 'How many gold coins and emeralds do you have now?' 'None.' 'So then what difference does it make? This will be more.' " Merrick smiled.

"I continued to harass him about it, trying to figure out if I'd be able to afford an Armani suit and an MP3 player, so he finally said, 'You can have as much as you can carry, and it'll be worth whatever people who want gold coins and emeralds will pay. Certainly enough to buy bread and clothes. Now drive before I decide to go with the wind instead of you.' "

She smiled. "To go with the wind? Meaning he'd fly?"

Merrick nodded. "I should've let him. Lysander's a musician, and sometimes he gets on a kick where he decides to be monogamous to one instrument and one composer. For five hundred miles, he played the same Vivaldi song on the violin."

She laughed out loud. "I love Vivaldi."

"That's because you've never listened to it for eight hours

straight. I tried to get the violin away from him, but you can't fight with an archangel in a moving car. Or in a car that isn't moving. Lysander said, 'You can choose the music on the drive home. If you survive.' I thought he was joking, meaning that if he didn't kill me before the trip was over. That's not what he meant."

"Oh, no. What then?" she asked, draining her glass.

"We drove around Omaha and the outskirts until he found the farm he was looking for, and he sent me into a barn, saying, 'Remember what I taught you, and you'll make it out.' "

She stared at him. "What was in the barn?"

"A demon with—I kid you not—a pitchfork."

"What was it doing? Baling hay?"

Merrick laughed. "Feeding on livestock. And humans."

"And Lysander sent you in to face it at sixteen?"

He nodded. "It was a lesser demon, and my training had to end sometime, but it was a bloody mess. I'm fast, but demons are faster and stronger."

"You were so young. You managed to kill it by yourself?"

He nodded.

"Was he proud of you?"

"Hard to say. He was sitting on top of the car, eating an orange. When I came out, he tossed me a towel to hold to my side where my kidney was sliced in half. All he said at first was, 'Good.' My knees buckled, there was blood pouring from the wound, and he put me in the car, adding, 'You've defeated a demon, Merrick. Something few men will ever do. It would be a shame to die in your moment of triumph, so don't.' "

"Good grief."

Merrick grinned. "I sweated through my clothes on the drive to the hospital while the car lurched over every bump in the road. And in a haze of pain and impending death, I heard him say, 'I dislike driving, Merrick. We'll stay in Nebraska until you're well enough to drive yourself back.' "

She shook her head incredulously. "No bags of gold or emeralds. Tricked into facing a demon that almost killed you. How are you still his friend?"

"Oh, there was gold, and he let me wait until I was

recovered to see how many sacks I could carry. Turns out I could carry a lot. And he was true to his word about letting me choose the music on the drive home."

She exhaled in exasperation. "How generous of him."

Merrick shrugged with a smile. "He also taught me to kill demons, which is a skill that's served me well. It's how I met you, remember?"

Chapter 25

Alissa had fallen asleep in Merrick's arms and woke in them. They were in the guest room that adjoined hers. She climbed carefully from the bed so she didn't wake him.

She had breakfast and worked all morning, but by one o'clock in the afternoon she knew they couldn't afford to leave much later, so she slipped into the room to rouse him.

Dragging him from sleep was more difficult than she expected, but when his eyes opened to slits and saw her, he pulled her head down to his for a kiss, then a slow smile formed.

"If I'm still dreaming, don't wake me." His fingers stroked through her hair to reach the back of her neck.

She kissed him once more, lightly, but resisted being pulled on top of him. "It's a long drive to the retreat center, and I need to arrive by five."

He rubbed his eyes.

"Think you can make it?" she teased, touching her fingertip to his forehead and pulling it away, then repeating the gesture a few times until he opened his eyes and cocked a brow.

"Unless you'd like to be teased in a much more interesting way, I suggest you cut that out."

With an expression of mock fear, she took a step back. "Come downstairs when you've showered and turned yourself into Len Mills."

To avoid distracting him, she left the room and descended for lunch. Merrick, efficient as ever, appeared twenty minutes later, dressed and ready, duffel in hand. She offered him tomato juice and food, but he shook his head.

"You need to eat something," she said gently.

"Unless you're on the menu, not interested."

Outside, he wore his dark sunglasses and sat in the passenger seat with it tilted slightly back. She drove them up the mountain, the sun and slopes breathtaking around every curve. She was looking forward to showing him the retreat center and to taking him on an excursion to her favorite place near it, a cave with glacial blue ice that she'd discovered and loved.

After a couple hours of uninterrupted silence, he straightened in his seat and retrieved something from his pocket. "Recognize this?"

"I'm driving in the outside lane of a mountain road where there's currently no shoulder, and, unlike you, I don't have superhuman reflexes."

"Here," he said, dropping the small object into her hand and taking the wheel. "I'll steer. You look."

She glanced in the rearview mirror. She hadn't seen anyone behind them the entire trip. The road was used solely as a route to the retreat center, and most of the guests were probably either already there or not coming until after five.

She stopped the car and put it into park. She lifted the small carved stone and froze.

"This is Phaedra's mark."

"Who's Phaedra?" he asked.

"A muse. An infamous one." Alissa brought the stone to her nose and thought she detected the smell of flowers and freshly cut grass. "Where did you get this?"

"Why is she infamous?"

"She had an aspirant who turned out to be a witch. This was a couple thousand years ago, so the accounts are speculative. Either Phaedra knew the girl was a witch and worked with her anyway, or the girl concealed that fact until she had what she wanted. They may have been lovers—or not. No one knows for certain. What is known is that the girl used

Phaedra's inspiration to create a spell that raised a demon. Being demonic, it killed villages full of people, including the witch. Phaedra, distraught, couldn't find a way to stop or bind it, so she walked off a cliff. The other muses she'd summoned to help found her broken body on the rocks."

"What happened to the demon?"

"Eventually it disappeared. No one knows."

"Lysander, maybe."

"Maybe. Anyway, all young muses learn about Phaedra's mistakes. Even if she wasn't aware at first that the girl was a witch, Phaedra should've recognized the danger of what the girl explored with the inspiration she was given. It's a cautionary tale for all muses. We aren't meant to be led. We must do the leading where our magic is concerned." She lifted the stone and inhaled. "It smells like something. Flowers and licorice and something cloying?"

"Demon ash sometimes smells like rotten licorice."

She turned it over in her palm and stilled at the sight of the tiny *H* etched on the bottom. The looping strands formed her mother's first initial exactly the way her mom had always written it. "Merrick, where did you find this?"

"I picked it up yesterday."

"Why didn't you show it to me yesterday?"

"You were late for the party."

It was the truth, but not all of it. His face gave away nothing, but intuition told her he held something back. If he'd been human, she would've known exactly what questions to ask, but with Merrick, it was like feeling her way down a dark hallway.

"Don't make me angry with you."

He quirked a brow.

"Unless I agree to it, don't conceal things that I have a right to know."

"Once I ask you whether you want to know something, you'll know it. No turning back."

"I want you to tell me about this. Everything about it. Where and how and when *exactly* did you find it? Was it in my house?"

"No."

"James." She stared into his eyes. "Please tell me," she said, infusing her voice with persuasive power.

He exhaled slowly. "You can't push me with your magic, Alissa. I feel when you try."

She rested the side of her head against her seat's headrest. "If you succumb to the push, it'll feel good," she said softly.

He stared at her mouth for a moment. "You don't need magic to get what you want from me."

"How about a bribe then?" she asked and leaned forward, brushing her lips over his.

He leaned back and shook his head. "Not for this." He licked his lips and swallowed. "I didn't want to tell you because I got it from Dimitri's safe."

"You said you didn't find anything."

"I implied that I didn't."

"Why?"

"Because you didn't want me to."

She sat back in her seat, understanding how she'd brought this on herself. "You're kind to me. You really are. I was wrong though to put you in a position where you had to protect me from the truth. If we're going to figure out what's going on, I need to know everything. No matter who's involved." She nodded to herself. "Promise me, no more secrets."

He shrugged, and she sighed.

"I know you don't want to hurt me, but whatever the truth is, in whatever form it comes, I can handle it."

"I never doubted that," he said. "But I came here to be your shield. Let me."

She reached out, but stopped before her fingers touched his face. She drew her hand back. "Don't get carried away by all this. It'll make it too painful when it's time for you to leave."

"Why do you assume you have to choose between keeping your life here and having whatever you want, including me?"

"Because that's reality," she said. He waited, and she frowned in frustration. "We could never keep it a secret. They'd find out about a real affair, and when they realized, they'd make me leave the Etherlin. My powers would weaken, and I'd lose my dad. I'm barely anchoring him to the world as it is."

"Maybe he'd be better away from the memories here."

"So he and I should do what? Leave the Etherlin and live in the Varden?"

"Not the Varden."

"But that's where you live. You're saying you'd leave the Varden?"

"Of course. I live there because you live here."

It was like a splash of cold water, shocking and unexpected. Could he be telling the truth? Had he really worked so hard to be near her when all she'd ever done was send him letters? Merrick didn't seem that romantic, but he certainly didn't seem like the kind of man to exaggerate his feelings either. In fact, he seemed like the kind to deny them altogether.

His confession should've worried her, but instead she felt strangely pleased. "Wow," she said. "You're a force with which to be reckoned on so many levels. You really shouldn't . . ."

"What?"

"Tempt me."

"I think that ship has already sailed." Everything from his wry amusement to the intensity of his gaze made her want to lean close, to kiss and touch and taste him until she'd had her fill, which might be never.

"Listen . . ." Her voice trailed off, and she cleared her throat. "I need to become Wreath Muse to save my father's life."

"I didn't know the Wreath had healing powers."

"In my dad's case, it does. When my mom died, the loss of that muse magic created a downward spiral that was dizzying. His wasn't normal grief. One day he was an even-keeled, if occasionally eccentric author; the next he was overcome with hallucinations and despair. The Wreath enhanced her magic, making it more potent, so its loss devastated his mind. Whenever I've worn the Wreath, he improves. That's why I need it. With steady exposure to magic fortified by the Wreath, he'll recover. And it's not only about him. Becoming Wreath Muse has been my life's pursuit. It's my connection to all the generations of North women, to that legacy. They wore the Wreath. It's what I'm meant to do."

"Are you happy?"

She swallowed hard. "Being a muse makes me happy. Yes."

"That's not what I mean. I'm not suggesting you stop inspiring your aspirants. I'm asking you if you're happy the rest of the time, living here with the scrutiny and speculation, under a mountain of rules."

Her breath shortened and her ears rang. Could she really even contemplate such a thing? Leaving the Etherlin? The possibility of a new life struck a frighteningly deep chord. Her mind reeled. "I barely know you."

"Leaving here isn't only about me. It's about you being able to breathe. A part of you wants me because of what I represent." He paused. "Freedom."

He wasn't wrong.

"I'm sure I seemed unhappy last night, but it's been an intense few months. Everything will get better when the competition ends, which it will tomorrow. Last night was an anomaly—"

"It's not about last night or the past few months. I've been reading your letters for five years. The truth about your life is there, between the lines. What makes you happier? Living here? Or being with me?"

She held out a hand to stop him and shook her head. "It certainly didn't make me happy to see Tobin's face, if you recall. This infatuation that we have for each other will pass. Basing decisions on how I feel right now would be short-sighted. My father, the Wreath, the Etherlin, they're my life."

"Your life so far," he said.

She shoved the door open and lurched out of the car, walking blindly away. She came to rest with her knees against the guardrail, staring out at the horizon. Was this how Phaedra had felt? So impossibly drawn by her attraction to someone that she'd wanted to throw caution to the wind?

Alissa set her hands on her head and felt the truth of her own soul unfold before her. A part of her had been suffocating for years, but admitting it just meant that she couldn't feign ignorance anymore. Denying how she felt had been her only refuge.

She heard the car door open and knew he was nearby.

I can meet someone else, someone who isn't ventala or a killer. I'll feel what I feel for Merrick with someone else. I just haven't met him yet. Not that she wanted anyone else. She wanted Merrick as much as her next breath sometimes.

"I have to use the Wreath to help my dad. I won't give up on him. I'd never be able to live with myself if I didn't see this through."

"That raises another question. I assume you'll be crowned, but what if you're not?"

She shrugged helplessly. "I'll make an appeal to whoever is the Wreath Muse. Once crowned, use of the Wreath will be at her discretion." She shook her head. "I wish I had a better relationship with the others, but the competition makes it hard."

"Where is the Wreath kept?"

She looked over her shoulder at him. "Are you suggesting what I think you are?"

"It would take some of the guesswork out of things. If you get what you deserve, great. If you don't, that doesn't have to be the end of it."

"They would hunt you to the ends of the earth."

"I'm aware."

She tilted her head. Was he joking?

"Of course, in that scenario, they'd be hunting us both," he continued. "On your own with the Wreath, you'd need a bodyguard."

"You think you're ready to make this job full-time and permanent now? That's very impulsive."

He shrugged with a shake of his head.

"It is! Of course, it is. You barely know me. You have no idea what I'm actually like. I could be a nightmare."

"I'll risk it."

They were silent for a moment.

"You don't know that it wouldn't be a terrible mistake."

"Sure, I do. I've known for five years. You gave yourself to me in those letters, and it made me want one thing."

She widened her eyes in question.

"More." There was no pleading or imploring in his tone. He wasn't trying to manipulate her into anything. It was the truth, delivered raw.

Emotionally fearless, she thought. *What is it like to live that way? And what would I risk to find out?*

There was a part of her—a large part—that desperately wanted more of him, too.

"Would you like another of my secrets?" she whispered.

"Always."

"Sometimes madness is contagious." She glanced at the deserted road. "You make me want to risk things, too." Turning, she rested her hands on his shoulders and slanted her mouth to his, warm lips against cooler ones. His arms closed around her, holding her against him.

She moved her lips along his jaw until her mouth was very near his ear. "There's only so much I'll ever be able to give you." His grip around her tightened. "We could have a real affair, but it would always be a secret. You'll never have all of me, no matter what you do. Can you live like that?"

"I already am," he said.

She exhaled, relaxing into his embrace. "All right, then, we'll have an affair and find out whether we were lucky to have that wall or not."

He answered her with a kiss, and she suspected if they hadn't already left the house for the retreat center, they might never have arrived.

During the last hour of their drive, Alissa grilled Merrick with questions. His responses were often laconic, but they opened the door on his enigmatic life. She learned about places he'd lived, books he'd enjoyed, and art he'd collected. She smiled at his casual confession that he and the Crimson bartender hosted a monthly dinner for the staff that was followed by games of poker and Halo, and that things sometimes deteriorated into challenges shouted loud enough to rattle the furniture. These arguments then led to rounds of sparring in the boxing ring that was part of the fitness center.

She shook her head, rolling her eyes. "Does every conflict in the Varden have to be settled with violence?"

"No," he said amiably. "Have you got a suggestion? A

needlepoint competition, maybe? The club can always use new pillows."

She laughed, picturing folksy additions to the Crimson's edgy décor. "That sounds like a good idea. Some cozy assassin expressions embroidered on them. 'A bullet in time saves nine.' Something like that work for you?"

He smirked.

She followed the narrowing road to the small gravel-covered parking area. There were several other cars and vans already parked. Her mood sobered.

"It's not much farther from here." She glanced around as she got out, her boots sinking into the powdery snow. The air was piercingly clean, but thin. "How do you feel? With your relative anemia, do you find it hard to breathe at these altitudes?"

He shook his head. "When I was a lot younger, Lysander had me help him carve a house into the top of a mountain. When you're ventala, and you work construction at eleven thousand feet for fourteen hours a day, your body either accommodates or collapses. After the first few days when I thought my heart was going to explode and my muscles were going to burst into flames, I got used to it."

"How did his house turn out?"

"Imagine if Michelangelo and the Mad Hatter designed the Bat Cave."

She laughed. "Explain that," she said, giving his arm a squeeze.

He opened the trunk and pulled out his bags. "The front juts out over a cliff, so in the living room you feel like you're going to free fall down the side of the mountain. There's an arched door on the roof, but most of the time he goes in and out through the enormous windows."

"Like Peter Pan."

He nodded. "There's a lot of wood and glass and exposed stone. He can create just about anything with raw materials. A throwback to his endless life. He's been a carpenter, a stone mason, a sculptor, and a lot of other things, apparently. The detail work defies description."

"It sounds incredible."

"He has a lot of time to kill between killing demons."

She smiled. "I was hoping you'd be impressed by the retreat center, but maybe you won't be. The Mad Hatter wasn't available, so we had to use architects and landscapers."

"How about ES? Were they consulted?"

She raised her eyebrows. "Of course. Why?"

"There's just the one road providing access up here?"

"Yes, but if there was a bad snowstorm while muses were in residence, we'd be perfectly fine waiting things out until the road could be cleared. We have our own cell tower and generators. There's fresh water, as well as a helipad."

His gaze swiveled from side to side as they climbed the stone steps.

"What is it?" she asked.

He shook his head, but she could tell he had more to say. She didn't press him with more questions for two reasons. The first was because she wanted to see his reaction to the retreat center. The buildings had lovely sloping curves painted in soft whites so they were in perfect harmony with their environment, and the generous use of windows allowed light to pass through many of the common areas unobstructed, adding to the communal sense of people in sync with each other and nature.

The other reason Alissa didn't ask Merrick questions was that as soon as they emerged from the wooded path, she spotted the two men in the Etherlin she could trust the least, Troy Rella and Theo Tobin, sitting together in deep conversation.

Chapter 26

He's going to regret not getting on a plane, Merrick thought when Alissa stiffened at the sight of Tobin sitting at a round stone table with Troy Rella.

"Don't forget I'm Mills," Merrick murmured to Alissa as the other two men watched them approach.

She didn't glance at Merrick, but the slight incline of her head acknowledged the warning. He needn't have worried. As always, in public she was grace under pressure.

Tobin rose from the bench seat with a word to Rella and hurried to the path. Merrick paused when Alissa did.

"Hey, Alissa. I need to talk to you. I found out something new since we talked last night," Tobin said.

She didn't answer at first, and when she did, her tone was frosty. "You seem to be really chatty lately, Mr. Tobin." Her gaze slid to Rella and then back to Tobin.

"Just a casual conversation about press photos," Tobin said quickly. "Listen, I've seen your itinerary. You're pretty booked up until dinner, but I'd like to get together after."

"It's a possibility," she said.

"Unless your schedule's too full," Merrick said. Mills wouldn't have interfered, and Merrick knew he should stay silent, but he didn't want her spending time with Tobin or staring at the guy's bruised face.

"You know, Mr. Tobin, I'd better see—"

Tobin stepped forward, and Merrick resisted the urge to shove him back.

Leave him, he warned himself. *Mills wouldn't overreact; if you do, it'll look suspicious. Besides, you don't want her seeing you get violent.*

Not ready to let it go, Tobin pressed on, and despite the fact that he whispered, Merrick heard what Tobin said. "They're interested in Phaedra's Legacy. They think it passed to your mother and you."

Phaedra again. That needs investigating, Merrick thought, watching Alissa's eyes widen.

"That's not possible," she said to Tobin, lowering her voice. "We're not descended from her line. She died childless."

Tobin shrugged and stepped back, saying in a normal voice, "There's definitely more to talk about. We can meet in the glass house, and I'll get some shots of you among the blooming flowers and plants. There's a security briefing, so we'll stay close. Hate to have ES getting twitchy." Tobin looked at Merrick, and after a moment, his head cocked. "No ES blazer? Easton won't like you being out of uniform." Tobin studied Merrick's eyes, which appraised him coolly. "I thought I knew all the ES guys who rotated on bodyguard detail for Miss North."

"Actually, this is Mr. Mills. He's a consultant."

"ES is using security consultants in the Etherlin?" Tobin asked.

Merrick forced himself to look away. Normally he never lost a stare down, but he recalled Victor's observation that his killer instinct was apparent in his eyes. Tobin's curiosity could prove dangerous.

Glancing at Rella didn't allow Merrick to relax. Rella's focus on Alissa was hawklike and hostile. Rage dripped into Merrick's veins, and he calculated the distance between them. He and Rella locked eyes, and Merrick saw something he recognized, a darkness.

Bring it, Merrick willed, but Rella kept his seat.

"I asked Mr. Mills to come," Alissa told Tobin. "He's been a valuable consultant on the West Coast, and I'm hoping to have a lot of travel in my future," she said. "I'll need a security officer with experience scouting and securing locations, and it will be convenient, once he knows my routine, for Mr. Mills to continue with me in the Etherlin as well. That's why he's here, to get some exposure to ES procedures in the Etherlin."

Merrick forced himself to look at Alissa. Serenely beautiful, she radiated control. He swallowed the urge to fight with Rella, a little surprised at the depth of that hunger. He was no stranger to violent impulses, but concern for a woman never provoked them. Until her. Everything had changed. He would have to deal with that.

"And will he be working for you or for the EC?" Tobin asked.

"Well, both of us. My interests always run parallel to those of the EC, Mr. Tobin. You know that," she said with a smile.

Smooth as satin.

"Sure, of course. I guess he's ex-military? Special Ops?"

"How did you know?"

"He's got that look to him."

It's in your interest and Alissa's for you to put Tobin at ease. But the easy charm Merrick often relied on would not come. Tobin had been party to Alissa's abuse, and now had the fucking gall to worm his way back into her life. *Destroy him,* the vampire instinct said, but the strategist in him quickly countered. *No. Would you risk being separated from her over Theo Tobin?*

"You can take the man out of training, but getting the training out of the man isn't as easy. Fortunately my skills have served me well in the private sector, too," Merrick said, forcing a friendly tone into his voice. "And speaking of a flexible skill set, you're obviously known for your candid shots of the muses, but I bet you're a good choice for shooting the retreat center. You've got a good eye for architectural aesthetics. I remember seeing some excellent pictures that you took of the Etherlin."

You didn't even choke on the words. Good job, he thought. *It's just like you were a famous enforcer once, instead of a guy too mesmerized by a girl to think straight. Plus, you've made an opening you can use. Now go get the name of the asshole who exploited her when she was a kid.*

Tobin nodded and smiled, acknowledging Merrick's compliment. "Thanks. Yes. Unfortunately, ES thought that was a security risk, so I don't shoot the muses' homes anymore."

Don't let the opening close. Get in there.

"I liked the way you composed your street shots," Merrick said. "There seemed an obvious hierarchy to the grandeur of the houses. The homes of the Etherlin Council members dwarf their neighbors' places. That council member you were talking to, Rella, his place was what, four stories?"

"Yeah, good memory, but he's actually one of the few. Most of the council members have large houses and estates, but not four stories. Rella inherited his grandmother's place and moved into it when he made the council."

"He looks young. How long ago did he join the council?"

"He was only twenty-three when he took the Rella seat about twelve years ago—"

Which would've made him twenty-four when she was fifteen. That fits. Now, who else is in the running with a four-story place?

"I'm so sorry to interrupt," Alissa said.

She sees where you're headed with this, Merrick thought, sorry his questions were about to be shut down, but not surprised she'd caught on quickly. He knew she was smart; it was one of the things about her that he liked most.

"We really should get settled in, Mr. Mills, so I can check my schedule," Alissa said.

"Of course," Merrick said with a quick glance back at the stone table. Rella was gone, but Merrick would catch up to him soon enough.

When they were out of Tobin's earshot, Alissa said, "You did a good job with the friendly bodyguard routine just now. Flattering the work of anyone who's creative goes a long way."

Merrick nodded.

"I had no idea you knew so much about Etherlin architecture. I thought I was the only thing in the Etherlin that interested you."

You are. He didn't answer. She was starting her own fishing expedition, and he was trying to decide whether he would let her have the truth about the fact that he was still after the name of the guy who'd exploited her.

"I'm surprised you remembered seeing pictures of everyone else's houses and decided to talk to Theo Tobin about them. What made you ask about Troy Rella's place?" she asked.

So she's coming after it, then. Despite Tobin, she's not afraid to challenge you. Good.

"Ileana Rella and her forebears are the muses of architecture. It wasn't a stretch to guess that Troy Rella would live in one of the biggest houses in the Etherlin," he said.

"Why did you ask when he got on the council?"

Merrick's gaze slid to Alissa's face, and he raised his brows slowly.

She stopped walking and glanced around before continuing in a low voice. "I asked you not to pursue that."

"You did, but threat assessment is part of being a good bodyguard."

"Right, so you're not going to act on the information? You're telling me that you're just gathering data?"

"You know," Merrick said, the corner of his mouth curving up. "If you want something tame, don't keep a lion for a pet."

"James," she said softly, making his pulse beat to the batting of her lashes.

"Don't try it," he said, but he didn't mean it. The pull of her voice made him want to give her anything that was in his power to give. *Fuck,* he thought, trying to steel himself against the urge. She was after another 'I won't kill a guy even though he hurt you' promise, and if he gave her that, he'd regret it later.

"James," she repeated, her voice a caress.

In the past, he'd never understood Samson or any of the men of history or legend who abandoned good judgment for the sake of a woman. He understood now.

He swallowed, and his muscles tightened reflexively. *She's five foot six and sweet as peaches. Are you going to let her bring you to your knees? What's next? A job as a florist?*

"People who hurt you aren't entitled to your protection, Alissa. I'm not going to let you tie my hands with promises."

"Do what you want," she said, her voice going as cool as the snowcaps. "If you'd risk bringing this relationship to an end before it really gets started, that's certainly your prerogative."

He clenched his jaw. He didn't like being threatened. But he liked the thought of losing her even less.

This is what it'll be with her. The better she knows you, the more intense the tug-of-war will become between what seems right to her and what feels right to you. Think you can handle that?

He should've followed the lead with Tobin when she wasn't around. Next time, he'd be more careful. Next time. He wanted a lot of those. "Extending the animal metaphors, I guess it doesn't make sense to fall for a dove and then expect her to be a vulture."

Her expression softened, twisting the arrow through his heart.

"I'm used to having to compromise, even when I shouldn't," she said. "I suspect you're not used to compromising, even when you should. Maybe we'll meet in the middle, and it'll be good for both of us."

Maybe, he thought, *but even if it doesn't turn out to be good, it won't matter.* After the kiss next to the guardrail, she could name the place; he'd meet her in the middle. He'd meet her anywhere.

Despite the tension when they'd first arrived, Alissa felt strangely elated to have Merrick nearby. He blended into the background, talking casually with ES officers during a series of staged photographs in various parts of the retreat center that featured her, Cerise, and Ileana.

When they finished, she completed the tour by taking him through the lounge area and into the private libraries and studies. She stopped in the main library to show him the portraits of the former muses, relating her favorite stories and memories of them, but she stopped when she recognized the antique walnut cabinet that had been in the Dome's library.

She hurried to it and tried the doors, unsurprised to find it locked.

"I've asked permission for full access to my mother's journals, but the EC hasn't granted it yet. When this cabinet was in the Dome, it held several original muse journals."

She rattled the handle, then looked over her shoulder at the corners of the room. "There are probably cameras."

"There are." He walked slowly around the room, seemingly to admire the portraits, but she knew he was evaluating the security, too.

When they left the room, she leaned her head close to him. "Do you think you could get into the cabinet without triggering an alarm?"

He nodded. "I'll see the layout of the security center at the after-dinner briefing."

"Which is when Tobin wants me to meet him. I thought I'd stall until you could come with me. I don't expect him to hurt me. Photographing me is a big part of how he makes his living. But maybe he's had a more lucrative offer. Your coming with me is assuming you're not too tired. It's been a long day, and I know this is when you usually sleep."

"I'm your bodyguard. I go where you go."

No response about whether he's tired, which he must be. He makes things so easy for me. She stopped in front of her door.

He opened it and stepped in, surveying the room. She closed the door and leaned against it, waiting. After a quick sweep, he returned to her.

"I hope it wasn't too awful—all that standing around, watching them set up the lighting and everything. Photo sessions are a lot more boring than people realize."

"Yeah, looking at you for a couple hours is a real hardship."

She set her palms against his chest, then moved one up to his cheek. "I miss your face. This new face is a great disguise, but it's such a tease. I've wanted to see you in the flesh for so many years. Now you're here, but you look like someone else."

Merrick glanced at the clock, then unbuttoned his shirt.

Speaking of making things easy for me . . .

"You don't have to do that."

Merrick lifted the medallion over his head and dropped it on the carpet. Suddenly, he was himself again, the handsome jaw stubbled with black whisker shadow and the eyes darker than night.

As her fingers traced his cheekbone, she exhaled slowly. This was the face she'd dreamt about. Her thumb rested just under his lower lip.

"If I kissed you, would we be late for dinner?"

"Let's find out," he said, reaching behind her to lock the door.

One kiss became two. Two kisses became many. They traded the wall for the bed, but before either of them was satisfied, the telephone's shrill ring interrupted. She grabbed his wrist to stop him touching her, so she could force her mind to clear.

She pulled away, breathless and laughing. "Hold on," she said.

"I'd like to," he murmured, which made her laugh again.

She put a finger to her lips to remind him to be quiet as she lifted the phone from its cradle.

"Hello?"

"Alissa, it's Dimitri."

She sat up straighter, moving her blouse to cover herself.

"Yes, Dimitri. Are you at the retreat center?"

"I am. Dorie just arrived." He paused. "She brought Richard."

Oh, God. Her blood plummeted with the shock, leaving her light-headed. From the corner of her eye, she spotted Merrick roll from the bed.

"She brought my father?" she echoed faintly, trying to concentrate despite the roaring sound in her ears and the dread rushing through her body.

"Yes. I convinced him to join me in the lounge where he'd be out of sight. You should come. He's not well."

"I'll be right there," she said and hung up. She put a hand to her head. All the precautions she'd taken to keep her dad out of sight until after the vote had been for nothing. Still reeling from shock and disappointment, she forced herself to stand and absently arrange her clothes. Dressed and back in his disguise, Merrick's fingers deftly redid the buttons he'd opened moments earlier.

She was grateful for his silence and for the efficiency with which he got them into the hallway. The lounge door appeared in front of her more quickly than she would've wished. She took a deeper breath and exhaled, pulling her shoulders back, a gladiator entering the arena.

In the lounge, her father busied himself in the kitchen area, making coffee, whistling the toreador song, and occasionally talking to an imaginary companion.

Dimitri, Cerise, and Dorie formed a tight trio at the room's center. Alissa heard bits of their conversation.

". . . to help you," Dorie said.

"I don't want that kind of help," Cerise hissed, and Alissa was grateful for that at least.

Spotting Alissa, Cerise strode over with a grim expression. "I'm sorry about this," she said, then she lowered her voice and tipped her head closer. "If you want to drive Richard home, I'll cover for you."

"It wouldn't matter," Alissa said. "I couldn't count on Dorie's discretion, and Dimitri can't deny what he's seen with his own eyes."

Cerise shrugged. "He'll find a way to help you. He always does."

Alissa blinked. Cerise's tone had been neutral, but the implication that she resented Dimitri's support of Alissa was evident. Would Cerise have been happier if Dimitri had abandoned Alissa like every other influential person had, including Cerise, in the immediate aftermath of her mom's death? Was Alissa supposed to have no one to turn to within the community?

"Good luck," Cerise said, and walked out of the lounge without returning to her family.

"Cerise!" Dorie called, hurrying after her.

"People call me the ice queen," Alissa said to Merrick softly, "but I'm a soft touch when it comes to the people I care about. Cerise, on the other hand, can hold a grudge forever. Dorie may be about to find that out." Alissa turned to her father, who was oblivious to all the drama.

Richard looked fit and handsome in his cable-knit sweater and jeans, with his recently trimmed hair neat and combed. To look at him, no one would've known how troubled he was.

Her dad approached, carrying two cups of coffee. He glanced to his left at an imaginary person and said, "I was not kidnapped. The girl tried to trick me by saying my daughter needed me, but I knew Andromeda was fine. Perseus was with her, after all." He turned to Merrick and held out a cup. "It's good Columbian coffee, but the machine's not great. Helene and I had our best cups of coffee when we lived in Spain for a year."

Merrick took a mug.

"Andromeda likes chicory coffee and beignets. You might take her to the Café du Monde in New Orleans. After you fight the Gorgon."

For heaven's sake, she thought.

"I'm her bodyguard. Between Gorgons, I'll go wherever she wants."

In spite of everything, that cheered her. Both Merrick's easy way with her dad and Merrick's rock-steady commitment to be with her no matter what happened. She smiled at him, and the corner of his mouth curved up. Her clamoring heart slowed, and the tension in her body eased a little. She'd done everything she could to control the situation with her dad, but now it was out of her hands. She tried to think of it as a step toward freedom from living a lie, despite the disastrous timing.

Her dad extended a mug to her. "Andromeda takes her coffee black."

"Like you," she said, taking the cup. She leaned forward and kissed his cheek. "Hi, Dad."

Dimitri, who had been watching the exchange, joined them. "This might not be the best place to have your coffee," he said to Alissa.

"No," Alissa agreed. "We'll go to my private study."

Her dad returned to the counter and filled a mug for himself, then he walked to the sofa in front of the fireplace and sat.

"Dad, this is a common area and might get loud. I'd love

to show you my private rooms. I've got a beautiful painting of Mom there."

"What about her journals? Did you find her missing journal?"

So he knew one of the journals was missing. Had he purposely started her looking for it?

"The EC has most of her journals and is keeping them safe," Dimitri said.

Her dad took a swallow of his coffee. "Keeping them safe from whom? Helene's writings belong to her daughter."

"You signed them over to the council," Dimitri said.

Alissa raised her brows. She hadn't known that they'd had her father sign anything. He certainly hadn't been competent enough to do that.

"I don't need her books. She is ever present, like salt in the ocean," her dad said. "You wanted to protect yourself, Dimitri. It didn't matter to me if you did. But now what was taken should be returned."

Dimitri rolled his eyes and looked at Alissa. "They wouldn't have been safe in his care. Helene's journals are an archive of her time as Wreath Muse. It would've been a problem if they'd been damaged or burned."

So Dimitri had been aware of her father's bouts of pyromania. Everyone seemed to know more than they'd revealed.

"I revoke my permission and transfer my signing power to Perseus."

Alissa gaped at her father, who winked at her.

"They bully you, Andromeda, but no knife to his throat will cow this Perseus. Let him help you retrieve what's yours."

"Richard seems to think you have a very close relationship with Mr. Mills," Dimitri said.

"He also thinks my name is Andromeda."

Unperturbed, her dad finished his coffee and turned to Merrick. "That which nourishes also destroys, but it's a magnificent destruction." He glanced at the ceiling, murmured something, and then lurched off the couch and slammed into the cabinet.

Alissa and Dimitri gasped. Dimitri grabbed Richard's arm, but as Alissa surged forward, Merrick drew her back.

"Let him," Merrick murmured near her ear.

Richard shoved Dimitri away and cracked the cabinet under his fist.

"Richard!" Dimitri snapped, dragging him back. "Stop this. You're not well. You'll hurt Alissa's chances for the Wreath!"

"Only a fool would deny her the Wreath, but then . . . we've been a company of fools, haven't we?" Her dad plucked a journal from the shelf, continuing to push Dimitri away. Richard opened it.

Merrick put a hand on Dimitri's arm. "Is it his wife's journal?"

Dimitri looked startled to have Merrick address him.

"Yes."

"Then why don't you let him and his daughter look at it? Seems like the mother's estate belongs to them unless her will said otherwise."

"A reduction," her dad announced and tossed it in the fire.

Alissa and Dimitri shouted, but Merrick moved lightning quick, retrieving the book from the flames before it caught fire.

Richard shook his head. "No need, Perseus." He walked to the counter and poured himself more coffee while Alissa and Dimitri recovered from their shock.

Dimitri turned and signaled to the corner of the room that everything was all right. Alissa glanced over, trying to spot the hidden security camera, but her attention was drawn back to her father when he spoke.

"It's not a bad forgery, but stripped of its secrets and her heart's blood, it won't be worth reading by anyone who knew her. Where is it?" Richard asked Dimitri. "Where have you hidden Helene's real diary?"

Chapter 27

Dimitri denied that the journal wasn't authentic, but Merrick could tell that Alissa wanted to dig deeper into things with the EC president. She asked Merrick to install Richard in the second room of the security suite next to hers, where Merrick was staying. Merrick didn't mind dealing with her father, but he didn't want to leave her alone in the lounge. Unfortunately, as Len Mills, he was supposed to be on her payroll, so he couldn't argue or ignore her instructions in front of Dimitri Xenakis.

In the room, Merrick set Richard's bags down. Despite the father's moments of pure madness, Merrick was inclined to believe that there was a problem with the journal. Why else would Xenakis and the Etherlin Council deny Alissa access to it?

Richard ignored the suitcases in the middle of the floor, not bothering to unpack. Instead, he sat on the couch with his messenger bag and retrieved a stack of manuscript pages from inside. He set the papers on his lap and slid a red pen behind his ear.

"I don't care that you're not what you seem," Richard said without looking up. "But they will. You should leave this place and take her with you."

"She won't go before the vote. She also wouldn't go without you," Merrick said.

"My wife is a muse. I belong to her and with her, in this life and the next."

"Your wife is dead. Your daughter's alive, and she needs you."

Richard's gaze went first to the ceiling and then lowered to rest on Merrick. "I'm a drowning man. She shouldn't wade in after me. This river is too deep."

"She believes she can rescue you."

Richard looked back down at his pages. "She should rescue herself."

Merrick's jaw tightened and he leaned forward. "Are you fighting her help, Richard? If so, you and I are going to have a problem."

Clear blue eyes rose to meet Merrick's. "No doubt your problems are just beginning, my friend."

Alissa flipped through the journal that was supposed to be her mother's. The handwriting looked very much like the way she remembered her mom's to have been. To discern if it was a forgery though, she'd need something she was sure her mother had written to do a side-by-side comparison.

She looked up to find Dimitri watching her. Setting the journal on the shelf, she turned to face him.

"There's a lot of mystery surrounding her death."

"It was a terrible tragedy."

"I thought for a while that you were keeping her papers from me because you were trying to protect me, but now I wonder if you were protecting yourself."

Dimitri's black brows drew together. "Your father sees conspiracies where there are none. He's clearly not in touch with the real world."

"He's generally lucid enough when it comes to her memory. It takes a bit of work to understand him at times, but there's a vein of truth that runs through the things he says."

"How could anyone spot it amongst the raving?"

"Practice." She paused. "He's not the only one who's told me there was more to the end of my mother's life than I realized." She leaned against the couch, studying him. "She spent a lot of late nights with you. I know that for certain."

Dimitri slid his hands into his trouser pockets and drew his shoulders back.

"Were you having an affair?"

"If we were, it's none of your business."

"It's my business if it led to her death."

"Helene was the most powerful muse in the world. She was phenomenally talented even before she was crowned Wreath Muse. She didn't always conform to conventional morality, so she occasionally had affairs, usually with her aspirants. But nothing as pedestrian as guilt over an affair would have caused her to commit suicide."

"Maybe my father killed her out of jealousy and made it look like suicide."

"Your father worshipped her. He didn't care about her affairs, as long as she lived and worked with him. He knew well enough that her passing infatuations with other men didn't last. He'd had twenty years of experience."

"I doubt Calla would've been so understanding. Maybe you had my mother killed to cover up the affair. Or Calla did out of jealousy. My mom's security detail was paid by the Etherlin Council, and you're in charge."

Dimitri choked out a laugh and raised his hands. "Can you really accuse me of such a thing? I've looked after you your whole life."

"If I can suspect my own father, I can suspect my surrogate one."

"No one murdered Helene."

"Then what happened to her? One minute she was happy, living a perfect life. The next she was desperately depressed and then dead. Something happened. What was it?"

Dimitri glanced to the corner and then drew her out of the room. "Let's enjoy the fresh air for a moment," he said, opening a door that led to a large patio. He sat on a bench and positioned himself so that his head was turned away from the security camera.

"Something did happen. Helene stumbled onto a memory

that caused us to investigate ancient lore, and we became convinced . . ." He shook his head, looking away. "If things had worked out, the discovery we hoped to make would've been of great benefit to mankind."

She thought about the stone with Phaedra's witch's symbol on it. It had been in Dimitri's safe. There was certainly potential for disaster where black magic was involved, but of course they would have both known that.

"Were you using black magic?"

His brows shot up. "Of course not," he said grimly.

"What were you—?"

"No," he said, holding out a hand to ward off her questions. "I'll never tell you or anyone else the details. It was her dying wish to have it concealed, to protect future generations from making the same mistake."

"I wouldn't do anything dangerous."

Dimitri shook his head vigorously. "I've told you all I can. I want you to know that she loved you and Richard. She loved this community and lost her life in service to mankind. She was my very dear friend, and I miss her every day."

"I don't understand why she would've chosen suicide if she loved everyone so much."

"Despair is a terrible thing."

"Despair over what? Over a mistake in the way she used her magic? Did someone get hurt or die because of something she did?"

Dimitri clasped Alissa's hands, holding them tight. "No one was hurt other than Helene."

"No one but me. And my father. And all her aspirants who never wrote again. She hurt a lot of people, actually, by leaving."

He sighed. "She dedicated her life to inspiring the talented. If she'd had a choice, she would never have done anything to harm them. And, of course, she never wanted to hurt you or Richard. You were precious to her."

"Why was I lied to? I was told that she was depressed for weeks and refused to meet with the council, but I know that's not true. She had a meeting at the Dome right before she died," Alissa said, following her instincts. "My father was so worried about it that he went along and waited while she met with them."

Dimitri nodded. "Helene was headstrong. The council felt she was recklessly pursuing knowledge that should have remained buried."

"About Phaedra?"

Dimitri held up a finger to warn her not to go too far.

"Why lie about the meeting?"

"We didn't want anyone looking into what she'd been doing before her death. Muses can experience intense passions and emotional swings when they become very involved with their aspirants, so that was the cover story."

"I want to know the truth. All of it. The wondering is like a hole inside me."

Dimitri took her face in his large hands and tipped it up. "I can't break my promise to her, and I wouldn't want to. I've spent the years since she died trying to protect you. I know that if she'd lived, you would've been Wreath Muse, and I've tried to help you achieve that status, at times ostracizing Cerise and my wife in the process. Do you think it's been easy for my family to see me favor you?"

"No. I realize now how much it's upset them, but you've helped Cerise, too."

Dimitri shrugged and let go of Alissa's face. "I'm faithful to causes that are just. Helene and I were ambitious, and we made a mistake together. She died because of that mistake. As the one left behind, I've been a father to her daughter. She would've done the same for Cerise and Dorie if I'd died instead of her." He glanced away to the clouds and nodded. "I honor her memory. You should do the same."

"Do you think I haven't tried to do exactly that?"

"In the past yes, but now you seem restless. I suppose managing Richard alone has taken its toll. You should've confided in me."

"But you'll have to report what you know to the council, and that will ruin my chances for the Wreath."

"To some it will be more proof that you could become unstable, but others will see it as I do, that you were strong enough to take care of a sick father while still exceeding every expectation we had for you and maintaining a pristine image. That should count for something, and it will."

"Maybe," she said.

Dimitri embraced her briefly and stood. "We need to change for dinner. I'll see you there."

Alissa stood, too, but spent a long time watching the sunset before she left the lounge. Seeing people in the hall who seemed to already know about her dad's condition frustrated and upset her.

Inside her room, she didn't take a dinner dress from her closet or retouch her makeup. Instead she paced, pausing occasionally to straighten things that didn't need straightening. When Merrick tapped on the door, she drew him inside.

"Thank you for getting him settled. He seems more comfortable with you than most people."

"He thinks we're kindred souls. He also thinks that now that I'm here to take care of you, any responsibility he had is gone."

She waved off the remark. "That's nothing new. I love him, but he hasn't taken care of me or himself for a long time," she said. She pushed her hair back from her face and held it at the nape of her neck. "Word traveled fast. I passed a couple of council members in the hall. They wouldn't make eye contact with me."

"I'm sorry."

"And Dimitri's hiding something. After the vote's over, I'm going to push him to tell me more about the days leading up to my mother's death. Tobin said the ventala syndicate thought Phaedra passed something on to my mother and me. I believe that my mother may have researched Phaedra's life and memories, but I haven't. Could the Jacobis be looking for the stone you found in Dimitri's safe? Could they want it and believe that I have it? And if they're trying to acquire it, why? Do they want to use it to raise a demon?" She walked to her makeup case and took out the stone. "It doesn't look old enough to have come from Phaedra's time."

"No, it's not worn enough."

Alissa dropped it back into the case and began pacing

again. "I've tried calling Tobin to move up the meeting, but he must have already gone to dinner."

"Speaking of dinner," Merrick said, nodding at the clock.

"You go. I don't feel like walking in late to a million whispers, and I don't feel like pretending that everything is fine." She fluffed the couch's throw pillows. "I also don't want to hover around my dad, fretting like I'm five minutes from a breakdown myself." She paused and shook her head. "He shouldn't be here," she said angrily. "But there isn't time to drive him back without missing a bunch of obligations, and what would be the point anyway?" she asked, arranging the pillows by color, then rearranging them by size.

"I apologize," she said, finally looking at Merrick. "I'm out of sorts. Please go to dinner. I'm not fit for company."

"Unless you think it'll make the tongue-wagging worse, I'll stay."

"Let them talk. If they suspect that we're having an affair, it'll likely sit better than the alternative, namely that I preferred to use my own security detail rather than ES."

"Are you hungry? They can send a tray for you, right?"

"I'm not hungry. I'll have something later. You know what I really want right now?"

"Tell me."

"To lock the door and just sit here with you. Talking. Or not talking. I don't care."

Merrick locked the door and took off his jacket, setting it on the back of the desk chair. Before he reached the couch, she held out a hand to stop him.

"One more favor?"

"The medallion?" he asked.

She nodded. He slid his tie off and draped it over the suit coat. He unbuttoned a couple of buttons and divested himself of the medallion, leaving it on the desk.

He sat sideways on the couch, so they faced each other. She studied him.

"You have more than a five-o'clock shadow now."

"It's later than five o'clock."

"It suits you," she said, running a finger over his jaw. "And having you here suits me, surprisingly." She traced her fingertip over his lower lip. "And not so surprisingly." Touching him caused an immediate shift in her thoughts. His magnetism and the jolt of their ever-present chemistry pulled her out of her turmoil and into the vortex of attraction that was always present between them. "Will you feel totally used if I take advantage of you to distract myself?"

"Absolutely," he said, mock affronted.

She moved closer to him. "Then you'd better stop me," she whispered, unbuttoning his shirt.

"Yeah, I'll do that," he said in a husky voice.

She quirked an eyebrow as she spread his shirt open. "Gorgeous," she murmured. Her palms slid over his chest. His hands rested at his sides, unmoving, as she unfastened his belt and slid it from his trousers. She set the belt aside and waited a moment, but he still didn't move. He only watched her with his characteristic intensity.

She rose from the couch and unbuttoned her shirt. "Are you planning to just sit there?" she asked, shrugging off the blouse to expose her scalloped lace camisole. "Letting me do all the work?"

"You're doing fine so far," he said, his low voice as smooth as a caress. "The part where I work is coming up."

She smiled and unzipped her skirt, letting it fall. It puddled on the floor, a halo of silky fabric around her feet. The cool air kissed her skin, raising gooseflesh. His dark gaze drank her in.

She stepped forward and knelt on the carpet at his feet. Her fingers stroked his lower abs and traced the path of his dark hair as it trailed down. She liked touching him, liked being so close. She unbuttoned his pants and ran a fingertip over his zipper. His muscles tightened, but his stillness reigned.

She watched his face through her lashes as she lowered the zipper. Darker than smoke, his gaze scorched her and their eyes locked. The corners of her mouth curved up as his cock jutted free of the fabric. He wanted her, but she would have him first. All that restrained power, the glint of danger just below the surface threatened, yet she knew she could do whatever she wanted.

You want what I represent, he'd said. Freedom.

Truer words were never spoken. And she intended to enjoy this freedom, to enjoy him, until nothing else in the world mattered.

She lowered her eyes as she leaned forward.

Every inch of him is beautiful. His father might have been a monster, but he'd given Merrick one gift. The preternatural perfection of the vampires. She closed her fingers around the base of him and licked the shaft then took it into her mouth. His muscles went rigid, and he exhaled hard. A drop of fluid salted her tongue.

Yes, he's mine, she thought and sucked as she bent forward, taking him deep.

Christ, Merrick thought. He had the most beautiful girl in the world, an Etherlin muse, on her knees servicing him. The plan had been for him to worship her body, not the other way around, but there was no arguing with those lips. She sucked like an angel, her soft, wet mouth a tight vortex around him.

He fought the building urgency. His hand cupped the back of her head to slow the rhythm, but she wasn't having the change of pace. Her small hands took hold of his wrists. She raised her face, licking her lips tantalizingly, and trapped him with cool blue eyes.

"Am I still doing fine so far?" she asked in a teasing voice that was pure sex.

He nodded.

"Then don't interfere."

He quirked a brow, but tugged his arms free and put his hands behind his head, tipping it back against the cushions so he could stare at the ceiling. "Have me however you want because when you're done that's how I plan to have you."

He felt her shiver, but her bold voice didn't betray nervousness. "When I'm done," she said, "you may not have enough energy to do anything at all."

His laugh was a low rumble. "Alissa, I've waited five years for tonight. No matter what you do or how well you do it, once is never going to be enough for me."

"Let's see you prove it," she whispered, her hot breath

tempting against his skin. He closed his eyes as Alissa drew him once more into the magic of her mouth.

Merrick didn't resist the driving pace she set, even though he would've liked for the experience to go on and on. There would be a lot more to savor soon, he thought as his pulse pounded. She'd questioned his stamina—had challenged him for a reason. She'd given him license to play games with her and he would. He'd enjoy it and would make sure she did, too.

He groaned and without thinking, he reached for her head. He caught himself before he touched her silky hair and yanked the hand back. He pinned it behind his neck, pressing his head against the couch cushion as he thrust.

Fuck, that feels amazing.

The surprises with Alissa never ended. He'd expected to find her pretty innocent; he thought he'd have to teach her how to enjoy her own body and his, but she was never what she seemed. She was always better.

His muscles clenched, his balls tightened, and he erupted.

She leaned back to catch her breath with her bright eyes alight like blue flames, and she said, "Now I want you naked."

"What a coincidence," he murmured, his heart just beginning to slow to a normal rate.

"Undress for me."

He released his hands from behind his neck and stretched his arms. He raised his head so he and Alissa could lock eyes.

"It's interesting how you think you're in charge," he said. He shook his head slowly, meaningfully.

He flexed his biceps, and she caught the movement, glancing at them.

Yeah, sweetheart, my arms are at least twice the size of yours, and they want something to do during the next round.

She set her hands on his thighs and pushed off them to stand. She was such a gorgeous vision in her pale lace underwear.

"You can't deny that you enjoyed me taking charge."

"Why would I deny it?" he asked, standing. He shrugged off his shirt and tossed it aside, never taking his eyes off her lithe body. He stripped to the skin in quick fluid movements then picked her up without breaking stride and took her to the bed.

Her fingers caught the hem of her camisole, but he stayed the movement with a shake of his head.

"I thought I'd help. As nice as it would be, we don't have all night," she said.

A part of her is still afraid of me. She wants to feel like she's directing things.

That didn't suit Merrick. If she were in control, she might try to hold back some part of herself. He wanted all of her.

I'm going to touch and taste every inch of you, and I'm going to take my time.

"People may interrupt—"

I dare them to try, he thought as he kissed her. He let darkness leak into his voice when he said, "The rest of the world can go to hell."

Alissa blinked, her cheeks flushing beautifully. He lowered his body next to hers and noted the scent of vanilla and muse blood and arousal perfuming the air. His gaze fixed on where the white cream of her breasts swelled over the top of the camisole's lace.

"James?"

"What?" he asked.

"Promise me one thing," she whispered, her voice soft and sweet and full of persuasive magic that didn't have a prayer of controlling the lust that raged inside him.

"Don't bite me hard enough to leave scars."

The ruthless vampire side of him wanted nothing to do with any promises of restraint. It wanted blood and sex, preferably at the same time. But there was another part of him that could never get enough of this girl and her letters. He wouldn't hurt her tonight and forfeit all the other nights he might have with her in the future.

His hand cupped her breast and pinched her nipple, slowly applying more pressure until her body arched and her pupils dilated in pained excitement.

"No biting deep enough to leave scars? That's all you'd bar me from doing?" His wicked smile made her lick her lips nervously. "You're going to have to learn how to negotiate."

He pulled the lace down to expose her nipple, now tight and dusky pink. His lips closed around it, and her fingers slid into his hair, beckoning him closer. He sucked the tip of her breast into his mouth.

"What would be the point of learning to better negotiate? Would you have allowed me to lay down a lot of rules?" she asked breathlessly.

He raised his face a few inches, studying the pink tint his mouth had left on her pale skin. *Strawberries and cream.* Her body's response to him would be a feast for every one of his senses.

"Rules?" he murmured, shaking his head. His gaze slid momentarily to her exquisite face. "If you want something tame, don't keep a lion for a pet."

Her fingers tugged his hair absently. "I don't want something tame. I want you."

"That's convenient since you're going to have me," Merrick said and bent his head again.

Increasingly warm and hungry for him, Alissa tried to tease Merrick into satisfying her quickly, but his infamous control continued. It was excruciating and delicious.

With one leg slung over his shoulder and her other knee pushed out by his strong hand, he spread her open and plundered her with his mouth. Licking and thrusting his tongue inside like he wanted to swallow every last drop of her, he brought her to orgasm, but never let her rest.

When they were completely nude and lying against each other, still tasting skin and exploring hidden hollows of tingling flesh, she forgot everything except what she needed from him. He made her wait, pinning her restless body, teasing her until she whispered begging words in his ear. Ruthlessly unwilling to finish, he brought her to the brink over and over until it was almost unbearable. She raked her nails down his back.

His hands slid over her ass and squeezed. "Finally a peach."

"Merrick," she rasped, half groaning, half growling a warning as he explored her creases.

When she was panting and writhing and would have promised him anything, including the last drop of her blood, he finally covered her with his body and sheathed himself inside her slick heat.

Cool and hard as stone, he thrust slow and deep, then fast and hard, riding her body through several mind-shattering orgasms.

He might be hers, she reflected afterward, but she belonged to him, too. And if anyone ever wondered why a woman might fall for a bad-to-the-bone ventala, they would only need to spend a night with Merrick to understand in vivid detail.

She lay spent for a while, her mind blissfully blank of anything but the aftershocks of so much amazing sex. Her muscles were warm and loose. Her flesh tingled and throbbed. Her entire body felt soft and sore and sated.

Eventually, she propped herself up on an elbow and looked him over. "Well, that wasn't smart," she said.

He didn't bother to open his eyes. "No?"

"I count two bite marks and six scratches on you, and I can't even see your back. I may have drawn blood."

"You may have," he said, his voice sexy and satisfied.

"Maybe next time, you won't tease me so long."

"Or maybe next time I'll tie your wrists to the headboard." She laughed softly and pressed her thumb against the corner of his mouth, which was curved into a wicked smirk. "Sure, if I'm too much for you to handle, but there goes your reputation." She bent forward and kissed his neck, then climbed from the bed.

"Where are you going, baby?" he asked.

"To shower. You rest."

She was only under the warm water for a couple minutes before he joined her.

"I thought I locked that door," she murmured.

"You did." He poured some shower gel into his hands and lathered her shoulders and back. She didn't pull away from his strong fingers, and her muscles thanked her for it.

When she turned and slid her slick hands over his body, the shower turned much longer than she'd intended.

Afterward, they dried and dressed in a silence as soft as the sheets.

She dropped a couple ice cubes from the ice bucket into a tumbler, added scotch, and squeezed some fresh lime that she'd asked the staff to stock in the small fridge.

She took a sip, then handed him the glass. After a couple swallows, he set the glass on the nightstand. She picked it up and took another sip, glancing at the clock for the second time in ten minutes.

"Tobin?" he asked.

She nodded. "I can go alone."

He retrieved the glass and swallowed the rest of the scotch and gave her another slow kiss. "We both know I'm coming with you." He put the medallion on, transforming again. He stretched his muscles before buttoning his shirt. "You want to check on your dad before we meet Tobin?" he asked.

"No, afterward is fine." She put her arms around his neck and kissed him, licking the scotch and lime juice from his lips. When she leaned back, his mouth chased hers and prolonged the kiss for a couple more minutes. It would be so easy to fall back into bed with him. At the moment, that was the only thing she really wanted to do.

"Later," she said with a smile as she extracted herself. "I need to hear what Theo Tobin has to say."

They finished dressing in a companionable silence, but she felt the intensity of his gaze on her.

Once they were outside on their way to the glass house, Alissa shivered. It had already been cold, and the temperature had dropped farther. Alissa burrowed her left hand deeper into her pocket for warmth while holding the rail with her gloved right hand. She glanced at Merrick, but he didn't seem bothered by the cold. She followed the winding cobbled steps upward. She could see the lit glass house at the top, sparkling like a jewel box.

Her foot caught on a step and she stumbled. Merrick grabbed and steadied her.

"Thanks," she said, pulling herself toward the rail. Her right foot caught again on something that wasn't stone. "James," she murmured, pressing the toe of her right boot gingerly on the obstacle.

With one arm around her waist, he moved her to a lower step behind him and turned on a small flashlight.

"Oh!" she gasped when she realized that what she'd tripped over was a pale stubby arm. Merrick leaned forward and spread some bushes apart to reveal Theo Tobin's lifeless face.

Chapter 28

Tamberi Jacobi had woken after surgery and insisted on being taken home immediately. Lying in her own California king bed with morphine dripping steadily into her vein, she felt light and cheerfully homicidal.

Cato sat next to her bed with maps opened over his lap.

"Hold them up so I can see them."

"Why the hell do you need to see them?" he growled.

She smiled. He was still furious that she'd been so badly wounded.

"C'mon," she said.

"No, you lie there and enjoy your buzz. We're going to have to find this place without you now, so I've gotta friggin concentrate."

"Told you what the demon tells," she slurred. "The girl will know the way by instinct. And without her, there's no point going. So if you can't find it after you touch down, make her show you. Bring the maps, and let's walk through the plan again. You're reviewing anyway. I may as well . . . may as well help."

"Yeah, you'll be a big help," he scoffed, but he grabbed the papers and sat next to her on the bed.

"Hope your boots are clean."

"Filthy," he said with a teasing grin.

"Push that downer—down arrow on the morphine drip. I need to focus."

He glanced at the pump and shook his head.

"C'mon! I can't reach it myself, and my head's spinning like a top."

"You'll be in pain."

"I've had my guts ripped open and put back together. I'm supposed to be in goddamned pain." She giggled. "Fuck. That's not supposed to be funny. Push that button."

He pressed the down arrow twice and then leaned back and spread the map open in front of them.

"Here's where we'll land," he said, pointing. "It's less than ten minutes to the meeting spot where he'll have the girl waiting."

"He'd better."

"If he doesn't, we'll go get her."

"And make sure there are no witnesses."

"I friggin know. Anyone who sees anything dies." He pointed. "We've got this ridge, so there's no way for anyone to get behind us, but we've got to be careful here because—"

"I think I'll come."

"What?"

"I can be on the helicopter. What difference does it make if I sit here or if I sit on the copter?"

"You're on a friggin morphine pump."

"We'll bring it."

"You're a goddamn lunatic, you know that?"

"Take that Sharpie marker and draw a bull's-eye on the wall, then give me your gun. If I can hit the center, I get to come. If I miss, I'll stay here."

"Tamberi, for fuck's sake."

"C'mon. You know you want me to come with you, and I don't want to miss a black ops trip into the Etherlin. Or the chance to see the opening! This was my goddamned plan."

"Then you shouldn't have let Merrick almost gut you."

"That bastard. I am going to cut out his heart before I cut off his head."

"Not if I get to him first."

Tamberi gave her brother's arm a squeeze. "Go on," she husked. "Go draw the bull's-eye."

* * *

Tobin's glassy eyes stared at them.

"He's dead," Alissa said breathlessly. "He must have fallen," she said, looking up the cobbled stairs. They'd been salted, so she hadn't found them slippery. "Or maybe someone pushed him."

Merrick skimmed the beam of light over the surrounding area, then he bent and patted the body, coming up with a cell phone. He pressed several buttons, eyes scanning, then he pocketed the cell. He clicked off the flashlight, plunging them back into darkness.

"Do you think he fell?" Alissa asked.

"No," Merrick whispered. "His body would've landed on the other side of the path if he'd slipped and fallen. There are scuff marks in the dirt where someone rubbed out his boot prints after dragging the body into the bushes. Follow me down," he said.

She stiffened, straining to hear any sounds, like the footfalls of a killer, but silence settled around them. She kept a palm on Merrick's back and moved as he did, carefully, quietly.

They were near the bottom when she heard voices and trampling feet hurrying toward the steps. Four beams of light bobbed around the path's curve. She paused, but Merrick continued.

"Mills," he said, announcing himself. "Escorting Miss North back to her suite." The beams swiveled up to Merrick's face. "I assume you're looking for the victim. He's twenty-four steps up. In the brush to the right of the path."

"Hang on, Mills," Grant said. "Alissa, are you all right? What were you doing here?"

She hesitated. "Theo Tobin asked me to meet him. We were on our way to the glass house when I tripped over his—body."

"Does your father have any reason to be angry at Theo Tobin? Has he done anything, taken any pictures, that would've upset your father?" Grant asked.

"What? No, my dad's had very little contact with the outside world until Dorie brought him here. Why do you ask?"

"Your father came to tell me about the body. There was a blood-covered rock in his pocket with bits of hair on it."

Her jaw dropped. "He had no reason to hurt Theo Tobin." *That I know of.*

"Do me a favor," Grant said. "Go to the central security office and wait for me there. You, too, Mills."

"Is my dad there?"

"Yes."

"This way, Miss North," Merrick said, nodding his head in the direction of the main building.

"Yes, okay," she said, cutting a path between the officers. Close behind her, Merrick was silent as a grave. She looked back twice to make sure he was still there.

When they were a few feet from the door, she heard something light hit the dirt to her right. She started to turn, but a hand on her back pressed her forward.

"Tobin's cell. We never had it or saw it."

"You looked at the messages. Were there any calls from the room that you and my father are staying in?"

"No, but I recognized one of the last texts Tobin sent. It was to Cato Jacobi's number at the syndicate. Tobin said that he was in, all the muses were here, and that he suspected that I was here, too, in disguise."

"He was working for the ventala?"

"So it seems."

"Do you think my dad killed him?"

"I don't know, but Tobin said he was in and warned them I was inside, too. The syndicate may be planning to take you from here. If they came from the northwest by helicopter, they wouldn't have to go over Etherlin airspace. They could land on the road or the helipad. The security detail here isn't like it is in the Etherlin. And the Jacobis may have another inside man. I don't think Tobin's the one who drove your car out the night you were drugged, because he called the Crimson to let me know he was coming through my territory. He had to know I'd ask questions, and he would've suspected that I'd come after you in the Jacobi territory. If he'd been in on their plan from the beginning, why would he have called me? I think Tobin was pulled in after the fact."

She looked around at the darkness, half expecting someone to lurch out of the bushes. "Well, the person who drugged me certainly wasn't my dad. He'd never knowingly hurt me, and he's not organized enough in his thinking to carry out some complex plot involving black magic."

"Agreed," Merrick said.

"The person who drugged me is probably the one who killed Tobin."

Merrick nodded. "Listen, if they interrogate you and tell you they know who I am, you're to say that you had no idea. You thought you were having a relationship with Mills."

"Why would they—Oh, we have to assume the other inside man knows from Tobin or Jacobi that you're here and could've told ES."

He nodded. "I paid Mills a lot of money to be off the grid for a few weeks, but ES isn't new to security. Mills turns up out of the blue as your new bodyguard. Merrick is missing from the Varden. Tobin is dead after just being on the other side of the wall. ES will dig."

Icy panic slithered down her spine at the thought of Merrick being caught in the Etherlin. "Then you should leave now. My father and I will go as soon as we've had a chance to talk with Grant. He can assign us a security detail for home."

"Remember what I said. No matter what they say, don't let them rattle you. As far as you know, I'm Mills, and that's what you answer every time they ask."

"I heard you. Now you hear me. I want you to take the car and go. I'll be fine here. They'll arrange my transportation down the mountain. I'll contact you as soon as it's safe."

Merrick leaned forward so that his mouth was close to her ear. "No."

"Don't you dare argue with me about this. It's just as dangerous for you here as it is for me."

"I'm the bodyguard, remember? I stay on the mountain until you're off."

"You were never just a bodyguard. I care about you."

He kissed her neck just below her ear, and his mouth lingered. Drawn in by the intimacy, she pressed close, inhaling his scent.

When he finally stepped back, the cold nipped at her nose and cheeks, a sharp reminder of where they were.

"If you want to help us, be the ice queen. If you act nervous or anxious, they'll think you're hiding something, and they'll keep you here until they've opened you up. Stay calm."

"I can handle myself. I don't need you to stay. In fact, I'll be better focused if I know you're gone and I don't have to worry about you."

He gripped her upper arms tightly. It didn't hurt, but it got her attention, quieting all the thoughts racing through her head. "Alissa, pay attention. Nothing anyone says or does will make me leave you here alone. Accept that and work from there."

"Why won't you leave, James?" she asked softly.

"You know why."

Her heart thumped, and she stared at his face, waiting.

"If something happens to you, I won't care that I got away," he said, then paused, staring down into her eyes. "If you don't come, I can't go."

Yes, emotionally fearless. She blinked away her tears and slid her arms around his neck. After pressing a kiss to the side of his face, she whispered, "All right. We stay together."

Chapter 29

Central security occupied a bigger area than Alissa had realized. She and Merrick were ushered into an interrogation room. The security officer who led them through the outer area into the back was friendly and apologetic toward her. He offered them drinks. When they declined, the young officer turned to her.

"You missed dinner, Miss North. The kitchen is sending a plate of the grilled salmon for you. Director Easton said to have them send one for Mr. Mills as well, so it's on the way."

"Mr. Easton said that my father was the one who discovered Mr. Tobin's body. May we see him?"

"I can take you to see him. Mr. Mills, would you have a seat here please? It shouldn't be much longer before someone's free to talk to you about what you saw."

"I'll stay with her," Merrick said.

"No, sir," the young man said, stepping forward to block Merrick's way. "Please have a seat."

Merrick's expression hardened. "Someone died under suspicious circumstances. As Miss North's bodyguard, I should stay with her."

A pair of officers entered the room swiftly. Alissa's gaze darted from them back to Merrick, but he remained perfectly still.

Stay calm. Merrick won't lose control.

"Mr. Mills," the young officer said. "Etherlin Security will be taking over Miss North's personal security until the conclusion of the investigation. You didn't have advanced clearance to be at the center. I'm sure you understand our need to be cautious." He gestured to a nearby chair. "We appreciate your cooperation."

Her heart thumped harder in her chest. Merrick didn't argue, but he didn't sit either. The intensity of his cool gaze on the security officers seemed to make them nervous because she noticed them widening their stances, fingering their weapons.

"Is the other interrogation room nearby?" Alissa asked, using her television interview voice, pleasant, upbeat. She didn't want to leave Merrick, but her instincts told her that if she stayed for them to fight over, things between ES and Merrick would escalate.

"Your dad's just down the hall," the young officer said.

Alissa forced a smile. "Lead the way." To Merrick, she added, "I'm sorry about this, Mr. Mills. I'm sure they'll sort everything out quickly. I'll be right back."

"It's no problem," Merrick said evenly.

As Alissa followed the officer, she heard one of the others say, "May we see your weapons, Mr. Mills?"

Damn it!

Alissa fought not to react. She held her breath, but she didn't hear Merrick refuse.

As they walked down the hall, they passed a lounge where Cerise, Ileana, Dorie, and Troy sat on couches. The flat-screen television played videos while they chatted and sipped gourmet coffee.

Dorie looked up, a curious expression alight on her pretty face, then a slow smile formed, shaping Dorie's mouth into a slight sneer. Alissa's heart beat faster, and she frowned. How had she not realized sooner what a bitch Dorie had become?

You're made of ice. Nothing penetrates. Alissa inhaled deeply and exhaled slowly. *Everything slides off without leaving a trace.*

The officer opened the door, and she found another ES man in the middle of fingerprinting her father.

Merrick had been sitting alone in the interrogation room for about twenty minutes. When the door opened, he smelled musky jasmine perfume and knew his visitor wasn't Alissa or more security officers. He glanced over as Dorie Xenakis sashayed in.

"Hi," she said, setting a soda down on the table in front of him. "I thought you might be thirsty."

"Thanks," he said, making no move to take the can.

"You and Alissa missed dinner," she said, sitting in the chair next to him.

This was a good sign. If they'd let another muse come in to talk to him, they must not suspect him of being a ventala. Of course, she might have slipped in on her own. She seemed to be good at taking initiative.

"Right?" she asked, nodding at the untouched plates of food.

"We didn't have dinner."

"Was Alissa upset?" she asked, leaning closer to him. When he didn't answer, she continued. "She's been lying to everyone about her father. I understand why. She thought if the council knew, they wouldn't give her the Wreath. But it would've been better if she'd just been honest, since they found out anyway."

Thanks to you, Merrick thought as a wave of cold fury rolled through him. He regretted the setting. There was nothing he could do to put a scare into her while under the watchful eye of Etherlin Security.

He stared silently at Dorie.

How far would you go to keep Alissa from getting the Wreath? Would you arrange for her to be taken by the syndicate? Maybe someone will show you the other side of the wall sometime.

Dorie stretched out her arm and fingered his watch. "Omega? It's beautiful."

Merrick left his arm flat on the table, watching her without answering. What was she up to?

"With everything that's happened, I'm sure that Cerise is going to be Wreath Muse now, and I bet Alissa won't be traveling much for a while." She rubbed the face of his watch with her fingertip. "You're with that security firm in California, huh? I guess you'll be helping with security for us when we travel there. Do you eat at the café across the street? What's the name of it?"

Testing me. "Pesce."

"I like the patio. It's really nice."

"Pesce is closed."

"Oh. That's too bad," she said, tracing the space between his fingers. "But times change. Maybe something new and better will move in." She looked up at him with doe eyes. "You have nice hands. Big."

The better to choke you with.

"People are saying that you and Alissa are involved. Is that true?"

"How is that your business?"

She smiled and went back to tracing the space between his fingers, moving her finger closer, so that it ran along his. "It could be," she whispered. "I'm more fun than she is. Guys in a position to know have said so." She glanced up and licked her lips. "You're interesting."

You have no idea how interesting I could become if you piss me off enough.

Dorie moved her hands under the table, and he expected to feel them on him the next second. He contemplated his reaction, from doing nothing to shoving her chair back hard enough to tip her onto her treacherous ass. But seconds passed, and she didn't touch him. Instead, she slid her chair a little farther away.

Blood.

Hunger roared through him. Rich, pure muse blood scented the air. His nostrils flared and his jaw dipped open, upper lips retracting. The involuntary response was strong. He snapped his mouth closed and clenched his teeth. His fangs descended, but with the glamour and his lips closed, they wouldn't be seen.

His senses heightened, the predator rising. He wanted to sink his teeth into her.

She brought her hands back onto the table. A drop of crimson welled on the tip of her finger.

"Pricked my finger on a thorn this morning. It keeps bleeding."

She extended her finger toward him, watching his eyes.

He moved his hand to the corner of the table, bracing himself against the urge to grab her.

"I wonder . . ." she murmured, standing up. "My sister, Cerise, and I met Len Mills in California. He was crazy for seafood," she said, glancing at the untouched plate of salmon. "Went deep-sea fishing every weekend he wasn't working. Raved about the restaurant across the street. Definitely didn't smell like magic." She looked Merrick up and down. "But you do."

He narrowed his eyes.

She sucked the blood off her fingertip. "You have a secret," she whispered. "If you do what I ask, I'll keep it for you . . . Mr. Merrick."

Chapter 30

"I don't want to go anywhere," Alissa's dad said, rearranging his manuscript pages for the fifth time. "I'm getting a better signal here than ever. Helene's communicating with me by satellite. It goes directly into my brain. It must be the altitude. Less cloud coverage and interference."

"It's not satellite transmissions from the afterlife, Dad. All four of the most powerful muses on Earth are in the retreat center, along with the Wreath. You're feeling concentrated magic. It reminds you of Mom."

"Andromeda, why are you here when you should be stealing fire from heaven?"

Stealing fire? A reference to the Prometheus myth?

"Heed Paddleford's advice. Never grow a wishbone, daughter, where your backbone ought to be. Make your choice. And if you choose anything over love, you're not the woman I wish you were."

She arched a brow at this simple, childlike perspective. If she succumbed to his suggestion of pursuing love at any cost, what would happen to him? He didn't seem to recognize that he might end up in a small padded room without windows if she stopped protecting him. Cut off from his books and her mother's memory, he'd spiral downward into misery. He'd done it before, and she'd had to rescue him. *So many times.*

"I don't have the luxury of only worrying about myself," she said, but he didn't acknowledge the remark. Instead, he glanced at the wall and nodded to the empty space as if it spoke to him.

"You're right, of course. The opening scene drags. I'm going to move the night march to the beginning and cut—"

"Dad, what were you doing outside tonight?" she asked impatiently.

"Tonight?"

"You were outside earlier. That's what they told me."

"Was I?" He paused. "That was tonight? Yes, I was working on a scene in the Bosnian woods, and I decided to stand outside without gloves to allow my hands to experience the cold. When I felt I had enough sensory details, I went up to the glass greenhouse to jot down some notes. On the way, I heard a noise. I thought it was an animal, and I wanted to see it, to watch the way it moved in the snow. My foot kicked the rock, and I picked it up. Warm and bloody. I didn't expect to stumble on a freshly dead body. Shocking," he said. "Really horrifying. Imagine how Sasha feels when he's staring at Irina's brother's body in the mass grave . . . terrible. Excuse me. I need to make some more notes," he said, and bent over his pages, scribbling furiously in the margins.

Alissa stared at her father. She wasn't even sure that he remembered who Theo Tobin was.

"Did you see anyone other than the dead man, Dad? Did you see the person who hurt him?"

Someone outside the room screamed. Alissa's head jerked toward the door as the screams continued. The security officers leapt from their seats, and she followed in their wake.

"Lock it down!" someone shouted. "Now! Now!"

Dorie stood in the hall surrounded by ES officers. Her blouse's torn shoulder gaped open, and she held it in place as she spoke frantically through occasional sobs.

"What's happening?" Alissa demanded, pushing into the circle.

"—bite me," Dorie said, tears dripping from round eyes.

No!

"Where?" Alissa said sharply, grabbing Dorie's hand and pulling it away from her throat and shoulder.

"Stop," Dorie snapped, yanking herself back from Alissa. "It's your fault."

Alissa recoiled, the shock and guilt slicing like a knife.

"It's your fault for bringing him here."

Alissa stepped back, her gaze sweeping over Dorie. There was no blood, no wound.

There's no bite. He didn't bite her! Alissa's hammering pulse slowed. *She's a lying little bitch.*

"Where are you bitten?" Alissa asked coolly.

"I didn't say he bit me. I said he tried to bite me. He's a filthy ventala." She broke down again, sobbing. The security officers fawned over her, and so did Troy and Ileana.

"Cerise!" Dorie said, launching herself at her sister as she approached. Cerise hugged the girl, who was the picture of fragility.

"What's going on?" Cerise asked.

Alissa walked away from them to the door of the large interrogation room. She pulled the handle, but the door wouldn't budge.

"Miss North, can you come with me?" an officer said.

"Let's look at the footage. There's a security camera in the room, right?" Alissa asked.

"He threatened me! He tried to bite me!" Dorie said shrilly.

A few moments of noisy chaos ensued. Alissa resisted being ushered back to the interrogation room with her father. Instead, she insisted on being taken into the control room to see the surveillance file.

"Something's wrong. It looks like—"

"What?" Alissa demanded.

"Somehow, the feed from that room wasn't being recorded."

"Convenient," Alissa said, folding her arms across her chest.

Dorie sniffed. "I told you what happened. Cerise, you said—you said he seemed different. That's why. He's under a glamour."

"That's ridiculous," Alissa said. "You misunderstood what happened. Or you're purposely trying to deceive us. Maybe in another attempt to sabotage my bid for the Wreath. Like kidnapping my father and bringing him here."

"Kidnapping!" Dorie scoffed. "You said he was fine, then you left him home. I thought you didn't know families were welcome. I brought him so he could be part of the festivities."

"Sure, and you didn't notice anything amiss? You didn't tell him I was in trouble to lure him into your car?"

Dorie glared at her. "You said he was fine. You lied."

"His condition waxes and wanes. It's near the anniversary of my mother's death, which is always a tough time for us. What I said was that he's writing again."

"He's completely crazy!"

"Is he writing again? Did he bring his manuscript to the retreat center? I bet he edited pages the entire drive."

"Don't try and twist things," Dorie said.

"I'm not the one twisting things." Alissa turned to security officers. "Unlock the door to the interrogation room. I want to hear Mr. Mills's side of the story."

"What's going on?" Grant asked as he walked into the central post.

It took a few minutes for Dorie to repeat her story. Alissa walked to the console and watched as Grant flicked on the camera.

Merrick, in the Mills guise, sat in a chair, legs stretched out in front of him, arms folded across his chest.

"There," Alissa said. "Does that look like someone who just attacked a teenage girl?"

"No, but actually, Alissa, he looks too calm. He must've heard the commotion in the hall and the doors lock."

Alissa lowered her voice. "Listen, Grant, I know she's lying."

"I am not lying!"

"You are."

"You weren't there," Grant said.

"Exactly. She doesn't know what happened," Dorie said.

"I know this much. Other than a torn blouse, there isn't a mark on her. I saw Merrick slay a demon in 2007. I witnessed a ventala attack at Handyrock's less than forty-eight hours ago. Ventala are blindingly fast, incredibly strong. If that man in there was ventala and he'd wanted to bite her, she would have been *bitten*. Period."

Dorie blushed. "He threatened and attacked me. He reacted to my blood. I'm telling you, Grant, he's not human."

"What blood?"

"I cut myself on a rose thorn earlier, and while I was talking to him, it started to bleed again."

"Just like that? It started to bleed again? Or with a little help from you?" Alissa demanded, rolling her eyes. She would not let Dorie get Merrick arrested. "Open the door, Grant."

"Open the door to the observation area only," Grant said to one of the security officers stationed at the desk.

Alissa fell in step behind him.

"No, you can watch from here, Alissa. I'm going to talk to Mills alone."

"He's my bodyguard. I'd like to come."

Grant stopped. "This is an ES matter. Your preference doesn't enter into it."

"Grant," she said imploringly.

He jerked filter earplugs from his pocket and put them in his ear canals, a precaution against her using her power to persuade him. Not a good sign.

"You heard what I said, Alissa. You wait here."

When Grant Easton came into the observation area, Merrick got up and tried the door. It was still locked. The reinforced steel had a silver overlay. Strong. Heavy. The sort of door that even a ventala couldn't break through. An interesting choice for a retreat center that was supposed to be remote and completely secure.

"Mr. Mills," Easton said.

"How are Richard and Alissa North?"

"They're fine. I was surprised to find that you'd been involved in an altercation."

"An altercation?" Merrick shook his head.

"What happened with Dorie Xenakis?"

"She talked and left."

"You didn't try to prevent her from leaving?"

"No."

"You didn't touch her?"

Merrick shook his head.

Grant leaned closer to the thick glass that separated the observation room from the interrogation room. "She says you did."

Merrick shrugged.

"We have sensors here that pick up magical energy. You set them off. What magic are you using?"

"A protection spell."

"Contained in an amulet or charm?"

"Magic's not outlawed."

"That depends on what you use it for."

"You know what is illegal? Detaining someone without cause," Merrick said.

"I have cause. Dorie Xenakis has accused you of assault."

"So arrest me."

Grant clenched his jaws.

"I didn't think so," Merrick said. "The girl's a liar. She's lucky she's a kid, or I'd see her in court. Now, open the door."

"Let me examine the magical object you're wearing."

"Link it to a crime."

"There are plenty of judges who will give me a court order based on what I have right now. A dead body. An accusation by a muse. An outsider who snuck into the Etherlin without ES clearance. I reviewed the checkpoint logs, and there's no record of you entering the Etherlin. If Alissa North didn't bring you through, how did you get in?"

"Have you finished questioning Alissa and Richard North?"

"Not your concern."

"I have reason to believe she's in danger. You can hold them at ES main headquarters in the Etherlin without compromising the investigation. And if you send them down the mountain, I'll be more cooperative."

"No one's going anywhere until things are sorted out."

"Then I should add that if you don't send them down the mountain, I'll be less cooperative."

"Meaning?"

Merrick walked away from the glass divider and sat down.

Easton leaned forward, lowering his voice. "I've spoken to Len Mills dozens of times. You're not him."

Merrick didn't answer.

"If you're ventala, you might as well get used to being in a locked box, because when I prove it, a cage is where you'll spend the rest of your life—which actually won't be that long."

"If you waste your night trying to break me and something happens to Alissa North, you and I are going to have a serious problem."

"Stop running your mouth about Alissa North. She is not now, nor will she ever again be, your responsibility."

Merrick turned his head slowly and locked eyes with Grant Easton. The stare was brutal enough to bludgeon a weak man. Easton blinked, but didn't step back.

"Do your job then. Protect her, Easton. Like your life depends on it."

"Jesus," one of the officers at the console said.

Alissa's heart pounded. *He is going to get himself killed.*

Everyone in the room stared at the screen, watching as Merrick leaned back in his chair. Her mind raced until it settled on one thought with perfect clarity. Even with his amazing control, Merrick would not be able to conceal who he was for much longer. He'd been under the thumb of the ultimate brutal authority figure as a child. That struggle to survive had shaped him. His whole identity had been built on his ability to absorb pressure without breaking under its force and on a need to openly defy anyone who tried to control him.

Grant burst into the room, pointing his finger at Alissa. "Did you know?"

"Know what?" she asked. "That Len Mills was tough, ex-military, and intimidating? I did suspect. I assumed that's why you contracted with his firm."

"You don't actually think he's Len Mills," Troy snapped.

"Of course I do," she said.

"Why does he want you off the mountain so badly?" Troy demanded. "He's obviously infatuated with you and—"

"Can ventala become infatuated?" Dorie asked. "They're animals."

Alissa glared at her.

"We'll find out what he is in the morning," Grant said. "Merrick is half vampire. When the sun rises, he'll slide into a comalike sleep. Then we'll go in and take off whatever magical objects he's wearing and see what we're left with."

No! Alissa felt ill and swallowed hard against the urge to be sick. She had to get him out of there.

"In the meantime," Grant continued, "the muses will stay together in the lounge. Troy, you take them there and stay with them. ES has a lot of work to do tonight."

"I want to talk to him," Alissa said.

"Absolutely not! Let's be clear about one thing, Alissa," Grant said. "Whoever or whatever he is, he's never getting near you again."

Cerise grimaced. Troy nodded. And Dorie smiled.

Chapter 31

The lounge was quickly arranged to accommodate Troy and the muses. Under ES supervision, the staff swept in, assembled temporary beds, covered them with fresh linens, and left a tray of drinks and snacks, baskets of toiletries, and sleepwear. The staff wanted to make a return visit to bring vases of flowers and some candles to "warm the space," but ES politely rejected the request.

Alissa sat in the corner, watching the activity, only half aware. The Wreath was lost to her now, but she was numb to that fact. Merrick's life hung in the balance. Alissa had to get her father and Merrick out of their interrogation rooms and away from the retreat center. It was all she could think about.

Concentrate. There has to be a way.

Grant and many of the ES officers were investigating the site of Tobin's murder, which allowed her a window of opportunity during which ES presence in the main building would be scarce.

What if Dad resists leaving? If you manage to free Merrick from the room, but Dad draws ES's attention during the escape . . . Merrick will be the one who pays the most for any mistakes.

As the others speculated about Tobin's death, Alissa went into the bathroom to be alone to think. A few moments after she'd left the lounge, the door opened and Cerise entered, her face grim and concerned.

"You okay?" Cerise asked.

Alissa shook her head, the urgency she felt spilling out. "Did you see what Grant was taking from the case when we left the security center? V3 ammunition. They aren't going to arrest Mills. They're going to execute him."

"If that's Merrick, then he's a syndicate assassin. He probably deserves whatever happens."

"Merrick saved my life twice."

Silence descended, then Cerise said, "I didn't know your dad was so sick. I'm sorry about that."

"Would it have mattered? You seem determined to hold a grudge forever."

Cerise shook her head.

"Look," Alissa said, "you were always the best dancer. When you auditioned, no one could take their eyes off you. I knew you should've gotten the lead."

"But I didn't look the part."

Alissa waved that away. "When they gave it to me, and you asked me to give it up, I should have. But Madame Joyce told me that we'd both be in trouble with the council if we defied their wishes. I was afraid of them."

"The council does love having its way and making us dance, even now," Cerise said, and rebellious energy flowed from her. Alissa absorbed it, thinking that she needed to act like an aspirant, to draw in creative energy and let it inspire her, to imagine the possibilities for getting Merrick and her dad off the mountain. She needed the Wreath.

"I told you I was sorry. You knew I regretted it. Why couldn't you forgive me for one mistake that I made when I was eleven years old?" Alissa demanded.

"I did forgive you. I just couldn't be your friend anymore."

Alissa stilled. She stared at Cerise's face. "Why not?"

"Because I couldn't watch you get everything I wanted for the rest of my life. I'm strong, but no one's that strong."

"How can you say— You're so gorgeous, so charismatic, so talented. What is it that I have that you don't?"

"Them," Cerise said, waving a hand toward the wall. "All

the most important ones. I had the worst crush on Troy when we were fifteen. He treated me like a kid while he flirted with you and snuck you into places the rest of us only dreamed of getting into. We were all crazy about Grant, and he chose you. Even my own father is in love with you."

"That's not true."

"C'mon. He'd obsessed with getting you the Wreath."

"He treats me like a daughter out of loyalty to my mom."

"His reasons don't actually matter to me. When I was ugly and awkward—"

"You were never ugly!"

"From eight to twelve, I was. There are pictures to prove it."

"Cerise—"

"Listen, I don't care. I grew into my looks. What I'm saying is that I could've used some reassurance from him. It would've been nice if he'd told me a few lies to boost my confidence. I do it for my aspirants. I'm sure you do, too."

"Of course."

"Now he wants to be close, but it's too late. I don't need his approval anymore."

"I'm sorry that you feel I came between you guys. I never intended for that to happen. I just needed a father, and he was there to fill the role. Maybe if you and I had been close, I wouldn't have needed him so much."

Cerise shrugged. "By the time I was secure enough in myself to be your friend, you'd moved on."

"What do you mean?"

"You changed. You became distant."

"That isn't true. As we got older, the circle around you became huge, and we were competing for the Wreath. You, Dorie, Troy, and Ileana were all friends. I couldn't reach out to you anymore. It was too painful."

Cerise frowned and shook her head. "You never said. You never let on that you still cared about being friends."

"Didn't I? Maybe not. I keep a lot of things bottled inside." Until him. Alissa glanced at the door. She needed to get moving.

"Things can be different," Cerise said. "Don't ruin your life, Liss, by doing something reckless over some guy who's obsessed with you. There will be another one along in five minutes. Let the man—or whatever he is—go. He got himself into this mess; let him deal with the consequences. You've earned the Wreath. You can still salvage things."

Alissa swallowed hard. "I hope that things will work out, but—"

"My dad and Grant and others will help you unless they suspect that you're knowingly involved with a ventala."

"If I don't get the Wreath, you will. I need you to promise me something."

"What?"

"If I'm not in the Etherlin and my dad is, I need you to watch over him."

"You'll be here. No matter who gets the Wreath, this is your home."

"Please promise me that you'll help my father."

"Ask me for something hard," Cerise said.

"I—What?"

"When we were little, your dad told me I would grow up to be a beautiful warrior queen. I thought he was crazy, but I hoarded those compliments like a stash of diamonds." Cerise smiled. "Your dad was such a great and charming liar during my ballerina-troll years, God love him. I'll never forget that. If he ever needs my protection, he has it."

Alissa smiled, her eyes burning with unshed tears. She swallowed, blinking them away, and gave Cerise's arm a squeeze. "Thank you."

"Come out and watch a movie with us. It'll probably be a comedy. I'm sure Troy's been outvoted."

"I won't be able to concentrate. I'm going to check on what's happening with my dad and Len Mills."

"You want me to come with you?" Cerise asked, which made Alissa tear up again. Seeing Alissa overcome with emotion, Cerise stepped forward. When Cerise hugged her, Alissa didn't want to let go.

"Thank you so much for the offer, but it's better if you keep your distance from me during all of this," Alissa said, dabbing her eyes until they were dry.

Cerise puckered her lips in distaste, then grinned. "Don't

worry about me. They need us more than we need them, and I'm not afraid to show them I know it." She shrugged her brows.

Alissa answered, and the truth was a relief. "Me either."

Alissa and Cerise returned to the lounge and found the lights dimmed. The others reclined on the couches as Alissa walked around the edge of the room to the door.

"Where are you going, Alissa? We're supposed to stay here," Dorie said.

"Mind your own business," Cerise said.

Alissa ignored Dorie and left. She saw three armed ES officers in the hall outside the large interrogation room that held Merrick. She wondered what they were doing there.

As she entered the control center, the lone ES officer looked at her, then back down at the monitor that showed the door and hall.

Alissa walked to the monitor that should've shown the inside of Merrick's room. The screen was black as tar. "He disabled the cameras?"

The officer glanced at her again. "Yeah. The ones in the room and the ones in the vents. It only took him five and a half minutes. We sent a guy in to stop him, but—"

"But?"

"The officer got a shot off, but that's it. We don't know if our man's alive or dead or how badly wounded Mills is because the cameras are out."

A fresh wave of fear rolled her belly. If Merrick had killed an innocent ES officer who was only doing his duty, there would be no saving him. Eventually, he would be brought to trial, and no one would believe that Merrick had acted in self-defense, even if he had. She wondered fleetingly if he was wounded, but set that concern aside. She couldn't let herself be overcome with fear or doubt. If she was going to see him through this initial jeopardy, she had to be as cool under pressure as he had been when he'd saved her life.

She walked to the manual she'd seen when she'd been in the room earlier. The retreat center had just opened, so they were still relying on their operation manuals.

If you want him out, you're going to have to make it happen.

"Director Easton?" the young officer said into a walkie-talkie.

"Yes?" Grant's voice crackled through the static.

Alissa found the section she was looking for and quietly opened the binder to the pages with the access codes.

"Should I call the Etherlin for backup?"

"And let rumors spread that we allowed a ventala to infiltrate the muses' retreat center on launch weekend? Absolutely not. There are fourteen of us and one of him. If he manages somehow to get out of that locked-down room, we'll be waiting for him with dozens of full V3 clips," Grant said.

"Yes, sir."

Alissa held her breath as she opened the binder's rings.

"Check on the status of the murder investigation. If the body has been moved to the secure location, have the rest of ES return to the center for new assignments," Grant said.

"Yes, sir."

Alissa folded the pages and slipped them inside her shirt.

"Are the muses asleep in the lounge?"

She turned quickly to block the officer's view of the binder, and reached behind her to close it.

"Miss North is here. The others are in the lounge, but not asleep," he said, glancing at her.

She schooled her features, hoping that her expression didn't show any traces of guilt.

"She needs to return to the lounge immediately. No one should be in the control center with you. Have Miss North's father locked down in his interrogation room so that we can free the officer who's with him for other duties, and call back a couple of ES officers right now to stand guard in the lounge. Their instructions are to keep the muses there for their own protection until I say otherwise."

Alissa cringed inwardly. She needed freedom of movement.

"Tell them to put in the filter earplugs, and you put some in, too. I'm sure the muses wouldn't misuse their magic, but under the current circumstances, ES needs to take every precaution."

Damn it!

Alissa hurried to the doorway, but by the time she got into the hall, the officers there were already putting in their earplugs.

She nodded at them. "I'll see myself back to the lounge," she said, knowing she'd be watched on the monitors the entire way.

"Mills, stop what you're doing," the bound ES officer said. "You're going to get yourself killed. Sit down and think this through. So far you're the only one who's injured. This can still be resolved without loss of life or prison time."

Merrick ignored him. The security officer was cuffed to a chair that was tipped back against the wall. Any attempt by the officer to right the chair and get his feet on the ground would allow Merrick plenty of time to subdue him.

Merrick slammed the butt of the gun repeatedly into the plasterboard, raining debris onto the floor. Once Merrick had the frame exposed where the door hinges were screwed in, he could disrupt the frame and take the door out of the doorway. The door that led from the hall into the observation area was not made of steel, nor was the frame reinforced. When he reached it, he could kick it open.

"They're in the hallway just outside the outer door. Even if you do manage to breach the hall, they will put you down."

Merrick's leg throbbed from the tourniquet. He bent and untied the strip of fabric he'd secured around his thigh. As blood circulated to his lower leg, it created sharp pins-and-needles pain. He moved his foot up and down to speed the return of flow and normal feeling. After a minute, he widened the hole in his trousers to examine the bullet wound. It was dry and almost healed, but that had cost him. The craving for blood had started, and the need to feed was becoming a distraction.

He rolled his shoulders to keep his muscles loose. This had always been a possibility. He'd fed deeply before entering the Etherlin, but the shoulder wound had bled so much, plus he'd forced himself to stay awake for so many daylight hours. Now a second blood loss from the through-and-through gun-shot wound to the thigh was taking its toll.

He resisted the urge to drink from the officer in the corner for two reasons. First, because male blood wouldn't satisfy the thirst for long and, more important, because it would come at the price of being able to deny who he was. There would be no way to claim the man imprisoned in the interrogation room had been Len Mills once Merrick dropped the glamour to feed.

Of course, the likelihood of getting off the mountain with the glamour intact was becoming more and more remote. He would try. For Alissa's sake. He ran a hand through his hair and exhaled slowly, returning to the plasterboard. As he worked, her words echoed through his mind.

Dear Mr. Merrick,

I learned yesterday morning that an anonymous donation has been made to the county hospital in an odd amount. The amount happens to be my birth date. I wonder if you keep your philanthropy a secret out of concern that your fearsome reputation would be compromised, or if you keep it a secret to protect someone other than yourself. If the latter, I appreciate your discretion.

There's something alluring about a private dialogue carried out in letters and gifts, in the form of books and flowers, donations and poems, don't you think? I hold our secret correspondence as close to me as my own skin . . . or deeper, since skin can be seen by the naked eye.

I was moved by your generosity to the hospital. Thank you for that and for this continued unconventional con-versation. I enjoy it more than I ever imagined I would.

AN

Merrick rested a hand on the steel door. After discovering Tobin's body, he could have gone through the woods to the parking lot and driven down the mountain. He also could have prevented himself from being shut into the interrogation room once he'd seen the door and its reinforced frame.

Self-preservation had demanded a single course of action: escape. But he couldn't go. Merrick, the legendary lone wolf, had fallen in love. Alissa didn't need to make him any promises. There would be no negotiations or discussions, no contracts or vows. He loved her, and he would do what love required. Whatever it required. Until he could do no more.

At the moment, he just wanted to get to her, to satisfy himself that she was all right, because with every second that ticked by, time seemed to be running out.

"Mills, listen," the security officer droned on.

Merrick looked over his shoulder at the man and pierced him with a hard look. "A tie makes an effective gag, but it's uncomfortable."

The man fell silent. Merrick turned back to the frame, raising the butt of the gun. He slammed it against the wall, peppering the floor and his clothes with the pulverized plaster.

Another two or three hours, he estimated, until he reached the outer door.

Chapter 32

Only a few hours until the sun rises.

"It's been a long night. Everyone needs his rest," Alissa whispered into the room, exhaling magic on her breath. It wouldn't affect the muses, but at least Troy, who kept looking over at her, fell asleep.

The ES guards, too, looked exhausted. They were leaning back in their chairs as she passed them on her way into the bathroom. As quietly as possible, she moved the velvet-cushioned bench away from the vanity mirror and counter. She unlatched the window, stepped onto the bench, and climbed outside.

She clamped down on her lip as the shocking cold swallowed her calves. The snow had drifted along the building, and it soaked her pants.

Alissa hurried toward the Wreath building, her heart thumping. Even if the officer in the control room hadn't seen her yet on the monitors, she knew the cameras would capture her and record what she did when she reached the door.

She clenched her teeth, the weight of her actions pressing down on her. She would never be able to go back, and if she couldn't get Merrick out, she would lose him anyway. This would cost Alissa her life in the Etherlin, and possibly her dad. Would it feel worth it if she didn't save Merrick?

Don't grow a wishbone where your backbone should be.

Her throat tightened, and memories of Merrick crowded

her mind, the shared secrets, the feel of his muscles under her fingertips, the intoxication of having him nearby. Longing gripped her, and she suddenly realized what her dad had meant when he'd said she should be stealing fire. It was a Delphine de Girardin quote.

To love one who loves you, to admire one who admires you, in a word, to be the idol of one's idol, is exceeding the limit of human joy; it is stealing fire from heaven.

She closed her eyes briefly, the hurricane force of her dad's passion galvanizing her resolve.

Yes, Dad, I am your daughter.

She stepped under the light that illuminated the door's landing, not lowering her eyes. She placed her palm on the pad and then keyed in the code. The door slid open. She walked inside, glancing at the muses in the portraits whose gazes seemed to follow her down the hall.

The center room was the shape of a hexagon, and Alissa's shoes clicked against the parquet floor. During the day, light streamed in through the bay windows, but at night there were only a few recessed lights in the ceiling shining on the center pedestal. Under faceted glass, the Wreath waited. Strands of gold and bronze formed interwoven twigs and delicate leaves, which were dotted with emeralds and peridots.

Alissa bent in front of the column that held the Wreath and dipped her hand inside her shirt. She extracted the folded pages and smoothed them. Her fingers trembled as she entered the multistep code.

With the final numbers, letters, and symbols entered, she waited. A soft whoosh of air, like someone exhaling, emerged from the case as the front glass pane opened. A shimmer of magic emanated from the Wreath.

She extracted it with care. Tipping her chin up so her hair flowed back to leave her forehead bare, she lowered the Wreath until it ringed her head like a crown.

"He came here to protect me," she whispered. "Inspire me now to do the same for him."

Ways to help Merrick didn't surface. Instead, a rush of images assaulted Alissa's mind, making her muscles contract and her joints lock.

She saw Phaedra among megalithic stones, bound hand and foot. Her aspirant, a freckled witch, spoke words as she scored Phaedra's hand, causing blood to pool in Phaedra's cupped palm. Tears spilled from Phaedra's wide eyes, and the witch tipped Phaedra's wrist, raining blood onto the ground as she said, "With a muse's blood, I command you to open." The witch shoved a small stone in the dirt and turned it like a key. A seam between worlds split, and darkness poured through it.

Alissa gasped as she was plunged into an oily, sulfurous fog. The witch hadn't just used Phaedra's inspiration to raise a demon. She'd used Phaedra's blood as part of a ritual to open a gateway to hell. Demons roared forth, and Phaedra screamed a verse to close the gate as one tore her flesh. A fierce pain ripped through Alissa. She grabbed the Wreath to drag it off, but her fingers cramped, clamping on her head.

New images roared through her mind, of her mother bathed in light at the mouth of a cave. Words in ancient Greek. "With a muse's blood and breath, I implore you to open. That I may discourse with the source." A glare of white light, the smell of floral perfume, heat to warm the coldest night. Soft voices. Alissa strained to see through the light's glare. Then harsh words and a pain pierced her mom's heart, ripping her soul from her chest.

Alissa's lower abdomen cramped like a fist closing on a razor blade. Fear, pain, and desperation tore through her. She sank to her knees, breath rasping in and out of her lungs.

She shook, tempted and wounded by the memories the Wreath offered.

This isn't the time! Merrick needs me now.

"I don't care about the past," Alissa cried. "I care about him. Guide me to save his life. Tonight. Right now."

Her head pounded painfully, her chest burning, then the pain eased to a terrible ache. She held herself still and forced her concentration onto Merrick.

"Help me have him," she said, then white-hot power flowed through her.

Oh, yes!

Alissa rose and left the Wreath building. She snatched up one of the decorative rocks that lined the cobbled path.

Continuing, she walked in the shadows to avoid the cameras. She positioned herself outside the spa center and launched the rock. The window shattered, and she heard glass rain down onto the floor of the yoga studio. She turned and broke into a run.

After smashing three more windows, she returned to the lounge bathroom, quickly wiping the melted snow from her skin. She entered the lounge quietly and noted that the two ES officers had left, presumably called to check the grounds and secure the buildings.

She hurried out of the lounge. In the hall that held her father's interrogation room and an empty one, she heard alarms sounding in the distance. Over them, Troy called her name. Alissa turned to find him and Dorie rushing toward her.

"What are you doing with the Wreath?" Dorie yelled.

Alissa stepped inside the empty interrogation room, knowing they would follow.

"I told you!" Dorie said triumphantly as they entered. "Tobin hinted that Mills was ventala and that Alissa knew all along. She helped him get in. He probably killed Theo Tobin to keep him quiet, and now she's trying to steal the Wreath."

"Alissa, what *are* you doing?" Troy demanded.

"Obviously, I'm using the Wreath."

"The vote—" Dorie cried, but Alissa cut her off.

"The council was formed so the attainment of the Wreath would be based on achievement, not popularity or nepotism. Who's done more this past decade to earn the Wreath than me? No one."

She moved slowly around the table, and they pursued her.

"I'm just as good a muse as you. All I need is more experience. The council might decide I'm the best choice of all of us," Dorie said.

"You really are clueless," Alissa said, rolling her eyes. Dorie flushed with fury. "You're lucky you're so young. Ventala are vengeful. To them, injuries must be repaid. You lied about him trying to bite you. Your deceit caused him to be locked in that room."

Dorie shrugged. "I'm not saying that I lied, but so what if I did? I'm not afraid of him. He'll be dead in the morning.

Grant promised. Will you wear black to his funeral?" Dorie sneered.

Alissa stared at her. How had a muse been born with so little empathy? Dorie relished the prospect of Merrick dying? And of Alissa's pain over his loss? Dorie enjoyed stabbing her friends in the back and then twisting the knife?

Alissa thought of her hapless father being made a spectacle, and her blood grew colder and colder, until it was roughly the temperature of ice-melt.

When Alissa was closer to the door than they, she infused her voice with persuasion and said, "Troy, help Dorie sit down."

Troy grabbed Dorie and forced her into a chair.

"No, Troy!" Dorie shrieked, thrashing.

"And for that, I didn't even use the Wreath's power," Alissa said.

"Troy, let go!"

"Don't let her go, Troy," Alissa said softly. Alissa and Dorie locked eyes for a moment, and Alissa inclined her head. "You see? All muses are not created equal."

"You're hurting me. He's holding my arm too tight!" Dorie screeched.

"Unfortunately, it's in Troy's nature to subjugate innocent young girls. Although if he hasn't tried with you before, maybe he finds you too wretched to be appealing."

Alissa closed the door on Dorie's shrieks of rage and keyed in a lockdown code.

Alissa knew it was probably too optimistic to expect that insults and the shock of being trapped would inspire a change in Dorie, but Alissa hoped for it. The girl's muse magic deserved to be used for good.

The Wreath's inspiration thrummed through Alissa. She strode toward the second hall, the alarms growing louder as she approached. Instinct told her to remove the Wreath. She slipped it off and concealed it behind her back.

Two ES officers still guarded Merrick's door, their guns ready.

She moved her mouth as if speaking and waved her free

hand wildly, the picture of distress. They yelled over the alarms, "What, Miss North? What is it?"

She feigned frustration until they removed their earplugs.

"You have to hurry. Grant needs your help at the spa building. Hurry!" she said, infusing her voice with power. They instantly grew dazed. She repeated herself, and they turned and rushed away.

The young officer appeared in the control-room doorway, his ears covered with headphones. She moved her lips, but he shook his head, not fooled.

"It's no use talking, Miss North. I can't hear you, and I'm not going to remove my earplugs or unlock those doors. That interrogation room is sealed under Director Easton's orders."

"He's overstepping his authority," she said, but the officer retreated into the control room, locking the door behind him.

She turned to Merrick's door and punched in the access code, but the red light blinked. They'd changed the code. She put the Wreath back on, walked to the fire-extinguisher box, and removed the ax. She hurried back to the door and swung the blade against the handle, which broke off.

The officer rushed out of the control room and grabbed her, but the interrogation room door swung open, knocking them back. She stumbled, but kept her balance, her eyes wide with surprise.

Sweat-dampened and covered in debris, Merrick emerged, rifle in hand. He knocked the officer down and cuffed his hands behind him. Merrick glanced around quickly. Finding no other threats, he looked at her and the ax she'd dropped.

"What have you been up to, North?"

"Exactly what it looks like," she said as relief at seeing him free overwhelmed her. She threw her arms around him, hugging him tightly.

He kissed the top of her head. "If this is the greeting I'll get afterward, I'll arrange to be locked up more often."

She smiled.

"Nice headgear," he said.

"I borrowed it," she said, glancing past him into the interrogation room where the massive inner door lay on the floor, the wall around it torn and jagged, plaster crumbling. She may have taken care of the guards in the hall for him, but Merrick would eventually have freed himself from the room.

As always, he's a force to be reckoned with, she marveled.

Letting him go, she said, "My diversion was only a few broken windows. Some of the officers will be back soon. Let's get my father and leave the retreat center as fast as we can."

Merrick nodded, retrieving the rifle, and they hurried to her dad's room. She keyed in the code, and the light turned green.

"That's a nice trick," Merrick said, but when she opened the door, Alissa's triumph was short-lived. The interrogation room was empty.

Chapter 33

Lysander woke from dreams of war to an image of Merrick raining blood onto the snow, then falling six stories onto a rock face. Dead eyes stared up from a shattered body.

"What the hell?" Lysander exclaimed, climbing from bed. He strode to the window and stared out at the clouds. The vision didn't recur, but he reviewed the details in his mind. It had lacked the hazy, surreal quality of his dreams.

A premonition then.

Merrick could be reckless, but he fought like he'd been born to the brotherhood of angels, and he could anticipate an enemy's attack as well as Lysander. So Merrick wounded and falling to his death was likely the consequence of his involvement with that girl. Lysander shook his head. *I warned him!*

Lysander rubbed his lower lip thoughtfully. For years, he'd thought the woman who could stand in the way of his redemption was someone he himself would foolishly become involved with, but he should've known better. Statistically, Merrick was far more likely to get dangerously entangled with a woman than Lysander was.

Lysander slid on a pair of leather pants, then pushed open a window. He dove out, plunging through clouds in the black sky. His wings burst from his back, and he soared around the mountain, whispering on the wind.

He had to separate Merrick from that girl before it was too late.

Alissa raced back to the cuffed young officer who'd been manning the monitors.

"Where's my dad?" she demanded, adjusting the Wreath, allowing its power to surge through her.

The officer ground his teeth together, shaking his head. Merrick reached out for him, but she waved off his intervention, knowing it might be brutal. She bent and took off the man's headphones and removed his earplugs.

"You want to talk to me," she whispered.

His lids drifted down.

"Where is Richard North?"

"Director Easton took him to the crime scene."

She stepped back, surprised, and glanced toward the control room. The alarms still rang. "He took him out in the middle of all this?" Why would Grant do that? She shook her head, her mind searching.

Show me the truth.

Alissa's mind unearthed a memory with sinister implications. When Grant had confronted Merrick through the interrogation-room glass, he'd said, "I looked at the checkpoint logs." If there were logs, the identity of the person who'd driven Alissa out of the Etherlin on the night of her abduction had been recorded.

Grant knows. He knows who took me . . .

Why wouldn't he tell me?

She hurried toward the door that led outside, her mind reeling back through her relationship with Grant. He'd never acted angry or suspicious, but he had become distant. *When was that?*

If he'd found out about her letters to Merrick, wouldn't he have confronted her?

The power of the Wreath buzzed through her, and her thoughts raced along as she started to run. No, Grant wouldn't have exposed her. He would have wanted to save face—his face. He wouldn't have wanted it widely known that a muse had chosen a ventala over him. He also wouldn't have wanted a woman he considered tainted to be crowned Wreath Muse.

Her whole body throbbed, and she knew Grant was the one, felt it to the marrow of her bones. She pictured Grant leaving her with the Jacobis. She saw her own unconscious body lying on the ground as he drove away, secure in the fact that he could alter the logs and that he had ES officers loyal enough to cover for him if he confided in them and perhaps showed them proof of her betrayal.

He'd left her for dead in the Varden, in the hands of his enemies. That was how much he hated her for even writing to Merrick.

Outside, she ran along the path. If Tobin had found out about Grant's involvement with the Jacobis, Tobin would have flaunted that knowledge. Secrets were only fun for Tobin if he could taunt someone with them. Grant wouldn't have tolerated that.

She ran up the stairs of the path, breathless when she reached the spot where they'd found Tobin's body. She looked around wildly. There was no sign of Grant or her father. She heard voices and lost her footing as she was pulled down into the bushes.

"Quiet," Merrick whispered.

She saw bobbing beams of light as security officers rushed out of the glass house toward the Wreath building. When they were gone, she whispered, "I think Grant Easton is afraid my dad witnessed him killing Tobin. We have to find them!"

Merrick was silent for a moment, his gaze flicking to the Wreath. "You think he's the one who betrayed you?"

She nodded. "He crosses into the Sliver and the Varden a lot. He'd have more access, know his way around."

"If Easton wants to get rid of Richard, he'll try to make it look like an accident. He won't want to be seen by the other ES officers who are crawling over the center's campus. You know the site better than I do, Alissa. Where would he take him? Someplace secluded, but not so far away that Easton would be gone too long for it to escape notice."

Alissa closed her eyes and let Merrick's words wash over her. The Wreath tingled against her skin, its inspiration soaking into her mind. She imagined Grant and her father tramping through the snow toward the ridge. One small push is all it would take.

"Northeast. Half a mile from the edge of the retreat, there's a cliff."

Merrick grabbed her hand and pulled her up. He led them over the rough sloping landscape. Once they reached the edge of the property, they ran through the snow with only moonlight to guide them. The ground was uneven under her feet, but the Wreath's magic coursed through her body, and her legs moved as sure as an animal's, as sure as Merrick's.

She slammed to a stop against him when they reached a downslope just before the drop-off. At first, she heard nothing except her pulse pounding in her ears and Merrick's harsh breathing. Then she heard her father's voice. Her head whipped to the side, and she saw a dot of light.

"This is good. Right here is good!" her dad said, his body lost among a thick group of evergreens.

"This isn't the spot. You need to see this view, Richard," Grant said. "Come this way."

Merrick let go of Alissa's hand and bolted toward the trees. She couldn't keep pace with him, but followed at a sprint, running toward the light.

When she was among the trees, she saw her dad and Grant, first spotting her father's red scarf through the snow-dusted green fringe. Grant didn't have a weapon in his hand, but they were very near the edge. Her heart pounded and her stomach churned. Grant could push him at any second.

"Richard North," she called, infusing her voice with power. "Break away from Grant and come to me."

Her father shoved Grant aside and started toward her, but Grant whipped out a gun and grabbed her dad from behind, one arm across her father's throat, the other pressing the gun to his temple.

"Stop!" she cried, and her father stopped trying to hit Grant with his flashlight. She strode toward them. "Grant, you don't want to do this."

"Take that Wreath off!" Grant shouted. "What did you do? Break in to the case?"

"Yes," she said. "I did."

Grant dragged her dad farther away, inching toward the ledge.

"Grant—"

"Take off the Wreath right now, or I will shoot him in the head."

She removed the Wreath and set it in the snow next to her. She couldn't see Grant's face. His head and body were completely blocked by her father's. She knew Merrick must be nearby, but he wouldn't be able to approach them without Grant seeing him.

"What's this about?" her father asked.

"It's about your daughter fucking a monster. Flirting and lying with a filthy criminal."

She winced, but found that the words didn't really hurt the way he'd intended. The only thing she felt was fear and dread that her dad would be shot or shoved off the cliff.

"What criminal?" her dad asked.

"He means Perseus," she said.

"Perseus is a hero," Richard said, dismissing the accusation. Her dad dug in his heels so that Grant had to drag him. "And he's quite a handyman, which is surprising. You can't win, Easton, by going to war with him. I've seen the sword he wields. Love is never conquered by insults . . . or gunpowder. Love is immortal."

Her dad surged forward, making them lurch. Grant's gun hand swung out and then back against her dad's body. The gun's report shattered the night.

Alissa's breath caught, her body frozen.

No!

Her dad fell forward with a cry, the flashlight dropping to their feet, but Grant yanked him back by the throat, replacing the gun's muzzle against his temple. Her dad wobbled but held his ground.

"I don't care if Merrick's in love. He'll die screaming, and so will she. Maybe I'll take him her head before I kill him." Grant moved his face out from behind her dad's to look Alissa in the eye.

The crack of another gunshot pierced the quiet. Grant's

head jerked back as the bullet entered his skull. He crumpled into the snow, her dad falling on top of him. Then their bodies began to slide toward the abyss.

She screamed and ran toward them, but Merrick flew past her from the left. His body sailed through the air, grabbing her father's coat. All three men disappeared over the slope.

She gasped, racing to the edge. She nearly lost her footing and had to drop and scramble for purchase. Digging her feet into the incline, she waited until her body was perfectly still to look over her shoulder. She squinted and spotted her father's ankle. She reached for it, inching down until she could grip it. She turned her shoulders slowly, getting her other hand around his calf, anchoring him. She couldn't see Merrick, and the stabbing fear that he'd fallen almost left her speechless.

"James?" She waited, holding her breath.

"Yeah," he said with strain in his voice.

"I have my dad's leg."

"Hold on to him," he said.

Suddenly her dad became much heavier. She tightened her muscles and held on, pressing her body hard against the incline. She slid a couple of inches down the slope and fought gravity, digging her toes into the frozen mountain as best she could.

It felt like hours before she saw Merrick's scuffed hands claw the ridge of rock and snow. As he pressed himself up like a swimmer coming out of a pool, she saw his torn shirt and the gash on the left side of his chest. He steadied himself, crouching down at the edge and grabbing her dad's leg.

"I've got him."

Her half-frozen fingers didn't move.

"It's okay, baby. Let go."

She bit her lip and nodded, uncurling her fingers slowly. She turned back toward the mountain and crawled slowly up the incline. When she was on level ground, she turned to find Merrick hauling her dad over the ridge. He bent and positioned her dad over his shoulder, then turned.

Merrick licked his pale lips, his breathing labored. She stretched out a hand to him, and he took it with one that shook.

He's weak!

She held his hand with both of hers and leaned her entire weight backward, using her body as a lever. Merrick got onto the flat ground and dropped to his knees, letting her dad slide from his shoulder.

"He's bleeding," Merrick said, his voice weary.

"You're not well either," she said, bending over her dad. His down coat was heavy and soaked on one side. "Oh," she murmured, wincing.

Merrick staggered away from them, dropping to hands and knees and inhaling deeply.

Alissa yanked her dad's shirt up and found a bullet wound in his side where blood flowed out in a steady stream. She pressed down hard to stanch it. Her dad groaned, and his lids fluttered open.

"Hey," she said.

He tried to push her hand from his wound, but she pressed down harder.

"Be still. I need to hold pressure."

"They're coming for you," he mumbled. "Go now, Moonbeam."

Her instincts flared, echoing her dad's warning. She wasn't safe.

"We're all leaving here as soon as we've had a minute to catch our breath." She glanced over at Merrick. His sweat-dampened hair curled at his collar. He dragged the Ovid Medallion over his head with a shaky hand and smashed it with his fist. Light shimmered, and he returned to himself. He tossed the fragments over the cliff.

As he drew in a breath, his fangs glinted in the moonlight.

"What's wrong, Merrick? Do you need blood?"

He didn't answer, but he panted like he'd just run a marathon.

"James," she said sharply. "Answer me. Do you need blood?"

His head, hanging a few inches from the snow, nodded.

She held out her arm toward him. "Then take some."

"You've been bled almost dry once this week. A second deep bite this soon could kill you."

"You won't drink enough to hurt me."

He made no move toward her.

"My dad is too weak to stand. I can't carry him to the car. Think, James. If one of us has to be weak and dizzy, it has to be me, not you."

"I might not stop in time." He sucked in air, swaying. "The hunger is bad. I'd be too rough."

She put her dad's hand over the wound and pressed down. "You hold that, Dad."

"Yesterday . . . all my troubles seemed so far away," her dad sang softly.

Alissa walked to Merrick and crouched next to him. She put her wrist near his mouth. "Don't make me slit my wrist open with your knife."

"Alissa, don't."

Alissa grabbed the back of Merrick's hair and pulled his head up with her right hand, dragging her left wrist across his fangs. Before she even felt the sting, his mouth clamped down, his fangs sinking into her flesh. She gasped at the sharp pain. His body lurched forward, knocking her back into the snow and trapping her beneath him.

Her heart banged in her chest, panic threatening to take hold. The merciless suction of his mouth drained away her adrenaline-spiked blood, making her heart race faster. Her wrist burned, the flesh bruising under the crushing force of his mouth.

She groaned and closed her eyes, thinking frantically, *You have to help him control this!*

"Easy," she said, her voice breathy. "Slow down." She tightened her fingers in his hair and tried to tug his head back, but it didn't give. She felt the corded muscles of his neck against her arm, solid and strong. She pushed power into her voice. "James . . . stop."

He groaned, grinding his body into hers. Attraction tightened her insides. Even dying, a woman could be smothered in lust under a feeding ventala.

"Merrick, stop!" she snapped.

Merrick's hand clamped on her left forearm and dragged it away from his mouth. He jerked his head to the side, breathing hard. The world swirled like she was on a carnival ride, moments melting away. She fought the urge to faint, digging her fingernails into her palms, focusing on her aching wrist. Focusing on the pain. On anything real.

"I know I hurt you," he whispered.

Her hammering heart finally slowed, the dizzying spin over. He licked his lips and eased his body off hers, finally looking down at her.

"I was too hungry to even try to roll your mind into wanting the bite. A muse's mind is unlikely to fall. I never wanted you to feel that pain," he rasped, examining her wrist. It hurt for him to handle it, but she didn't allow herself to wince. Her arm rested in his hands. "I tore the skin. It'll scar," he said and clenched his jaws. "I'm sorry."

She raised her other hand, laying her palm against his neck. "We're both all right. That's what matters."

He ripped a strip of fabric from his shirt and wrapped her wrist, cinching it tight enough to stop the blood from oozing. His gaze slid to her face again. "I love you."

She smiled, resting her palm against his cheek. "I know. I love you, too."

Her father's Beatles rendition stopped, and he said, "They were coming. Now, they're here."

Alissa heard the sound of helicopter blades chopping the air.

Chapter 34

Cerise straightened her tank top and untwisted herself from the sheets. Ileana sat up as Cerise climbed off the couch.

"Why the hell are all the lights on?" Cerise mumbled.

"And where is everyone?" Ileana asked.

Cerise strode into the hallway. A thumping sound drew her to an interrogation-room door. Had someone left Richard North alone in the room? She tried to yank the door open, but it didn't budge. The light on the security pad blazed red.

"Hello," a man said.

Cerise jumped, scowling. "Damn, you scared—" As she turned her head toward him, the words died on her tongue. She had to look up to see his face, which almost never happened. Dark blond hair spilled over broad shoulders. His bare chest was scarred but wicked beautiful. Incredibly, inexplicably, the light seemed to fracture around him, as though he were made of crystal instead of flesh.

"Who are you?" she demanded.

"I'm not available for conversation. I'm looking for my friend."

She cocked a brow.

A slow smile curved his lips. "You smell like oranges." He took a step back, pushing the hair away from his heartbreaking face, then he frowned and shook his head. "Which is actually an unwanted distraction." For a moment, he lapsed into a language so ancient, she couldn't translate fast enough to follow what he said. Returning to English, he managed, "My friend Merrick might be with a muse named Alissa."

Of course, he's beautiful. He's one of them, she thought furiously. She didn't even have a weapon to defend herself. "So you're Merrick's friend, huh? It's illegal for ventala to be in the Etherlin. It carries a death sentence. Did you know?"

He shook his head. "Laws made by men are—"

She lunged and grabbed the knife sheathed at his hip. He caught her wrist and launched himself forward, slamming her against the wall and pinning her body with his.

"Get off me," she said, shoving his shoulder with her free hand.

"You're strong and soft," he murmured, staring at her mouth. "An unusual combination—which I don't have time to contemplate." He grabbed her left wrist and forced it up against the wall so both her arms were pinned over her head.

"Let go," she snapped, trying to knock him off balance. When her forehead banged against his chin, he jerked his head back, then he spun her body so she faced the wall and was crushed between it and him.

His cool breath blew against her ear, matching her own ragged breathing.

"You smell too good to be part demon, so you're not my sworn enemy. Calm yourself," he said.

She was still for a moment, waiting for her chance to throw him off, but his muscles never relaxed. She exhaled hard, frustration thrumming through her.

"You attacked me without cause," he said. "You should ask my forgiveness."

"You can kiss my ass."

His knee rose to nudge her butt. "Be careful what you demand. Someone may accommodate your request."

"You son-of-a-bitch!" she snapped, whipping her head back to slam it against his face.

A moment later she was free, and she spun to face him. He was several feet away, rubbing the swollen corner of his mouth.

"I don't have time to teach you a lesson, but your ferocity deserves one."

"You're trespassing."

He smiled, and she hated that it had a devastating impact on the part of her that noticed beautiful things.

"You don't own the world," he said. "I trespass where I please." He turned. "Now, I need to find my friend before he gets himself killed." He sprinted down the hall in a blur of speed that left her breathless.

She rubbed her wrists.

Who the hell was that?

Merrick moved Richard into the trees and was glad that Alissa was well enough to walk despite being winded. From the cover of the evergreens, Merrick put several rounds into the side of the helicopter, but when it suddenly lost altitude, it was over a clearing, so there was no fiery crash.

Ventala syndicate members poured out.

Merrick shot several before the remainder rushed into the woods. The gun battle lasted ten minutes, and Merrick would've cleared a path if a second chopper hadn't landed behind the first.

"If I go out, they might think I'm alone. If they come in after me, they'll find the two of you," Merrick said.

"If you go out, they'll kill you," Alissa said.

Merrick shrugged. "I'm almost out of ammunition. When they realize it, they'll be coming in after me anyway." He grabbed Richard and placed him under the low-hanging branches of an evergreen. He waved for Alissa to join them, and she did. "Stay out of sight. I'll see if I can reach a fallen ventala to get a loaded gun."

He cleared away their tracks as much as possible, then moved forward. Within moments, he was pinned down by their attackers' cross fire.

Alissa pressed her hand against her dad's side, which was bleeding again, and tried to soothe him.

A branch lifted, and she froze.

"I smell blood," Cato Jacobi said with a menacing smile.

She scrambled to the far side of the tree, drawing him away

from her dad. Jacobi pursued her as she crept along the ridge. There wasn't much space.

"Fall," she said, but when Cato stumbled, he didn't go over the cliff.

He lunged and grabbed her, slamming them both to the ground. They slid down the incline. She grabbed at the ground, but her hands trailed through snow and over ice.

Over Cato's shoulder, she saw Merrick sprinting toward them. He dove and she reached. A terrible pain in her shoulder made her shriek when Merrick yanked her toward him as Cato held on.

Cato swung his free arm around and buried a knife in Merrick's thigh, holding tight to the hilt. Merrick's fist slammed into Cato's face, and Cato lost his grip on her. Merrick yanked her up and away from the incline, then shoved her down flat into the snow just as a bullet ripped through him. Cato jerked the knife free of Merrick's leg and barreled forward.

She grabbed for Merrick, but caught only air as he fell sideways over the ridge. Her scream pierced the night. Cato climbed over her body to reach level ground.

"Hold your fire. He's gone! I've got the girl!" Cato half-carried, half-dragged Alissa to a waiting helicopter.

Alissa fought to free herself—to get back to the ridge and Merrick—but couldn't. Her mind replayed the last moments over and over.

Everything had happened with mind-blurring speed. Cato kept a hand over her mouth as he climbed into the chopper with her.

"Well, if it isn't Bitch Barbie," Tamberi Jacobi said with a smile.

As tears slid silently down her cheeks, Alissa stared out of the open helicopter doors. Merrick was gone. Her dad was bleeding under a tree. She was captured. It was too much.

She tried to leap out as the helicopter started to rise, but Cato dragged her back inside and slid the door closed.

"Don't worry, you won't have time to mourn Merrick. You're not long for this world yourself," Tamberi said.

"Pilot, crash," Alissa said, infusing her voice with power. The helicopter lurched.

"Motherfucker!" Cato said, jumping on top of Alissa and shoving a hand over her mouth while Tamberi screamed at the pilot. After several breathtaking swerves, the helicopter's erratic flight returned to normal.

"What the fuck did I tell you? Tape her goddamned mouth!" Tamberi screeched at Cato.

Cursing and yelling the entire time, he covered Alissa's mouth with duct tape.

"You reach for that tape, and I'll break your jaw," he said.

Alissa sat cross-legged on the floor, staring daggers at them. She willed herself to come up with a plan to kill them both, but her mind kept returning to Merrick falling. It wasn't fair. After everything they'd been through . . . in the end, they'd had so little time together. Her throat tightened and tears welled in her eyes.

He's gone. Her mind rebelled at the thought, but she had lost him. And not only Merrick, but also her father, the Wreath, and soon, her life.

Anger and frustration burned through her. She wouldn't die alone. She would find a way to take the Jacobis with her.

Perched on a ledge, Lysander glared at Merrick, whom he'd saved from a deadly fall.

"Take me to her!" Merrick rasped, coughing up frothy, bright-red blood.

"You need a hospital," Lysander said, kneeling over him. "I didn't come here to let you die. I need you to fulfill that prophecy, and you're—" Lysander reached out to pick Merrick up.

Trying to catch his breath, Merrick shoved Lysander's hand away. Blood poured from Merrick's wounds. He didn't have much time left before he'd be too weak to help her.

Lysander reached again.

"Don't!" Merrick shouted. "You'll take me to Alissa, or you'll take me nowhere."

"You're my friend!" Lysander shouted back. "My one

friend. I won't lose you over a girl, no matter how good they smell!"

Merrick choked down a bloody breath. "You *are* my friend, Lyse. You are," Merrick said and coughed again, spraying the snow with specks of crimson. "I would fight to the death alongside you. You know that. But this woman . . . she's—" Merrick shook his head, suffocating. "She's my heaven . . . what I want to live for." Merrick's head buzzed, getting light. *Not yet!*

"You're a brother to me, Lysander. That's how I know—" Merrick stopped to catch his breath. "You'll take me to her. You'll help me fight them to save her life."

Lysander scowled. "The last time I went against my better judgment to save a brother, I was cast out of heaven."

Merrick dragged himself to a standing position, drawing in a wheeze of air. "This time, I promise the fall won't be nearly as far."

Tamberi directed the pilot toward a small ravine. The helicopter landed, and Cato hopped out with a duffel bag.

"Hurry!" Tamberi said, then dissolved into giddy laughter. "Let's get this party started!"

Another ventala climbed out of the helicopter and carried Alissa to the mouth of an ice cave. Cato yanked a hammer and a set of spikes from his bag and worked quickly to drive them into the rock in a formation she recognized. Her limbs would be bound as Phaedra's had been.

"Don't secure her until after you anoint her with the vampire ash."

Vampire ash?

To raise a demon, why wouldn't they use the ash or some aspect of a demon? Unless they were trying to raise something else. Alissa stared into the duffel and saw a small stone with Phaedra's mark, the one Alissa knew had been used as a key in different types of rituals.

Alissa turned her head to the mouth of the cave, remembering what Merrick had said.

No one ever proved that the shapeshifting vampires came from a mutation.

What if those shifting venomous vampires hadn't been an evolution of the species? What if they'd been a different breed of vampire that had been brought forth?

By muse blood or breath.

The syndicate would spill her blood to open a gate not for demons, but for their vampire sires. And the world would be under siege again. Millions of people would die, starting with everyone in the Etherlin.

No!

She wouldn't allow herself to be used for that purpose. She couldn't let them anoint her. There were other gates that could be opened. She'd seen it in the vision of her mother. Dimitri had said that Helene was the only one hurt by what she'd done. Whatever her mother had brought forth had destroyed her and no one else.

With her left hand, Alissa grabbed the tape and ripped it off her mouth. With her right hand, she snatched the Phaedra stone. She lunged into the mouth of the cave and dropped to her knees. She cut across the bandage and wounds from Merrick's bite, dripping her blood onto the dirt. Then she jabbed the stone's nub into it and turned it like a key, blowing her breath into the cave.

"By my blood and breath, I implore you to open that I may discourse with the source."

A creamy light shimmered, appearing as if it were being filtered through an opal. It brightened and brightened until it blazed through the cave and bathed her in it.

She squinted until her eyes adjusted, and she saw a collection of women with green and gold wreaths woven through their flowing hair. Their diaphanous gowns blew in the breeze and warmth radiated from them.

They spoke the Greek of the ancients, and she recognized them from their portraits. They were the original nine muses, beautiful and glorious, crowding together near the opening, obscuring all but tiny glimpses of the opulent room behind them.

"You've returned, Helene," Clio said.

"No, not Helene. She's new. She's whole," Euterpe said.

"I'm Alissa. Helene's daughter."

"And do you have a child of your own?"

"No."

"Good," Clio said. "There's no daughter to keep you there. Come and join us."

The warmth and the light were wonderful. She eased her tired body toward them.

"Yes, come. Hurry, now."

From behind her, she heard Cato's voice yelling to his sister that there was too much light.

"Get her! You have to get her," Tamberi shouted.

"He won't," she mumbled, hurrying forward. But something—Cato's hand—caught Alissa's ankle and dragged her back.

The muses shrieked, and Alissa kicked, trying to free her leg.

"There's poison in this cave. A man of tainted blood," Thalia said.

"Part man, part enemy," Clio said. "He has her. Quickly, give me a weapon for her. Quickly, sisters! And raise the light. Burn him! Blind him! Turn him back!"

"But the girl! Our new sister!" Thalia said.

Alissa fought Cato's grip, and the light intensified until Alissa's eyes stung. She clenched them shut.

Cato wailed, and Alissa smelled smoke. He dragged her back, then lost his grip. She scrambled forth, but he caught her leg again.

Something clattered on the ground at Alissa's feet. She bent and felt it. A sword.

"Free yourself," Clio urged.

She clutched the sword by its rough hilt. Her hands trembled with the effort of raising it. Sharing blood with Merrick had left her weak, and the sword was heavy.

You have to free yourself!

"Let me go, Cato, or I will kill you."

His grip didn't loosen. "You bitch—"

Alissa swung the sword in an arc dictated by her instincts. The blade sliced through air and through muscle and bone. Alissa heard Cato's head thud to the ground, felt a chill as his fallen soul hissed past.

She pressed the sword tip into the ground, leaning on it to steady herself, trying to catch her breath.

Her knees wobbled, and her body sagged as water dripped onto her head and shoulders, the light's heat creating puddles of melted ice.

"You're so very tired. Come to us, darling girl. Let us comfort you," Clio said.

"We'll stroke your temples."

"And braid flowers through your hair."

"Come now."

She would feel so much better on their side; all her pain would be gone, the past forgotten. She imagined a different life, a peaceful life. An end to loneliness. She only had to walk a little farther.

"Another enemy comes! Run, Alissa. Run to us."

She dropped the sword with a clang and lurched forward.

"Alissa!" Merrick yelled.

Merrick!

She turned, unseeing, toward him.

"You must come to us! You'll be among the strongest sisterhood in existence," Clio said. Alissa felt a wave of comforting warmth wash over her. She wanted to cross the portal and join the other muses.

"You'll be powerful, and wielding the inspiration will bring an ecstasy you've never known."

Alissa's skin tingled as though stroked. She shivered.

"You'll be loved and worshipped," Thalia whispered in a silky voice.

"You'll be immortal," Clio said, dripping joy over Alissa.

Yes, that would be so wonderful . . .

She stepped toward the light, and Clio's soft hand clasped hers.

"Alissa, no!" Merrick shouted, but his voice sounded very far away. "Come back. I can't walk into that light." He hissed in pain, and she heard sizzling and smelled smoke and something acrid.

Clio tugged her, and Alissa inched forward into a place between worlds. Memories as vivid as bright paint splashed over Alissa's mind. Merrick's smile. His bare chest. His deep voice.

Whispered words. Hot caresses. Shared secrets.

Letters. Gifts. Love.

Heaven's Fire.

Don't leave him.

Stay.

"I can't," Alissa said, tears filling her eyes. "I can't join you. I'm sorry. I belong with him." She tried to back away, but pain blazed through her chest as if her soul were being pulled out through her fingers. Alissa gasped and grabbed Clio's wrist, squeezing hard. "Please stop. Let me go."

"You can return to him, but your power stays here. That's the price of opening this door."

An image burned Alissa's mind. Her mother clutched her chest and fell. She lay pale and close to death on the cave floor, surrounded by ice and light. The first muses had taken Helene's magic, and its loss had driven her mother into despair. They were responsible for her death.

Clio's vise grip prevented Alissa from escaping. The pain tore at Alissa's chest and she cried out.

"James," Alissa croaked as her knees buckled.

She heard him shouting, but couldn't make out the words as icy wind blew across the gate.

"James! Put the sword in my hand. Please," she yelled, reaching back.

"No!" Clio screamed. "Close the gate, sisters. Close it!"

Alissa thrust her right hand back, stretching it as far as she could. Golden flames licked her skin as she felt the hilt. She closed her fingers around it and slammed the end of the sword hilt against Clio's arm. Losing her grip, Clio screamed. Alissa threw herself backward, away from the portal.

Everything blazed white before bleeding to black. Alissa's heart stuttered, threatening to stop. She gasped for breath, squeezing her eyes shut. Then her pulse thrummed again, a heavy, steady throb.

She coughed and rolled onto her side, feeling her way to Merrick's body. Hot and blistered, his skin smelled charred.

He'd walked into the burning light for her. She felt for his lips with her fingertips, then put her cheek next to his mouth. She felt nothing. He wasn't breathing.

"James," she sobbed.

She pressed her lips to his. "You want to breathe," she said, infusing power into her voice. "Breathe."

He coughed, then sucked in air with a whistling wheeze.

"James?" she whispered.

His arms closed around her, pulling her against him. "Yeah, I'm here," he said in a rasping voice. "Wherever you are, that's where I'll be."

Chapter 35

The breeze blew in with the sound of the surf. Soft light from a nearby lamp cast shadows, and Alissa rolled onto her side, catching Merrick's scent on the sheets. She inhaled deeply, squinting. She had not fully recovered her sight yet, but she wasn't completely blind as she had been in the first days after escaping the ice cave.

She thought it had been two weeks since that night, but wasn't sure. The nights blended together, a soft haze of precious moments in a precious new life.

She climbed from the bed, finding her silk robe with her hands. She slid it on and tied it by feel. She left the master suite and trailed her hand over the furniture as she walked toward the patio where she knew she would find her men.

"Yes, I do say you cheat, old man! Merrick, you saw him deal that card from the bottom of the deck."

"Sorry. If he did, I missed it."

"You miss nothing." Lysander thumped his fist on the table. "I'm surrounded by liars and cheats. Why don't I just keep company with demons?" he asked, slapping down his cards and lapsing into Latin.

"Would a glass of wine make him a better loser?" her father asked.

"Not that I know of," Merrick said with a smile in his voice. She heard ice clink against Merrick's glass. Scotch and lime for him. Merlot for her dad. Orange wedges, sometimes soaked in vodka, but usually not, for Lysander.

"I'll have a glass of something," she said.

Merrick's chair scraped over the deck. "Here's my good-luck charm," he said, his voice drawing closer. He kissed her lightly on the mouth, tasting of expensive scotch and delicious Merrick. "Deal me out this hand, Richard."

He led her into the kitchen.

"What time is it?" she asked.

"Night," Merrick said. "But I'll make you whatever you want for breakfast."

"Crepes with melted marshmallow meringue and toasted coconut?"

He chuckled. "Sure, but we'll need help from Richard the experimental gourmet for that."

Merrick was a shadowy figure before her eyes, the clanking sound of pots and pans occasionally punctuating his movements.

"What's this?" he said.

"What?" she asked, straining her eyes. She saw the dark blur of his body approach.

"Something for you," he said, pressing a box into her hands.

She felt a satin ribbon and untied it. As soon as she removed the lid, a wave of power rolled over her. She leaned back reflexively, but it didn't burn. She dipped her hands inside, and her fingers traced the delicate filigree loops and small gemstones of the Muse Wreath.

"Where did this come from?"

"I found it in the snow."

She smiled, knowing he was being intentionally vague. He and Lysander had obviously made an illegal trip into the Etherlin.

"I won't keep it," she said, but lifted it from the box and lowered it onto her head. A pulse of light flashed behind her eyes, and the room swam into focus. "Well, just as I said all along. There's a little bit of healing magic in this old thing."

"Yeah?" he asked, snapping the frying pan so a crepe sailed into the air and flipped over before landing again with a sizzle.

His casual response didn't fool her. Even though she knew he'd been telling the truth when he said that he'd make sure she was happy whether her sight returned or not, she'd also overheard what he'd said to Lysander. She shouldn't have been able to hear from two rooms away and over the sound of the ocean, but since the ice cave, her other senses were remarkable.

"I got there too late to save her. She had to save herself, and it cost her her sight," he'd said.

"I guess you're right," Lysander had replied. "That's what you get for fooling around while drowning in your own blood after that gunshot wound to your chest. You should've dragged down a military helicopter with the force of your will and slaughtered a pack of armed ventala with your bare hands. Really, Merrick, I don't know how she puts up with you."

"Fuck off," Merrick had said with the barest trace of amusement under the surface.

"I never know what that actually means," Lysander said. "But I think when I find out, I may want to break your jaw."

Merrick had laughed softly, and she'd been grateful again for Lysander, who'd first gone back to rescue her dad and later forced Merrick to leave her side long enough to get his own burns and wounds treated. Apparently, Merrick hadn't been kidding when he'd said it was impossible to fight with an archangel.

As her vision sharpened, her eyes drank in the sight of Merrick, dark and beautiful, his skin healed and unscarred, the stubble on his jaw the exact length she liked it.

Behind him on the counter, nestled between a bottle of seventeen-year-old scotch and a bowl of bright green limes, there was a small black velvet jewelry box.

"What's inside that little box?" she asked, nodding.

He didn't answer. He only stared at her face and smiled. "Spotted that, did you? If you take the Wreath off, will your eyes work as well?" he asked.

She shrugged and removed the Wreath. Her vision immediately began to fade. "It seems pretty good," she lied.

She jerked a little when his lips touched hers. She knew he'd darted forward with that inhuman speed so that her other senses didn't have time to compensate.

Having been caught, she smiled sheepishly. "Lysander's right; he's surrounded by liars and cheats." She paused. "I exaggerated a little, but aren't I allowed to be optimistic? My vision's getting better bit by bit. I'm sure in a few weeks I'll be back to normal. And even if I'm not, how can I regret what happened? If I hadn't opened the portal to the ancients, the Jacobis would've killed me and let a plague of vampires into the world. I nearly lost my father, my magic, and you." She shivered and shook her head. "If my vision is the price I pay for remaining a muse and having a life with you, I say . . . worth it."

His mouth settled on hers for a deep kiss. Her heart thumped heavy against her ribs. He was such a skilled kisser . . . lover . . . everything.

When he returned to the stove, she said, "The Wreath really should go back, Merrick. My magic's stronger than ever after the cave. I have enough power to do everything I need for my aspirants. The Wreath should be kept in the Etherlin where it can do the most good. Also, I don't want ES hunting us for it. I want a life with you. I want to be left alone. Will you see that it's safely returned?"

His silence was telling. She sighed and stood. When she reached him, she pressed her body against his and slid her arms around his neck, trailing her fingers over his scalp. She felt his body's response.

"Do we need to have a battle over this? You know in the end you'll give me whatever I want," she teased.

"You are as persuasive as advertised," he mumbled, exhaling slowly as she moved her hand down and ran her index finger over his zipper. She heard him move the pan to another burner and felt his arm extend to turn off the flame.

When he turned, he picked her up, and in a few short strides they were alone in their room.

He made love to her for hours, like time was as endless as what they felt for each other.

Close to sunrise, half asleep, she sensed him leave and then, moments later, return.

"You asked me once what I needed," he said.

"I remember."

"It's you. Since we met, it's been you." He brushed a strand of hair back from her face. "I'm yours. Until my last breath . . . and probably long after, if Richard's to be believed."

She smiled.

"You don't have to promise me anything." He paused.

"But?"

"But if you felt like marrying me, Lysander is willing to be my best man. And Ox could be an usher. Or a flower girl. He owes me plenty of favors."

She laughed, then rested her head against the pillow again.

"Throughout this whole affair," she said, "you let me have you on my own terms, so I'm sure that to keep you I don't have to promise anything . . . but I want to." She extracted her hand from under the pillow. "I promise you everything," she murmured, raising and extending her left hand.

The ring glided onto her finger, and, with her other hand, she felt its facets and contours. An antique, she realized, which was what she'd wanted. Had she mentioned that to him? Or had he unearthed her heart's desire on his own, as he often did?

"This ring was worn by women who lived great lives and who were deeply loved," she whispered as her instincts chased memories that threaded back through the years. She rubbed the band with her thumb; she'd enjoy unraveling its history . . . when she was done unraveling her husband's. "It's the perfect ring for me. Thank you, James."

He kissed her slowly.

"When we get back to Colorado, I'll pick out a beautiful ring for you," she said.

"You know what I'd rather have from you?"

"What?" she asked.

"A letter."

She smiled. "That I'll fill with my darkest secrets and innermost thoughts?"

"Exactly." His satisfaction hummed against her skin.

"All right," she whispered, knowing instinctively that their longing to be together would never fade. "I'll fill it with the things I would never tell anyone . . . except you."

Keep reading for a special preview of

KIMBERLY FROST'S

next

NOVEL OF THE ETHERLIN

Coming summer of 2012 from

Berkley Sensation!

Cerise froze as if she'd been doused with slush. The sounds of the party receded as she stared down at her phone.

Can't face people after last night. Plz don't blame yourself for not being able to help, C. I can't keep it together without Griff either.

Cerise exhaled through pursed lips, chilled as if it weren't late spring. Two of Cerise's secrets were thinly veiled in Jersey Lane's text message, but seeing them displayed wasn't what concerned Cerise most.

Cerise slipped the phone into the pocket of her gunmetal gray silk pants as she glanced around. She forced a smile when she made eye contact with friends, but her gaze didn't linger. She searched until she spotted Hayden Lane slouched against the wall. He was laid-back and shy, unusual for a rock star, but he'd been poured from the same mold as his older brother, Griffin. Pain skewered Cerise's chest and tightened her throat. Even Griffin's name alone could still ambush her. But this wasn't the place to get emotional about Griffin, and it definitely wasn't the time.

Cerise tipped her chin up a fraction as if daring fate to sock it again. She strode across the room, weaving through people and reaching Hayden a few moments after her sister, Dorie, did.

Dorie's new nose and pencil-thin brows had transformed her cute face into something vaguely plastic. Her hips, however, continued to betray her, despite a diet completely devoid of everything that tasted remotely decent. If their parents let Dorie get body-sculpting liposuction as a teenager, Cerise would be sick. Of course, the blame wouldn't rest solely on their shoulders. One of Cerise's assistants had described Dorie as a Machiavelli princess in the making. Cerise had fired him, but later there'd been moments . . . Cerise could understand lying to steal a little freedom. All the muses did that from time to time. But lying to hurt another muse? Ever since seeing evidence of that at the retreat center, Cerise hadn't felt the same about Dorie. And Dorie, who seemed to sense it, had been trying too hard. Tonight though, Dorie glued herself to Hayden, which gave Cerise a bit of peace. But also didn't. Hayden had already been through a lot.

"Hayden, I got a text from Jersey. She's not coming," Cerise said.

"I figured."

"What happened last night?" Cerise asked.

Hayden shuffled his feet. "All week, she kept forgetting lyrics in rehearsals, so she was a nervous wreck last night. She decided to have a drink to calm down, but on an empty stomach . . ."

Cerise grimaced. Already petite, Jersey had lost weight since Griffin's death and was probably all of ninety pounds at the moment.

"She got wasted off two vodka cranberries," Hayden said, frowning. "She slurred her way through 'Sympathy' and went word-salad on 'Burn It Down.' I jumped in even though I don't have the voice to do it. People were pissed. They started yelling for her to get offstage." He shrugged lean shoulders. "She did."

"It hasn't even been a year since Griffin died," Cerise whispered.

"I know, but drunk people get annoyed."

"She's torn up inside," Cerise said, knowing that feeling all too well.

"Everybody misses him. You. Me. Jersey. But so do the fans, and we can't charge people money and then fuck up his songs because we're too wasted to sing."

"You're right," Dorie said. "Griffin wouldn't have wanted that. She should respect his memory."

Cerise didn't spare Dorie a glance. Her sister, the sudden expert on Griffin Lane, had met Griffin for a sum total of about twenty minutes.

"Where is she?" Cerise asked.

"At the apartment."

"Griffin's place here in the Etherlin?"

"Yeah."

"Let's go check on her," Cerise said.

"Oh, come on," Dorie said. "You guys can't leave the party now. Dinner's about to start. How would that look to the council, Cer?"

I don't care what the Etherlin Council thinks. Haven't for years.

"Besides," Dorie continued hastily, probably at the sight of Cerise's stony expression, "Jersey will never pull herself together if everyone gives her a ton of attention every time she screws up. If she's going to sulk, ignore her."

Cerise turned a frigid gaze on Dorie, who blanched, and then Cerise glanced back at Hayden.

"I'm worried about Jersey," Cerise said. "I have a bad feeling."

Hayden's shuffling ceased, and he straightened. "Okay, let's go," he said.

Dorie fell in step with them. "Considering how you and I are the only Etherlin muses here tonight, if you're gone, they'll probably hold dinner till you get back. So it won't matter if I go out, too."

Neither Cerise nor Hayden said anything.

"I'll come with you," Dorie added.

"No," Cerise said.

Dorie narrowed her eyes. "Why not?"

Because I don't trust you. "Because this isn't your business," Cerise said.

* * *

Even while not dancing, Cerise's fluid movements seemed to recall her ballet training, Lysander noticed. Her fingers extended gracefully as if reaching for something beautiful. Like a stolen moment.

With the beat of massive wings, Lysander rose from the tree's bough that overlooked Cerise's house. Her scent didn't reach him that far up, but it didn't need to. He remembered it too well, along with the warmth of her body and the fierce way she'd fought to free herself when he'd restrained her.

She's nitroglycerin wrapped in the softest skin, he thought as he swooped across the sky, skimming the treetops of roof gardens. Cerise's wild passion awakened his own.

Enough.

Enough of watching the girl. Enough of thinking about her.

The more a preoccupation is fed, the more powerful it becomes.

The prophecy—the one that pertained to his only chance for redemption—contained several parts, including a warning that getting involved with a woman could make him fail. He'd never risk that no matter how beautiful she felt or smelled or danced.

He flew over the Etherlin, so named by her kind, the descendants of the ancient muses. They were the only remnants of the lofty society of the Olympians, the superhuman creatures who had once been caretakers of the world. Until their hubris and their manipulation of mankind had led to their exile from Earth.

Exile.

Lysander knew all about exile. But he was hoping to make his own a distant memory.

Movement below caught his eye. *There's a child on that roof.*

A little girl. Eleven or twelve, perhaps?

With an unsteady gait she wobbled across the concrete.

It's dark. Why is she there alone?

She climbed onto the ledge. Bare feet shuffled over the faded artwork that someone had painted. He hovered in the clouds.

"Be careful," he whispered.

She rubbed her arm and swayed.

He held his breath. Archangels weren't allowed to consort with humans. As an arcanon—a fallen angel—Lysander wasn't barred from it, but he avoided people out of habit. He also avoided them to resist the temptation that beautiful women presented.

The girl teetered.

She's not my responsibility. I've let myself get too entangled with human beings lately. I shouldn't—

She pivoted too fast and stumbled, her eyes wide with shock and terror as she fell.

He dove, a torpedo through the air, until he caught her. Her eyes rolled back and her head hung toward the concrete street that would have destroyed her skull.

She's unconscious and barely breathing, he realized.

Opium-scented breath emanated from a fragile body. She was small, but not a child after all. He landed and laid her on the doorstep under a large awning.

"Opium tastes like heaven, but isn't," he said, resting her head gently against the step. Her bleached hair fell away from an unlined forehead. Under cherry lipstick her lips turned dusky blue.

She goes, he thought. "You'll see the difference soon."

The click of heels in the distance made him look over his shoulder. He recognized the cadence of those footfalls.

Cerise.

Lysander straightened, very tempted to stand his ground, to wait for her to arrive. No law forbade him from talking to her.

The scuff of other shoes was paired with her heel strikes.

There's someone with her.

Who? A man or a woman?

He ducked around the building into shadow and waited.

From a roof's edge, an icicle hung like a dagger ready to fall. Spring had arrived, but then receded, like a virgin clambering under the covers on her wedding night. Two days of freezing rain had claimed the Etherlin, but a new warm front was steadily melting the ice.

As Cerise walked with Hayden, she drew her shoulders forward, huddling them together against the chill.

I'm so cold. Why is it always like this when I think about Griffin?

Memories of him gushed like a flood . . . Griffin's sandy brown hair and the crooked smile that could transform his expression from angelic to devilish in an instant. The collection of vintage rock T-shirts that he and Cerise had shared between them. The "morning" coffee they'd drunk upon waking at six p.m.

Cerise dug her nails into her palms. *He's dead almost ten months. You have to deal with it and move on.* The problem was she couldn't.

The final night with Griffin was a hazy blur that haunted her. And the holes in her memory stretched back insidiously. She couldn't remember the songs they'd worked on. She couldn't remember their last fight, but she knew they'd had one.

Worst, and most important, her magic had been damaged. The power she used to inspire people had melted like so much snow. She'd been faking it since then, kept expecting it and her memory to return after the pain receded, but it never did. After ten months, she felt worse than ever.

Some of her aspirants suspected, and it was only a matter of time before the council realized, too. If only she could unlock her mind. If only she could review the steps she'd used to tap into her power in the past.

I need Griffin's missing songbook. I need to see the flow of ideas, to relive the way the magic worked. The missing pieces are on those pages. I know it.

Instincts more powerful than any she'd ever felt outside of her muse magic were driving her to find the book. She dreamed about it constantly.

Unfortunately, she and the band had been searching for Griffin's songbook since they buried him. The journal had contained all the songs that Cerise and he had worked on during his last year. There were thirty-seven songs in total, including a dozen that Cerise had known would be number-one hits.

After Griffin died, Cerise couldn't remember a single lyric or melody from all that work, which had left Griffin's band, the Molly Times, without their lead guitarist and unable to record new material. They'd begged Cerise to work with them, to inspire them, to come to rehearsal and jam with them. But without her magic, Cerise couldn't help. It broke her heart. Hayden and Jersey had lost their brother; they should've at least had his final musical legacy. Cerise couldn't even help them retain that much.

"I don't know what's going on with Jersey. She *knows* the songs," Hayden said as they walked. "She hears a lyric once and remembers it. Always has. Do you think she's screwing up on purpose?"

"No."

"Not even subconsciously? As a way to get back at him for dying?"

Cerise flushed. Hayden wasn't only asking about Jersey now. *Maybe.* "I don't know. I'm not a psychiatrist."

"I wish she'd let me take her to one. She needs to talk to someone about how she really feels. It might help."

"Maybe," Cerise murmured, reflecting on her own failed experience. She'd seen a therapist in secret, hoping that through hypnosis the woman would be able to unlock Cerise's memories and free her muse magic. For a few moments of their session, Cerise had seen a glimpse—a very unsettling glimpse—of the past, but then it had deteriorated and Cerise had been back in the dark and more troubled than before.

Cerise pressed her fist against the side of her thigh. When Griffin had died at twenty-seven, he'd deprived Cerise of more than her favorite aspirant; he'd been the guy she was crazy in love with, the one with whom she'd been having a secret affair.

That Griffin's death might have been partly Cerise's fault was a detail that no one knew. Except Cerise, who could not get over it. She never let on how much she still hurt, but the pain was there, just below the surface.

"I've been writing," Hayden said.

"That's great. I can't wait to see what you've been working on."

"Yeah, sure . . ." He paused.

"What?"

"Dorie's cool. I thought maybe I'd show my songs to her."

Cerise's gaze slid to him. He wanted to replace her with Dorie? Cerise's blood ran cold. "Is that right?"

"Well, she's a muse, too. And I thought—"

She raised a brow, but said nothing. He flushed and clenched his teeth. She might have admired the way he was trying to assert himself if he hadn't been in the middle of stabbing her in the back.

"Look, we can use all the help we can get right now. Things are falling apart. You and Griffin were amazing together, but talking to you doesn't light my mind on fire like it did his. If anything, it brings me down and makes me feel— I don't know, exhausted. Kind of like I'm hungover or something."

The words crushed her, but before she could respond, she spotted Jersey's body. Jersey was the same blue color Griffin had been that morning at the bottom of the ravine. Cerise recognized it as the color of death.

To distance himself from the frenzied attempt to save the girl, Lysander had flown to the roof. He stood at the edge looking down, unable to tear himself away. The girl's death was bringing Cerise pain, which made him want to comfort her, to touch and reassure her.

Don't interfere.

He stepped down from the ledge so he wouldn't be able to see Cerise any longer, and in doing so noticed the graffiti. There was very little of it in the Etherlin, but the place where the girl had tread so unsteadily was covered with elaborate artwork. The white ledge had been painted with the tangled green of a woodland scene. He studied it and, within the tendrils of vines, he spotted a blackbird. He froze for a moment, unable to believe . . . But yes it was there.

He flapped his wings and rose, hovering above so he could

see the entire thing at once, could stare at the swirling patterns, and he spotted what was buried. A message woven into the vines. The letters emerged in one long string.

Sadly talks the blackbird here. Well I know the woe he found: No matter who cut down his nest, For its young it was destroyed. I myself not long ago Found the woe he now has found.

The verses were from a ninth-century poem called "The Deserted Home." Lysander knew who and what had inspired it. Reziel.

Lysander's muscles locked, and his gaze darted side to side as if expecting his former brother to appear. But, of course, Reziel wasn't lurking nearby. Lysander would've known, would've felt him. Still there was the message . . .

Had the demon invaded the dreams of an artist? Or maybe one of Reziel's followers lived in the Etherlin. It didn't matter how Reziel had accomplished it. What mattered was that it was part of the prophecy: *Watch for a sign. The message left by your betrayer marks the beginning of the end.*

With stunned triumph ringing in his ears, Lysander thought, *This is it. After thousands of years of waiting, the prophecy has finally begun.*

The largest tombstone in Iron Heart Cemetery was also the newest. Twelve towering feet of carved marble announced that Cato Jacobi had been laid to rest in the fresh grave. No one mourned him more than his sister, Tamberi.

A vicious kick launched the flowers that lay at the base of the headstone. Cato couldn't have cared less about dead plants, and Tamberi didn't want anything touching Cato's grave that she didn't put there herself.

From her tote bag, she extracted a one-of-a-kind Venetian vase, created nearly a hundred years ago. She clenched her jaw and flung the vase against the headstone. Shattering, its shards rained down like multicolored tears and joined the pile of fragments from what had once been Tamberi's quarter-of-a-million-dollar Italian glass collection. Since she'd buried Cato, she'd smashed a piece each day against his headstone, marking time, creating a testament to the fact that nothing else mattered except that her brother was food for worms.

Tamberi shoved her bangs back from her eyes. She liked to keep her black hair buzzed to an inch or two long, but she'd vowed not to cut it until her brother's death was avenged.

She snagged a half-empty bottle of bourbon from the wet sod. She swigged deep, then while she caught her breath between swallows, she poured a generous amount onto the grave.

"Do you think the third time's a charm?" she asked, splashing drops of bourbon over the headstone. "A new demon contacted me," she whispered.

The sound of a throat being cleared startled her, and she went still and silent. She inhaled and recognized the cologne.

"So you're the one who's been killing the grass," his voice said.

She didn't bother to look over her shoulder at the interloper. "Hello, Dad."

"I've left you a lot of messages," he said, his voice low with fury. "Given the mess you and your brother made, I'm under a lot of pressure. Invading the Etherlin? You must have been out of your minds. At least you were hopped up on morphine, but what the hell was Cato thinking?"

She turned slowly, her eyes narrowed to slits. "He was thinking that Merrick was never going to bring us that muse that we needed for the syndicate's plan—your plan—to work. Cato was thinking that we'd go in and get the job done ourselves."

"And he got himself killed."

"Yeah, he did. But at least he had the balls to try to get out from under their thumb."

Victor glowered, his lips retracting to show his glistening fangs. "If you don't want to get thrown in a fucking cell, you'd better straighten up. And I've already told you there cannot be a blood feud. Not now. So Merrick and that bitch muse are off-limits until everything quiets down."

"I wanted the rock-and-roll muse. If you'd agreed to let us snatch Cerise Xenakis, the wrong portal would never have been opened. Cato would still be alive."

"The North girl was the smarter choice. She was more isolated. And Cato would still be alive if he hadn't gone off half-cocked into the Etherlin."

"That plan worked," Tamberi hissed. "We slaughtered every Etherlin Security officer that we came in contact with. There are no living witnesses in the Etherlin to prove we were there."

"The choppers were seen."

She shrugged.

"And Alissa North could testify."

"Not if she dies before she gets the chance."

"I'm so fucking sick of fighting with you about this!" Victor snapped. "It's like you're deaf, and—" The words that would've followed choked and died on his lips as two V3 bullets ripped through his heart.

"I heard you. Every time," Tamberi said as he crumpled backward, clutching his chest. She slid the gun she'd whipped out back into the pocket of her coat.

She walked behind the headstone and grabbed the sword whose blade was buried to the hilt. She unsheathed it from the earth, sending clumps of dirt flying.

She stalked to her father. Victor's eyes were wide with shock, his bloodless lips moving silently.

Her jaw was set. "I'm tired of fighting about this, too," she whispered. "You think it's only about Cato, and it mostly is about him. He's dead, so they need to be dead, too. But it's also about something that started a long time back. And I can't afford to have you or anyone else getting in my way anymore. You always said you can tell how committed someone is to a goal by what he's willing to give up for it." She swung the sword and didn't let herself blink as her father's head rolled free of his body. The bullets probably would've killed him, but decapitation was certain.

She swallowed hard and retrieved the bourbon bottle she'd dropped on the ground. She swiped the dirt away and took a burning swig, glancing up at the overcast sky. After a moment, she forced her gaze back to where blood pulsed, then trickled, and finally oozed from her father's severed neck.

"I have a goal," Tamberi murmured. "And I am *completely* committed to it."

Cerise tightened the belt on her purple trench with shaky hands and walked toward the side door of the urgent care center where they'd stabilized Jersey Lane. An ashen-skinned Hayden was at Jersey's bedside, so Cerise stepped out for a moment to escape the bleach-scented air and the sight of Jersey's tiny body covered in wires.

Jersey's alive. You got there in time, Cerise told herself, trying to stop her heart's frantic pounding.

But she was blue. We had to do CPR. What if she's brain-damaged? What if she ends up a vegetable? It might seem like we got to her in time, but maybe we didn't. Maybe I was too late to save her. Just like I was too late to save Griffin.

In a flash, she recalled Griffin's lifeless body, followed instantly by Jersey's on that doorstep. Cerise's stomach churned. She swallowed gulps of air and squeezed her eyes shut.

Do not get sick. Do not.

She spit out excess saliva and slowly eased herself down the bricks to sit on the ground, her back against the wall.

In the early days after Griffin had died, the pain had been so bad she'd started to meditate, focusing all her concentration on her next breath. She did that now, listening to her breathing, clocking the beat of her heart as it throbbed in her temples.

Better. Just breathe.

Her heart slowed, and her stomach settled.

She rested against the wall until the door opened, and Hayden called her name.

"I'm here," Cerise said, shooting to her feet. "Is she worse?"

"No," Hayden said, and a lopsided grin claimed his face. "She's awake. The little brat." He grabbed Cerise in a fierce hug and nearly sobbed. "If you hadn't said we should go—"

"It doesn't matter now."

"Yeah, it freaking does. And it always will." His bony

fingers tightened against her back. "I was so stunned when we found her. If I'd been alone, I might have just stood there in shock."

"No, you wouldn't have."

"The way she looked. I don't know if I would've thought to try to save her. And when you used the power of your voice on her—if you hadn't been there, she would've died. I'll never—I'm sorry about what I said earlier. The Molly Times only works with one muse. Ever. No matter what happens, we're with you and no one else."

Her eyes misted, but she blinked away the tears and swallowed against the tightness in her throat. "We'll figure things out," Cerise said. They'd gotten a second chance with Jersey, and Cerise wasn't going to lose her. Cerise would find a way to help the Molly Times again even if it killed her. "Everything's going to be okay."

Hayden nodded with a wobbly smile.

"Let's go back in. I don't want her to be alone," Cerise said.

"Yeah, c'mon." Hayden's hand clung to her arm, and Cerise wondered if that was to steady her or to steady himself. Maybe both.

They walked down the sterile-smelling hall to Jersey's room, and Cerise braced herself with a deep bleach-scented breath before she opened the door.

Inside, Jersey looked like a little doll whose makeup had been applied by a child. Smudged black eyeliner haloed her light eyes. Smeared scarlet lipstick at the corner of her pale mouth looked almost like blood, as though she were a tiny blond tribute to the undead.

"Sorry, Cerise," Jersey said. "I'm so sorry. I just wanted to sleep and forget about everything. I guess—" Jersey had a clear high voice that could be mesmerizing when she sang. Even wavering as it did now, it was irresistible. "I guess I took too much."

"I guess you did," Cerise said, sitting on the edge of the bed and clutching Jersey's hand. "You almost killed yourself and us along with you. You scared us to death."

"Sorry."

"How do you feel?" Cerise asked.

"I'm okay." She tried and failed to stifle a yawn. "Tired."

"I bet."

"When I was dying, I saw an angel, and I heard Griffin."

"You did?" Cerise asked, brushing the platinum hair away from Jersey's face.

"Griffin said, 'I'll tell you where it is. Songs among the rafters. In the falling playground above the stage.' Something like that," she murmured. "Isn't that crazy that I heard his voice? It was nice, though, to hear it again." Jersey's lids drooped. "I miss him."

Cerise ran a shaky hand through her hair. She continued to watch Jersey, but her thoughts were elsewhere. In the last six months of his life, Griffin had been obsessed with heights. Climbing them or avoiding them, depending on his mood. He'd been fixated. "The farther it is to fall, the more I love it, Cherry. And the more I hate it," he'd said to her.

Griffin's mood swings had upset them both. Cerise hadn't probed into the cryptic things he'd said because he'd been a powder keg of emotions. She'd tried not to pressure him because questions set him off. She'd thought he would talk to her when he was ready. Leaving him alone had been a mistake; his struggle ultimately consumed him. Now he had plenty of space to brood. And she and the Molly Times had plenty of space to grieve.

Cerise shivered, withdrawing from those thoughts. Instead, she concentrated on what Jersey had said.

Songs among the rafters. Above the stage.

Griffin had sometimes written music in one of the top boxes in the performing arts center that was named for her mother. He'd liked the place's outstanding acoustics.

Could he have left his songbook there? But if he had left it in a box, someone would've found it and turned it in. Or kept it and sold it. The kind of money collectors and fans would pay for a journal of Griffin's would be a serious temptation to most people.

Cerise frowned at the thought of someone trying to profit from that book when she and the Molly Times needed it so much. It was the last piece of Griffin they'd ever have.

Griffin wouldn't have left his songbook lying around in plain sight. If he'd left it in the auditorium at all, he'd have put it someplace where no one would stumble across it. He would've hidden it.

I have to check.

Cerise rose. "She's asleep again."

"Yeah," Hayden said with an affectionate roll of his eyes. "She nearly gives us heart attacks and freaks me out so much I may not get a good night's sleep again ever, then five minutes after she wakes up, she's out again like she's got a clean conscience. How's that for irony?"

Cerise smiled and gave his arm a squeeze. "You watch her. There's something I need to do."

He nodded. "Sorry about you missing your dinner party tonight."

"No worries," she said, walking out of the room. *That celebration party was a sham anyway.*

The trees lining the walkway were strung with small blue and white lights. Grecian colors, Cerise thought. From the outside, the Etherlin appeared to be all things pearly and bright. Home to women who had descended from the ancient muses. Women who were inspiration made flesh, as the saying went. Maybe the fact that Cerise spent a lot of time with rock stars who were subversive and athletes who battled for their bread made Cerise harder to placate, harder to control. She didn't see the Etherlin as a glittering Garden of Eden. Like all things of great power and beauty, it had a dark side. Ambition and the quest for perfection made people dangerous even if they lived in the Etherlin.

And, of course, some darkness came from the shadows cast by the Varden. It was just outside the Etherlin's walls and home to the ventala. One of the Varden's fallen creatures had recently seduced a muse and the community was still reeling in the wake of her defection. Some couldn't accept that Alissa had been seduced. They believed she'd been taken.

Cerise was sure her former friend had left voluntarily, but sometimes women loved men who later caused them endless pain. Alissa was in the hands of one of the most dangerous men in the world. If Alissa decided she wanted to leave him, would Merrick let her go? Cerise doubted it. That was a thought that kept Cerise awake at night. What if Alissa regretted her choice? Did Alissa think that the Etherlin Council would never let her back after what she'd done on the night she'd left?

Cerise planned to talk to Alissa. She couldn't cure Alissa of an attraction to the wrong man, but she could make sure that one of the most talented muses in the world knew that she had the support of the other one. If Alissa wanted to come home, Cerise would fight to make that happen.

Cerise approached the Calla Xenakis Center for the Performing Arts. It was a building of alternating blue and white glass with reeds of silver in between. Musical instruments and notes were etched into the frosted panes, making it playful yet elegant.

When Cerise unlocked the door, music floated down to her, and she slowed as she stepped inside. The building was dark. There were no scheduled performances or rehearsals. Sometimes students or staff musicians requested use of the building, but Cerise hadn't wanted to run into people tonight, so she'd checked the schedule and found it bare.

She ventured deeper inside and opened the door to the main auditorium. The dark stage was empty, but light drifted down from above. She stepped inside and looked up. The illumination was very faint. From a candle or small lamp? In one of the upper boxes? Why would anyone be playing up there?

It's him, she realized. *The Etherlin's version of the Phantom of the Opera.*

For months, there had been rumors of a performer who some of the staff called the young maestro. They claimed he played the guitar as well as Hendrix and Clapton, that on sax he was sublime and on violin unparalleled. She knew it had to be an exaggeration, but it made her curious.

The music always came from the upper boxes, and initially, some of Griffin's fans thought it was his ghost, but Griffin had only played guitar and never as well as Hendrix or Clapton.

So who was the young man who turned up out of nowhere and left the same way, never tripping the building's alarms? He was suspected to have fixed a hole in the roof caused by a lightning strike. There'd been water all over the floor, but when the workmen went up to patch the leak, there were new shingles nailed in place.

His presence had been confirmed as real rather than fantastical when the center's director had found a cash-filled donation envelope midstage during the center's annual fundraising drive. The note had been done in writing that was more calligraphy than cursive. It read: *The welcome this space offers to music is admirable. A visiting musician offers compliments to the designers and builders of this place.*

After the note, the hunt for the center's young phantom had redoubled, but he was more slippery than ever according to the students who sometimes hid in the upper boxes in hopes of spotting him and getting to listen to him play for more than a few moments. They caught glimpses of him and said he was tall and blond, but they couldn't tell much else.

Knowing the sound of her boots against the stairs would travel, she sat and removed them. Setting them aside, she ascended in stockinged feet. Three flights up, his playing stopped her. In his hands, a violin was more than a violin. It was the voice of countless generations. It was the soul of the whole world. "Beethoven's Fifth" transitioned to Bob Dylan's "Hurricane" which gave way to "Rock You Like a Hurricane." She crept higher into the building and opened the door. She closed it silently and didn't dare move farther because she would rather have fallen down the stairs than have him stop playing.

She recognized Steppenwolf's "Born to Be Wild," which turned into Nirvana's "Smells Like Teen Spirit." Then a blazing "Flight of the Bumblebees" transitioned into "Dance of the Goblins." She cocked her head. His lightning speed had such clarity and precision that her jaw dropped. She slid down the wall to sit on the floor. Closing her eyes, she followed the music, not bothering to identify any more songs.

When the music stopped, Cerise had no idea how long she'd been sitting on the floor. And she didn't care. She uncoiled her limbs and rose. This mystery man was the most talented violinist she'd ever heard, and she wanted him for an aspirant. No sound that pure and amazing should be played for an empty auditorium. The world had a right to hear it. She would make him understand.

She followed the soft glow, enjoying the smell of sandalwood. She was surprised to find that the candle wasn't in a box. It was in the middle of a girder. And lying next to it was a book she recognized. There in the center of a steel beam several stories above the stage was Griffin's lost songbook.

She heard water slosh and turned her head sharply. When she did, she froze. The tall shirtless blond creature drinking from a jug of water was stunning in a host of ways, not the least of which was that she'd met him before.

The meeting had been on Alissa's last night in the Etherlin when the ventala had infiltrated the muses' retreat and had murdered ten members of Etherlin Security. including its director, Grant Easton, whose body had never been recovered.

She should have been afraid of the blond intruder, but she wasn't. No sixth sense warned her to retreat. She actually wanted to crowd him, to challenge him. In was an inexplicable instinct.

"It can't be you," Cerise said, staring at him.

He quirked a brow. "It can be me. In fact, it can be none other." He finished off the gallon of water, his skin glowing from the ferocity of his earlier playing. "And hello. How have you been?"

"I've been fine. How did you get in?" she demanded.

His gorgeous smile widened. "I'm not obliged to answer your questions and choose not to."

Oh right. Now I remember. He's impossible. "You're an incredible musician."

"I know."

She fought not to scowl. He might be an arrogant jerk, but for a talent like his, allowances would have to be made.

"Thank you for the compliment," he added, sliding a large duffel bag from the shadow of a corner and putting the empty water jug into it.

"Where did you train?"

"Many places, and the sound quality here rivals them all."

"What school? Who was your teacher?"

"Ah. I've not had instruction. I teach myself."

Of course you do, you bastard, she thought with an inward sigh.

He wrapped his bow in a worn cloth before putting it in the bag. His violin joined the bow after being covered with a frayed towel.

"You need a violin case. An instrument like that deserves better protection."

"The violin has never complained," he said as he zipped the duffel. He looked up through strands of dark blond hair and added with a slow smile, "Which is why it makes better company than some people." He looked so young and heartbreakingly handsome that her heart thudded in her chest.

She noticed the *Crimson* logo written in bloodred script on the side of the bag.

Crimson is Merrick's bar.

"What's your name?" she asked.

He shook his head. "It's better if I don't even give you that much. It'll only make you want more."

She laughed. "You are so full of yourself. I've met rock stars who were more down-to-earth than you."

"That's certainly true. Being down-to-earth is not something to which I aspire."

Aspire. She'd been determined to make him an aspirant. Was she still? He had the talent, but he would be a nightmare to work with. Still, his playing . . .

"I'm Cerise Xenakis." When his expression remained blank, she rolled her eyes. The fact that she was world famous could not have escaped his attention, especially when he was in the Etherlin, for God's sake. And how was he still inside? When he'd smiled, she hadn't seen fangs. Was he ventala or not?

"I'm the Etherlin muse who inspires musicians."

She waited for him to respond and he finally said, "Congratulations?"

She scowled. "This center belongs to the Etherlin community."

"It was built for great music. That's what I bring."

She held out a hand. "I know. I'm not going to give you a hard time for trespassing. You clearly deserve to be here. I want to talk to you about your aspirations. What do you want to do with your music?"

"Play it?"

Smart ass. She smiled. "Nothing beyond that? C'mon," she said. "You could've snuck into an auditorium anywhere in the world. You chose one in the Etherlin. Wasn't some part of you hoping to be discovered by a muse? By me?"

"Definitely not," he said flatly. "I chose this place because it's the best place to play that's close to where I live."

"Close to where you live? Where is that?"

"Will you excuse me? I should go."

"So go." She had no intention of leaving him alone. She wanted to see how he was getting in and out.

"I need to snuff the candle. To leave it burning would risk a fire."

His turn of phrase seemed odd at times. Where was he from originally? Not the Varden. His speech was too precise and too archaic to have been born of its mean streets.

"I tire of waiting," he said.

She glanced at the girder. The drop was dizzying. She didn't blame him for wanting to avoid any distractions when he walked out there to get the candle, but what idiotic impulse had caused him to put the candle there in the first place? Maybe he'd gone out there to have a look at the book?

"Sorry, but I'm not leaving," she said. "I came to retrieve the book that's sitting next to the candle. Since you're getting the candle, it would be cool of you to bring me the book. That way both of us don't have to walk out there."

"Step aside," he said.

She glanced at the end of the beam. There was plenty of room for him to get to it without her moving out of his way. "I'm not going to touch you," she said.

"Of that I'm certain." He ran a hand through his hair, adding more chaos to locks that already defied a style. "Nevertheless," he said with a gesture for her to move.

She held out her hands in surrender and backed up. "Take all the space you need. I'll wait here. You can just drop the book as you go past."

He turned and strode out onto the beam without a moment's hesitation or fear. She glanced at his legs and noticed for the first time that his feet were bare. She also noticed the scars on his back. There were many of them. Mostly thin lines where bladelike cuts had been made, but there were also two thick vertical lines just inside his shoulder blades that didn't look like the other scars. They weren't flat and shiny white as the others were. They looked like golden brown grooves. The tops and bottoms of the vertical scars came to points that were unnaturally perfect.

What the hell are those marks?

She studied them and then her eyes lingered on his waist and down to the seat of his leather pants. He had an athlete's butt. Griffin had been good-looking, but he'd been somewhat androgynous. This mystery musician had a stunningly beautiful face, despite its scars, but there was nothing pale or fragile about his body. He could probably play a piano; he also looked like he could lift one. The appeal of that combination was not lost on a muse who inspired great athletes as well as great musicians.

She watched his sure footwork as he turned and strode back toward her, candle and book in hand.

"Do you dance?" she asked, her gaze fixed on his well-defined stomach muscles.

"Often and well."

"Is there anything you don't do well?" she asked dryly.

"I don't lie well. Sometimes it would be convenient if I did."

She glanced at his face. "You're odd."

"That's the other thing I don't do well."

"What?"

"Blend."

He walked to his duffel bag.

"Hey," she said.

He glanced over his shoulder.

"You forgot to give me the book."

"No, I didn't," he said, zipping the duffel over the candle and Griffin's songbook.

"What the hell?" She rushed toward him, but he shouldered the bag and sprinted away. Her socks slipped on the floor, but even if they hadn't, despite being able to run a five-and-a-half-minute mile, she wouldn't have been able to keep pace with him.

By the time she rounded the corner, he'd disappeared. She looked around and up. She heard a rustle of wind, but by the time she raced back to where she thought the sound had come from, he was gone. She checked the stairwells, but there was no sign of him.

Where the hell did he go?

She swore in frustration. Griffin's songbook had probably been sitting on that beam unattended for almost a year, and on the night she'd finally seen it, she'd had the bad luck to run into Merrick's eccentric friend. The other bizarre thing about the night was that for the twenty minutes she'd spent talking to him, despite being aware of the songbook, she hadn't thought about Griffin or been pained by his memory.

That still didn't mean she could leave the songbook with the mystery musician. She needed to read it and then she needed to turn it over to the Molly Times.

Cerise put a hand to her forehead and grimaced. The only thing she really knew about the phantom musician was that he was a friend of Merrick's. It looked like she would be talking to Alissa sooner than she'd intended.

Cool air grazed Cerise's cheek, and she glanced heavenward. Everything slammed into place.

The children of men will not recognize him for what he is unless he reveals himself. They will look, but not see.

"In the rafters . . ." Cerise murmured. "Not in the *falling* playground. In the *fallen's* playground above the stage."

Ventala don't have scars, and they don't have vertical grooves on their backs that could conceal wings.

Merrick's friend is a fallen angel.

From national bestselling author

KIMBERLY FROST

Halfway Hexed

· *A Southern Witch Novel* ·

Pastry-chef-turned-unexpected-witch Tammy Jo Trask is finally ready to embrace her mixed-up and often malfunctioning magic. Too bad not everyone wants her to become all the witch she can be. One thing's certain: this would-be witch is ready to rumble, Texas style . . .

Praise for the Southern Witch series

"An utter delight."

—Annette Blair, national bestselling author

"Full of action, suspense, romance, and humor."

—*Huntress Reviews*

penguin.com
facebook.com/ProjectParanormalBooks